The Lizard
and the Fly

Robert Edward Levin

The Lizard
And the Fly

Copyright ©1997 by Robert Edward Levin
All Rights Reserved

Library of Congress Card Number 98-90470

ISBN 0-9665127-0-7

Manufactured in the United States of America
First Printing 1998

This is a work of fiction. Names, characters and places are the product of the author's imagination or used fictitiously and any resemblance to actual persons, living or dead, events or locales is entirely coincidental.

Without limiting the rights under copyright reserved alone, no part of this publication may be reproduced, stored or introduced into a retrieval system or transmitted in any form, or by any means, without the prior written consent of both the copyright owner and the publisher of this book.

Published by
VOYAGE BOOKS
5325 Elkhorn Blvd.
Suite 8071
Sacramento, CA 95842

Produced by
PPC BOOKS
Westport, CT

Other Titles by Robert Edward Levin

American Meat
(ISBN 0-533-12101-9)

ACKNOWLEDGEMENTS

I would be remiss not to acknowledge Christopher Watson, whose patience and professionalism allowed this book to happen, Seth Mindell, for being the good doctor he is, Dan Sutton and Robin Richards, great friends indeed, my nieces and nephews, Melissa, Jessi, Brett, Bryan and Jason–the purity of their thoughts and enthusiasm help sustain the flutter in my own wings of youth; and lastly, the girl whose golden brown hair, cat-eyes, and radiant smile fills each day with the stunning beauty of a Jamaican sunset.

To Chase Dean Richards, a little boy who flies with the angels.

THE STORY OF THE LIZARD AND THE FLY

Once upon a time there was a baby fly buzzing around a lizard. The lizard was sunning itself next to a tree, seemingly unaware of the little buzzing fly. Since the mother fly never explained lizards to her baby, the fly never learned that in the blink of an eye, a lizard could snap out its long, wiggly tongue and snatch it clean out of the air.

But then it happened...

And the baby fly was no more.

CHAPTER 1

PRESENT DAY:

The rain that pounded the ground for most of the day and night suddenly grew quiet. A warm, steady breeze pushed through the clouds and eased the charcoal gray sky into black. All that remained was for the night to slip into morning.

Police Detective Max Cougar slid the bedroom window open and let the August weather rush in around him. He dismissed the night air as it brushed against his half naked body and filled his nose with the outside. The rain poured out of the sky like a giant shower to wash the city streets, and yet, when it was over Max couldn't decide if what he smelled was a musty odor emanating out of the steamy darkness, or worms baking on the sidewalk. He fixed his eyes on two dimly lit porch lights decorating a house down the street. They reminded him of the yellow stained whites of two sleepy eyeballs hung up on a black face. He stared and they stared back. Unsettled rainwater spilled from the gutter to the ground below with the sound of a summer night beer piss splashing against a tree. It broke the quiet.

Like so many other nights when Max held his sleepless gaze over the neighborhood streets, he knew that somewhere a murder was taking place. What he didn't know was that the murder being committed on this particular summer night would change his life forever.

CHAPTER 2

SEVEN YEARS EARLIER:

The night he'd been planning for the last 12 months finally arrived. Yet, instead of waiting in the one bedroom slab house he rented, Hank, as his friend knew him, decided to wait outside. At least outside he wouldn't feel like a caged animal.

It was an unusually hot June night. The moon hung from the darkness like a single pearl, while its light suffocated under the thick humidity, melting Hanks shadow in the process. Mosquitoes were everywhere.

The rented house sat alone at the end of a dirt cul de sac. There were three other houses scattered down the street, and at least a dozen times over as many months, during all hours of the night, Hank walked the property of each of them, studying the views and angles in good weather and bad. And it always turned out the same. The houses were too far apart from one another to see anything more than the simple fact they existed.

It was another fifteen minutes before Hank spotted the 89 Camaro his friend borrowed earlier in the evening. It was easy. The headlights looked like they were bouncing from the end of a rubber cord because his friend was obviously going slow in order to avoid the many potholes and ruts carved in the dirt road. Yet, it was the same slow driving that served as the signal for Hank to make his way over to the large weeping willow tree beside the driveway. What a big, beautiful, droopy tree it was too. Big enough to enable Hank to crouch down out of sight like a big game cat poised to leap on its prey.

And soon enough the car turned into the drive and the seconds began to tick. One thousand one...one thousand two.

Hank thought of the simple terror his friend was about to come to know. He relished the thought and laughed quietly to himself.

One thousand three...one thousand four.

His friend had no idea of the madness pending. Hank's fingers dug in the ground and his forearms twitched. Otherwise, he was as still as the night.

One thousand five...one thousand six.

His friend pulled the car even with the weeping willow and got out. He trudged along the gravel drive on his way to the front door, each step marking his precise location.

"Lucky Seven!" Hank popped out loud. He sprang out from behind the tree, and before his friend had a chance to turn around, seized him by his hot, sticky throat. His long fingers dug deep as he began to squeeze.

His friend thrashed and jerked wildly. His mind raced with confusion. Then fear. He tried to call out but his voice could not get beyond the grasp of his assailant. His eyes bulged.

Hank churned his teeth and squeezed harder. Blood pumped viciously through his strong, tapered arms.

Forwards - backwards - forwards - sideways. His friend continued to thrash and jerk about.

Hank stayed focused, squeezing with such force he thought the palms of his hands would touch.

His friend tried to reach back with his hands and grab his assailant's hair, face, ears, an ear, anything. He got nothing.

Hank squeezed harder. His arms shook. The veins in his forehead looked like a 3-D road map. The rage spilled out of his body like the sweat poured out of his back.

Knife sharp spasms ricocheted throughout his friend's body. He convulsed. His arms danced, then dangled at his sides. Snot hung from his nose. Milky white saliva ran down his chin.

In one final fury Hank snapped his neck in two. It sounded like the cracking of dry tree twigs.

His friend crumpled to the ground. He would no longer swing his arms. He would no longer kick or thrash about. He would no longer breath. Hank stepped away from the fallen body and cocked his head to one side. He lingered in thought as the stale, misty night air engulfed him. He was glad he broke his neck. A little fuss, no mess, and really not that painful, he decided. He didn't want it to be painful. After all, they were buds. Hank allowed himself a hardy laugh.

Mosquitoes were everywhere.

CHAPTER 3

Hank tried lifting the body over his shoulder, but as strong as he was, found the weight of his dead friend to be a bit much. As a result, he resigned himself to dragging the body inside, where he laid it face down in the bathroom and proceeded to empty his dead bud's pockets. And wouldn't ya know it? The law school I.D. card he was looking for was the first thing he pulled out. Now all Hank had to do to order "his" law school transcripts was have the identification number handy. "Great country we live in. Don't you think so?" Hank smacked his dead bud in the head and bellowed a short, but hardy laugh.

The tongue and groove floating parquet wood floor pieced together like a puzzle. It pulled apart much the same way. And after Hank used a pair of bolt cutters to disconnect his dead friend's fingers and thumbs, he disconnected certain sections of the wood floor until exposing the homemade grave it took him two weeks to make. It wasn't easy to make either, what with having to saw-cut a three-by-six foot section of concrete slab. Oh well. When it was all said and done it still served as the ideal resting place to bury his bud. And frankly, nothing else mattered.

Aside from being perfect, the plan was really quite simple. With Hank's bud dead, buried, and by morning, hermetically sealed, the old lady could rent out the house again and no one would ever suspect a thing. Since his dead bud had no family, and except for Hank, no friends, no one would come looking for him either. Besides, there wouldn't be any reason to look for him because, through Hank, his dead bud still had a future practicing law. Hank would see to it. He planned to use his new law school I.D. number to have the administration office send out as many transcripts as it would take to land himself a job.

As for Hank, no one would find him because he wasn't Hank. Hank was a guy who stood just over six feet tall and was thin, but athletically built. He wore dark brown hair, had dark eyes, a mustache, closely cropped light brown beard, and when it served his purpose, went by the name of Hank Conners. He rented a house from a little old lady and paid the rent and his utility bills with money orders.

But he was not Hank Conners. He did not have brown hair, a mustache or a beard. He had blond hair and was clean shaven. And, unlike his dead bud, who recently graduated law school, he quit law school after two years. He was a young man with a past. He was a young man with a bag full of fingers and a plan for the future.

His name was John Henry Stevens.

CHAPTER 4

PRESENT DAY:

Kathy and Jack Reed had been married four years and had a two year old son named Matthew. He was named after Kathy's brother, Max. Earlier in the day Jack's parents stopped by the house to pick up Matthew for the weekend. Although Kathy wasn't sure if Matt understood he would be staying with his grandparents for two nights - "two whole nights" - she couldn't resist the opportunity to get some time for herself and her husband, so she was willing to experiment. She figured if the weekend went off without a hitch they could do it again. And again. And again.

It was 6:30 p.m. before Jack strolled through the door. "Anybody home?" Jack greeted his family with the same question every night. All he ever got for an answer, however, was the noise of his son running through the house and his wife in pursuit. A few seconds later Jack called out again. "Kathy, Matty? Where is everyone?" Kathy's Jeep was parked in the garage so he knew they were home. He figured they were in the other room playing a game and didn't hear him come in.

"Matthew's staying with your parents for the weekend," Kathy finally called out to him from the family room.

"Oh really? What's the occasion?"

Kathy could tell her husband was smiling. She figured it was the thought of a weekend alone. "They volunteered, what was I gonna say?" Kathy was smiling as well.

Jack proceeded to walk over to the bar in the library and make himself a drink. It was Friday and Jack always had a drink on Friday. As he reached for the bottle of Crown Royal it suddenly occurred to him that maybe his son would not be happy staying with his grandparents for the weekend. He knew Matthew was crazy about them, but the strange bed and all. "Maybe we should call over there and see..."

"I just got off the phone with your mother," Kathy broke in. "Everything's fine. Matthew and your father are watching The Lion King."

Kathy always found it interesting that her husband was the first one to preach the importance of Matthew's independence, but the last one to let Matthew out of his sight. It stemmed from his own loving upbringing. An upbringing she wasn't as fortunate to have had.

Kathy's father died of a heart attack when she was 9 years old. And her mother, she may as well have died then too. That's because her mother spent the next 12 years of her life walking around only because she was still breathing and had no choice but to live another day. She ate little, didn't bathe with any degree of regularity and never seemed interested in conversation, no matter the topic. She took odd jobs when she had to and family handouts whenever they were offered. As for her children? She showed them all the interest of a blank stare. The only family Kathy ever knew was her brother Max. Even though he was only three years older, he took it upon himself to raise her after their father died. He watched out for her, cooked for her, helped her with her homework, and gave her an allowance from the little money he earned from his after school jobs. When Kathy turned 16 and started dating, Max even made it a point to meet all her dates beforehand, although after Roger Sharp it wasn't necessary.

Roger Sharp was a senior in high school and the shortstop on the baseball team. He was also either cocky or stupid because when he went to kiss Kathy goodnight on their first date he tried to feel her tits. Kathy fought him off, but lost her shirt in the process. And ol' Roger Dodger? Three days later he showed up at school with a broken nose, fractured cheekbone and separated shoulder. After that, it wasn't necessary to meet Kathy's dates beforehand. Max did anyway.

Kathy Cougar Reed was wearing one of her husband's expensive Armani double breasted suit coats. She was naked underneath. Armani probably didn't design the coat thinking it would be worn in such a fashion, but she figured her husband certainly wouldn't mind. Assuming, of course, he ever came in the room to give her a kiss hello.

When Kathy and Jack were first married, Jack came home after work one day and didn't kiss her hello. She didn't know why, and would never try to explain it anyway, but it somehow made her feel empty and alone the entire evening. After that Kathy made it a rule in their house. Whenever Jack left for work in the morning he kissed her goodbye, even if it meant waking her up. When he came back from work at night he kissed her hello. It was the only thing she ever held him to.

"What do you want to do about dinner?" Jack asked.

Kathy didn't answer. Instead she waited for her husband to walk into the room, then unbuttoned the Armani...slowly.

Jack took a large swallow of his drink.

They never ate dinner.

CHAPTER 5

It was two o'clock in the morning and dark. The streets were quiet, and except for John Henry Stevens, lifeless. But that wasn't anything unusual because he came to life at night. It was his time to play.

John Henry Stevens was parked across the street from the Reed house in a 1992 midnight blue pickup truck he stole earlier in the night. He sat there, just as he did every night for the past two weeks, watching the house and neighborhood traffic, all the while thinking about the family inside. The mommy, the daddy and the little boy. Tonight was different though. Tonight he was going to introduce himself to the family inside. And as the darkness grew thicker over the neighborhood street John Henry burst with anticipation. It was time. He hopped out of the truck, and like a shadow, disappeared inside the darkness while making his way to the back of the house. It's a good thing the Reeds never built an addition to their house either. Otherwise the fat tree that carried him to the roof probably wouldn't be there.

As a kid John Henry never believed in Santa Claus. There were no presents growing up, the family never went to Church, and Christmas dinner could have either been a cold hot dog or a fat lip sandwich. Christmas for John Henry Stevens was really just another day to get locked up in the crawl-space basement by his mother, or the closet by his aunt and uncle. The only thing he knew for sure about Christmas was that there was no way a fat piece of shit in a red suit, dragging an equally fat bag of gifts over his shoulder, could get down a chimney, even in a house with a double wide stone fireplace like the Reeds. But, John Henry wasn't fat, he wasn't Santa Claus, and he wasn't bearing gifts for the family. If anything, when John Henry lowered himself inside the chimney, he resembled a snake doing a mating dance.

Down a few inches. Stop. Down a few inches. Stop.

His body sounded like worn out sandpaper sliding across wood.

Down a few inches. Stop. Down a few inches. Stop.

Soot spotted his black jeans and black sweatshirt. It also made his hands feel greasy. But John Henry would not wear gloves, even if it meant getting soot on his hands. It took away from the feel. He needed to feel the flesh, the sweat, the blood and the fear. He would not compromise the feel. He would not wear gloves. He did in his younger days, but he didn't have to now. That's because no one would ever know it was him.

Down a few inches. Stop. Down a few inches. Stop.

John Henry figured the summer weather would preclude the use of the fireplace. Besides, like most people, the happy couple probably stopped making fires after their first winter in the house.

"Oh look honey, it has a fireplace."

"Yes dear, isn't it wonderful. I can chop the wood outside, carry the wood inside, and together we can build a cozy fire and cuddle up when it's cold."

What a bunch of bullshit, John Henry thought.

Down a few inches. Stop. Down a few inches. Stop.

He was right. The fireplace pit was empty. John Henry Stevens squatted down like he was hiding behind the old weeping willow tree, and other than eye movement, remained motionless. He surveyed the room and found shadows from the moonlight playing along the curtains and walls, as if dancing to the music of the daddy's loud snoring. He maneuvered the free standing bronze fireplace door just enough to slither by. He was careful not to make a sound. When he stood up he felt a hot flash rush through his body. It was followed by a cold chill. John Henry ignored them both and proceeded to peel the duck tape off the inside of his forearm where he had secured his six inch switchblade. It wasn't his greeting weapon of choice, but he wanted his Santa Claus entrance to leave the police with a lasting impression. A bigger or bulkier weapon could've given him problems in the chimney. He wouldn't risk it. Besides, he always had, and intended to use, his bare hands.

After taking the library phone off the hook John Henry followed the sound of Jack Reed's snoring until he stood just inside the master bedroom. Introduce yourself to the daddy first, John Henry told himself. The daddy was the head of the household. He deserved a certain measure of respect. Meeting him first only seemed like the right thing to do. And you do want to do the right thing.

Jack Reed slept with his body sprawled across two-thirds of the bed. His wife Kathy slept curled up on her side. She was facing her husband. John Henry Stevens moved into the room until he stood over the daddy, his strength growing stronger with every breath of darkness.

Now!

In a single motion John Henry Stevens released the blade into a locked position and plunged it the full six inches into Jack's chest. The blade pierced his heart.

Kathy shot up from the bed at the very moment she heard the dull thud, but before she could react, John Henry moved around to the other side of the bed and had her throat wrapped securely in his hands. He yanked her out of the bed like she was a ten pound rag doll and threw her head first against the wall. She fell hard to the floor, but she was not dead. Still, John Henry was amused at the sight of her bloody, broken nose. "You look sick mommy. Are you sick?" he mocked in a child's voice.

Kathy raised up her head. Her eyes burned with hatred and fear. And with death. "Fuck you," she forced out.

John Henry was no longer amused. He pulled Kathy up from the floor and started punching her in the face until her head hung like it was a bag of sand.

He could feel her warm blood running over his hand. Her eyes were glassy and red, and she could no longer see images. Her mouth hung open. John Henry found himself getting aroused from all the excitement and decided to take her. Kathy wanted to die and would offer no struggle. She thought of her husband. She thought of her brother Max. She thought of her son Matthew. She died before John Henry finished. He didn't know it, so he choked her to death anyway.

Now it was Matthew's turn.

However, no sooner did John Henry storm into his room when he discovered the little shit was nowhere to be found. "Ahhhhhhhgggg!" he roared from deep inside his belly. All dressed up in rage and no place to go, John Henry staggered over to the little shit's dresser and hurled it forward. He barely waited for it to crash to the floor when he turned and grabbed the nightstand sitting next to the little shit's bed. He rammed its legs into the wall over and over until the drywall cracked and broke open. He threw the nightstand off to the side and reached for the stuffed bear sitting on the little shit's bed. He squeezed it like he planned to squeeze Matthew's neck. The head tore off and the stuffing came out. He dropped the bear to the floor.

Finally, the rage that swelled up inside John Henry like a wild river began to recede. He rested his hands on his knees and took several deep breaths. But it wasn't until his sweat dried that he felt in control.

John Henry Stevens left the house through the front door.

CHAPTER 6

It was 10:30 in the morning when the phone rang.

"Zack it's for you," Susan called out from the kitchen.

Zack was lying down on the couch reading the sports section and in no mood to get up. "Who is it?" he asked, without lifting his eyes from the paper. He was in the middle of an article about how the Illinois football team would stack up against the other Big Ten teams.

"It's Captain Whitaker," Susan returned.

Knowing Captain Whitaker wouldn't call him on a Saturday unless it was important, Zack sprang up from the couch. He was still carrying the sports section when he hurried into the kitchen to take the call. Zack Darwin loved sports, especially football. Until he ripped up his knee in spring practice when he was a sophomore at Wisconsin, he was the second string tailback. He never played again. Instead he changed his major to criminology and ultimately became a detective with the Chicago Police Department.

"Cap, what's up?"

"Beast, I hope you're sitting down."

The first time Max Cougar and Zack Darwin ever met, Max nicknamed him Beast. Max never told him what prompted the nickname but it stuck. Zack always figured it was because his last name was Darwin. The real reason was because he had a pair a shoulders that looked more like a wing span.

"Why, what's up?" Zack asked.

"Max's sister..." Captain Whitaker began softly.

"What about her?" Zack interrupted. His voice was quiet, almost tentative, like he really didn't want an answer to his question. He leaned forward on the kitchen counter and rested his muscular upper body. He tossed the paper to the kitchen table.

"She was murdered," the Captain finally said.

Zack was silent. He instantly thought of Max. His eyes became moist and his square jaw quivered slightly.

Captain Whitaker figured words might come slow to the Beast so he continued talking. His tone was flat and his sentences deliberate, but as usual he sounded in control. "I'm at the scene. Have been for about thirty minutes. Don't have any details yet, but I've got a team on its way to meet me now."

Zack remained silent.

"It was bad Beast. As bad as I've seen in a long time. Maybe the worst ever." Captain Rudy Whitaker had been with the Chicago Police Department for the past 27 years. And even though he'd been around some awfully brutal murders over that time, he really couldn't remember which murders were worse than others. Still, like most of the cops Zack knew, when the Cap said it was bad, it was bad. End of conversation.

Zack met Susan's gaze, but the cheery brown eyes and easy smile he walked into the room with were nowhere to be found. "Max's sister was murdered," he said. Zack had to fight to get the words out.

Susan gasped. She knew Kathy fairly well. Worse yet, she knew how devastated Max was going to be and the thought of it overwhelmed her with tears.

Zack needed to find his composure. The Beast had business to tend to. And though he wanted to hug and comfort Susan, he didn't.

Susan understood, and took hold of his outstretched hand instead.

"Does Max know?" Zack asked. His voice was still quiet but he could no longer afford to be pensive. He wanted an answer to his question.

"No I don't think so," Captain Whitaker began, "and I haven't tried to contact him. I wanted to talk to you first."

"I understand," Zack said.

The Beast and Max had been best friends ever since they became partners 12 years ago. Even though the Police Commissioner split them up a year back, they were still the best of friends. Max was certain to be overcome by the news. The Captain figured Zack would know best how to tell him. He was also hoping Zack would be able to corral Max's temper if it became necessary.

"How did you find out Cap?"

"The guy who cuts the grass called the department. Sergeant Olson took the call. I happened to be standing next to him when it came in. Olson recognized the address. Evidently he had been to the house before for dinner."

"Yeah, he was. We both were about a week ago," Zack confirmed.

"Anyway," the Captain continued, "this guy, this gardener, he says he was over there to cut the grass and when he finished he was hoping to get paid. He said he started banging on the door but got no answer. He goes around to the back and sees that both cars are still in the garage so he figures that someone had to be home. He decides to try the front door. Turns out the front door is unlocked. My guess is this guy didn't think anyone was home and decides to break in on the spot."

"Do you think he had anything to do with it?" Zack asked.

"No. I'm here and we've talked. This guy might be a petty thief but he's not involved. He just happened to be the person that found the bodies."

Zack heard the Captain mention Max's sister. He didn't recall hearing him say "bodies" before and it suddenly registered. The words spilled out of his mouth. "Matthew, the little boy, was he..."

"No. There's been no sign of the boy," the Captain interjected. "Just Max's sister and her husband."

The Beast cried.

CHAPTER 7

Ever since the Police Commissioner forced Max Cougar and Zack Darwin to split up as partners they started taking Saturdays off. That way they could at least get in some guy time over the weekend. Saturdays usually meant a ballgame or a pool hall and a few beers. Today Max and the Beast were going to meet at Harvey's Tavern around 1:15 p.m. After a quick burger they planned to head over to Wrigley Field and find a couple of bleacher seats for the Cubs game.

It was approaching 12:00 p.m.. Max planned a quick detour to his sister's house on his way to meet Zack. Having spent the night at Clare's he was close enough to pop in and see his nephew.

The weather station called for rain, which would have meant game cancellation and an entire afternoon drinking beer. Yet, as Max turned off the avenue and headed west for Kathy's sub, enough sun was in the sky to cause him to pull his sunglasses out of the console and put them on.

The Reed house was stuck on Hardy street deep inside the subdivision. Max always liked the choice of house his sister and brother-in-law made. The neighborhood traffic seemed minimal, and if nothing else, made it safer anytime Matthew was outside. But today was different. Today Max didn't find himself driving on a long, winding street. Instead, he found a street that carried all the markings of a crime scene.

The police barricade was still some 50 yards away from where Max was, and the actual crime scene was probably 25 yards farther than that. Nevertheless, Max sensed that something was terribly wrong and immediately parked his Bronco and walked towards the barricade, taking note of the other houses locked inside its boundaries. "Let it be someone else God. Please let it be someone else," he pleaded in a whisper. Five more yards, Max broke into a trot. Ten yards later he was at full speed.

The two uniforms guarding the perimeter of the barricade were facing the crime scene and talking. Only policeman and other authorized personnel with the proper identification were to be given access. Once inside they were to report to Police Captain Rudy Whitaker. He'd been directing the investigation throughout the morning. Residents were to be escorted directly home. Max knew the rules but made no effort to slow down. He jumped over the sealed off perimeter and ran by the two uniforms like they were invisible. Max ignored their pleas to stop. One of the officers broke into pursuit.

Zack was standing just inside the doorway when Max exploded into the house. He was sweating and breathing hard, but didn't pause long enough to catch his breath or say anything. Instead he headed straight for the commotion at the other end of the house. Zack hung his head and started to follow, until a uniform burst in.

"Where's the guy who just came in here?" he demanded. He was looking to Zack for an answer.

Zack put up his hand. "It's okay," he said to the officer in a quiet, reassuring tone.

"I have orders to keep a log of all people that come into the area. I need to see that guy's identification."

"It's okay," Zack repeated, aware that the officer was just trying to do his job. "He's a cop. His sister is the female victim."

The officer stood silent for a minute and glanced around the room. Up until he followed Max through the front door he hadn't been inside the house himself. "That's fine," he said looking at Zack again, "but I'm still gonna have to see his I.D. I have to include it in my report with all the others."

The Beast did not have patience for this. He wanted to go find Max and this uniform, with his rules and regulations, was pissing him off by keeping him from doing that very thing. He shifted his weight into his large chest and peered into the officer's shallow blue-gray eyes. A blank expression sat on the officer's face. Sweat was resting on his buttoned shirt collar and his hat was off, exposing short, curly brown hair. "How long you been a cop?" Zack questioned, his voice sounding raspier than normal.

"Look, I'm just trying to do my job," the officer protested. He suddenly looked uncomfortable standing in the house.

The Beast ignored the uniform and continued. "Let me introduce myself. My name's Zack Darwin, but most people call me Beast. Whether you know it or not you owe me a big favor 'cause I probably just saved your life."

The officer cocked his head to one side not quite sure what this Beast guy meant. The Beast explained, "Had you tried to stop him he probably would have killed you. I'm a little kinder. I probably won't."

The officer swayed his upper body back like he was shocked another cop, one with a ponytail to boot, would talk to him that way.

"Probably," the Beast repeated. He gave the officer a hard look. "Now I think it would be a real good idea if you head back outside. Whadaya think?"

The officer stood silent. Zack sensed he either felt bad or was just plain stupid because he suddenly had that "aw shucks" look on his face. Zack wasn't sure what else to say so he turned his back and headed for the bedroom to be with his friend.

Captain Whitaker squeezed Max's shoulder as he brushed by him on his way into the bedroom. The Captain motioned for everyone to clear the room so Max could have some time alone. The investigative team had finished taking pictures but were still in the process of dusting for fingerprints and taking blood samples for DNA testing. Nevertheless, the Captain knew Max wasn't in the room to touch anything. He just wanted to say goodbye.

The Captain stood out in the hall discussing details with the Coroner, Dr. Samuel Murphy, and the Assistant District Attorney, Tyler Lake, when Zack approached. Zack greeted the Coroner and the Assistant D.A. with a nod and a solemn handshake. He had already seen the Captain, but until now, hadn't noticed just how tired he looked.

"Would you two excuse us?" Captain Whitaker waited until the two men walked away before he fixed his eyes on Zack. "Ya know," he said, shaking his head in disgust, "I drag my black ass out of bed every freekin' morning knowin' I may see something like this. But after 27 years I gotta tell ya, it's gettin' harder to take. I don't know how much more I've got left in me." He pulled at the gray hair sitting on his head.

"What's up Cap? I know you didn't excuse those guys to tell me that."

Captain Whitaker sighed the sigh of a large man. "He's gonna want to be part of the investigation Beast, and I'm not sure that's wise."

Zack shrugged nonchalantly. "I don't know if it is either Cap. But I know if ya don't make him a part of it he's gonna go lookin' for this maniac himself. So will I."

"Yes, I'm fully aware of that. I just hope you didn't forget that you guys got pulled apart once before."

"No Cap I didn't forget," Zack said, clearly annoyed at the reminder. "I doubt Max has either."

The Captain studied Zack's face for several seconds. He rubbed the poorly shaved whiskers on his loose chin. "I'll square it with the Commissioner," he said, "but you make sure to keep yourselves in line. Make sure Max doesn't cross over."

"Yes sir."

Captain Whitaker and Zack walked over to the bedroom entrance and watched Max. He was sitting on his knees gently rocking back and forth. His arms were folded tight across his midsection like they were going to keep him from throwing up. He was mumbling to himself.

"Get him outta there Beast. He ain't doin' himself any good sittin' there like that."

Zack Darwin walked into the bedroom, restraining his usually long strides. He placed his hands by Max's arms and gently tugged until Max rose to his feet. At six-one and 190 pounds Max was two inches shorter and 35 pounds lighter, but somehow Zack always thought they looked the same size. When the two men faced each other the confusion and anger buried in Max's deep blue eyes was obvious. So too was the fact that Max hadn't cried. Nor did the Beast expect him to. Max would grieve on his own time, it was as simple as that.

Zack wrapped his arms around Max and said, "I'm so sorry my friend."

As Max returned the hug he spoke in so faint a whisper the words were barely audible. "The fuck's gotta die, Beast."

"I know Max, I know."

CHAPTER 8

Almost two weeks had passed since the murder of Kathy and Jack Reed. Matthew was living with his grandparents and seemed to be adjusting well. Max was not as fortunate. Ever since the murder he ate little and slept even less. For the first time in his life Max wasn't able to protect his sister when she needed it and the guilt followed him like a shadow. The image of her dead body was locked in his mind. Unless he looked at a photograph he couldn't remember what she looked like, the way she walked, or the way she slapped him high fives. He couldn't even remember the way she smiled, or the sound of her voice when she talked or laughed. And when he was alone at night he felt an emptiness kicking deep inside his belly.

It was on a Wednesday afternoon when Clare Adams was finally able to talk Max into letting her cook dinner for him at his apartment that night. She'd been wanting to see him everyday since the murder, but Max always claimed to be too busy with the investigation, or too tired for company. Clare didn't believe him and Zack confirmed for her what she thought to be the truth. Every night Max was holed up in his apartment, isolating his mind from everything except his sister's killer and the bottle of whiskey he happened to be drinking from. Still, as desperate as she was to see him, Clare was afraid if she pushed too much she might isolate him even more. Instead she waited for his okay.

During much of dinner Max sat quietly and listened to Clare talk about the upcoming school year. She taught English at Lincoln Elementary and was relaying a few of the juicy rumors she'd heard about some of the other teachers. Clare realized Kathy would never stray too far from Max's thoughts, she was simply hoping to give him something else to think about, even if only for the moment.

She did too. Although the stories had nothing to do with it. It was the sparkle in her violet colored eyes and the way she twisted the ends of her long dark hair when she spoke that did it.

Max loved Clare and was glad she was with him. He was glad she stayed the night too. It was the first time in two weeks he'd gotten a decent night's sleep.

CHAPTER 9

In the twelve years Max had been a cop, the last eight as detective, he never saw a murder scene as messy as his sister's reveal so little. And as he sat in the conference room waiting for Zack and the Captain, he couldn't help but think how the last couple of weeks provided him with little more than a waste of time. He was glad when the door finally opened. It meant he could stop thinking about it.

"Hey bud," Zack tossed out.

"Hey," Max returned.

Zack walked over to the table and sat down. "How was lunch?" he asked.

Max pushed himself away from the table and leaned back in his chair. "Clare had to cancel. School Board shit, ya know? I ate a turkey instead. You?"

"Not bad. I had a turkey too. Susan ate something green." Zack thought for a second, then added. "I hate salad."

"I'm not crazy 'bout it myself."

"No Max, you don't understand. I mean, I really, really hate salad. Even the thought of it gets me all shook up." From there Zack went straight into his *I'm all shook up!* Elvis impersonation, complete with voice and hip gyration. He even tried to curl his lip and make it quiver, but couldn't, so instead added a couple more shakes and wiggles.

Max cracked up. Then again, the sight of a no necked, square jawed, 225 pound man with a ponytail, dancing while he sat in his seat, would do that to just about anyone. It was the first time in some two weeks Zack heard Max laugh. It was a good sign. A sign that meant the cruel impact of his sister's murder was beginning to thaw. It would never die, Zack knew that for sure. But maybe Max was returning. Zack certainly hoped so, and would do all he could to speed up the process. Even if it meant making an ass of himself for the sake of a few good yucks.

By now Captain Whitaker was standing in the doorway watching. He was wearing his blue suit minus the jacket. His white shirt looked like it had to be stretched in order to cover his stomach, and his pants were baggy in the ass. His maroon and blue speckled tie clashed with the beige colored stain that was both large and obvious as it sat smeared just below his shirt pocket. His shirt sleeves were rolled up exposing his thick black wrists.

"Am I missing something?" The Captain made sure his deep voice could be heard above the laughter.

Max and Zack turned to face him. The Captain might appreciate a good joke, but since the Elvis impersonation was one of those things you had to be there for, Zack just said, "No Cap, we were just discussing lunch." His laugh faded to a smile. His teeth looked like an even row of white.

Max choked back his own laughter. "What happened to your shirt?"

Captain Whitaker frowned. "I ate a goddamn salad for lunch and spilled goddamn Thousand Island dressing all over it. Goddammit!" he bellowed.

Max arched his head back and cracked up all over again. His long dark hair hung suspended in the air. Zack dropped his head into his large palms and tried to keep it to himself. His broad shoulders shook.

"Cougar what the hell is so goddamn funny?! Beast, goddammit!"

The Captain closed the door behind him and walked over to the far end of the table. He too was glad to hear Max laugh. Yet, with another meeting scheduled in some thirty minutes, enough, as they say, was enough. "Okay," he said, dropping his open palms on the table, "let's get it in gear."

This was the first time in weeks Max didn't have the liquor from the night before pounding drumrolls in his head. Not only that, he finally got the kind of sleep that turned his eyes from sleepless red to bright and blue. And his voice, generally a mix of just enough restraint and confidence to make a person trust and fear it equally, was no longer a phlegm filled scratchy mess. Yet, as he spoke to the Captain he sounded almost apologetic. "There isn't much Captain." Max read down his list like he was reading the ingredients for a recipe. "Because of the semen sample, we obviously know the killer is male. Unfortunately, the sample produced no identifiable match with what we have on record. As far as fingerprints, we picked up several clean ones, but again, no match. We believe the killer is extraordinarily violent and irrational, not only because of the brutality involved in the murders, but mostly because of the way he dismembered my nephew's stuffed animal." Max paused and took a deep breath. When he continued his tone was soft, but sure. "We also believe the killer is strong because of the deep, yet clean knife wound in my brother-in-law's chest cavity. It went in with force Captain. The deep bruises around the point of entry and all." Max stopped talking and took another deep breath. He was determined not to break. If he intended to find this madman, he couldn't afford to.

The Beast figured his best friend and partner might want a minute to wrestle with his composure so he took it upon himself to continue. "I took the measurements of the chimney interior to Charley Dunlop over in forensics. I was hoping he'd be able to give me a real good read on this guy's size. Ya know what I mean?" Zack waited for the Captain's nod of approval. When he didn't get it, which he didn't really expect anyway, he added, "nothin'. Same shit we got now...which is nothin'."

The Captain pulled out a chair and sat down. "I'm not sure what that would do for you anyway."

"In all likelihood, nothin'. It was just a stupid idea coming out of a crazy situation," Zack offered. "Especially since we already know the little cocksucker is probably small enough to hide behind a fat tree, but too big for Max to stuff in a mailbox."

"Fuck that. I'm gonna stuff him in a garbage disposal." Max leaned forward to meet Zack's clenched fist with his own.

The Captain rolled his eyes. "What about blood samples?"

"DNA tests indicate the victim's only," Zack shot back.

Unlike Max or the Beast, the Captain didn't waver when he got an answer he didn't like. He just went on with a different question. "What about shoe prints?"

"None. Although," Max was quick to add, "we don't think this madman really cared what he left behind. Kinda like he's daring us to find him."

Between the Captain's long sighs and the way he kept rearranging his body, it was obvious he was restless in thought. "Well, where's that put us?" He finally asked.

Max leafed through the folder sitting in front of him until he found the information he was looking for. Two names were written down. Each name had a case number, a year penned beside it and a case synopsis. "Well Cap, do you remember Harry Weeble?"

The Captain remembered, but didn't respond. Max was going to tell him anyway, so what difference did it make?

"Beast and I busted him about 7 years ago. We knew he sodomized an old lady in her 70's but we couldn't prove it. The old lady couldn't identify him. There was never a semen sample. It was a fuckin' mess. The D.A.'s office plead him out on a B & E and an assault. He got eight years but he was out in six. He's been on the street for about a year now."

"So?" When Captain Whitaker rubbed his chin it made his puffy cheeks look puffier.

"So he swore he would kill me and Zack," Max responded.

"Gee, there's a surprise. I mean for god sakes, didn't you two beat holy hell out of him when you busted him?"

Max knew the question was coming and shrugged his shoulders. "Yes Cap, we tagged him. But nothing more than what he had coming. And no, it wasn't the beating that caused him to make the threats. He was just plain nuts. Probably still is. Besides that, it's his body size. He's kinda scrawny. He may fit the bill Captain."

The Captain studied Max's face for several seconds then locked onto Zack. "Beast?"

The Beast raised his eyebrows. "Max is right about the guy. It's as good as anything we got to go on Captain."

"That it?"

The Captain's question didn't sound like he was putting a whole lot of stock in the direction Max was heading in, and Max could hardly blame him. Still, it was better than nothing. "No Cap, there's another."

Captain Whitaker traded glances with Zack. "Who?"

"Louie Hart. Beast and I got him two years ago. He raped and killed two little girls. They were sisters. One was ten and the other eight. He got life. He's also got a younger brother who we think was in on it. Problem was Louie Hart said he did 'em both and the D.A. went with it."

"And?"

"And we think the brother who never went to jail may also fit the bill. Hell, we always figured him to be crazier than Louie. At the time he was thin, probably still is. And I'm willing to guess he's still quite nuts," Max concluded.

"What's his name?" Captain Whitaker asked.

"Eddie," the Beast offered.

The Captain leaned back in his chair and stared at the ceiling. Several quiet seconds later there was an abrupt knock on the door. "What!" Captain Whitaker barked, as he let the chair fall forward.

The door swung open and Bernard Forest, Attorney at Law, strutted into the room. He was a short man with jowls for cheeks and a belly so round he couldn't see his penis when he pissed. His ego was large, his clothes expensive, and his year long tan a golfer brown. He and his partner, T. Rubin Gary, were known criminal defense lawyers. They wanted to be well known.

"Is there something you want Mr. Forest?" the Captain asked. He didn't like Bernard Forest but tried not to make it so obvious.

"I was in the building getting a copy of a police report for one of my clients. While doing so I thought it best to stop in for a brief moment and see you Captain. Believe me, if I wasn't already here I wouldn't be making a special trip. Although now that I did, I'm glad to see you have your two infamous detectives with you," Bernard Forest added in his well manicured voice.

"What and the hell do you want?" the Beast growled. He made no effort to disguise his contempt.

"We're in the middle of a meeting so you can leave." Max added. It was obvious he didn't like the strutting peacock of a man either.

The Captain motioned his detectives to remain silent. "I'll ask you again, is there something you want?"

Bernard Forest bent over a short distance and set his alligator briefcase on the tile floor. The exertion from having to bend over and straighten back up so quickly caused him to grunt. Zack snickered. Max shook his head in disgust.

"I'll be brief," he announced. "My client Billy Turner. You all remember Billy, don't you?" Bernard Forest arched his eyebrows and waited for a response. Although, ever the pontificator, he didn't wait long. "Well, as we all know Mr. Turner was wrongfully accused of drug possession, possession with intent to sell, carrying an illegal firearm, kidnapping, rape, and most wrongfully, of resisting the arrest by the two questionable law biding detectives you have sitting at your table." The short, fat lawyer paused to take a deep breath.

Zack was wondering what it would be like to roll him down a hill. Max, on the other hand, just wanted to punch away at his belly until he fell backwards and died.

"Yeah, so what about him?" the Captain inquired.

The attorney cupped his hands together and rested them on his belly. "Well, as you know, since last year I've been appealing his arrest and subsequent incarceration on the grounds that your two worldly detectives here violated his Fourth Amendment rights. It was a brilliant appeal, I might add." The balloon shaped lawyer might've been looking at Captain Whitaker, but he was motioning to Max and the Beast. "To say it in your tongue, which is rather simple, it was an illegal search and seizure and I got everything thrown out. After one year in jail the State Supreme Court reversed the lower court's decision. He's out." Bernard Forest was swaying back and forth on the balls of his stubby feet. His teeth were barely visible when he smiled.

"How long?" the Captain asked.

"Four weeks to the day," came the lawyer's response.

A cold chill ripped through Max's body but he wouldn't move an inch and risk giving Bernard Forest the satisfaction of knowing the news bothered him.

"So why are you telling us?"

Bernard Forest began his answer with a long, exaggerated sigh. "Well Captain, it was your two detectives who were found to have violated my client's constitutional rights. It was your two detectives who were questioned about their arrest tactics. And," the lawyer concluded as though it was a closing argument, "your two detectives who were split up by the commissioner as a result of those tactics. Now that he's out I want you to make sure they don't harass him. Partners or no partners."

Zack was ready to leap out of his chair. He figured with one strong push he could land on top of the lawyer without his feet even touching the floor. He looked at Max instead.

"Is that all?" the Captain asked. He'd grown tired of the lawyer's presence and wanted him out of the room.

Bernard Forest said nothing. He bent over for his suitcase, grunted when he straightened back up, then turned and left the room. He was proud of himself.

"His client's another one that fits the bill Captain."

"Then check him out. Check all three of 'em out," the Captain snapped.

CHAPTER 10

HARRY WEEBLE, SEVEN YEARS EARLIER:

Harry sat on a curb and studied the Twilight Retirement Home through the midnight darkness. He was searching for shadow movement in the windows.

"Ain't gonna see nothin' though. Damn home's filled with a bunch of old wheelchaired cocksuckers who probably never make it past the evening news anyway."

A cool October breeze was blowing but it didn't bother him near as much as the steady drizzle. He didn't have an umbrella with him, though it suddenly dawned on him that it would look good with the rest of his outfit. He made a mental note to bring one the next time he went out stylin', even if it wasn't raining.

Harry sat there like a skinny tree stump wearing a size 8 cotton dress, long johns underneath, black socks, running shoes and a lady's red haired wig. His purse matched the dull brown and gray pattern of his dress. His face was painted with a combination of blush, eye shadow, mascara and red lipstick. Harry loved wearing makeup. It was his stylin' paint. He wanted it to last.

Harry stood up from the curb and arched his back like a rainbow so he could stretch out the stiffness. It had been two weeks since he quit his job as a Twilight Home nurse's aide and he wondered if the set of keys he had copied before he quit would still fit in the door.

"If not, no matter. I'll just break in through the mother fucking window just like all the malcontent neighborhood pricks that live around here. Only difference is, they're just as happy stealin' $5.00 from an old lady's purse as they are strippin' her naked. I ain't."

The dampness from the curb soaked through Harry's long johns so he lifted up his dress and peeled them away from his ass. He wiggled around like he was trying to shake day old shit from a diaper, and farted. After a hurried look around the street, Harry squinted his eyes and started his trot over the three acres of ground separating him from the front door of the Twilight Retirement Home.

Harry loved running in his dresses. Ever since he was a kid he would steal them from his five older sisters, put them on and run around the neighborhood. He used to run in all kinds of weather so a little rain certainly wasn't gonna stop him now. Not even if it meant getting his socks wet because his shoes could no longer absorb the rain water. Not even if it meant leaving shoe imprints in the soaked grass. He didn't worry about it. In fact, the imprints never even occurred to Harry. The only thing he was thinking about now was naked old ladies.

By the time Harry reached the front door his wig was wet and the matted red hair was hanging in his eyes so he flipped it to one side like an actress doing a shampoo commercial. His mascara was running but he ignored it. It was time to get inside. He dug deep in his purse and pulled out his Playtex gloves. After he stretched them over his small hands he fumbled through his purse again and pulled out the set of keys that he hoped would work. He slipped the front door key into the cylinder.

"So far, so good."

He turned the key until he heard the deadbolt fall back into the empty door cartridge. Harry was almost giddy. Everything was turning out just like he wanted, except that his stylin' paint was getting messy. No matter. He was still standing in the foyer of the Twilight Retirement Home and that was the main thing.

"No forced entry or nothin'."

He rewarded himself by taking a deep breath and inhaling the medicinal odor that filled the hallways.

"Damn that smells good."

Harry's shoes were soggy but the carpeted stairs muffled any chance of them squishing too loudly as he climbed up to the second floor. Mrs. Florence Berry was in the first room on the right. Harry remembered her. She was either 78 or 79, a widow for 15 or so years and a real bitch. She always complained about the lack of hot shower water.

"Like it was all my fault, for god sakes." It reminded Harry of his goddamn sisters when he was growing up.

"You used all the hot water."

"There isn't anymore hot water."

"Who took a shower last?"

"I can't take a shower without hot water."

"Get out of the bathroom before you use up all the hot water."

Oh well, no matter. For all the bitchin' about hot water he was still right where he wanted to be. And better than that, he was gonna see Mrs. Berry naked.

"Can't wait."

The doorknob turned without making a sound but the door squeaked when Harry started to push it open. He immediately stopped and stood like a statue. His thin eyebrows burrowed forward. His little black eyeballs swung from side to side, looking, searching. He listened for anything. He heard nothing.

"Whew! That was close. Gotta be careful."

Mrs. Florence Berry was sound asleep. A little night light was plugged into one of the light sockets and Harry noticed her eye glasses on the nightstand next to the bed.

"Wonder if she'll be able to see my face under the messy stylin' paint? Nah! Not a chance in hell. The old bitch'll never know."

Harry moved over to the side of the bed. The blanket was pulled up to Mrs. Berry's neck but the night light made it possible for him to see the wrinkled contours of her face and the blue tint in her otherwise gray hair.

"Nice lookin'."

Harry was glad he decided on her. Actually he was glad she happened to be the first door on the right because that was the only criteria he used for making his decision.

Harry inched as close as a lover could, then...Zap!

Mrs. Berry's eyes bugged open and her body filled with fear. She wanted to look away, but her eyes were so full of life because she was so scared of dying, she found herself unable to. She had no idea that she'd ever seen this person before, let alone know him. As a matter-of-fact, the only thing Mrs. Berry knew at that moment was that a monster with long, stringy hair, wearing what looked like a house coat and clown-like makeup, had her in his grip.

Harry balanced himself on one leg while he propped his other leg up on the bed and placed his knee squarely over Mrs. Berry's worn out chest. It would help to secure her for the time being. He reached in his purse and grabbed the two sweat socks wrapped in a tight ball. Harry removed his hand from Mrs. Berry's mouth, but before she could even think about uttering a single noise, he stuffed the socks deep into her mouth. She gagged. "Don't worry, ya ain't gonna die, you good lookin' hag you."

Harry secured the socks in Mrs. Berry's mouth by stretching a piece of duct tape from one cheek to the other. He reached back in his purse and grabbed some pre-cut pieces of thin nylon rope. In a single move, Harry lifted his knee off of Mrs. Berry, placed his arms underneath her and flipped her over on her stomach. He was not rough. He was not gentle. Harry was just plain crazy.

After tying her hands behind her back, Harry straightened himself up. He admired how quickly he had been able to subdue her. He admired his handy work. He admired his plan. More importantly, he admired the naked bodies of old ladies. Harry grabbed her nightgown collar and slipped it over her shoulders and down her back. He then grabbed her bottom hem and pulled it up over her thighs and buttocks. He yanked Mrs. Berry's underwear down around her ankles.

Florence Berry was trembling and sweating profusely. Even though her nose was left uncovered she was still having difficulty breathing because she was lying with her head face down on the bed. Darkness was all around her. She was weeping. She was helpless. Worse than that, she knew it.

Harry reached in his purse of tricks and pulled out his battery operated rubber dildo. He turned it on and left it humming on the bed while he pulled his own dress up and his long johns down. He was excited by the view of the old lady's wrinkled ass and became hard in a matter of seconds. Harry started stroking himself and soon was dizzy from the warm feeling of his own erection.

"Hot damn."

He picked his toy back up and instantly thought he was holding the keys to life. In one hand he held himself. In the other, his dancing dildo. He felt whole. He felt spiritual.

"Hallelujah Brother."

Although Mrs. Berry could hear the sound of a soft buzz she really had no idea what it was until Harry drove it up inside her anus. She would have grunted from the shock and utter pain but was too overcome by a lack of oxygen. Harry worked the dildo in and out, and with each stroke of dildo masturbation he stroked himself. But, just when he felt like he was gonna explode, he stuffed his penis back in his long johns.

"Can't wet her. It's against the rules."

Instead, Harry turned the dildo on its highest setting and pushed it in as far as he could. He delighted in watching the old lady's body shutter with pain. He rubbed his erection through his clothing until he could no longer hold back.

Harry left that night with sticky long johns.

"That was a helluva good time. I love this stuff. I'm comin' back. No two ways about it."

CHAPTER 11

The Twilight Retirement Home was located on Lincoln Street in a quiet middle class neighborhood. It sat far back from the road surrounded by acres of green grass and large trees, mostly Maple and Evergreen. It was the kind of setting that on any typical October day the trees would twist in a crisp breeze, the leaves would flutter and the sunlight would wash out old colors with new colors. It was the kind of setting that on any typical October night people took long walks under the brightness of the late evening stars. It was the kind of setting where people like Florence Berry didn't have to worry about being assaulted.

Until now.

By the time Max and the Beast arrived at the crime scene the area was in the process of being sealed off. They avoided the convenience of cutting across the lawn and walked the long driveway up to the front door. Besides, it was apparent that some evidence may have been located on the grass because the police were pointing to various spots, making notes and talking softly and nodding to one another.

If at all possible, Max and the Beast wanted to talk to the victim first. They would get with the other police later. As they continued up the long drive the Beast kept his head turned so he could watch the local news reporters and their camera crews scurry around like bloodhounds looking for a scent to follow. Any scent would do, just so long as it had an odor.

"How could this happen?"

"Was her family involved?"

"What about drugs?"

"Doesn't this place have any security?"

"Where were the police?"

The more the Beast witnessed, the quicker his disheartened mood hardened. Max tried to ignore the whole thing by keeping his eyes focused on the driveway in front of him.

The Beast elbowed Max lightly in the ribs. "Only thing missing is a call to 1-800-Lawyer."

Max pointed across the lawn. "Wrong," he answered with a sigh.

The Beast scanned the direction where Max was pointing until he located the personal injury attorney whose chubby face often appeared in TV Guide advertisements and on the backs of bus benches. His name was T. Jay Silver and he was known around legal circles as the Doctor Slick of slip and fall. He was also despised by every legitimate law firm in the city.

"And you didn't think we'd be safe," Max muttered sarcastically.

The Beast took a deep breath and slowly exhaled. The thought of the personal injury attorney wandering around a crime scene like a scavenger and the fact he could do nothing about it was itself criminal. The Beast said nothing. Instead he kept his eyes focused on the driveway leading to the front door.

Until the criminalists were satisfied that all the evidence from Mrs. Berry's room was recovered they would continue to invade it. As a result, Mrs. Berry was moved to another room at the end of the hall. Dr. Thorngood was sitting on the edge of the bed when Max and Zack entered. The stethoscope hanging around his neck gave him away.

"How is she?" Max's voice was as soft as velvet.

Dr. Thorngood turned his head to see the two detectives. He had that Marcus Welby look. Content but concerned, prepared to listen but ready to respond with a fatherly sermon. The gray hair on his head matched the gray hair growing out of his ears. "Physically she'll be fine," Dr. Thorngood reassured them. He turned back towards his patient.

Max walked closer to the bed and searched Mrs. Berry's face. He wasn't sure what to expect, he was just hoping to see some sort of reaction. He got none. Her pale skin sagged around her cheeks and under her chin. Her hair was stretched out in different directions like she slept on every part of it during a winter long hibernation. Her pupils were dilated from the medication and looked like shiny little black saucers. They floated back and forth between the wall and the floor.

"I just sedated her. She'll be asleep in a couple of minutes." Dr. Thorngood took Mrs. Berry's hand and started to measure the beat of her pulse against the second hand on his watch. "I assume you two gentlemen are with the police."

"Yeah, I'm Detective Cougar and this is Detective Darwin."

"I'm Dr. Thorngood," he announced. He never turned to see which one was Cougar and which one was Darwin. He continued measuring the beat of Mrs. Berry's pulse. "Once she falls asleep, she'll most likely remain that way until morning. It'll probably be the same thing tomorrow." The doctor placed Mrs. Berry's hand back on the bed then stood up and brushed at the seat of his pants. Dr. Thorngood was medium height and carried a slight pot belly. "Problem is, I don't think she can tell you anything anyway."

Max pulled at his chin. He realized that it was a difficult time for Mrs. Berry and the last thing he wanted to do was make it worse by asking her to relive the experience. On the other hand, a sick pervert was on the loose and if he wasn't caught soon another old lady might be similarly assaulted. Whatever she could tell him might not be much, but it would be something. Max decided to press on. "Do you think she'll be in good enough condition to answer a couple of questions tomorrow?"

"Like I said detective, she'll probably be sedated again. Let's take a wait and see approach because I don't want her rushed," the doctor cautioned.

Zack moved closer to Mrs. Berry. She reminded him of his own grandmother. He stared at her but listened to the conversation between Max and Dr. Thorngood.

"Why don't you think she'll be able to tell us anything?"

"Because I don't think she knows anything, detective." The doctor wasn't trying to sound like a smart ass.

"But why?" Max was curious and until the doctor gave him an answer he could live with, he wasn't going away.

"I've been here since the police first came in to take Mrs. Berry's statement. I don't remember who they were but..."

"Officers Gordon and Conway," Zack interjected. He remembered the morning police schedule.

"Yes, that's right, Gordon and Conway," Dr. Thorngood said.

That son-of-a-bitch has a good memory, Max thought to himself.

"Anyway..." Dr. Thorngood continued, "they came up to take a statement and Mrs. Berry kept muttering about a clown, or maybe it was a clown face. I don't recall specifically. Frankly, she was quite incoherent so I didn't pay much mind to it. Obviously that's why I sedated her."

Max pulled at his chin again and stared at the tile floor. He was thinking about what the doctor said until his attention was suddenly snapped up by Zack's question.

"Dr. Thorngood, does Mrs. Berry have any family?"

"Yes a daughter. She and her husband are vacationing in Florida."

"Florida? Why and the hell would they be vacationing in Florida at a time like this?" Zack was incredulous.

"Did someone contact her?" Max inquired.

"Yes, the administrator here and I both talked to her."

"And..." Zack said in a manner that invited the doctor to continue on with the story. His eyebrows were arched up high on his protruding forehead.

Dr. Thorngood held his palms open like he was waiting to catch something from the sky. His bushy eyebrows locked together over the bridge of his nose as he spoke. "Mrs. Berry refused to go to the hospital."

"So what does that mean?" Max asked. A scowl crossed over his face like an afternoon shadow. It gave him a hard, impatient look.

"My understanding is that when the administrator contacted Mrs. Berry's daughter to let her know what happened, she told the administrator to take her to the hospital. She said that she would see her when she returned from Florida...in four days. When the administrator told her that her mother refused to go to the hospital, the daughter summoned me to check her out here."

Zack massaged his temples. "Am I missing something here?"

"No, not at all. You're hearing this right," the doctor reassured him.

"That's hard to believe."

Dr. Thorngood waved his finger in the air like it was a sword. "Listen detective, I've been their family doctor for 32 years. All I can tell you is as horrified as I am by what happened, I'm not surprised at the daughter's reaction. Knowing her, she probably figured she'd be of little use here so why come in and ruin her vacation."

Zack looked over at the helpless old lady on the bed. It suddenly dawned on him that he owed his grandmother a visit. First chance he got, he thought to himself.

"Doctor, do you have a card by chance?"

"Sure." Dr. Thorngood withdrew a card from his billfold and handed it to Max.

Max studied the raised lettering for a couple of seconds then stuffed it in the inside pocket of his leather bomber jacket.

"Let's go see what they got downstairs Beast."

The Beast offered a sympathetic smile to the old lady but by now she was asleep. "Yeah, okay," he said softly.

The two detectives headed for the stairs. Dr. Thorngood sat back down on the bed beside his patient. He massaged the bridge of his nose and closed his eyes. At that moment he hated his job.

Max slid his hand across the railing for balance and eased down the stairs in four fluid strides. When he reached the bottom he turned to see Zack still standing on the second floor.

"You Comin'?"

"Yeah."

Zack moved slow. His steps were heavy, like his large body was too much to drag around. When he got to the bottom he made a half-hearted attempt to smile. It made his face look heavy and sad.

"What's up man?"

"Nothin'." Zack's tone was somber.

"Something's up," Max countered, before leading the way out the front door.

He stopped on the porch and surveyed the commotion outside. The weather was clearing up. The shadows from the gray clouds had pretty much been chewed up by the sun so he pulled out his sunglasses and put them on.

"That goddamn old lady looks like my grandmother. I'm lookin' at her but I'm seeing my gram. It makes ya start thinkin'. Ya know what I'm saying?"

Max nodded as though he understood. But he didn't. He couldn't. Max never knew any of his grandparents. Max never even had time to know his own parents. His father died when he was just a kid. And his mother – Christ, she was a basket case altogether. The only family he ever knew was his sister Kathy.

He wished he grew up with a big family like Zack did. Maybe one day he'd have one of his own. Oh well, at least he had his sister.

Zack on the other hand could not remember a time when his gram didn't live with him and his parents. From the time he could shit without wearing a diaper, until the morning he left for the University of Wisconsin on his football scholarship, she was there. Hell, when his mom and dad were off working during the day it was gram who watched him. She took care of him, fed him and clothed him. She even disciplined him when he needed it, which, come to think of it, couldn't have been very often because the way he remembered it, he was just a goddamn perfect little peach of a kid. Zack felt a pit in his stomach the size of a grapefruit. His gram's arthritis had been getting worse over the last year and for some stupid reason he'd been visiting her less. Now when she could use some help getting fed, or clothed, (damn if she'd stand for any disciplining), he was nowhere to be found. Most of the time it seemed like he was working. And when he wasn't working, he was out playing. Holidays. On goddamn holy holidays he saw her. Christmas. Easter. Thanksgiving. What an ass, he thought to himself. "Ya know, I haven't seen my gram in a little while. I think when we're done here I'm gonna stop by her house. You mind?" Zack knew Max wouldn't care but he asked him anyway.

"Why and the hell would I mind?"

"Cause you're driving, remember?"

"No, I don't mind."

Zack put his paw on Max's sturdy shoulder and the two detectives marched down the porch steps into the open arms of the crime scene outside.

"Ya know, by the time we get oughta here it'll be somewhere around noon. We oughta take your grandmother to lunch. I'll even buy," Max announced in an attempt to draw a rise out of Zack.

Zack lifted his hand off of Max's shoulder like he was touching something hot. He smirked. "Oh no. If you gotta buy then I'll never hear the end of it. Life's too short for that kinda shit. I'll do the buying."

"Okay, fine," Max quickly agreed. "But I tried," he added, feigning his disappointment. His eyes sparkled when he said it.

The Beast stuffed his hands in his jean pockets. The pit in his stomach disappeared as quickly as it first appeared. A wry grin replaced his smirk. "Max Cougar, you've always been a cheap motherfucker. But now you're taking it out on grandmothers. Have you no shame boy?"

Max was about to respond when he spotted Officers Gordon and Conway. He pointed to the opposite end of the drive leading up to the Twilight Retirement Home. "Come on, they're over there."

"Yeah, I see 'em."

Officer Johnny Gordon had been with the Chicago Police Department for almost two years. He was tall and thin, with pale skin and light brown hair. He also had a nervous twitch around his right eye, which at times made it difficult to tell which direction he was looking in.

Officer Randy Conway had been with the Chicago Police Department for about two and a half years. He was built just the opposite of Johnny Gordon, which is why the two officers always looked out of balance when they stood next to each other. Randy Conway was short but had a robust chest and an equally robust stomach. He also had a case of dandruff which he hated so much he shaved his head bald every ten days or so. It made him look menacing, especially when he had a thin cigar dangling from his mouth. He referred to it as the "Kojak" edge.

"Gordy, whataya got?" Max called out.

"Hey Max, hey Beast," Officer Johnny Gordon responded. His voice was mild, almost meek sounding.

"Connie, how you be?"

"Pretty good Zack. Pretty good." Officer Randy Conway always sounded like he was winded.

"Which one of you girls has the pregnant wife?" Max inquired.

"Yo," Johnny Gordon signaled.

"Congratulations. I'm proud of ya papa to be," Zack said.

"Yeah. Now we can stop wondering if he really has a dick." Randy Conway chaffed.

Max stuck out his chin and began to stroke it like he was pondering one of the great mysteries of life. He nodded his head when he spoke. "Hell, I never wondered that about Gordy. I never wondered that about any woman's husband. You ever wonder anything like that Beast?"

"Naw, not me. I never wondered that Max." Zack was grinning from ear to ear.

"What about you Gordy. Did you ever stop and wonder if you had a dick?"

"No. Frankly, I can always remember one being around."

"Aw fuck you guys," Conway said jokingly.

One of the first unwritten rules Officer Johnny Gordon learned was never to laugh out loud at a crime scene. It implied disrespect to the victim. But since this was Max Cougar and Zack Darwin he took the liberty. Randy Conway joined him.

"Yeah, yeah, okay," Max said, motioning with his hand for the officer's to keep it in check. "So we know he's got a prick. We still got some biz to get down to. Whata we got?" He asked casually.

Officer Gordon grew attentive. "So far not much."

"We gotta have something Gordy," Zack said. His tone was friendly but unemotional.

"Well obviously it's still too early to know if we got any prints. And as far as a cursory inspection goes, there doesn't appear to be any seminal fluid. But that's not a certainty at this point either." Officer Gordon studied the faces of the two detectives like he was trying to guess which one of them would ask the next question.

Max motioned to the Retirement Home's sweeping front lawn. "What'd they find on the grass?"

"Looks like we may have some good shoe prints," Officer Conway offered.

"Evidently the grass was nice and wet. The stupid bastard must not have realized it when he was crossing it," Johnny Gordon added.

"Either that, or he didn't care," Zack said.

The two officer's mumbled their concurrence.

Zack and Max glanced at each other. They both understood that stupidity was one thing. Not caring was something different altogether. It was a characteristic possessed only by the worst of criminals.

Max thought back to what Dr. Thorngood said about a clown. His concern was reflected in the darkness of his voice. "What about this clown shit you guys heard? The victim's doctor said you were in the room when the victim was talking about it."

Officer Conway shuffled his feet and shifted his weight back and forth. "Actually she said something about a clown face. But that's all she said. We just figured whoever was in the room was wearing a clown mask of some kind." Officer Conway suddenly felt bad he and Officer Gordon didn't pursue it a little more when they had the chance. He looked over at Johnny Gordon as if to ask him why. Johnny Gordon's right eye started to twitch.

Zack folded his arms. "You're probably right - though it could be paint or makeup, or some other kind of crap like that," he concluded.

Max arched his neck and gazed at one of the tall trees standing guard at the Twilight Retirement Home. "Damn," he whispered to himself. "I don't like it." His eyes slowly drifted back down the body of the tree until they rested on Officer's Gordon and Conway. "What about forced entry?"

"Doesn't appear to be Max."

Max studied Conway's round face for a moment. There had to be a break-in somewhere, he told himself. "They check all points of entry Connie?"

It was plain to Officer Conway that Detective Max Cougar was growing more concerned with this crime by the minute. There was nothing casual about his demeanor anymore. He responded accordingly. "Yes sir."

Max kicked the toe of his running shoe at the ground.

"Strange," the Beast said in his low, raspy voice.

"Strange unless it's somebody with a key. Maybe an employee or ex-employee," Max guessed.

Zack ran his fingers through his thick hair a couple of times. Each time it fell back to his head in a different direction until it finally looked like it had been in a wind storm. "You guys make sure you get records of all the people who've worked here for - oh, I figure - say the last twelve months." Zack pondered his own request then added, "Whataya think Max?"

Max nodded. "Yeah that should do it. That should be good."

Max turned to see the Twilight Retirement Home. Like a fortress the three story brick exterior stood tall and firm, seemingly unscathed by the crime scene commotion sucking on its perimeter. But it was not a fortress. Like a ghost Harry Weeble left his dark spirit to fester in the empty hallways, burrow inside the cracks of walls, and chip away at the interior until the very foundation rotted away.

CHAPTER 12

Harry Weeble turned in front of the door length mirror so he could get a better view of the new women's underwear he purchased at Bloomingdales that afternoon. At the same time he couldn't help but admire his tight little ass.

"God these feel good. I'm gonna wear 'em all the time."

Harry rubbed his buttocks for a minute but had to stop because he was beginning to get aroused. He couldn't afford to be late for his 6:00 p.m. janitorial shift at the Towers Office Complex. He walked into the closet, which used to be the bedroom until he converted it, and searched out his blue coveralls. They were hanging in his blue section, stuck between two blue and red print dresses. He yanked them off the hanger and stepped into them.

"I hate this janitor bullshit. Five hours a night, seven fucking days a week. Maybe I should quit and get a job in a woman's store somewhere. Hell, I know more about fashion than most of the other bitches in Chicago. They'd have to hire me."

Harry browsed his shoe rack and pondered which one of the dozen pair of cheap running shoes he would put on. At first he grabbed the same pair he wore the night of his date with Mrs. Berry, but on closer inspection, decided against it. They still had a bunch of grass stains and Harry wanted to go with something a little whiter. When he finished tying his laces he went to look at his face in the vanity mirror one last time. He rubbed at the smooth skin on his cheeks hoping to wipe out any signs of blush still there from his afternoon stroll. His thin lips were still a little red. "Hell, that could be from a cherry popsicle. Ain't a big deal."

Harry rotated his head to check the different angles of his face. His eyebrows were plucked thin but his face was bony enough so they didn't look out of place. When he spotted one of his rubber dildos in the reflection of the mirror his green eyes twinkled - and he smiled, exposing a black, rotted tooth. He pulled at the few remaining strands of red hair just to make sure they covered as much of his head as possible. Perfect as perfect can be. Now he was ready. Harry sauntered by the combination living room/dining room but stopped just before he reached the front door. He twirled around to admire the carnival like colors splashed across the ceiling one final time before he left for the evening. "Beautiful, just fuckin' beautiful. Leonardo Di Angelo got nothin' over me."

Harry locked the front door behind him, pranced down the apartment stairs and headed south on Brotten Street to begin the two mile trek to the Towers Office Complex. He nestled his hands deep in his pockets and whistled the theme song from Snow White.

Harry was happy...

In two more blocks he turned west on Broadmoor Avenue, moved his hands around in his coverall pockets a little bit, and changed his tune to the theme song from Beauty And The Beast.

Harry was satisfied.

The Twilight Home profile list compiled by Officer's Gordon and Conway included four ex-employees. The first one moved out of state four months prior to the Berry assault. The second got married to her boyfriend of eight years, and the third gave birth to her first child. Harry Weeble was the last of the four to be checked out by Max and Zack.

The wind kicked up just about the time Zack turned his jeep north on Brotten Street. It was one of those autumn nights when at dusk the moon was about three quarters up, the sun was about three quarters down, and the combination made the blue sky look like it was about to pack it in for the day.

"What's the address Max?"

Max looked down at the open file on his lap. "According to this he lives at 273 Brotten, apartment 201. It's gotta be one of these piece of shit apartment buildings. Should be on your side."

Brotten Street was a garbage littered, rat infested side street that resembled an alley. Except for the occasional drunk who decided to take up residence on a piece of concrete for the night, it was little traveled and not well lit. Had the detectives arrived much later it would have been too dark to see much of anything without walking around with a flashlight. As it was, Zack had to bring his jeep to a steady crawl just so they could study the building addresses. Zack took up all of his window space so Max leaned towards the dashboard to get a better look out of the driver's side of the windshield. He stretched his arm out in front of Zack's chest and pointed at the buildings as they slowly passed them. "Nope," he mumbled. "Nope, that's not it either. Should be comin' up...should be right over....there. See it?"

"Yeah." Zack calmly steered his jeep to the other side of the street. He intentionally parked about twenty yards from the building entrance. When he shut off the engine the two detectives automatically looked at each other. "Think he's home?" Zack asked.

"I dunno, but I guess we're gonna find out."

"How do you want to handle it?" Zack was referring to the method he and Max would use to illegally search the premises if Harry wasn't there. Either he would go in and Max would play the lookout, or vice versa.

Not having a search warrant had never been an issue with Max and Zack. Getting caught for intentionally conducting an illegal search was. They'd likely get indicted. Plus, any evidence found during the illegal search would get thrown out of court, making a conviction impossible. So far they'd been lucky.

"We don't know what this guy looks like," Max cautioned.

"I know. That's why I asked you how you wanted to handle it."

"I dunno..."Max offered..."but this place is kinda fucked up looking. I think I'd just as soon see both of us go in as I would one of us. Hell, I'd rather have you standing behind me than have to wonder who else might be."

This street does have that kind of look to it, Zack thought. But at the same time Max's idea was pretty risky.

Max could see the concern in Zack's eyes and understood his hesitation. Still, he figured it would be better if they were able to focus on searching Harry Weeble's place without having to think about some drug induced, penny ante thief looking to steal $5.00. Besides, they'd probably only get one crack at this so it was important to make it count.

"Look - we'll blow through there as quick as we can and keep our ears open for someone coming. Hell, what else can we do?"

Zack stared out the window. The most important thing is finding out if this Weeble character was the one who assaulted the old lady. Max is right, what choice do we have? I for one can't think of any. Zack turned back to his partner without the look of concern. "Okay. Let's do it."

Although Max would never admit it, he was relieved to hear the Beast agree with him. It made him feel stronger because now they moved as one. He clenched his fist and held it out for the Beast to meet with his own.

"Besides," Max said, in a tone of voice as serious as the look in his eyes, "we can always kill the guy if he catches us."

Zack shrugged. "If he ends up being the guy the world'll probably be better off."

Max snickered. "Ain't no probably about it."

A faint light burned at the top of the second floor landing just enough to direct Max and the Beast up the stairs. The stairs were carpeted but the carpet was old and frayed and the steps underneath creaked from years of wear and tear. The chipping plaster walls were either marked by an artist with a crayon or a gang member with a message. The smell of urine filled the stairway.

Harry Weeble's apartment was the first one at the top of the second floor. Max knocked on the door. "Mr. Weeble? Mr. Harry Weeble?" His voice was friendly but firm.

Zack kept his eyes glued to the stairs and hallway.

Max knocked again. "Mr. Weeble, if you're home please answer the door. I have a delivery for you." Obviously Max realized he was supposed to identify himself as a cop, but if Harry Weeble wasn't home, why bother. He planned to break in anyway so what would be the point in identifying himself and take the chance someone else might hear. He held his ear to the door to see if he could hear anything on the other side.

Nothing.

Max kneeled down and studied the lock. "Let me have the picks," he said quietly. He waited for the Beast to fill his open hand but there was no response. Did he forget to bring the picks? Max suddenly wondered. Nah! He probably didn't hear him ask for them is all. Max repeated himself a little louder this time. "Let me have the picks." Still the Beast did not respond. No way he could've forgotten them, Max assured himself. He turned his head and looked up to find Zack standing directly behind him. "You got the picks, right?"

Zack could hear traces of panic in Max's usually calm voice. He flashed his partner one of those, "Uh-oh, I forgot," kind of looks.

Max's eyes slightly bulged. "Zack you've got to have the picks. You've got to."

Zack winked at him. "Gotcha."

"Cocksucker," Max whispered.

Harry Weeble's door had one of those typical button locks that popped out. The only problem would be if the lock guts were rusted. Still, if a key could open it, Max figured he could too. He was right. The thin steal pin slipped inside the lock hole cartridge, and with one magic push and turn..."Bingo."

From the start the whole idea was simple. The detectives would talk to Harry Weeble if he was at home. If not, they didn't plan to waste anymore time by wandering around and looking for him. If Harry Weeble was the one who assaulted Mrs. Berry they wanted to know about it now while they had the chance. It was time to forget about red tape. It was time to sidestep rules. It was time to think about Mrs. Berry. If that meant searching Harry Weeble's apartment without a warrant, or his consent, they were prepared to do it. If that meant finding inculpatory evidence and obtaining a search warrant, without ever revealing that they'd already conducted an illegal search, they were prepared to do that also. It wasn't pure, but it wasn't supposed to be.

Then again, neither were the criminals they hunted.

CHAPTER 13

Captain Whitaker was getting ready to phone his wife when Max pushed the door open and poked his head inside the Captain's office. "Cap, you busy?"

The Captain always thought of his office door as a shield against unexpected or unwelcome visitors. He hated to be bothered out of the clear blue. If you had an appointment great, no problem. If you didn't, you best make one. Whatever you do, don't barge in unannounced. Max was not expected. Worse than that, he was not welcome. Captain Whitaker slammed the phone receiver down hard. It was a small miracle it didn't break in half. "What? Whataya want Cougar?" he growled.

Max knew right then he'd made a mistake. He had no intentions of making a bigger one by staying any longer than necessary. Where and the hell is Beast, he wondered. "If this is a bad time Captain, then..."

"Cougar goddamnit - what?!" The Captain bellowed.

"It's about the Berry woman Captain. The Twilight Home thing."

"What about it?"

Zack Darwin spotted Max leaning in the door to the Captain's office and walked up behind him. He secured his hand on Max's shoulder, balanced himself on the balls of his feet and poked his head in the door just above Max's.

Their two heads looked like big game trophies stacked on top of one another. If I only had an elephant gun, the Captain thought.

"Hey Cap," Zack said casually.

Oh terrific, Max thought. Now we're gonna hear it.

"Son-of-a-bitch! Goddamn son-of-a-bitch!" The Captain pounded his hand on the desk. "What and the hell do you two want?"

"Did I come at a bad time?" the Beast whispered to Max.

Max responded by planting an elbow in his gut. As hard as his stomach was, it still took the Beast by surprise and caused him to grunt out a cough. Max swallowed hard and for the time being was able to suffocate his amusement and force out an answer for the Captain. "We need to speak to you about the Berry investigation Captain. Won't take but a minute."

"Prick," the Beast whispered.

"Fine, then come in the goddamn office and talk," Captain Whitaker commanded. "You got ten minutes."

Max pulled the door open and started to walk inside. The Beast was right behind him.

"Cougar!" Captain Whitaker snapped.

Max froze in his tracks. The Beast bumped into him from behind. "Yes Captain?"

"Ten minutes!"

Jesus Christ, enough with the attitude already, Max thought. He looked at the Captain and nodded. "I understand." Max planted another elbow in Zack's gut and proceeded. The Beast rubbed his midsection and followed.

Captain Whitaker was sitting behind a cheap Formica desk. It was decorated with two family pictures and a stack of files and phone messages. To the right of the desk stood a pair of file cabinets. To the left stood a large potted plant that died three weeks earlier. In front of the desk were two guest chairs. Max pulled one out and sat down. He fidgeted for a minute, trying to get his ass accustomed to the unforgiving plastic seat. Zack declined to sit and leaned against a side wall instead.

Captain Whitaker leaned forward in the big leather recliner he filled so easily and peered at Max. "Well?" His voice was loaded with impatience, but at least he stopped yelling.

"Captain, it's been ten days since the assault. We haven't come up with any fingerprints or semen samples. The lack of fingerprints is explained away by gloves. But the fact that no semen was found in the room, well that's kinda different." Max waited for the Captain to react.

The Captain glanced at the clock hanging crooked on the wall. "You got nine and a half minutes Cougar."

Max figured that was enough of a reaction so he continued. "Well the victim's doctor said there wasn't any penile penetration."

"What the hell's that mean?" A curious look filled the Captain's drained eyes.

Max moved his hands through his long hair. He knew the answer because of what he and the Beast discovered in their illegal search of Weeble's apartment, but could say nothing. The entire situation disgusted Max and he struggled to keep the composure in his voice. "Well, I guess it means something else was put inside the victim. The hard part's gonna be proving it. I mean we all know that the Berry woman was sexually assaulted. I'm just not sure we'll be able to prove it."

The Captain massaged his meaty chin. It was apparent he had calmed down somewhat because he was now concentrating on the Berry case and not the intrusion into his office. "You talk with the D.A.'s office?"

"Yes sir."

Captain Whitaker knew all to well, if the D.A.'s office gave his detectives anything positive they wouldn't be in his office at that very moment. He asked anyway. "And?"

"They said if some artificial instrument was used for anal penetration...then in all likelihood it would be impossible to get a sodomy conviction." Max rolled his eyes. "In other words, we can't get the little son-of-a-bitch 'cause he didn't use his own dick, Captain." Max thought back to the illegal search. He knew it was an artificial instrument because it was one of the two dozen dildos he and the Beast found in Harry Weeble's closet. They were stacked on top of each other like a case of beer bottles in a refrigerator.

Captain Whitaker grimaced. "For God's sake, where is the damn sense in that?"

"There isn't any," the Beast offered. "The law doesn't make an allowance for an artificial instrument. The guidelines necessary to determine if the crime's been committed can't be met." The Beast paused. He understood all the words but they still made no sense to his way of thinking, especially since he knew Weeble sodomized the old Berry woman with a dildo. "I mean, what the fuck," he added out of frustration.

Captain Whitaker rubbed his eyes like he was just waking up in the morning and leaned back in his recliner. The chair groaned.

"That's not even the worst part of it Captain. Beast and I have been over to see the victim three times now and she either can't, or won't talk to us. The D.A. said without her cooperation we probably can't make a case for any kind of sexual assault, let alone sodomy." Max's efforts to disguise the frustration in his voice only made him sound desperate.

The Captain traded glances with the Beast and Max before resting his eyes on the open office space. "So far you've told me everything except where we're at."

Max looked over to Zack as if to say now the bullshit begins. Zack understood the look, as well as the bullshit. He held out an open palm, inviting Max to continue.

"We're not sure where we're at Captain. To date we've compiled a profile list of anyone who's worked at the home for the last year." Max paused and gleaned his notebook for some relevant facts to feed to Captain Whitaker. "We've come up with 22 people, 14 of them are females. They're still employed there – nurses, office help, that kinda thing. We don't think any of them fit the bill. Of the remaining 8 people, 4 are still working there. All four are male. One of them is the administrator. He's been there for the last seven years. Another is his assistant. He fills in the blanks around the place. He's been there as long as the administrator. They're known to be lovers. We don't think they fit either." Max stopped and waited for a reaction from the Captain.

"I'm still listening Cougar."

"The other two are full time maintenance. One's been there eight years and one's been there since the place has been in business. We haven't come up with anything on them - and frankly Captain it doesn't make sense that either of them would suddenly go nuts."

"You haven't ruled them out, have you?"

"No, they're just not at the top of the list," the Beast piped in, tongue in cheek.

"Well what's at the top of the list?" The Captain's expression was blank but his tone of voice was sharp.

The Beast suddenly felt like a schoolboy who shot out a sarcastic answer to a perfectly good question. Now he had to pay for it by having the teacher suddenly give him all the attention he didn't want. If I'd only keep my fucking mouth shut, the Beast thought. He rolled his eyes and proceeded. "Of the four ex-employees, one moved out of state before the assault, one had a baby, one got married, and one we know nothing about - except he quit working at the home some three and a half weeks ago." The answer made Zack want to gag but he finished what he started. "At this point he's the one that tops the list. At least we wanna check him out."

Max figured if he sat in the plastic chair much longer his ass was gonna go numb. He stood up.

"Who is it?"

Although Max was quite tempted to say Daffy Duck, he held back. "His name is Harry Weeble."

"Whataya got on him?"

Max pinched the bridge of his nose before giving the Captain the type of answer that was no answer at all. "Nothin' much. According to his employee file he's 33, single and basically moves around some. Does odd jobs for awhile and leaves. He evidently quit his job about two weeks before the assault. Gave no reason. Gave no notice. He just up and quit."

"That's all ya know about him? That's it? What the hell you two been doing all this time?" The Captain was more surprised than he was angry.

Max ignored the last question. "Well there isn't anything unusual about him in his file or from the people we talked to..." Max let his answer hang in the air unfinished.

"But?" Captain Whitaker asked.

Make it good partner 'cause if we don't get the search warrant we got nothin' except some crazy motherfucker still on the loose, Zack said to himself.

"Well Captain..." Max began..."Zack and I went over to see him a couple of times. The first time he wouldn't even open the door. He told us to get a search warrant or get lost." Max paused.

"So?" Captain Whitaker prodded.

"Well as much as we may have wanted to Captain, we couldn't very well kick the door in and yank him outside."

"Why, it wouldn't be the first time you two got carried away." Captain Whitaker was annoyed that his two detectives occasionally developed convenient memory syndrome. "What about the second time?" He asked.

Max immediately flashed back to Harry Weeble's apartment. The ladies' dresses and underwear, the makeup area in the bathroom, the bright lights and all the red wigs, the dildos, the Barbie dolls, the wild colors painted everywhere, the running shoes with the grass stains. It wasn't thirty minutes into the illegal search before Max and Zack knew that Harry Weeble was a major league nut who liked to play house. It wasn't much more than an hour before each one of the detectives could piece together what they believed happened on the night of the Berry assault. "Well...the second time we never quite made it to his door. When we went there we believe we saw him walking across the street wearing a dress and makeup." Max hesitated for a second. "And running shoes."

The Captain's eyebrows tried to touch each other as he spoke. "So what the hell does that have to do with anything?"

Max shrugged his shoulders before he answered. "Well the makeup he was wearing kinda made him look like a clown. And the running shoes, I don't know Captain, but we found a half a dozen shoe prints outside of the Twilight Retirement Home. The casts we took of the sole imprints seem to indicate an athletic shoe of some sort."

So far the Captain didn't like what he was hearing. "Look it," he said firmly, "just where and the hell are you two going with this?"

God if they'd just change the fucking system and let us go after the goddamn loony tunes, me and Zack wouldn't have to go through all this shit, Max told himself. He hated having to lie to the Captain. But what he hated worse was when he didn't lie the sick perverts they were chasing were at a constant advantage. By now Max was agitated. He hoped it wasn't obvious when he spoke. "Well the Berry woman mentioned a clown and when me and Zack saw him he reminded us of one. Plus the running shoe thing. Are his shoes the same as the imprints we got from the crime scene? We don't know for certain but maybe with a search warrant we could find out."

Captain Whitaker didn't respond right away. Instead he fidgeted in his chair for a couple of seconds before straightening back up. The chair groaned again. A look of confusion filled his eyes. "Let me make sure I've got this right. You want me to see if I can get you a search warrant because some guy, who you believe was this Harry Weeble, was wearing a dress and makeup?"

"Well Captain..." Max started to respond.

"Wait a minute Cougar, I'm still talking." From the tone of Captain Whitaker's voice it was obvious that he was getting mad again. "Now you said the Berry woman mentioned a clown, and because this guy needs a lesson in putting on makeup you think that's enough probable cause to get a search warrant?"

"Don't forget the running shoe thing Captain," Zack suggested.

Captain Whitaker dropped his forearms on the desk. It sounded like a slab of beef hitting the floor. He cupped his hands together and stared hard at the Beast. He couldn't believe what he was hearing. "Oh yeah your honor, besides the fact that he needs a lesson wearing makeup, my detectives have brilliant eyesight and saw him from across the street wearing running shoes. Maybe the shoes my detectives saw from all the way across the street are the athletic shoe imprints found at the crime scene." Captain Whitaker slouched back in his chair and let his words soak in the silent filled room for almost a minute before he continued. He tried to sound friendly. "Look, I know where you guys are going with this. Your instincts tell you this Weeble character might've had something to do with the Berry woman mess. Maybe he does, I don't know. But I do know that based on the information you've given me we can't even make a bad argument for probable cause. The D.A.'s office will get thrown out of court before they even get in."

"We were really hoping you'd convince the D.A. to try anyway," Max said, wanting to sound apologetic even though he wasn't sorry.

"Look-it Max, there's no freakin' way the D.A.'s gonna embarrass himself or his department by going to court with what you two have. Right or wrong isn't the issue here. The D.A. just isn't gonna do it," the Captain said matter-of-factly.

"But Captain, with a search warrant we can find out about this guy in an hour...that's all we're trying to do," Zack pleaded.

Here they go, the Captain thought. One starts up, the other one finishes. One asks, the other one begs. One circles overhead, the other one sneaks in underneath. They never stop. Captain Whitaker leaned forward in his chair again, and once again the chair groaned. "Forget the damn search warrant. It isn't gonna happen," he chided.

Son-of-a-bitch! Now this fucking puke's gonna get a crack at another old lady and we gotta wait for it. I hate this fucking job, Max thought.

One day I'm gonna grab that D.A. and shove a baseball bat up his political ass...see how he likes it, Zack thought.

"Maybe you two ought to give some thought to a stakeout," the Captain half suggested, half demanded.

"We already have Captain."

CHAPTER 14

Max was slouched down in the passenger seat of Zack's jeep staring out the window. "How long you think he's been up there?" He asked, more to help pass the quiet than anything else. His eyelids felt like ten pound weights as he strained to keep his dried out blue eyes focused on Harry Weeble's apartment building.

"Don't know. How long we been sittin' here?" Zack responded. His raspy voice sounded more tired than it did raspy.

"About an hour, and didn't you ever learn not to answer a question with another question?"

"I can't remember, what about you?" Zack asked sarcastically. He wanted to see Max's reaction but found himself semi-numb from a combination of the soothing early morning darkness and his own tired body, so he was unwilling to lift his head from the headrest and look over at him.

It had been five days since Detectives Cougar and Darwin went to see Captain Whitaker about obtaining a search warrant, and four nights since the Harry Weeble stakeout began. What started out as an illegal search designed to help enforce the law, turned into a legal stakeout designed to allow the commission of another crime. It was that good old constitutional thing; and it would remain intact, pure and simple, blind or ugly. Detectives Cougar and Darwin couldn't do anything about Harry Weeble until Harry Weeble decided to break the law, again. Wonderful kind of shit, Max thought. He continued watching the apartment building while Zack's jeep got spanked with rain water every time the early November wind reared up its ugly head and lifted it out of the street puddles.

"Who's relieving us tonight?" Zack asked. He was tired and the sooner somebody got there to relieve him, the sooner he'd be able to get some sleep. He found the idea appealing.

"Tracy and Hollins," Max quietly answered, referring to the two first year detectives.

Zack rounded up enough energy and turned to face Max. "What time you got?" His mouth was dry and the words sounded like they were stuck to his lips.

A dim glow from the lone street light filtered through the darkness but it was still dark inside Zack's jeep and difficult to see. Max brought his hand up in front of his face and peered closely at his watch. "1:25, and why don't you buy a fucking watch already?"

"Don't have to," Zack said, as though the notion never crossed his mind. A slight smile curled at the ends of his mouth.

"Why not?" Max asked, knowing he was about to get a smart-ass response.

He popped his eyes wide open like he was trying some shock treatment to wake them up.

"Cause if I bought one you wouldn't have anything to buy me for my birthday," Zack deadpanned.

"How do you know I'd buy you a watch anyway?" Max asked, as if the answer was a deep, dark secret.

"Frankly, I don't," Zack replied, like a layman imitating an aristocrat.

"Well until that magical day comes why don't you get this fucking clock fixed?" Max tapped the dashboard with the toe of his running shoe for emphasis.

"Don't have to," Zack retorted. A slight smile returned to the corners of his mouth.

"Why not?"

"Because I can't tell the time anyway."

Max laughed.

Zack watched him for a couple of seconds before laughing quietly himself. Bantering with Max was one of those great intangibles Zack enjoyed most about their friendship. As much as he wanted it to continue he also realized the Harry Weeble stakeout was neither the time, nor the place. He turned and focused on the apartment building outside. "What time are they supposed to get here Max?"

"Bout an hour." The tone in Max's answer sounded as deflated as the tone in Zack's question.

The Beast was suddenly curious about the change in personnel. He and Max hand picked Detectives Scroggins and Sheppard and after three days a new team was now getting involved. "Why Tracy and Hollins?"

Max yawned before answering. "Not sure, but I hear the Captain wanted Scroggins and Sheppard in another part of town."

Zack frowned. "Don't tell me the Captain put 'em on that Zorby investigation just 'cause they're black?" Zack was referring to Arnold Zorby, a black teacher accused by the parents of a white eight year old girl of sexual assault. It was the new media darling case.

"I don't know. I guess." Max sighed.

Zack turned to face Max again. "I think the Captain's thinking too much. Whata you think?"

Max sat up in the passenger seat. The stiffness he was feeling was turning into dull spasms so he rotated his shoulders to loosen up. "He probably figured somebody in the Zorby clan would scream some kind of racist bullshit the first chance they got. You know, two white boys show up to investigate, ask some meaningless question the ACLU doesn't like, and boom, they're off and running. So..." Max paused to yawn again, "we got stuck with the white boys and Zorby got stuck with the black boys. But this way when they ask the same meaningless question it'll have been asked from the proper color so the ACLU won't bitch about it too much."

"Yeah but Scroggins and Sheppard are good," Zack protested, although the emotion in his voice was so slight nobody else but Max would have been able to tell that it really bothered him. "We don't know a thing about these other guys but we gotta get stuck with them 'cause they're white. That's such a bunch of crap. I wish I could understand it."

"Me too man, me too." Max settled back into the passenger seat and tried to get comfortable.

Zack decided on some coffee so he reached around his seat and grabbed one of the two thermoses sitting on the floor mat in the back seat. "Coffee?"

Max grunted.

Zack unscrewed the thermos and the steam danced out like a cobra out of a basket. The aroma filled the jeep. He couldn't help but take in a deep, exaggerated breath. "Ahhhhhh. That coffee sure does smell good honey," he said, pretending like he was in a commercial for Maxwell House Coffee.

Max was half amused and laughed like it. His shoulders jumped forward once and air shot out his nose. "You missed your calling. You should've been a fucking moron when you grew up, not a cop," he said in jest.

Zack poured the coffee. "Your just jealous you don't have my talent, that's all," he asserted.

"Yeah, I'm sure that's it," Max agreed sarcastically. Max took one of the cups and for the next thirty minutes the two detectives sat in silence drinking coffee. They focused on the apartment building, the darkness and anything that moved in between. The most important thing was to stay awake while the November night drifted along.

"You ever think about getting married?"

The words fell from Zack's mouth out of the clear blue and caught Max off guard. He looked at Zack but the darkness inside the jeep made it difficult for Max to read his face. "I don't know, I guess...I don't know," Max said, somewhat uncomfortable with the subject matter. "Why do you ask?"

Zack leaned his powerful upper body against the jeep door and rested his head against the cold window. He was no longer looking at Harry Weeble's apartment building. "I don't know...I guess 'cause I think about it from time to time and was just wondering if you ever did too." Zack didn't know why but his answer suddenly made him feel uneasy. If it was light outside and Max could see his face he would've been embarrassed.

The more Max thought about it, the more he got that far away look in his eyes. His voice was kind of out there as well. "It would probably be nice. I mean I never grew up with much of a family...ya know there's my sister Kathy, but that's it."

Listening to his friend made Zack wish he never brought up the subject.

On the other side of Brotten Street Detective Tracy slowed his car when he spotted, what he calculated to be, Zack Darwin's jeep parked a clear distance away from the Harry Weeble Apartment Building. "That's gotta be them," he said to Detective Hollins.

"Flash the signal and we'll find out for sure," Detective Hollins responded. He was referring to the signal he and Detective Tracy concocted between themselves on their way to the stakeout.

Detective Tracy nodded dramatically and proceeded to engage the signal. He flashed his brights and counted to three - flashed his brights and counted to three - flashed his brights, and stopped. He was prepared to repeat the signaling process two additional times. If he didn't get a response after the third time he was prepared to pull up to the jeep and check it out.

Detective Hollins monitored his watch to make sure no more than 90 seconds went by before his partner engaged the signaling process for the second time.

Zack's attention was quickly swallowed up by the blinking headlights. "Hey. You catch that?" His raspy voice sounded full of life.

Max nodded his head. "Yeah, I got it. I'd say our white boys are here."

"I'll say this, if no one knew we were sitting out here before, they sure know it now." The Beast was definitely agitated. "I mean we sit with no lights on trying to make it difficult for someone to see us, and he comes down the street like a fucking pinball machine to let everyone know we've been here all along. What the hell is the matter with that dumb son-of-a-bitch anyway?"

Max was equally perturbed. "Better drive over there before he sends up a goddamn flare."

The Beast wrapped his paws around the steering wheel like it was a big donut, only the wheel didn't fall apart when he squeezed it.

Detective Tracy studied the jeep's slow, but certain movement. "They don't have their lights on but it looks like they're coming this way."

Detective Hollins looked up from his watch. "Flash your lights to let them know we copy their presence."

Detective Tracy nodded dramatically and proceeded to flash his headlights at the approaching jeep.

The Beast clenched his teeth.

A stakeout's bad enough without letting every Tom, Dick and cocksucker who happen to be looking out a window know you're on one, Max thought. Still, he knew the Beast had no choice but to finish the short distance to their car. With these two detectives turning around would only create more havoc.

"I'm gonna kill the motherfucker," the Beast mumbled as he reached the vehicle. He maneuvered his jeep alongside of Detective Tracy's door.

The two rookie detectives met Max once before but never Zack, so

Detective Tracy rolled down his window for introductions. "Detective Tracy," he said with a mouthful of starch. "To my right is Detective Hollins." He pulled out his shield and displayed it for Zack's inspection.

The Beast bent his head a little and got a fair view of the detectives because they had the interior car light on. He ignored the badge altogether. From the looks of his shoulders Detective Tracy appeared to be of medium weight. He had short brown hair that looked like it was combed and sprayed three days ago, eyes set back away from his nose and small ears with large earlobes that hung like chandeliers. A look of grave concern decorated his face from forehead to chin.

Detective Hollins, on the other hand, appeared to be a large man. He was sporting a blond crew cut over a square head, wide cheekbones, a wide nose, and because of the darkness, dull eyes that were barely visible. His face was as expressionless as the darkness. It was there, nothing more.

"What and the hell are you doing?" the Beast asked in a harsh whisper, hoping not to disturb the silence of the empty street.

Detective Tracy found himself taken aback by the question, as well as the tone of voice used to ask it. Still, he reasoned, the best way to handle the situation was with total and complete professionalism. Remember, keep a level head, and always, keep emotions out of it. "Detective Hollins and myself are here to relieve you."

"You do remember, don't you?" Detective Hollins added. He had a deep voice, that coming from the passenger seat, sounded like it echoed.

The Beast couldn't tell if the two detectives were patronizing him, but either way he didn't like it. He turned his back on them and looked at Max. "You better jump in if you don't want me kicking his stupid ass from one end of the street to the other," he muttered.

When Max saw the look of anger and astonishment mingling in his eyes, he knew his partner's patience had been compromised. There was no other choice. "Sit tight. I got it," he assured the Beast. Max leaned towards the driver's window and looked at Detective Tracy. Zack moved over as far as he could to give him as much room as possible. The problem was Zack's body was half the size of the jeep so moving over accomplished little more than almost putting Max on his lap.

"Your first name is Dick isn't it?" Max asked calmly.

Detective Tracy looked at him like he didn't know what Max was talking about. After all, he met Max just the other day. Surely Max remembered his name.

"You know, as in Dick Tracy," Max volunteered.

"Ha!" shot out of Zack's mouth before he had a chance to choke it back. Max felt his breath hit him in the side of the head.

Total and complete professionalism, a level head and no emotions, Detective Tracy reminded himself. Besides, Detective Max Cougar was a veteran. Play it smart, say nothing, he decided.

"Don't tell me I'm the only one to ever call you Dick, Dick?"

"Ha!" shot out from Zack's mouth again. Again Max felt his breath hit him in the side of the head.

Total and complete professionalism, a level head...but I don't have to sit here and get insulted. Detective Tracy planted a stern look across his face. "It's Barton. My name is Barton Tracy. In the future I would appreciate it if you would remember it."

"Hell, I'd rather be called Dick," Zack whispered to Max.

Max set Zack's comment on the back burner and continued to focus on Detective Barton Tracy. "You want me to remember your name?"

Detective Tracy said nothing. Instead he wrestled the stern look off his face. Total and complete professionalism was what he would strive for.

"Do you?" Max repeated. He asked in such a way that Detective Tracy knew he had to provide an answer, even if it wasn't much of one.

"Yes I do."

"Fine, I'll remember. But in turn I want you to remember something for me."

Again Detective Tracy said nothing.

"Are you hearing me Barton?"

"I'm hearing you. What is it you want me to remember?"

Max wagged his finger at Detective Barton Tracy. "The next time you're on a stakeout and you flash your lights for the whole fucking world to see, the two of you are gonna get together with the two of us for a little dance. And that's regardless if me and my partner are even on the case. Understood?" Max's question sounded more like a warning.

Detective Tracy looked like he wanted to say something, but didn't.

Detective Hollins leaned forward and peered out the window. Even then his eyes looked dull and his head looked as flat as Frankenstein's. "Detective Cougar I don't think you understand just what we were attempting to do. I think..."

Before Detective Hollins could utter another word, Max emptied his shoulder holster and had his arm out the window and his revolver planted not 6 inches from Detective Tracy's nose. He moved it just enough to let Hollins know the gun was also pointing at him. Oh Christ, Zack thought. He knew Max wasn't gonna do anything, he just wasn't sure how Detectives Tracy and Hollins would react. Would either of them reach for their guns? Zack doubted it. So far they looked frozen. Heart attacks were more likely, which was a good thing because Zack was hemmed in and wouldn't have been able to help Max anyway.

"I don't care what you think detective. As a matter-of-fact it's quite obvious to me you don't think. Now this is not the time or place to lose a debate with me. I think you should concentrate on that little bastard that lives upstairs there. That's why you're here." Max nodded in the direction of Harry Weeble's apartment building. "Are we clear?"

Detective Tracy looked like he was shaking. He said nothing.

Detective Hollins nodded his head slowly. Sweat was running down his temples. "We're clear."

"Good." Max said. He pulled his gun away and searched the faces of both detectives. Detective Tracy exhaled and it reminded Max of air being let out of a balloon. Detective Hollins had his eyes sealed shut, like he was in deep prayer giving thanks.

"Now before me and my partner leave I want to remind you, if you see Harry Weeble, contact the precinct immediately. Even if all he does is look out his window. They'll know where to find us." Max's tone was calm, almost friendly. "Are we clear?"

Detectives Tracy and Hollins remained silent.

"Good," Max concluded. He fell back in the passenger seat and took a deep breath.

"You okay?" The Beast asked.

"Think I got carried away Zack?"

The Beast didn't answer immediately. He pulled away so the two first year detectives could recover from their encounter with Max and get on with the Harry Weeble stakeout.

Max looked at him and waited for an answer.

"If they never do that type of shit again then you didn't go too far. But," the Beast cautioned, "if they do that kind of shit again, then maybe we have to do more."

It was obvious by the look on Max's face he didn't understand what the Beast was saying. "Meaning what, we blow their fucking heads off next time?"

Zack found his partner's question a little irritating. "No we don't blow their heads off. All I'm saying is we'll go see the Captain and try and get them reassigned to the desk. I mean what choice do we have. Otherwise, sooner or later they'll get someone killed."

Max nodded his head. "Yeah, I guess."

The Beast turned west off Brotten Street and headed home. By the time he arrived some 50 minutes later, Detectives Tracy and Hollins were sound asleep.

Fifteen minutes after that Harry Weeble strolled out the front door to go stylin'.

CHAPTER 15

It was 7:00 a.m. when the telephone blared out like a siren. Max had been asleep less than 3 hours so when he first heard it his eyes popped wide open and his body shot straight up from the bed. It took him a couple of seconds before he realized where he was and could answer the phone. "Yeah, what?" His voice was groggy with sleep.

"Our boy made it out last night."

Max shook his body like he just got an electric shock. "Say what Beast?"

"Our boy made it out."

Max snapped to attention.

"Olson contacted me a couple of minutes ago. Some old lady called the police about 5:00 a.m. to complain about a break-in at her house. They send some cop over and first she's ranting and raving about a woman, then she's ranting and raving about a man dressed like a woman, then something about a red wig falling off. You get the picture."

"What time is it?" Max asked.

"About 7:00 and before you ask me, Tracy and Hollins are just finishing their shift. Need I say more?" It wasn't a question that required an answer. The Beast shook his head in disgust. He woke up with a headache and he knew it was gonna get worse before the day was out. He pawed at his thick hair in the hopes of pushing it into some kind of shape because he knew he wouldn't have time for a shower.

"Great." Max rubbed the sleep wrinkles out of the side of his face. Something told him he wouldn't have time for a shower either.

"After Olson got a look at the cop's report he sent a squad to pick her up and bring her in."

"How much time do we have?" Max asked.

"None."

"Fuck."

"I'll see you in about 45 minutes."

When Max saw Mrs. Shirley for the first time she reminded him of a little china figurine made in the 1950's. Her thin white hair was brushed to the side in such a way that she was able to hide her baldness. Her facial skin was wrinkled and hung loose but she did her best to disguise it with a heavy dose of white facial powder and makeup. Her hands were small and bony, but the nail polish was evident as she cupped her hands together and held them in her perfectly postured lap. She wore glasses that, by looking at the narrow, pointed frames, had to be 30 years old.

"Mrs. Shirley, please meet Detectives Cougar and Darwin," Sergeant Olson said, in as hospitable a tone as he could pull out of his mouth.

Max smiled and bowed his head a little. "Nice to meet you ma'am."

Zack followed suit. "It's a pleasure Mrs. Shirley."

"Do I need a lawyer?" she snapped. Her voice was high pitched and strong.

In as much as Mrs. Shirley never asked Sergeant Olson about a lawyer while the two of them waited for Max and Zack, he was slightly stunned to hear her ask about one now. "Why no ma'am, you don't need a lawyer," he answered gingerly.

"Because I won't talk to anyone if I need a damn lawyer," she bristled.

Max and Zack looked at each other at the same time. They both grinned.

"No ma'am, you don't need a lawyer," the Sergeant reassured her.

"Why don't I? Hell they always have 'em on television. Seems to me lots of those stories are real. Maybe I ought to have one."

"Please ma'am, let me assure you, you won't need one," Max broke in. He was half entertained and half delighted to be in the presence of such a feisty old lady.

Mrs. Shirley looked Max over from head to toe like she was examining him to make sure he was good enough for her granddaughter.

"Cougar, huh? Like the cat or the car?"

"Excuse me ma'am?" Max didn't know what else to say because he wasn't really sure what the old lady was getting at.

"Sweet Jesus, honey, get the damn wax out! I said like the cat or the car. Your name for cripe sakes."

"Sorry ma'am. Like the cat, just like the cat."

"Don't be sorry honey. I haven't liked the car since they changed the model in 74." Mrs. Shirley swung her tiny head back and cackled.

Max stood amused. The Beast and Sergeant Olson each wore a look of disbelief.

Mrs. Shirley pointed her bony little finger at the Beast. "Who's that big fella next to you?"

"That's my partner, Zack."

Mrs. Shirley shifted her head back and over to one side like she was trying to get a full view of the Beast. "You gotta last name big fella?"

"Darwin, ma'am."

"Darwinmaam?" Ever since Mrs. Shirley's 80th birthday, she didn't always understand things as clearly as she used to. Sometimes words needed to be repeated two or three times before they started to make sense to her.

"Darwin."

Mrs. Shirley ignored Zack's answer, as if forgetting she even asked him a question. Instead she searched the office for a window. When she couldn't find one her eyes settled on the wall opposite where she was sitting. Suddenly she looked sad and confused, and before anyone knew it, she was answering questions not yet asked. "I have a dog named Lucy. I got her about 7 years ago. I needed the company and wanted the protection. She's a dobie."

Max pulled out one of the chairs and sat down. Sergeant Olson and Zack remained standing.

"I think it was about 4:30 in the morning. I didn't have my glasses on so I'm not sure, but I think that's right, 4:30 in the morning. Anyways, Lucy must've heard a noise 'cause she came to the side of my bed. Lucy won't make any noise when she hears something. I never have figured that out. She just comes next to wherever I'm sittin' and stands there and looks at the place where she heard the noise."

At that moment Zack realized the dog saved Mrs. Shirley from being assaulted and a sense of relief flushed out his tension. Zack had a doberman as a kid and his dog did the same thing. It would hear a noise but it wouldn't make any noise itself. Then one day some neighborhood kid decided to test out the front door. It was open so he walked in. The dog waited until he was all the way inside before he came out of nowhere and ripped into the kid's thigh. The kid couldn't walk for a month. He never tested the front door again either.

"I could feel Lucy breathing on me so I wake up. As soon as I do, I see something standing in the doorway. I hurried to find my glasses and when I did I saw it was a woman. I could tell 'cause I could see she was wearing a long dress and had long hair."

Max thought back to all the dresses and wigs he saw in Harry Weeble's apartment and his stomached tightened in knots.

"So I put my nightlight on, but then I wasn't sure what I saw. Lucy wasn't sure either but she went after whatever it was. The woman started to run but she must've fallen down 'cause I heard a loud thud and I knew it wasn't Lucy 'cause I could still hear her growling and carrying on like nobody's business."

Max closed his eyes. He wasn't sure he wanted to hear the rest of the story. Zack folded his arms securely and Sergeant Olson belched.

"By the time I got into the other room I saw this man. At least I think it was a man. He was wearing this dress and he was holding a big purse and his hair was on the floor next to him. It was red. It must've fallen off when he fell to the floor. Anyways, he's layin' there and shaking so bad you would've thought he was standing naked outside in the middle of a Montana blizzard. He looked up at me, only for a second though, 'cause I think he was too scared to look away from Lucy. His face was all marked up too. Colorful, if I do say so myself."

Sergeant Olson glanced at Max and nodded his head. Had to be the same guy, he thought.

"Did Lucy do anything to this man?" Max asked.

"No. He just laid there shaking like I told you. He had his hand up in front of his face like he was gonna protect it if she went after him. But she didn't, I think 'cause she sensed how helpless he was."

Harry Weeble, helpless? Not in this lifetime, Max thought.

"How'd he get out of your house ma'am?"

Mrs. Shirley looked over at the big fella. "Well after some minutes he started dragging himself along the floor real slow till he got to the front door. Lucy stayed right with him. Then all of a sudden he jumped up, kicked at Lucy one time and ran out the door."

"Did he take his purse and wig, Mrs. Shirley?" Max asked.

"Boy he had a hold of those things like there was no tomorrow. You bet, he took 'em. Nice lookin' bag too. Would've made a fine purse."

"I'm sure it would have ma'am," Zack agreed. "Now do you think you might be able to recognize him from a picture?"

"Well fiddle-dee-dee and drumsticks, I can sure try. Yes siree, I sure can do that. But he had an awfully strange lookin' face. It might be hard 'cause of all the color's he was wearing. Besides, I don't know if I see as good as I used to."

"I think you do pretty well Mrs. Shirley. Now you sit tight and Sergeant Olson is gonna bring you a couple of books to look through. It won't take too long, okay?" Max asked.

He sounded so warm and friendly, Mrs. Shirley thought. And he was good lookin' too. She nodded her head.

Max pushed his chair away from the table. "Mrs. Shirley, would it bother you if maybe me or my partner, or some other police officers keep a watch on you for a few days?"

"Well maybe you and that big fella," she said, pointing to Zack. "But I'll be damned if I want a bunch of strange cops walking around," she snarled.

Max smiled. "Well they wouldn't be walking around. Maybe they'd be sitting outside in their cars during the night."

Mrs. Shirley searched for that window again, but when she remembered the room didn't have one her eyes settled back on the wall opposite where she was sitting. She looked concerned. "You think he's coming back, don't you?"

For the first time Max could hear the fear in Mrs. Shirley's voice. He could have kicked himself for scaring her. He tried to sound reassuring when he answered. "No ma'am, I don't think so. But we do want to be sure. And even if he does, we'll be there to help Lucy catch him."

Mrs. Shirley rolled the thought around for a couple of seconds. "Okay," she concluded abruptly.

"Good," Max said. "Now we're gonna go outside but Sergeant Olson's gonna bring a couple of books back in here. You take as much time as you need when you look through them. And if you see a familiar face you let the Sergeant know, okay?"

Mrs. Shirley nodded, but after they left the room she searched for the window again.

By mid afternoon it would have been obvious to anyone with eyesight that the crime business was flourishing. The precinct was bustling with the kind of activity normally seen at a Wal Mart blue light special. Max and the Beast hoped to search out Detectives Tracy and Hollins but Captain Whitaker had other plans. Besides, the Captain assured the two detectives that Tracy and Hollins would remain on the Weeble stakeout.

The wacko business must have also been flourishing because until Captain Whitaker phoned Dr. Wasserblock personally, Max and the Beast couldn't get in to see him. Not that they really cared. Had it been up to them, they wouldn't have wasted time searching out the shrink of police, (as the Beast liked to refer to him). Problem was, it wasn't up to them. Seeing the good doctor was the Captain's other plans.

Dr. Maury Wasserblock was medium height, ate three sizeable meals a day, including desert, and hid behind a full grey beard and bifocals. He was also one of those criminal psychiatrists who never seemed capable of giving a straight answer. "The mind is a very deep and very tricky thing," he would say. Except he would articulate it with the restrained arrogance of a well known doctor. Concurrence to his psycho babble was generally automatic, even if misguided. Max and the Beast hoped to hear Dr. Wasserblock tell them Harry Weeble would definitely be making a return visit to Mrs. Shirley's. What they got, after sitting for over an hour with nicely folded hands and polite faces listening to the doctor pontificate about the virtues of Freud and the criminally insane, was if in fact the intruder was to return, he would do so in the future.

"That was enjoyable," Max uttered sarcastically after he and Zack left Dr. Wasserblock's office.

"Indeed it was my good man. Indeed it was," Zack returned.

Harry Weeble sat cowered in a corner, his arms draped tightly around his upper body like he was the gift and his arms were the wrapping paper. He'd been that way ever since his early morning return from Mrs. Shirley's house 12 hours earlier. He felt defeated. He felt dirty. Worst of all, he felt unfulfilled because he was unable to fulfill the needs of Mrs. Shirley. Finally, he cast his eyes down at the small pink and green throw rugs scattered around the wood floor. Nothing. He looked at the walls, the pictures. Nothing. He searched the interior of his apartment. The furniture, the little trinkets that made him blush and giggle. Nothing. He gazed up at the ceiling. It was a ceiling that sang and danced with the colors of life. It was a ceiling only another great painter like

Leonardo Di Angelo would've appreciated and hailed with reverence, if he was still alive. But now something was strangely different. The colors on the ceiling began spiraling smaller and smaller into darkness. Harry found it maddening. He sealed his eyes shut, hoping that would make it stop. He was wrong. The colors on the ceiling grew farther and farther away.

"Noooooooo!" he bellowed, banging his head against the wall.

The colors continued to get smaller.

"Nooooooo!"

The colors were a mere speck.

"Goddamnit Noooooooo!"

The colors were suddenly gone. Only the blackness of an empty hole remained in his head.

Harry's bloodshot eyes popped open and sailed around the room. The walls, the furniture, the pictures, the trinkets, the walls, the furniture, the pictures, the trinkets.

Harry was growing dizzy with confusion and hungry with rage. He couldn't make it stop. He didn't want to make it stop.

The walls, the furniture, the pictures, the trinkets.

Harry jumped to his feet and started pacing in tight little circles. His eyes were bugged out but he wasn't seeing anything. His fists were clenched, exposing the kind of veins only a junkie could love.

Harry Weeble was set to erupt.

"Motherfucker! Motherfucker! I'm killing that fucking dog," he growled. "I'm gonna fuck it too. Gonna make that bitch watch. Then I'm fucking her. They'll never - ever fuck with me. Never goddamnit it. Not ever!"

Sweat poured out from Harry and soaked his undershirt. He took a deep breath and exhaled quickly. "I'm goin' back out stylin' tonight." He pumped his fist like he just sank the winning putt at the U.S. Open. "Goddamnit! Yes! Yes! I'm goin' stylin' tonight!" A sparkle flickered in Harry's eyes. He gazed up at his ceiling and found wild colors dancing before him.

"Now what am I ever gonna wear?"

CHAPTER 16

Max and the Beast were parked six houses down from Mrs. Shirley's, approximately 50 yards away. They were prepared to wait there all night if necessary. If they needed sleep, which wasn't likely since they were both suffering from adrenaline poisoning, they would alternate 20 minute naps.

Detectives Tracy and Hollins were parked just down the street from Harry Weeble's. Earlier in the day they sought out Max and the Beast and apologized for their rookie stupidity. They also expressed sincere remorse upon having learned Harry Weeble got by them the night before.

When Max heard the apology he figured he had no choice but to offer a simple, if not direct response. "I'm glad 'cause we don't have time for anymore bullshit."

The Beast was a little softer in his approach. "Don't fuck up again," he warned.

They understood.

At 1:00 in the morning Harry Weeble finished filling his stylin' bag and wanted to add a couple of finishing touches to his outfit.

"The pearls and earrings should complement each other nicely."

Harry never went stylin' much before 2:00 a.m., but tonight he was so excited about all the good stylin' ahead of him, he couldn't wait any longer.

It was an unseasonably warm night for November. It rained early in the evening and the humidity caused blotches of light fog to drift along the ground. Still Harry figured to walk. It wasn't cold and he only had to go a few miles. As he headed for the door he momentarily thought about taking an umbrella, not because of the rain, but because it matched the red and blue print dress he was wearing. "Nah! Maybe next time."

Harry Weeble's apartment building was constructed in the 1930's, a time when the city fathers allowed a single entrance and exit to be used for the entire building. It might be a fire hazard by today's standards, but it made following Harry Weeble a lot easier. Detectives Tracy and Hollins knew if he was coming out he'd have to come out the door not 30 yards from where they were parked across the street. The two first year detectives sat upright, almost rigid. They kept their eyes glued to the door.

They didn't have to wait long.

It was clear by his troubled expression that Detective Hollins wasn't sure what he was looking at when Harry strolled outside. But it did cause him to feel for the security of his gun.

Detective Tracy followed directions like a robot. He secured the receiver in his hand and made contact with Detectives Cougar and Darwin. His eyes never left the figure walking down the street.

"Stay with him, but stay far enough away from him so he doesn't know it. And don't forget Tracy, unless it's something you absolutely can't avoid, yours and Hollins' job is to keep tabs on him only," the Beast calmly directed.

"Man oh Man..." Detective Tracy muttered..."You don't have to worry. I don't think I want this guy."

Max took the receiver from Zack and leaned towards the center of his jeep. "Tracy, now he's only got about 3 plus miles to old lady Shirley's house so I want you to stay in contact. Okay?" Max didn't wait for Tracy to answer. "How you guys doin'? How's Hollins?"

Detective Hollins appreciated Max asking the question, especially since Max had a gun in his face the night before. He smiled to himself and nodded to Tracy. "He's fine, we're both fine. It's just...I mean we've been on stakeouts before but nothin's ever happened on our shift. At least nothin' like this." The trepidation in Detective Tracy's voice was obvious.

"Don't worry. Just stay focused and don't let Weeble see you. It'll work out fine."

The plan was simple. It called for Mrs. Shirley to take her dog Lucy and leave the house several hours earlier. Since Lucy didn't bark the first time Weeble wouldn't expect to hear her the second time, so taking her out of the house wouldn't alert Weeble to anything different or unusual. Once they were gone Max planned to play the part of Mrs. Shirley and wait in the bedroom for Weeble. The Beast, on the other hand, would follow Weeble into the house. Between the two detectives they planned to give Weeble a nice little "howdayado." There was one problem though. At the last minute Mrs. Shirley decided she wasn't going to leave. No rhyme, no reason. She just decided to stay put. That also meant Lucy wasn't going to leave and she didn't appear to be real friendly.

The back up plan wasn't quite as simple, simply because they didn't have one. To complicate matters Detectives Tracy and Hollins lost Harry Weeble halfway to Mrs. Shirley's house when he suddenly decided to cut through a side street. Tracy wasn't able to maneuver his car fast enough without making it perfectly obvious he was giving chase. Max and the Beast were understanding of the situation and remained calm, although their sense of readiness was replaced by a sense of urgency. It was like sitting on pins and needles, only now the pins felt like nails and the needles felt like ice picks.

Zack took a deep breath of November night air and flashed back to the time his doberman tore into the neighborhood kid. He wanted no part of that kind of action out of Lucy. "What about the dog, gun-butt?" he asked, with the kind of nonchalance reserved for someone who knows the answer to their own question.

"Yeah. No sense having to deal with her too."

The Beast steadied his eyes in the rearview mirror and watched for movement. Max fixed his eyes on the area in front of the jeep. For the next twenty minutes the two detectives sat motionless, their minds racing, their thoughts still.

There! The Beast saw something. He didn't utter a sound, he just followed the direction to make sure it wasn't just another void, mysterious shadow caused by the moonlight.

Again! Thirty-five, maybe forty yards away. Zack pulled at his shoulder holster to make sure it was secured across his large chest. "I got him Max. He's on my side at 7:00 o'clock."

Max found him through the back window. Harry Weeble appeared carefree, almost cavalier. He zigged and zagged his way down the neighborhood street across the front yards of houses, oblivious to the vehicles parked along the curb. As he closed in on Mrs. Shirley's house, he started running in the shape of a halfmoon, moving farther away from Zack's jeep.

"Whoa baby. This guy's fucked up Max."

"I'm gettin' out. I don't want him inside her house without me bein' right behind him. Make sure he doesn't come out the back door Beast."

Zack grunted.

Max nodded to his partner the kind of nod only partners and best friends understand, then eased out of the jeep and slipped through the darkness like a ballerina.

Zack followed. He got out of the jeep and headed in the opposite direction. Once he was out of sight from the Shirley house his powerful strides churned evenly across the back alley. Streams of air pushed through the darkness from his hard, but steady breathing. He hadn't sprinted 50 yards since his football days at college and was glad to find he could still do it without getting too winded. As he approached the fence separating Mrs. Shirley's back yard from the alley he came to a stop. He would wait there until Max either made his next move, or until the Beast thought the next move should've been made. He did not plan to let much time go by without making sure Max was okay.

Back in front of Mrs. Shirley's house Max kept his distance somewhere between not being able to smell Harry's perfume, and being able to see the crazy son-of-a-bitch in a long dress and wig creep along the front porch and search for a way inside. He would have enjoyed nothing better than taking Harry Weeble down right on the spot, except he knew he couldn't. They'd never be able to prosecute him for anything more than a misdemeanor if he wasn't allowed to break into the house. Max was glad he made it easy for Weeble. "The door's unlocked you dumb bastard. My little gift to you. Now turn the fucking knob and let's get on with it," he muttered to himself.

Harry Weeble hemmed and hawed like he was deciding on whether to have a lemonade or an ice tea. "Let's see now. Should I try a window this time? Ya know, maybe I oughta come in through the back door. Sneak up on that fucking dog this time steada it sneakin' up on me. Oh what the hell anyhow. I'll come in through the front."

Harry found the gift Max left him. He was inside.

Max moved at a quick, but deliberate pace and reached the front porch within seconds. The floor boards creaked loudly from the sudden impact of his weight. Too late to do anything about it now, Max determined. He drew his revolver.

Harry was tiptoeing to Mrs. Shirley's bedroom but wasn't five feet from the front door when the noise outside grabbed his attention. He froze like a deer. His eyes flickered.

Mrs. Shirley hadn't been able to sleep. She was sitting upright in her bed when she also heard the noise. That detective said he and that big fella were gonna be around. It's probably them, she figured. "Officer Cougar is that you?" She called out softly, almost like she used up all her voice strength earlier in the day.

Max didn't hear the old lady so he couldn't respond.

Harry heard the old lady all too well. He twirled his head and glared at the front door. His breathing grew furious. He reached in his duffel bag style purse, pushed aside his stylin' toys and pulled out a pickax.

But what if it ain't them, then what? Mrs. Shirley wondered. She suddenly realized the mistake she made in calling out for the detective. Her heart pounded as she struggled to locate her glasses on the nightstand. Confusion raced through her weary soaked mind and her head began to throb. Her bedsheets would soon be soiled because of the fear and old age that consumed her.

Lucy remained next to the bed. Her weight shifted into her chest cavity, her snout quivered and she bared her teeth.

From the backyard the house still appeared dark and quiet. Enough of this crap already. I'm going in, Zack decided. He hopped the fence and hurried towards the backdoor.

Harry knew the outside light would filter in as soon as the front door opened, so he darted back and crouched down just around the corner from the front hall closet. He held his pickax like a spear.

Max turned the knob and pressed on the door. He let it swing open on its own. He stood in the doorway for what seemed like an eternity and battled the room darkness while he eyeballed for movement. Finding none, he stepped inside and felt along the wall for the light switch he located during his inspection of the house earlier that day.

In the blink of an eye Harry Weeble sprang to his feet, lunged forward and thrust the pickax at Max's head. "Die Bitch, Dieeeeeee!" he wailed.

Max swung around so quickly he lost his footing. He fell back by the front door, which actually saved him because the pickax slammed into the wall at the exact spot where he was standing.

Lucy bolted from the bedroom, saw Max on his back and zeroed in, teeth and all. Max rolled to his right and got to his knees. He whirled around and backhanded the gun-butt into the side of Lucy's head before she was able to rip away at his flesh. She fell over easily.

Harry didn't like his options and made haste for the backdoor.

"Beast!" Max yelled out. He pulled himself up and followed.

Zack heard the warning but Harry already turned the corner and was heading straight for him. The Beast got in a three point stance and rushed Weeble. He planted his shoulder into Weeble's gut and lifted him off the floor. Like a freight train the Beast plowed forward and slammed him against the wall. Weeble crashed hard and dropped to the floor like dead weight. His wig fell off. The Beast backed up to admire the clean, hard hit. The only problem was he didn't know just how hard a shot Harry Weeble could take, so when Weeble pulled himself up the Beast was somewhat surprised.

"Harry honey, why not come back out this way?" Max politely offered. Harry Weeble turned to find Max standing behind him with a shit eating grin on his face. Harry sneered at him. He straightened his stylin' dress and took a quick look at the Beast. Christ, that guy takes up the whole fucking hallway, he thought. He glanced back at Max, all the while trying to catch his breath. That guy's not as big. If I can freeze him for even a second I might be able to squeeze by him and get outside. Once I do it's long distance baby. They'd never catch me then, he concluded. Harry made a mad dash towards Max.

Max was ready. Like a small cannonball his fist lodged deep into Harry's rib cage. Harry would've dropped from the blow but Max wouldn't let him fall. He grabbed hold of him under his chin, squeezing hard enough to hold Harry in place while he delivered two more devastating shots to his ribs. Harry doubled over and Max pushed him in the direction of the Beast.

The Beast caught him before he could fall and threw Harry against the wall. He punched him in the face and a combination of blood and spit flew out of Harry's mouth. He was gasping desperately to catch his breath. Each time he inhaled he felt like he was being cut in half with a giant pair of scissors. "I'll.....I'm gonna.....I'll kill you," he spat from between his bloody lips.

The Beast punched him again, only this time he could feel Weeble's cheekbone crack. Blood gushed from his nose and he dropped to the floor.

Max stood him up and drilled his knee into Harry's groin. "That's for Mrs. Berry!" Harry Weeble crumpled back to the floor, numb with pain. When he did, Max reared back and kicked him in the rib cage one last time. "That one's for Mrs. Shirley."

Two weeks after Harry Weeble's arraignment Assistant District Attorney Kenneth Brueger sat at the end of a conference table with a solemn look etched on his face. He was attempting to look concerned while explaining to Detective Cougar the plea bargain agreement he entered into with court appointed counsel for Harry Weeble.

The reality was Assistant D.A. Kenneth Brueger knew Weeble was a real head case but couldn't have cared less. He was quitting his job to open up a titty bar with his wife's first cousin, so all he wanted to do was clear his desk of files as soon as possible. If that meant portraying the facts in such a way that a plea bargain agreement appeared like the only viable option, even when it wasn't, so be it. Besides, Kenneth Brueger wanted to impress Kelly Turnbull, the new Assistant D.A.. She was an attractive brunette with legs that reached for the sky. She was also fresh out of law school and hung on every legal word, theory and argument like each one by itself would fill her virgin intellect with an orgasm. Kenneth Brueger didn't care if she learned anything. All he cared about was getting in her pants, which is why he invited her to sit in the room with Detective Cougar and himself. He figured a little showboatin' might help the cause.

Max was leaning against the door. "Let me see if I have this straight," he said, like a student pondering a teacher's answer to a question. "You get that bastard Weeble to plead guilty to one count of Breaking and Entering and one count of Assault, correct?"

"Yes, uh-huh, that's correct."

Max nodded his head like he had that part of it down pat. "And for that you agree to drop one count each of Aggravated Battery, Assault With Intent to Commit Rape, Sodomy, Assaulting a Police Officer, Resisting Arrest, and, last but not least, Assault With Intent to Commit Murder." Max stopped and locked eyes with Kelly Turnbull. "And for your information, I was the one Weeble tried to kill," he added with emphasis.

Kenneth Brueger always found the cops he worked with so willing to concede all matters of criminal law and procedure to him that he was fairly pissed off at this cop's sharp reply, especially since it was unnecessary. The plea bargain agreement was already part of the court record. It was signed, sealed and delivered, and nothing Max Cougar did was going to change it. Still Kenneth Brueger felt the need to respond. (After all, he was a lawyer). "Listen Detective, I don't expect you to understand all the intricacies of evidence, but you guys had nothing. No semen sample from the Berry woman, no identification from the Berry woman, not a damn thing from the Berry woman." Kenneth Brueger waved his hand like he was swatting a fly. He glanced at Kelly Turnbull to see if she was watching him.

She wasn't.

"As for the Shirley woman, Christ! You got him breaking into the house and then find him with some of the same items he had when he was at that Twilight old folks home. Big deal. A pair of running shoes. Some rope and duct tape. Three dildos. At best it's circumstantial. And some of it isn't worth a shit at that!" Kenneth Brueger held his hands out like he was presenting Max with a gift. "Look detective, I saved your ass. Do you realize the embarrassment you and your partner could've caused the department if I wasn't able to negotiate this deal? You go ahead and use excessive force...strike that, excessive force to the third degree. Then you act like none of that matters. Well I've got news for you, we'll still be lucky if he doesn't sue the whole damn city of Chicago."

Max's face was red with anger. His eyes burrowed into the eyes of Kenneth Brueger. "Why don't you get off that mountain of yours. You wanna sell the court a bill of goods go right the fuck ahead, that's your problem. I might not be able to do anything about it but that doesn't mean I gotta stay here and listen to anymore of this crap."

Max slammed the door on his way out. He would have preferred going to the dentist with Zack.

CHAPTER 17

PRESENT DAY:

The door to the parole office buzzed to signal Max's entrance into the small lobby.

"Sign in at the counter," called out a female voice over the sound of a typewriter. She sounded annoyed, like she was fed up from having said the same thing to the last 1000 people who walked through the door.

Max leaned over the counter where he found a black, heavyset woman sitting behind her desk typing away. Since she appeared to be in no hurry to stop, and since Max had no intentions of waiting for her to get off her fat ass, he decided to introduce himself. He pounded his open palm on the countertop like it was a gavel. "Excuse me, I'm Detective Cougar, Max Cougar. I've got an appointment with Dennis Hurley."

The lady peered over the bifocals sitting halfway down her round nose. Her stubby fingers rested on the typewriter keys like they were the keys on a piano. "May I help you?" Her attitude was littered with petulance.

"I said I'm here to see Dennis Hurley. I'm Detective Cougar, Max Cougar." He pulled out his badge to show her.

She ignored the badge. "Yes I'm sure you are but you'll have to sign in if you want to see him."

Max knew he'd be standing at the counter until he either signed in or broke down the office door. At this point breaking down the door was not an option. "Where?" Max squinted his eyes and pretended to smile.

"Where what?"

"Where and the hell do you want me to sign in?"

"The sign in sheet, where and the hell do you think?" The fat lady was determined to stand her ground.

"Where and the hell is the sign in sheet?" Max did not try to mask his growing anger.

She motioned her eyes and nodded her head in the direction of the clipboard hanging from a nail on the wall next to him. "Right there," she said pleasantly.

Max turned and yanked the clipboard off the nail and the nail out of the wall. He grabbed the attached pen and scribbled in the name of Dr. Winston T. Boogie. He offered the clipboard back to her. She stood up from behind her desk and waddled back into the office area, leaving Max holding the clipboard. He watched her double door size ass bounce from side to side. "What a bunch of crap," he muttered loud enough for her to hear. Max tossed the clipboard on the floor, leaned on the counter and waited to be let in to the office area.

A couple of minutes later the fat lady waddled back to her desk and sat down at the typewriter. She never looked at Max. "You can go in. His office is the last door on the left." She took a deep breath and started typing again.

Dennis Hurley sat behind his old carved up wood desk feeling like the proud captain of a ship. With a big head, sloping shoulders, and what looked to be 190 pounds resting between his stout chest and thin ankles, his appearance was anything but. He had been a parole officer for fourteen years, and supervisor - The Captain - of his eleven person office staff for the last three. Dennis Hurley answered to no one but the District Parole Board. He liked it that way.

Max knocked lightly on the frame of the open doorway. Dennis Hurley assumed it was the detective whose sister was murdered, but at the moment was enjoying his Playboy and made no effort to put it down. Max waited several more seconds, even cleared his throat while he was standing there, yet Hurley kept the magazine locked in front of his face.

It was one thing to require Max to come all the way down to his office just so Max could get a three second answer to his three second question. But, it was quite another to go out of his way just to make Max wait for it. In two angry strides Max was standing over Hurley. He ripped the magazine out of his hands and fired it towards the nearest corner. It smacked against the wall and landed on the floor next to a stack of Playboy magazines and a small wastebasket filled with Kleenex. Startled and outraged, Hurley bounced up from the chair. He wanted to stand nose to nose with Max but knew he wasn't tall enough. Instead he planted his contempt filled eyes on Max and stuck his chin forward in defiance. Little beads of sweat were forming on top of his shiny scalp. "Just who and the hell do you think you are and what and the hell do you think you're doing?" Dennis Hurley's voice sounded like it swirled around his big empty belly before going off like a loud bomb.

Max scowled at him. He wanted to squeeze Hurley's chin like it was a ripe tomato but figured it wouldn't be worth the effort. He decided to just get on with his business and be gone. "Like I told you over the phone, it's about my sister's murder. I wanna know about Harry Weeble." Although his pulse was racing, Max kept his voice under control.

Dennis Hurley kept his eyes fixed on Max. He had no intentions of letting this cop come into his office - His Ship - and dictate anything. Hurley was Captain. He answered to no one, and he wasn't going to start answering now. Not for this cop. Not for any cop. "I asked you a question. Just who and the hell do you think you are?" Hurley demanded, as though he was scolding a child.

Max closed his mouth to hide his clenched teeth. Don't do it, he thought to himself.

"You deaf?" Hurley prodded.

In a flash Max grabbed Hurley around his polyester tie and yanked him forward until Hurley collided with the side of his desk and stumbled to the floor.

Hurley was still. He wanted to appear unfazed but the look on his face suggested he just danced with a ghost.

Max kneeled down and planted his knee so hard into Hurley's chest, Hurley thought it was gonna come out the other side. He tried to wrestle Max's knee off him but Max just dug it in harder. Hurley coughed and his belly shook.

Max snarled. "I said I'm here about my sister's murder. I wanna know about Harry Weeble." There was no forgiveness in Max's voice. There was no forgiveness in his knee. "Now I'm gonna let you up and then you're gonna tell me where I can find Harry, understood?" Without waiting for a response Max lifted his knee, and in a single motion stood up, dragging Dennis Hurley and all his weight with him.

This was his ship! Hurley reminded himself matter-of-factly. This cop could threaten all he wanted but this was still his ship. Not the cop's, not his fat secretary's, not some other parole officer's - but his! He was Captain! If there were any buttons to push, he'd be the one to push them. This was his ship and no one was gonna tell him different! Not now! Not ever! Having regained his sense of bravado, Hurley looked Max square in the eyes and once again stuck his chin forward in defiance. "You son-of-a-bitch! Don't you ever..."

Max threw his palms into Hurley's shoulders and drove him backwards until the wall met the weight of Hurley's body and there was a loud thud. Hurley gasped. If Max didn't keep him pinned he would've dropped to his knees. A picture of a sailboat fell off the wall. "One last time. I want to know where I can find Harry Weeble. If you don't know, find out - but find out quick 'cause I'm runnin' thin on patience, and believe it or not, you're runnin' thin on luck." Max backed away and watched as Hurley's legs buckled beneath him.

Fifteen city miles away Zack finished running down a lead on an unrelated investigation he was finishing up when he headed back to the precinct office. He'd been sitting at his desk for about 10 minutes scanning a Sport Illustrated when Desk Sergeant Mike Olson came over. "I think there's a phone call you might want to take," he whispered to Zack. Since no one else was in the room the Sergeant didn't have to whisper at all.

"Who is it Mike?" Zack pushed the magazine off to the side.

Sergeant Olson shook his head from side to side. The creases forming around his eyes suggested he was trying hard not to laugh. "It's Dennis Hurley from the parole office. He asked for the Captain. I didn't say nothin' about the Captain not bein' here. Better take the call. Sounds to me like our boy's in full dress."

By the time Sergeant Olson finished talking he was grinning from ear to ear. His bushy eyebrows were arched high, where they sat buried under his thick head of dark hair. A faint hope and understanding filtered through his otherwise tired brown eyes. The Sarge worked with Max and the Beast ever since they broke in with the force twelve years ago. Over the years he'd grown quite fond of the two detectives. He took Kathy Reed's murder harder than most. Every night he prayed her killer would come to know a cruel death. The Sarge would help Max find the madman any way he could, even if it meant giving Captain Whitaker's phone call to Zack Darwin.

"Thanks Mike, I appreciate it."

The Sarge tipped an imaginary hat to Zack in return.

Zack waited until the Sarge shuffled back to his office before he picked up the phone. "Yes may I help you?"

"Is this Captain Whitaker?" Dennis Hurley inquired.

"What can I do for you," Zack politely responded.

Dennis Hurley held the telephone receiver tight against his ear and paced back and forth behind his desk. "This is Dennis Hurley from the Parole Office," he announced. "You have a detective by the name of Max Cougar in your precinct?"

Zack wasn't sure if Hurley was making a statement or asking a question so he remained silent.

"Well I think you should know that the son-of-a-bitch assaulted me. He should be brought up on charges. There should be a goddamn investigation. That cop's a son-of-a-bitch!" The panic in Hurley's voice was obvious. His fear was a given.

Zack was ready to explode with laughter, but couldn't with Hurley on the other end. He took several short breaths and concentrated on sounding concerned. "Do you want to press charges sir?"

There was silence at the other end of the phone.

Zack noticed the Sarge watching him from across the room. He placed his hand to his forehead like a visor and shielded his eyes. His voice sounded rigid when he forced the words out again. "Do you want to press charges?"

Before Max stormed out of Dennis Hurley's office he promised Hurley that his head would be separated from his shoulders if he even thought about pressing charges. Although Hurley tried to remain undaunted by the entire episode he was actually scared shitless.

Dennis Hurley stopped pacing behind his desk. He had Captain Whitaker on the other end of the phone, yet all he could see and hear was Max Cougar. Hurley played the threat over and over in his mind, but never heard any trepidation in Max's voice. He pictured Max snarling at him, but couldn't see any apprehension in his eyes either. Hurley moved the phone away from his mouth, took a deep breath and inhaled the reality of the situation. He exhaled slowly before answering. "No, I'm not gonna press charges. I just thought you oughta know Captain, that's all. Thank you for your time."

Dennis Hurley hung up the phone and took notice of his stack of Playboy magazines. He took another deep breath and rotated his shoulders back and forth. He needed to relax. He closed his office door and grabbed a Playboy from the pile. The Kleenex was in the top desk drawer.

Zack placed the receiver back into the telephone cradle and immediately looked up to find the Sarge still watching him. Zack hailed him with a thumbs up and the two men laughed.

CHAPTER 18

Max went straight from Dennis Hurley's office to visit his nephew, Matthew. An hour later he called Zack. "According to Dennis Hurley, Harry Weeble's some kind of preacher at a place called Church Of The Three Angels," Max declared over his car phone static.

Zack's conversation with the Parole Board Officer hung fresh in his mind. He snickered at the thought of Dennis Hurley calling "good ol' Captain Zack" to complain about the roughshod treatment he got from a detective named Max Cougar.

Max continued. "It's in Addison, on the southwest corner of River Drive and Third. I can be in Addison in about 50 minutes. Shouldn't take me much longer to find River Drive and Third. Can you meet me there?"

Zack contemplated the location for a minute. "Yeah, if I don't get lost I should be there in about an hour...on second thought, let's say an hour and fifteen to be on the safe side. Wait for me."

Ninety minutes later the two detectives were standing in front of a building, that except for the pale yellow door, dull green awning, and hot pink letters that spelled out Church Of The Three Angels, bore all the characteristics of an old brown shoe. Max looked at the color of the sign, and for the first time in seven years, memories of Harry Weeble swelled up inside him. He recalled Weeble's face in the bright makeup and red wig and it made him feel like he was standing in Harry's apartment for the first time. The closet full of dresses, the running shoes, the dildos neatly stacked. They were all there, mixing in his head like watercolor paints.

"Ya know, to this day the motherfucker still makes me think of my grandmother," Zack said to quietly break the silence. "God I wish I saw more of her when she was alive."

For whatever reason Zack's comment caused Max to think about Detective Hollins. He thought about the night he stuck his gun into the rookie's face to scare some sense into him. He recalled how they ultimately became friends and how he and Zack would drag Hollins away from his wife and baby girl and take him out drinking. Then he remembered the night Detective Hollins was shot and killed during a stakeout three years ago, and he was saddened. For Max the sadness was like a seed, stirring up images of his murdered sister. His eyes moistened.

The Beast looked over at his friend and would have guessed him to be thinking about Kathy's recent murder. He slapped him on the back like he was trying to get him to cough out the thought, and at the same time propel them both forward. "Let's go inside," he said.

Max nodded and the two men walked inside to find the small empty warehouse resembling anything but a church. The floor was a combination of concrete and brown linoleum tile, but the tile was so old and dirty that its color looked as gray as the concrete. The recently painted white walls were chipping because the walls were never scraped before the new paint was put on. A single light fixture/fan combination hung from the center of the ceiling. The light was minimal and the fan struggled to turn. Two rows of folding chairs were stacked beside an open doorway and just as Max started to head in that direction, Harry Weeble appeared. He was wearing khaki pants, a dark blue shirt, work boots and a Chicago Bears hat to cover his skinny little head.

"Detectives," he called out like an old friend. "I've been expecting you."

That cocksucker Hurley told Weeble I was coming to see him, Max thought. "Remind me to stop by and say hello to Hurley after we leave here," Max mumbled.

If Zack thought he could have gotten away with it he would've shot Harry dead right then and there. No particular reason, just for old time sake. Problem was he couldn't lay a single hand on the little fuck, let alone kill him. Zack had to make sure Max didn't touch him either. Orders made loud and clear from Captain Whitaker. Weeble was perfectly safe. Worse yet, he had to stay that way.

"Come on in my office." Harry made an about-face and disappeared from the doorway before the two detectives had a chance to reach it.

Max and the Beast glanced at each other and proceeded cautiously. They found Harry sitting behind a dusty metal desk. Next to the desk stood a lady trying to hide the fact that she was in her seventies by dressing like she was in her twenties. She wore jeans so tight they looked like they were painted on, a tight pullover to expose her large, floppy breasts, and black cowboy boots over her pants. (She still looked like she was in her seventies). She would have also worn a cowboy hat but she didn't want to get hat head. Besides, it was quite obvious she was trying to straighten her otherwise curly, white-blond hair because it hung on her head like wet, stringy plaster.

Harry stood up. "I'd like to introduce you to my wife, Marilyn."

Zack couldn't help it. He started to laugh. Max couldn't help it either. He joined him.

"May I ask what's so funny?" Marilyn's tone had all the trappings of an uppity bitch. Since she spent her entire adult life living in a trailer getting drunk, pregnant, and ducking the right hand of every man she ever knew, she had to work hard to sound that way.

Max stopped laughing. "Frankly no. This doesn't concern you," he said curtly.

Harry Weeble stood up. He was about the same height as his wife but she was easily twenty pounds heavier. "You're looking for your sister's killer. Until now, my wife didn't know that."

"How and the fuck did you know it?" Zack shot back.

"My parole board officer." Harry looked at his bride and winked. She smiled in return. Her deep red lips curled upwards, but her plump cheeks, painted heavily with circles of blush, sagged below her chin.

"Look officers, I did my time. I was a bad apple, I admit. But I went to jail for it. I'm not like I used to be. I found Jesus. Found Marilyn too." Harry dropped back down in his chair behind the desk. "Did I tell you how we met? Her son Timmy and me were cellmates my last two years. We hit it off from the moment we saw each other."

"And a lovely couple you are," Zack said sarcastically.

Max showed up at the Church Of The Three Angels hoping Harry Weeble was the one who murdered his sister and brother-in-law for two reasons. The first, because he'd be done searching for the killer. The second, because he'd be in the very process of killing Weeble with his bare hands. As it turned out, even if Max tortured Weeble for the next three days it wouldn't have made a difference. Shortly after he arrived he came to the realization that Weeble had nothing to do with the grizzly murders of his sister and brother-in-law. It wasn't because Harry Weeble was now married, wore normal looking clothes, or claimed to be on the straight and narrow. It wasn't even because he professed himself to be a preacher. Quite frankly, Max still figured Harry Weeble to be a dirty little fuck. The realization came when Max remembered just how weak Harry Weeble really was. Max's sister might have been able to kick Harry's ass in a fistfight. More importantly, Harry Weeble was not even close to having the kind of strength forensic test results concluded as being necessary to inflict the degree of penetration, type of wound, and size of bruise caused by the chest stabbing of the victim, his brother-in-law, Jack Reed.

Zack knew it too, but until Max was ready to give up on Weeble, he was prepared to circle the wagons.

"A wasted fucking trip," Max muttered to his partner as they hit the daylight outside. "It's one thing when you realize he ain't the guy, but it's another thing when you start remembering all the bad shit just because you see his goddamn face."

"Yeah but look at it this way, at least we got to meet his wife. Quite a looker, I'd say." The two detectives continued walking in silence for a few seconds. Finally Max looked over at his partner and started to laugh.

As soon as Harry knew Max and the Beast were gone he stood up to tug at the woman's thong underwear crawling up his ass. Marilyn watched her man with pleasure.

Later that same night when Susan was walking to the townhouse she and

Zack recently purchased, she heard a soft whistle somewhere out in the darkness. She stopped, but as soon as she did there was silence. When she started walking again the whistle started back on the same lonely, dark melody. One more time she stopped, and one more time the whistling stopped. On the third time Susan turned around. The street was empty and silent, but this time Susan could feel the presence of cold, penetrating eyes and she knew someone was watching her.

Someone was.

John Henry Stevens.

CHAPTER 19

LOUIE & EDDIE HART, TWO YEARS EARLIER:

The first time Eddie Hart ever saw Rebecca Anderson she was coming out of the Phar-Mor Drugstore. With long, blond hair, a thin waist, beautifully sculpted, silicone endearing breasts, and the ability to move her ass like it was an invitation to do a slow grind, even though her face said hands off, she was easily the most beautiful woman he'd ever seen.

Eddie Hart was in love.

But hell, she'd never go for him. He was just a mechanic. Even when he wasn't working, the soiled jeans, ripped tee shirts, loosely tied work boots, and axle grease aroma that clung to his body made it impossible to tell.

Just the same, Eddie was in love.

He hopped out of his green and rusted out pickup truck and maneuvered his way through the parking lot until he was walking towards Rebecca Anderson. She looked in every direction but his. Still, Eddie was determined to get a date. He licked his grimy fingers and ran them through his dirty black hair. Without a mirror to look in Eddie was really just hoping his hair would all fall back in the same direction. It didn't. His hair was so oily that combing it with his fingers only caused it to stand up at different angles. No matter, as Rebecca got closer the gyration in her walk got him so excited Eddie forgot all about his hair.

Probably the quickest way to find out is to just come out with it. That way I'll know where I stand right off, Eddie figured. "Excuse me Miss, or should I say Mrs.?" Eddie stopped walking and flashed a generous smile. His brown eyes squinted in the afternoon sunlight.

Rebecca Anderson ignored Eddie altogether. The bounce in her step picked up as she hurried past him on the way to her car.

Eddie followed her with his eyes. "No need to be rude, you purdy little thing you. Just wanted to innerduce myself," he called out cheerfully.

Rebecca Anderson glanced over her shoulder and saw Eddie standing there with his mouth hanging open. How disgusting, she thought.

Christ, he only wanted to split a six pack with her. Even a cup of coffee and a jelly donut would have been okay. Eddie shook his head, partly because he felt dejected, and partly because he couldn't get over how great lookin' her ass was.

Since Eddie would have scaled Mt. Everest just to get a date with Rebecca, following her home to find out where she lived was certainly no big deal. He hustled between the parked cars to get back to his green and rusted out pickup. Eddie didn't want Rebecca to know he was following her so he stayed a safe distance behind her Cadillac. It mattered not. Rebecca Anderson was smack dab in the middle of a nasty divorce, and with the money and custody battles to consume her every waking moment she had no room left to concentrate on anything else.

Eddie had been following her for some fifteen minutes when it dawned on him that he left his older brother Louie waiting for his valium prescription in the drugstore. But Eddie didn't care. He hated his older brother. He thought Louie was just a big, stupid pig, holding Eddie back every step of the way. Besides, he knew Louie would still be waiting, no matter how long it took before he returned.

Eddie was right. An hour later he found Louie leaning against a parking meter across the street from where he first left him. His large head was cocked to one side, his mouth was open, and his eyelids were half closed. He looked like he was in the middle of understanding an answer to a question he asked five days earlier. In reality, Louie just realized for the first time that parking meters don't make change.

CHAPTER 20

Rebecca Anderson lived in a 5,000 square foot English Tudor in an upper middle class subdivision of Highland, Illinois. Rebecca and her husband purchased the home ten years ago when she was 30 years old and he was 42. She continued living there with her two young daughters, even though her soon to be ex-husband was still fighting her every step of the way for permanent custody of both the house and the girls. The only thing Rebecca's husband conceded to giving her in the four months of shouting matches, often reaching the depths of gut wrenching, utter hysteria, was the family dog. It was a toy poodle, and between its little red ribbon, manicured cut, perfume odor, and the way it pranced around the marble floors, he hated it like poison.

For the past two weeks Eddie drove by Rebecca Anderson's house everyday on his way to work. He'd wake up earlier than usual and drive 10 miles out of his way just for the chance to catch a glimpse of her. Eddie figured if he was out and about at 7:00 a.m., the rest of the world was also. But, in two weeks the only thing he saw was the family dog taking a poodle size dump, hardly worth going out of his way for. The worst part of all was that Eddie hadn't seen Rebecca Anderson since that one time at the Phar-Mor drugstore and he was missing her something awful. He was in love, so the longer he went without seeing her, the more miserable he got. Moping around was one thing, but now it was starting to make his heart feel like there was a big hole right in the middle of it.

Lunch hour. I'll go by then. Maybe she'll be home. Got nothin to lose, Eddie concluded.

It was noon by the time Eddie pulled himself away from the engine of an old Dodge. He'd been thinking about Rebecca all morning and the schoolboy smile he wore almost covered as much of his face as the grease did his clothes. Eddie wiped his dirty hands on an equally dirty towel, hitched up his pants and made haste for the pickup.

Rebecca Anderson lived in one of those subdivisions where every house flirted with elegance. Trees and bushes sat in sculpted shapes. Lawns were manicured with the kind of attention reserved for the greens on a golf course. And old green and rusted out pickup trucks - well, let's just say since Eddie was the only person in the sub with one, it looked about as out of place as an old green and rusted out pickup truck could.

But Eddie didn't see it that way. As a matter-of-fact, after he started walking up Rebecca's drive he looked back to admire how nicely his truck shined from the recent wax job his brother Louie gave it. That's the one good thing about Louie. He does whatever I tell him, Eddie thought. Eddie smelled the roses Louie ripped out of the neighbors garden for their mother, shook his head with delight, and proceeded up the half-moon shaped drive like a man on a mission.

Eddie had to ring the bell a couple of times before the maid finally answered. She opened the door just enough to poke her head outside. Her name was Carmen. She was a heavyset Mexican import with bad skin and worse English.

"Howdy. Is the Miss in?" Eddie politely asked.

"No. No can see you now," Carmen answered, like she was shooing a fly away.

Eddie wasn't quite sure what the ugly maid meant. Did she mean no, the Miss wasn't in? Or no, the Miss couldn't see him now? He pursed his lips and thought about it for a couple of seconds.

Carmen eyeballed Eddie closely. She certainly didn't know every American custom, although she thought one of them was to shower once a week, something the man at the door didn't look, or smell like he did.

Eddie couldn't draw any conclusions from Carmen's answer and figured to have no choice but to repeat the question. "Is the Miss in?" He was hoping to hear a different answer and his eyes opened wide with anticipation. His normally taut forehead formed ridges as his eyebrows strained upwards towards his scalp.

Carmen repeated her answer. "No. No can see you now."

For the entire morning all Eddie Hart could think about was seeing his sweet Rebecca Anderson. It added a bounce to his step and a buoyancy to his mood. But now, with the speed of a second hand, Carmen's response changed all that. Eddie's eyes turned to narrow slits, his eyebrows looked like crossed swords, and his pointy chin became even pointier when he jutted it out. "Listen you stupid Jamaican, is she in the house or not?" Eddie's voice snapped with urgency. "I ain't got all day ta be standin' here tryin' ta figger out what the hell yer talkin' about."

Eddie talked so fast his words hit Carmen all at once and she couldn't understand what he was mad about. Still, she didn't like the tone of voice in any language so she frowned at him.

Carmen never spent enough of her spare time trying to learn the English language. Instead, she was content uttering non-descript words and broken sentences. The only thing Carmen figured she had to understand was how much money she would make for cleaning the house and how often she would get paid. Since Rebecca Anderson wanted a house spotless enough to grace the cover of Better Homes and Gardens Magazine, the only thing she cared about was making sure Carmen knew how to clean. Rebecca couldn't care less if Carmen held up her end of a conversation, simply because she didn't want to talk to her anymore than was necessary. It was a system, that until now, never gave either of them cause for concern.

Eddie was beside himself. Here he was, after the longest two weeks of his life, with the chance to finally see his true love. It didn't matter that Rebecca didn't know how much he loved her. Eddie would change all that. He would tell her. He would show her. Eddie expected Rebecca to love him back in no time at all. Maybe as much as he loved her. Who knows? Maybe even more. But first he had to see her and all this ugly maid could do was make ugly faces when he talked to her. This is bullshit! I ain't got time fer dis, Eddie decided emphatically. He took two steps back, then threw his upper body forward. Even though he was on the tall and skinny side Eddie was certainly strong enough to push the door open and knock Carmen on her ass in the process.

    Eddie stepped inside. His eyes scanned the marble floor foyer, the entrance to the dining room, and the circular stairs leading to the bedrooms. Carmen scurried along the floor towards the opposite end of the hallway.

    Eddie ignored her. Like a dog outside when the wind's blowing, he curled his long nose and took several short breaths. The smell of perfume made him all the more hopeful Rebecca was home. What Eddie didn't realize is that he was smelling air freshener, not perfume. "Anybody here?" he called out loud and enthusiastically. Eddie hoped someone, anyone, besides the ugly maid would answer.

    Carmen stopped moving when she bumped into the wall at the end of the hallway. She started talking in a language Eddie never heard before. The words jumped together and Eddie couldn't tell where one word stopped and another one began. Her eyes swirled around almost as much as her head swung from side to side, and her hands moved so fast Eddie wasn't sure if her arms would be able to keep up.

    "Why don't you shut the hell up!" Eddie barked. He forgot he was carrying roses and unwittingly squeezed them until the stems collapsed.

    Carmen was frightened by the troubled look that filled Eddie's eyes. She never saw that kind of look before and quickly disappeared inside the kitchen so she wouldn't have to look at it anymore.

    "Anybody here?" Eddie called out again, this time at the top of his lungs.
    Nobody answered.

    Eddie waited a full minute before he found himself overcome by the reality Rebecca wasn't home. His stomach churned and tied itself in knots. His chest settled back into its usual, uninspired flatness, his shoulders drooped a little, and his head hung low. Eddie was so distraught he didn't bother going back to work. Instead, he headed home.

    As soon as Rebecca returned to the house Carmen started to carry on about the Eddie Hart visit. She sounded so frantic, and her hands and body moved with such frenzied animation, anyone who didn't know her would've thought a bee flew up her blouse. Rebecca knew better. She also knew she'd be standing there for the next half-hour waiting for Carmen to put the right words in the right order, so she pooh-poohed the attempted explanation before Carmen got out of control. Besides, Rebecca already concluded it was just her husband trying to give her another hard time.

It all started several months ago on a Tuesday afternoon when Barry Anderson came home from work unexpectedly and found his wife tongue massaging the inner thighs of Miss Trinket, the 27 year old fourth grade teacher at the elementary school Rebecca and Barry Anderson's daughters attended. From that day forward he did everything he could to prove to the court his wife was an unfit mother. For Barry Anderson that meant taking certain liberties to help further the cause. Three times in the last four months when Rebecca was home alone, Barry had the house ransacked and his wife bound, blind folded and groped by intruders. At least a half a dozen times he saw to it his wife was either harassed by some friendly neighborhood whores, or solicited by their pimps. Barry even made sure Rebecca received the occasional death threat by an anonymous typewritten note wrapped around an equally anonymous late night brick.

Although Rebecca held to the firm belief that each instance was tied directly to her husband, she was never able to prove it. Even when her lawyer appealed to the court after each of the first two occurrences it was Rebecca who came off as both a liar and hopelessly paranoid, exactly what Barry wanted.

Thereafter it was simple. Rebecca could either remain calm and do absolutely nothing to help her husband's custody claim along, or go to court after each episode and try to prove her allegations. So far she was zero for two, and with the custody of her kids hanging in the balance, the answer was simple. As a result, Rebecca ignored everything her husband tried to do. When intruders broke into her house and put their hands on her body, she never uttered a sound. Whenever she was harassed by whores or solicited by their pimps, she acted like she was invisible. When occasional death threats came crashing through the window on the tail of a midnight brick, Rebecca simply had the window fixed the following day. She could have even made Barry pay for it because, pending their divorce, he was still responsible for its maintenance. It would have been the perfect irony. Instead, however, Rebecca found more satisfaction knowing if she acted like nothing at all happened, her husband's curiosity would grow into immense frustration, never sure if what he was paying people to do was actually getting done.

It was certainly no way to live. But, like all things, it too would pass.

CHAPTER 21

Dottie Hart stood five-two when she was standing. Yet, for much of the past year she was on her back, wheezing and hacking from emphysema, and withering into death.

Eddie yanked the door open and walked inside the trailer he shared with his mother and older brother Louie. The aluminum door slammed back hard to signal his return. "Anybody here?" It was obvious from Eddie's crisp tone of voice he no longer felt dejected about not seeing his Rebecca. Now he was just plain mad. It didn't matter that Rebecca had no way of knowing he was stopping by. In Eddie's mind she should have been there just the same. For god sakes, it's been days, even weeks since he last saw her. How was he ever gonna prove his love to her if she was never home. Worse yet, if she was ever gonna love him back, she was gonna have to start by waiting around for him. That wasn't asking so much, was it? Eddie certainly didn't think so.

"In here." Louie Hart responded in the kind of deep, clumsy voice one would expect to hear from a guy who was six-four and weighed a soft 280 pounds.

Eddie didn't have to walk into the other room to know his big, stupid brother was standing vigil over their mother, who no doubt would be laying on her mattress, carrying on about how she sacrificed everything just to be a good mother. In between cigarettes, coughing and spitting up phlegm, Dottie Hart often talked until the roof of her mouth became so sensitive, portions of it would split open and blood would wash over her gums.

The entire trailer wasn't forty feet deep so walking through the living area, (which also served as Eddie's bedroom), into the kitchen, where he grabbed a beer from the fridge, didn't take Eddie but a couple of seconds. He twisted off the cap, tossed it on the counter, where it landed next to the other beer bottle caps, food crumbs, dirty dishes and empty pizza boxes, and took two long swallows until he drained the bottle. Eddie grabbed himself another one before going into his mother's room.

"Hi," Louie said. No matter the situation Louie was always happy to see his brother.

Eddie ignored him and walked over to Dottie, where he pulled the non-filtered ciggy from her fingers and put it to his own lips. He inhaled hard enough to suck a few blades of tobacco onto his tongue. He spit them back out on his mother's bed and let the smoke stream out his nostrils.

Dottie surveyed her son as close as her lousy eyesight would permit. She didn't think anything of Eddie spitting the tobacco back on her bed. She did it all the time herself. Dottie was more interested in the way Eddie's eyes looked. She was afraid the wild look was setting in. Eddie would get that look and sure as hell his mean streak would come out. Sometimes it would last for an hour, sometimes a week. There was no way of knowing when it was coming and no way of knowing how long it was likely to stick around. Dottie's husband used to get the same look. Of course, the only place it landed her husband was in the ground. One day he got that look and the next thing Dottie knew the police showed up at the trailer to tell her, her husband was shot dead trying to rob a grocery store. It was thirty-four years ago. Louie was two years old at the time and Eddie was still sitting in her belly.

Life for Dottie was not pleasant. She was forced to raise two sons by herself. Her own family lived in other parts of the country, or simply didn't give a shit about her. Either way, they never offered any help. As for her husband's side of the family, they too never offered any help. Come to think of it, the first and last time Dottie ever met her in-laws was on her wedding day. They showed up for the free ham sandwiches and stayed until the keg of beer ran dry.

"Ain't it kinda early ta be drinking beer?" Dottie knew if Eddie was drinking at the same time his wild look was setting in there was a possibility he might do something crazy. It didn't happen all the time, but when it did, Lord have mercy.

"No, it ain't too early. It's the middle of the afternoon. Hell, ya both oughta be drinkin' with me."

Eddie usually didn't invite Louie to do anything, much less share his beer. So when he offered, Louie broke into a smile like a little kid on Christmas morning. "I'll have me a beer with ya," he said cheerfully.

"Shut the hell up, you will not," Eddie snapped.

Sad, disappointed, crestfallen - however you want to describe it, that's how Louie felt. Eddie loved it. "Shit I was just kiddin' Lou. You can have the resta this one." Before Eddie handed his brother the bottle he took a long swallow from it. "I'll just get myself another."

As nasty as Eddie could be when the mood set in, it never interfered with Louie's affection for him. He followed Eddie around like a lost puppy dog. The bad part was that Louie couldn't hide it. The pathetic part was that Eddie took advantage of it. Louie took the bottle like he was being handed a crisp one hundred dollar bill. "Thanks Eddie. Thanks bunches."

"Anytime Lou, you know that," Eddie replied spuriously. He left the room to retrieve another beer. "You want one ma?" he called out. Dottie couldn't talk loud enough for Eddie to hear, which is why he waited until he was standing in the kitchen before he made the offer. He chuckled to himself.

Dottie watched helplessly as Louie emptied the bottle in front of her. She didn't want any beer for herself, but she didn't want Louie to have any either. For years now there was nothing she could do about Eddie, so she stopped trying long ago. But Louie was different. His man-size body was half filled by that of a child and Dottie hated when Eddie tried to get him to drink beer, whiskey, smoke ciggies, or even use cuss words.

Back out in the kitchen Eddie reached for the pint of Canadian Club sitting on top of the fridge. He twisted off the cap, tossed it on the counter with all the other garbage, and took a swig from the bottle. It felt hot as it ran down his throat. When it hit his belly one of his eyes started flickering and his head whipped from side to side. "Damnit-all, that shit's good. Damnit-all," he said, as if the proud founder of a newly discovered taste.

The rest of the afternoon went by quickly. Dottie Hart spent it in bed smoking her non-filtered ciggies. Louie spent it watching his mother cough up an assortment of blood, phlegm and puss. He also shared two more of Eddie's beers. He felt sad his mother was in such a bad way, but at the same time was happy because Eddie offered him beer. And Eddie? He spent it drinking and wondering why Rebecca wasn't home to greet him the last time he was over there.

It was somewhere in the early part of the evening, a pint of whiskey and six beers later, to be exact, when Eddie got the silly notion that Rebecca was home waiting for him. He decided to visit, but first wanted to check in on his mother. He knew she was dying, that's not what bothered him. He was hoping she died soon 'cause he spent enough of his life sleeping in the living area of the trailer. Eddie wanted her bed, so as soon as she kicked the ol' bucket, he intended to take over her room.

Dottie Hart lay propped up against a couple of sweat stained pillows. Her eyes were veiny, (though not so veiny she couldn't see that Eddie's wild look had set in good and deep), and the bags underneath them stuck out like black paint because her skin was as white as the paper on her cigarettes. She held a ciggy in one hand and a dishrag in the other. Whenever she spit up she used the rag to wipe herself off. Louie had been doing it earlier, but he didn't know his own strength. Everytime he tried wiping her mouth Dottie felt like her jaw was coming apart and her teeth were caving in. It got so bad, she had to take over. Louie whimpered, but Dottie figured his whimpering was better than her suffering.

Eddie glanced at his brother. He was sitting in a corner of the room sleeping. "Beer got him, huh?" he said to no one in particular. Eddie found the concept amusing, and snickered.

"You know he can't drink that stuff," Dottie said, her voice a scratchy whisper.

Eddie looked at his mother. She was only 57 years old, and even though Eddie didn't know what 100 years old looked like, he was sure his mother looked it.

For the last year Dottie refused to see a doctor. She realized she was dying but gave her doctors all the money she planned to. All she had left was a $20,000.00 life insurance policy and the trailer, but there was no way she was going to borrow against either of them. Dottie planned to leave the money and trailer to her sons. She just prayed Eddie would do the right thing.

Dottie Hart didn't pray hard enough.

CHAPTER 22

Rebecca Anderson climbed into the bathtub at 8:00 p.m.. She took a glass of wine with her and for the next hour planned to soak the day's events away. Barry Anderson picked up the girls a half-hour earlier. He was supposed to have them back by 9:30 p.m. at the latest, but Rebecca knew the moment she kissed them goodbye the son-of-a-bitch wouldn't drop them back off until 11:00. It didn't matter if it was a school night. Barry Anderson got to see his daughters twice a week and each time he made sure to let them stay up later than they should. It made them happy, and at the same time pissed off his soon to be ex-wife, which, in turn, made him happy.

The house was quiet. No kids to answer to. No television blaring away. And no Carmen. Rebecca closed her eyes and rested her head against the neck of the tub. The hot water was soothing. So was the Merlot. Rebecca sipped it steady until it was gone. She set the empty glass down on the edge of the tub and let her hand slide through the water across her breasts, over her stomach, and down to her vagina. She massaged herself softly and thought back to her afternoon rendezvous with Judy Trinket. Too bad they had to stop seeing each other, Rebecca thought. She massaged herself a little harder, and moved her fingers in a little deeper. I'll call her once the divorce is final, she decided. A tiny smile curled up at the end of her lips.

On his way over to Rebecca Anderson's house Eddie stopped off at the liquor store to buy a six pack of Bud and another pint of whiskey. He preferred Canadian Club but didn't want to spend the money, so he settled on some cheaper brand he couldn't pronounce. While in the store he also decided to steal a pack of non-filters. Fuck it. If the guy in the store isn't gonna pay attention, why the hell not?

For a while the whiskey was going down so smooth and easy Eddie stopped paying attention to where he was going and took a wrong turn. Fifteen miles later he figured out his mistake, only to blame Rebecca. "Fucking bitch cunt," he muttered between clenched teeth. The street was empty and the bald tires screeched loudly as Eddie wrestled the truck into a U-turn. Once back in the right direction he grabbed the whiskey bottle from the shotgun seat. There was a quarter pint left, which he promptly chug-a-lugged down. Eddie rolled down the window and waited for an oncoming vehicle. He would have preferred a motorcycle but planned to settle for the first thing that came along. When a car finally approached Eddie tried to time his throw so the whiskey bottle would hit the windshield.

What the hell. It was all in good fun, wasn't it?

Eddie watched the car swerve out of the way...but damn if he wasn't close! "Lucky cocksucker!" he shouted.

Eddie pulled a camel from his pocket and lit it with his own butane. Eddie didn't realize it, but whenever he lit a cigarette he was fortunate the grease he'd collected on his hands, body and clothes, didn't catch on fire. It would have been different if he showered and changed his clothes with some degree of regularity, but he didn't. Maybe ten times a year - a dozen tops.

The ciggy hung between his lips and the smoke spewed from his flared nostrils. Eddie grabbed one of the two beers left from the six pack. By now the beers were kind of warm - and Eddie despised warm beer. "It's that goddamn bitch's fault. If she was home the first time, I wouldn't be out here now gettin' lost. And if I didn't get lost, the damn beer wouldn't be warm. It's that goddamn simple!" Eddie said vehemently.

There was no logic to Eddie's way of thinking, but, then again, that's why he was Eddie.

"And I better not get no lip 'cause I'm showin' up late. I won't tolerate no fucking lip. If I get any, I may just up and smack the shit clean outta her," he concluded.

Eddie didn't stop cursing Rebecca until he pulled into her driveway, a full 90 minutes after he started out for her house. By now Rebecca was in her robe, the stereo was pouring out tunes from the Big Band Era, and her wine glass was refilled a second time.

It was dark outside, which made the truck more difficult to see than if parked at the curb under a streetlight. Not that Eddie gave it any thought. All he could think about was getting inside to see Rebecca. As he approached the front door the muffled sound of music could be heard coming from the inside. Eddie and his whiskey soaked mind didn't think twice. He wrapped his jacket around his fist, walked around to the back of the house, where he stood like an innocent shadow among the tall trees, and punched the family room window until the glass gave out.

The house was consumed with The Glen Miller Orchestra and Rebecca never heard a thing. She was in the walk-in closet looking to see if she got back the same amount of dry cleaning she took in a week earlier.

Eddie pulled his lanky body inside the large opening, studied the room interior for several seconds, (taking special note of the portrait of Rebecca and her two daughters), then followed the lights and music upstairs. Eddie's long strides allowed him to take the carpeted steps two at a time.

The bedroom lights were on in one of the girl's rooms so Eddie poked his head inside to see what he could see. All he found of interest was a plastic Raggedy Ann mask sitting on the bed. Eddie slipped his oval shaped head inside the elastic string, and though it was snug, it still wasn't too bad a fit for his narrow face and compressed eyes. Eddie grabbed himself a look in the mirror. Man-o-lordy-man. Wait'll she gets a load of me. She's gonna love me sure, he thought. Raggedy Ann Eddie followed the lights down to the end of the hall. When he got to her room Rebecca was just setting her glass of wine down on the nightstand. Her back was to the doorway.

Dottie Hart was right. When Eddie had the wild look and started drinking, sometimes, something ugly happened.

This time something ugly turned out to be Rebecca Anderson.

Eddie snuck up behind her and tapped her on the shoulder. The sudden touch startled Rebecca and she gasped, jumped and turned all in a single motion. When she saw the six foot tall Raggedy Ann her body grew paralyzed with fear.

For the next hour, Eddie Hart was long and strong.

Rebecca grunted and panted only when she couldn't help herself. Otherwise, she stayed true to the belief that the assault was the doing of her husband. She thought of her daughters, her babies. There was no way on God's green earth her husband was ever gonna find out she got raped. There was no way she was going to accuse him of anything. That's what the son-of-a-bitch wanted. Accuse him again and look like a fool in front of the judge again. But it wasn't going to happen this time. Whatever sacrifice it took was still better than losing custody to her husband. After all, they were her babies. She brought them into this world, and she was going to keep them. No way her husband was gonna get them.

No way!

CHAPTER 23

Dottie Hart died in her bed four days after Eddie's little tryst with Rebecca Anderson, a time when Eddie was just getting over his headaches.

Eddie got headaches whenever the wild look disappeared from his eyes. Now, with the death of his mother, Eddie knew that sooner or later he was gonna get his wild look again, which meant it was only a matter of time before the headaches came calling again.

Eddie usually got the wild look when he was distressed over something, like running out of whiskey when a ballgame was on the black and white, or Rebecca Anderson not being home when she was supposed to be, or having to take care of his big, stupid brother because his cunt mother suddenly decided to push up daisies.

It wasn't as if Eddie felt bad about getting the wild look. On the contrary, he relished it. It made him feel strong and confident, the way a real man should feel. It was the headaches Eddie couldn't stand. They always snuck up on him real slow. At first an incessant, dull vibration would fill his ears. After a little time, maybe a day or two, the vibrations would get louder and louder until his head felt like it was being invaded by a jackhammer. From there it settled into a steady pounding, like there was a little guy with a tattoo on his forearm running around inside, beating on his brains with a mallet. Sooner or later the headaches just died out. Eddie always figured the little guy with the tattoo got tired and couldn't swing the mallet anymore. But, until that happened, there were occasions when the pain in his head would get so intense, his eyes would flicker and Eddie would either have trouble maintaining his balance, or he'd black out altogether. He preferred the latter. It was the only time he was free of the staggering pain.

Dottie Hart's estate was simple. She left the trailer and $20,000.00 from a life insurance policy to be split equally between her two sons. Dottie wanted to leave everything to Louie, but figured his only chance to make it from day to day was if Eddie watched over him, and she knew Eddie wouldn't do it for free.

Dottie didn't think Eddie was worth a damn. Often times she couldn't stand the sight of him. Just the same Eddie was still her son and she figured to trust him with the estate more than she did some banker or lawyer. There was only one small condition. As long as Louie was around, half the money had to be used for his well-being. That included the proceeds from the sale of the trailer, if Eddie decided to sell it.

It wasn't as if Louie was retarded or anything. He was just slow, the result of Dottie Hart's heavy alcohol and periodic valium consumption during pregnancy. After Louie was born Dottie learned her lesson. When she was pregnant with Eddie she cut out the beer and valium and confined herself to whiskey, (okay, so maybe she had an occasional boilermaker, but only once in a while). That's why Eddie was lucky. He wasn't slow at all. He might've gotten stuck with the wild look and some brutal headaches, but he was capable of normalcy, at least on the days when he wasn't nuts.

Eddie Hart was leaning against the fingerprint smudged, grease stained fridge having a beer. Louie was sitting on his bed, whimpering over the loss of his mother. The cunt's dead and buried. What the fuck could he be crying about, Eddie wondered. "Shut the fuck up! You sound like a goddamn puppy dog," he snarled. If that fucking cunt thought I was gonna spend the rest of my freakin' life babysittin' ol' dumbo, she was sadly mistaken, he thought. Eddie downed the rest of his beer and threw the can in the direction of the sink. It hit the counter, rolled back off and landed on the yellow and white checked linoleum floor. Eddie ignored it altogether. He was beginning to sweat and wanted to get outside. "I'll be back," he snapped.

Louie inhaled deep and hard in an effort to suck the snot back up his nose. He got half of it. The other half he wiped on his shirt. "Where ya..." his voice cracked just a tad ..."where ya goin Ed? Can't I go too?" Whenever Louie talked the words sounded like they were bumping into each other.

Eddie hated to be called Ed. "Stay the fuck inside and shut the fuck up!" The inside of Eddie's head was still a little tender from his last batch of headaches. Getting mad at his big, stupid brother wasn't helping the pain much either. Eddie softened his approach. "I'm goin' outside for awhile. I'll be back when I get back." What a fucking asshole, he thought. Eddie massaged his temples and walked outside. The fresh October air helped to dry his sweat.

It was another ten days before the insurance money arrived. By the time Eddie tore open the envelope and saw the check his pulse was racing so fast he thought blood might shoot out of his body like the water out of a fire hose. He never saw that much money before. He certainly never had that much money before. Make no mistake. Eddie had no intentions of using any portion of the $20,000.00 on Louie. Eddie had other plans for good ol' dumbo. Had 'em since the day he read the old cunt's will.

It was the same day he got the wild look back in his eyes.

CHAPTER 24

It was a bright Tuesday afternoon and the school buses were lined up in parade formation, yellow to yellow, bumper to bumper, exhaust to exhaust.

Eddie was sitting behind the wheel of his dead mother's 86 Impala. Originally the car was misty blue but a couple of years ago Louie painted it black. It didn't help. The car still looked like an 86 Impala.

It was the second time in the past week that Eddie parked in front of the school. The first time was to make sure he had the right place. It wasn't as though Rebecca Anderson was going to tell him. Eddie figured since it was the closest elementary school to Rebecca's house, her daughter's probably went to it. Eddie turned out to be a master of the obvious. He also discovered that instead of taking the bus, the two girl's walked the four blocks home. Eddie liked that part of it most of all. It was going to make his job that much easier.

Louie was sitting in the passenger seat with a wayward look in his eyes and a carefree grin splattered across his beachball size face. His hand's were folded over his crotch, but they were so big it looked like a catcher's mitt was sitting in his lap. Whenever Louie sat down he put his hands in his lap. Besides taking a leak it was the only other time his crotch was ever touched, (which would explain why Louie always liked to be sitting down).

Louie wasn't sure why he and Ed were parked in front of a school. Hell, Louie couldn't even remember Ed driving to the school. For some inebriated reason the last thing Louie remembered was eating eggs. Indeed he did. Eddie fried them the good ol' Eddie Hart way, crushed up valium in place of salt and pepper, and plenty of beer in place of orange juice and coffee.

It was, to be sure, a breakfast fit for a king, or in this case, a court jester.

There was still another ten minutes to go before school let out, and since Eddie had no intentions of passing the time by making idle chit-chat with Louie, he reached behind the driver's seat and grabbed a fifth of Canadian Club. Eddie knew if his brother stopped drinking he'd fall asleep for sure. He always did. A couple of beers, and boom, it was nighty night for good ol' dumbo. Eddie hoped to take Louie beyond the couple of beers and lights out routine. A little whiskey, maybe a couple more valium, and who knows, Louie might just stay awake long enough to pass out.

Eddie smacked Louie on his jumbo size arm. It actually stung his hand a little when he made contact. "Hey Lou, have a swallow." Eddie made the offer as though Louie was his best friend.

Louie's body was numb from the valium and beer he'd already consumed, so when he turned to face Eddie his head bobbed back and forth in a half circle. Still, Louie couldn't remember a time when he felt better. Here he was sittin' with Ed, his best bud in the whole wide world, and for the first time since his mother died, Lou didn't feel like crying. "Okay, sure Ed." He wrapped his huge paw around the neck of the bottle and lifted it to his mouth.

What a fucking jerk, Eddie thought. "Say Lou, ya might wanna unscrew the cap before ya try drinkin' her."

Louie pulled the bottle away from his mouth and looked at it like he was waiting for it to do a trick.

"Just unscrew it Lou, it ain't gonna do ya any good if ya keep holdin' it in front of your face - 'sides, the whole world don't have ta know we're sittin' here drinkin' the shit."

Louie moved the bottle closer to his lap. He tilted it sideways and looked at it like maybe it would do a trick from that angle.

Eddie watched his brother with disdained curiosity, until, for no reason at all, Louie exploded into booming laughter. The sudden bellow took Eddie by surprise and his body jumped a notch. After his nerves settled back into his skin Eddie smacked Louie on his arm again. "Say Lou, that shit ain't gonna do nothin' for ya if ya don't swallow some of it."

Louie unscrewed the cap, lifted the bottle and gulped down enough for two guys, (not counting the whiskey that spilled out the sides of his mouth).

Good thing I brought a few bottles, Eddie thought.

Louie glanced over at his brother. His big brown eyes were red and glassy, and his head bobbed back and forth just enough to make his thick, scraggly hair fall from side to side. He wiped the sides of his mouth with the back of his hand before handing the bottle back to Eddie. "You're gonna have some yerself, aren't ya Ed?" As Louie waited for an answer his mouth fell open, exposing a gap where two of his bottom front teeth used to be, the result of an accident he had when he was 13 years old. It seems Louie had a toothache in one of his back molars and Eddie took it upon himself to play dentist. It was the first time Dottie Hart ever saw Eddie's wild look turn into something ugly.

Eddie grabbed the whiskey bottle by the neck and rushed it to his mouth. He took a considerable gulp, his saliva mixing with all the little drool bubbles Louie left around the bottle opening. Eddie pulled the bottle away, swallowed down the mouthful he was holding in and wailed, "Eeeeeeee-heeeeeee! Damnit you big tub, damnit if that ain't good!" Eddie shook his head fiercely and bounced his upper body back and forth against the car seat. "Eeeeeeee-heeeeeee!"

Louie chortled, but that only triggered a wicked cough from deep inside his big, soft belly.

Eddie stopped bouncing once it sounded like ol' dumbo was beginning to choke. Not that Eddie cared, mind you. He just wanted to make sure Louie's gut didn't burst in half until he was finished with him. "Lean forward Lou."

When he did, Eddie swatted him on the back until the coughing stalled out. "Gee, you okay Lou?" Eddie mocked.

Louie took a deep breath and blew the air out of his mouth like he was blowing out birthday candles. His head felt like it was full of water and the water was swishing around whenever he moved. Just the same, the coughing attack appeared to be over with so Louie nodded his head in response.

Eddie snickered and stuck the bottle out again. "Hell, then have some more Lou. Shit's good for ya."

Louie took the bottle and gulped down another mouthful. He wanted to imitate Eddie's wailing, but when he tried, some of the whiskey came back out of his mouth. His face contorted and his shoulder's cringed. He started to cough again.

What a fucking jerk, Eddie thought. (Seems Eddie thought that a lot). "Gotta go slower Lou. Sip it down if ya have to, don't gulp it. If ya gulp it and end up spittin' some of it back up, ya get more on your shirt then ya do in yourself. At that point, there ain't no point in drinkin' it."

As soon as Louie stopped coughing he turned glum. He was suddenly afraid Eddie wouldn't let him sit and drink with him anymore. The sad look made Eddie want to laugh and make fun of his brother, but he didn't. "Just drink it slow, it'll be fine," he said in as reassuring a voice as his acting abilities would allow.

Eddie's reassurance did little to spark any life back into Louie. He just sat there like a big, stinky pile of elephant shit.

Eddie was growing impatient. "Here gimmee the sucker, I'll show you." Eddie grabbed the bottle before Louie had a chance to offer it to him. "Like this." Eddie proceeded to sip the whiskey slow, but steady. After several easy swallows he pulled the bottle away from his mouth and handed it back to ol' dumbo. "See Lou, it's easy. You can do it for sure."

"I just gotta go slower, don't I. I mean we got all day to be drinking together, don't we Ed?" The thought that Eddie might say no, we don't have all day to be drinking together, caused a look of concern to adorn Louie's face.

"Now you got the picture Lou. Damnit you big tub, now you got it." Eddie flashed a wholesome smile at his big, stupid brother.

Louie was happy again. He held the bottle back up and tried to emulate Eddie's way of sipping whiskey. Other than his drooling, he had it down pretty good.

Eddie refocused his attention on the school because the kid's were beginning to wander outside. His wholesome smile vanished.

It wasn't long before they appeared, Rachel and Jody, as pretty as the faces in the portrait hanging in the Anderson's family room. Rachel and Jody Anderson were both skinny and kind of short for their respective ages, but each one had beautiful long blond hair just like their mother. Maybe Rebecca was a true blond after all.

I bet they're spoiled as all get out, Eddie concluded. Standin' there doin' nothin', like they're too good for all the other little stinkin' brats.

It was true, while most of the other kids dillydallied their way on to a school bus, Rachel and Jody Anderson quietly stood off to the side, out of the way. There was a time when they'd play with all the other kids. But not anymore. It was the divorce thing however, it wasn't because they were spoiled. As a matter-of-fact, neither of the Anderson girl's felt like they were good enough for the other kids. Between the pending divorce of their parents, and having a bunch of the other kids always making fun of them because their mother was with Miss Trinket - naked - Rachel and Jody were ashamed, embarrassed, and at the same time, felt like they were responsible for it all and had to apologize for something, (although they never knew what). They no longer got invited to any of the other kid's houses, and none of the other kid's ever came over to their house. If Rachel and Jody didn't have each other, they would have had no one.

The situation made them very loving sisters. At the same time it was creating a very hateful childhood.

Eddie planned to wait until Rachel and Jody were a fair distance down the street and out of sight from the school before zeroing in on them. He still had a little time so he reached over and grabbed the whiskey bottle from the clutches of Louie's blubbery lips. Eddie took a healthy swig. The whiskey felt like it melted his throat on its way down to meet his gut, where it landed like a ball of fire. "Eeeeeeee-heeeeeee! Damn-damn-damn! Boy howdy, that shit is for me!" Eddie winced and shook his head wildly.

"That shit's for me too, Ed."

"Good then have some more Lou." Eddie shoved the bottle back in front of his brother.

Louie didn't react near as quick in taking hold of the bottle as Eddie was in shoving it in front of him. Consequently, it took a couple of seconds before Louie's big, mushy hand got a feel for it. At which point, he brought the bottle to his mouth just like he was a baby and the bottle was his mother's tit.

Uncoordinated fucking jerk, Eddie thought.

Louie still had no idea why he and Ed were parked by a school, which would explain why the expression on his face was the color of blank. Yet, with his best bud in the whole wide world sitting next to him, Louie was having one of the best days he could remember. Since his memory was as limited as his I.Q., that meant Louie was having one of his best days in the last month.

Eddie reached in the backseat and grabbed his Raggedy Ann mask. It was the same mask he wore on the night he had his fling with Rebecca. As he adjusted the mask over his face Eddie could feel the sweat on his hands building up. It wasn't because he was nervous about what he planned to do with the Anderson girls. Hell, Eddie's wild look was off and running and nothing could make him nervous. The moisture on his hands was due to the vinyl driving gloves he was wearing. He'd been wearing them from the moment he stepped inside the Impala. Not because it was cold outside, but because he planned to keep his fingerprints to himself.

By now Eddie determined Rachel and Jody Anderson were far enough along. It was time to fire up the Impala. The car engine didn't turn over the first couple of times, but when it did, the exhaust pipe belched out a cloud of charcoal gray smoke. As the car sat idling, its relentless sputtering vibrating the frame, Raggedy Ann Eddie turned to face Louie. "How do I look?"

Louie looked at his brother. "Ya look fine Ed, real fine."

Raggedy Ann Eddie put the car in drive and began his quest.

As slow as Eddie maneuvered the Impala down the street it still didn't take long before he turned the corner and caught sight of the girls.

Rachel and Jody were holding hands and skipping along the sidewalk, oblivious to the sounds of the old car as it closed in. They were too busy singing the words to a song they made up one night after listening to their parents scream at each other for the umpteenth time.

mommies love their babies...daddies love them too...
if we could be babies again...then ours would love us too.
mommies are so pretty...daddies are so strong...
but ours live apart...'cause we did something wrong.
your little girls are sad...your little girls cry...
please be our mommy and daddy...please try, try, try.
we'll be good little girls...we'll do whatever you say...
please be our mommy and daddy...please say yes today.

In another three houses the girls would be turning the corner again. Eddie planned to take them before they got to that point. He gunned the Impala and the bald tires turned and burned until the car burst forward.

Rachel and Jody stopped skipping and turned in the direction of the screeching tires. Since the Impala had all the appearances of a car speeding up the street the girls didn't think anything of it. Instead they turned back around and started singing again.

mommies love their babies...daddies love them too...
if we could be babies again then......

Out of nowhere the old Impala barreled up the mouth of the driveway, moving over the lawn and across the sidewalk. A bomb could have exploded and the girls wouldn't have been anymore startled. For a brief moment Rachel and Jody stood suspended from movement, just like two doe when they hear the crackling of a tree branch during hunting season.

Then they saw Raggedy Ann Eddie bolt from the car. Instinctively the girls ran. Unfortunately they ran side by side, making it much easier for Eddie to corral his prey.

For Louie, all the commotion was like looking at a collage. The more he saw, the less he understood, and the less he understood, the more he sipped his whiskey.

In the matter of a few long strides Raggedy Ann Eddie absorbed the space between himself and the girls. He grabbed hold of Rachel's long blond hair and Jody's skinny arm almost simultaneously. He pulled on Rachel's hair so hard her feet almost left the ground. In between crying and gasping to catch her breath Rachel tried to punch and scratch Eddie's hands so he would let go. Jody was screaming and trying to fight her way loose, which consisted mainly of attempting to wiggle her arm free. But the screaming and fighting was all for naught.

Nobody heard them. Nobody saw them. Nobody was going to save them.

And somehow when Eddie stuffed them in the backseat of the car, they seemed to understand that.

CHAPTER 25

At one time Mckenzie Elementary was considered the school of the future. That was until the school district's resident's started voting down every school millage making its way on to a ballot. Oh, they wanted the school alright. Indeed, educating their children was of the utmost importance. They just didn't want to pay for it, that's all. Since then the school's been up for sale. One day it was bound to make another office building. Until then, it would remain as quiet as a graveyard.

It was getting late, well past the time when Rachel and Jody Anderson should have been home. Much past 4:30 p.m. and Rebecca immediately started to blame her husband, Barry. It wouldn't be the first time he picked them up after school without checking with her. When that happened Rebecca wouldn't get the obligatory phone call until 6:30 p.m., after she was certain to have dinner prepared and waiting, but still several hours before Barry Anderson saw fit to bring his two girl's home. Generally, it would have been the perfect prelude to another thirst quenching, gut wrenching argument. Not this time.

When Eddie first pulled into the school the sun looked like it had enough play left inside it to dance with the clouds for another hour or so. Sometimes the sun looked like it was leading the dance and sometimes the clouds looked like they were leading. Either way the combination brought sweeping shadows over the tall, unrestrained weeds and grasses. By the time dusk settled a perfect chill had crept into the air. Not quite cold enough for someone wearing the right kind of jacket, but certainly cold enough to cause the skin to stand rigid if it was left bare, or as in this case, naked.

The Impala was parked between the swings and monkey bars, tarnished momentos the abandoned school was once decorated with a playground. Louie had his back propped up against the front bumper and his big ass settled comfortably in the dirt. A bottle of Canadian Club stood upright between his legs. It was the first time that day he wasn't interested in drinking. Ol' dumbo was more interested in staring at the two naked girls lying on the ground directly in front of him. He never saw naked girls before, let alone two at once. Indeed, this had become one of the best days Louie could ever remember.

Rachel and Jody Anderson were sprawled out beneath the darkening skies, the result of being fed enough valium to fill a grown man the size of Louie.

Eddie was sitting on the hood of the car casually drinking a beer and smoking a camel. He looked at Rachel and sneered. "Not so sassy now, are ya? Ya spoiled little brat." When Eddie first attempted to stuff valium down Rachel's throat she tried to bite his fingers. All it did was piss Eddie off and he punched her in the side of her head.

Jody was different. As soon as she saw Rachel get whacked she couldn't swallow the valium fast enough.

Eddie finished his camel and flicked it on the ground. He jumped down from the car and grabbed the bottle of whiskey from between Louie's legs. "Lotta good it does ya sittin' there." Fuckin' jerk, he thought.

Eddie's words floated through Louie's ears like his head was a dark, empty cave and the only sound it could grab hold of was the echo of a blowing wind. He turned his head towards Eddie, but said nothing. Louie didn't have to. The dazed look in his eyes and the aimless expression on his face said it all.

Eddie sealed his eyes tight and took a long pull from the whiskey bottle. When he reopened them it was as if his eyes were a different color. They weren't. It was just his wild look getting set to do something crazy. Eddie planted himself alongside the blanket and stared down at Rachel. Her eyelid's quivered open and closed. When they were open Rachel was able to see foggy images in front of her, though she could no more tell if the images were of a man, Raggedy Ann, or a rock. When they were closed she felt like she was spinning around in a pool of warm black water.

Eddie probed deep inside Rachel with his glove covered fingers. Since her body had been rendered senseless from the valium it made it impossible for her to feel anything or offer any resistance. Not that Eddie cared. He simply dug away, clawing and scratching at her young purity. Eddie snickered. "Hey Lou, ya like what I'm doing here?" Eddie didn't wait for ol' dumbo to respond. Instead he pulled his fingers out so he could make room for the head of the whiskey bottle. As he moved the bottle in and out of Rachel's vagina the whiskey spilled inside her.

Several minutes later Rachel started to bleed from inside. For Eddie it was an invitation to drive the bottle in faster and harder.

Louie watched with his mouth hanging wide open.

"Ya like this Lou? Ya like what I'm doin'? Wanna try it with yer peeter? Ya do, don't ya?" Eddie found the thought of his big, stupid brother pounding away at the insides of the young, helpless Rachel Anderson, amusing. He laughed accordingly.

Louie's mouth was still hanging open but no words came out in response.

"Gotta get yer pants off Lou. Y'ain't gettin' the bottle. Gotta use yer cucumber."

It was all Louie could do to struggle to his Bozo The Clown size feet. When he did, his body swayed back and forth like he was trying to maintain his balance on a boat in high seas.

Eddie was kind of surprised ol' dumbo was able to stand up.

Louie grappled with his belt until the buckle came loose. It only took five minutes. His pants were another story. Once he got them unzipped and forced them down over his big, lumpy ass he lost his balance and fell forward. It was like watching a tree fall over, except Louie grunted on impact.

"Figures," Eddie mumbled out loud. He pulled the bottle out of Rachel. A mixture of whiskey and blood was swirling around the bottom. "Have a drink Lou." Eddie held the bottle out until dumbo bungled his way into a sitting position and grabbed it. He drank the red whiskey until the bottle was dry, then offered it back to his best bud in the whole wide world.

"No thanks Lou. You can throw that one away - I'll get us another from your car."

As soon as Eddie started to walk back to the Impala Louie crawled over to the Anderson girls. He looked like a St. Bernard dog without the barrel around his neck. Louie might have slobbered more, but the dog was definitely smarter.

Eddie planned to feed his brother more whiskey, but what the hell, he figured. Them spoiled brat's ain't feeling nothin', plus it looks like ol' dumbo has hisself a stiff one. Eddie decided to grab himself a beer, fire up a camel and take a seat on the hood of the Impala instead. He wasn't disappointed with the entertainment.

Louie rested his 280 pounds on top of young Rachel Anderson and bulldozed his peeter in until it reached her pelvis. He wrapped his hands over her shoulder blades for leverage and hammered away, snarling and grunting like a ravaged dog, while blood spurted out from between Rachel's legs.

When he finished, minutes later, Louie moved his big hands over Rachel's young, fragile chest cavity and pressed down with enough force to push his largeness off of her. He cracked four of her ribs and pierced one of her lungs.

Ten year old Rachel Anderson slowly wheezed into death.

Thirty minutes and a bunch of whiskey later Louie was ready again. He slapped at Rachel's legs a couple of times but there was no movement. "Try the other one Lou. She's just as pretty as her sister." Eddie took a long drag from another camel and leaned back on his elbows for support.

Louie didn't respond, he simply followed directions like a robot. He dragged his naked ass across the dirt and climbed on top of little Jody Anderson. The valium was far from wearing off but Jody could still feel a burning sensation every time Louie tried to force her vagina to widen. The feeling caused her muscles to contract, prompting Louie to grab hold of her buttocks like he was ready to rip it in two. He plunged inside of her, and for the next twenty minutes, moved in and out like a battering ram. When Louie finally exploded, she gasped, her body first shuddering, then falling as still and as silent as a bean bag doll. It was the moment her spine snapped in half. It was the moment eight year old Jody Anderson died.

Killing the two Anderson girls wasn't what Eddie originally intended, but hey, what the hell ya gonna do?

Eddie stuck around long enough to finish his last two cans of beer and have a smoke. He looked at ol' dumbo, who by now had passed out next to the dead Anderson girls, and snickered. He'd fed the stupid jerk enough valium and whiskey to keep him that way until the following morning.

    At 5:30 a.m., Eddie, the anonymous jogger, called the police department from a pay phone to report seeing three naked bodies during an early morning run. "It was pretty dark and hard ta tell, but from where I was it looked like three people. I didn't stray too close. There was a car there too. It was kinda spooky lookin' so I didn't bother gettin' close enough to look inside. I don't know if anybody was in it or not. The others, they might be dead though. I don't know, but ya might wanna check it out. Like I said, it's that school they closed up awhile back, ya know, Mckenzie Elementary."

    Eddie knew the cops were gonna wake up big stupid Louie, only to find out he wouldn't remember a thing. Not one fucking thing. He liked that part of it second best of all. Eddie liked the part about having the $20,000.00 and trailer home all to himself even better.

CHAPTER 26

After Louie Hart was hoisted into the ambulance Carl Pita and Brian Dexter were instructed to park it some thirty yards away from the dead bodies of the two young girls. The only thing they didn't do was strap Louie in. "What's the difference," Carl told his partner. "The ankle straps aren't worth a shit, and besides, the guy's so goddamn comatose, he's not goin' anywhere. It'll be fine, trust me."

A short time later, 7:30 a.m. to be exact, Max Cougar and Zack Darwin arrived at the Mckenzie Elementary playground. Usually they didn't get to work for at least another hour, but on this particular Thursday morning Captain Rudy Whitaker made himself loud and clear over the phone. Like the Captain said..."It ain't Sunday so ya don't get to sleep late. And even if it was Sunday, you don't go to church anyhow, so get the hell over there, now!" As Max sidestepped the area marked off by yellow tape and joined the festivities inside the criminal arena he made every effort to look straight ahead, although he couldn't help but notice Assistant District Attorney Tyler Lake out of the corner of his eye. He nodded in the D.A.'s direction. Tyler Lake responded by shaking his head in disgust. The doleful expression on his face should have been enough to warn Max of the horror he was about to view. It wasn't, but then again no facial expression would be. Beast was consumed by the insanity and presence of the local news station so he failed to notice the Assistant D.A.. Instead, he pointed his finger at some fat guy with a camera as if to say, "stay the hell away from me." Judging by the agitated look in Zack's eyes and the way he squared up his shoulders, it was highly unlikely any person from the news was going to test his warning, let alone the fat guy with the camera.

The only thing Max and the Beast knew about the crime before they arrived at the school was it involved the apparent rape and possible murder of two girls. That in itself was pathetic, but for Max to bear witness to something he couldn't imagine, not even in his wildest dreams, was altogether different. The instant Max peeled the coroner's blanket away to gaze down at the little Anderson girls his stomach started to shake and cramp up, and his throat swelled and convulsed forward. Dry heaves were only a moment away. Max sealed his eyes tight and immediately turned away from the bodies. He scurried several feet in the opposite direction and bent over, his palms resting on his trembling knees. Over and over he took deep breaths, letting the air back out slow and sure until his insides felt like they settled back into place.

The Beast, who had been several yards away from Max, was more concerned with his partner than with viewing the dead bodies so he hustled over and kneeled beside him. He put his paw on Max's upper back and searched his face. "You okay?"

Max turned his head. His eyes were red and moist, like he'd been punched on the bridge of his nose. It wasn't from crying. It was from the pain of having to fight off the frenzy in his own guts after seeing the two young girls, (little kids for Christ sakes), dead on the ground. Max shook his head, "Yeah, I'm fine. I guess I just didn't expect it, ya know what I mean?"

"Yeah, unfortunately I do."

Max straightened up and arched the tenseness out of the small of his back. "They got anything Beast?"

"Don't know yet Max. Wanted to find out how you were first."

Max lightly slapped at the Beast's chin, and said, "Thanks man," then promptly turned away and headed for the Coroner. He thought Zack was right behind him, but he wasn't. The Beast lumbered over to the naked dead bodies instead. His reaction wasn't much different from Max's, except he wasn't able to hold back.

Dr. Samuel Murphy had been the Deputy Coroner for the past twelve years. He was smart, but didn't try to sound like an intellectual, and in his early fifties, only the stress from his job, coupled with the gray hair on his head and the wrinkles cut deep into the sides of his full cheeks and across his forehead made him look seventy years old at best.

"Hey Doc," Max said extending his hand as he closed in on Sam Murphy.

After twelve years of crime scenes, cops and lawyers, shaking hands had become so routine Dr. Murphy didn't realize he was even doing it, which explained his flaccid grip. "Not a pretty sight, is it Max?"

Max figured Dr. Murphy was referring to the little bout he just had with the dry heaves. "It doesn't appear your partner thinks much of it at any rate."

"Huh?" Max asked. His tone of voice was quiet and uncertain, almost like the doctor threw him a verbal curve ball and he didn't know how to hit...or rather, respond to it. Max turned and found the Beast bent over about ten feet from the dead bodies. His hands were resting on his waist and he was slowly shaking his head.

"Beast?" Max called out.

Zack didn't look up. Instead he acknowledged Max with a wave of his hand.

"He'll be okay," Dr. Murphy said. The doctor had a steady confidence about him. Whenever he spoke his words seemed to put Max at ease.

Max nodded his head automatically. "Yeah," he mumbled.

"There were three of them..." Dr. Murphy began..."the two poor little girls and the one in the ambulance." Dr. Murphy knew Max well enough to know his head was filling with questions. He decided to provide all the information he could and save Max the trouble of asking. "He's a large man, even bigger than your partner, Zack. When we first arrived we found him passed out next to the victim's bodies. He was breathing but we weren't able to get him up, so I sent for EMS to cart him off to North View Hospital. They arrived a short time ago."

"Is he gonna die, Doc?"

"No, his vitals checked out. He's stable."

"Good then make sure they don't take him anywhere until I give the okay," Max instructed. His voice was quiet, but firm.

Dr. Murphy nodded. He'd anticipated that exact instruction from Max, which is why the ambulance was still there. He continued talking as though Max's interruption never happened. "I don't know what else he might have inside him but I could smell whiskey the moment I approached the area. To say the least, the smell was all over the three bodies. I'm sure there's more to it than whiskey though - the officer's found an empty bottle. The label was missing but the bottle type comes straight from the pharmacist. I'd be willing to bet whatever was in the bottle was in the bodies." Dr. Murphy paused to sigh.

It was just enough time for Max to fire out a question. "The two girls, whataya figure..."

Dr. Murphy hated to be asked the cause of death before he'd had an opportunity to administer a complete examination. It was a premature question that wore out its welcome years ago. "To be honest I'm not quite sure, and as you saw for yourself, they're in rough shape. It's gonna take a little time in the lab before I know anything. I can tell you this, from all appearances they were sexually assaulted. As to how they died, at this juncture, I won't speculate. Yet, in the same breath I would guess that the deaths were painful, possibly sadistic in nature."

The Beast approached. He looked a little peaked to Max, but probably no more peaked than Max looked to him. "The Doc figures they were raped, but he doesn't know how they died, at least not yet. Evidently the guy who did it was passed out when the cops first got here. They weren't able to get him up so they called EMS to ship him off to North View. He's inside the ambulance now."

"Is he awake Doc?" Zack asked.

"No, not the last time I checked, which was about 10 minutes ago. The ambulance crew is supposed to let me know if there's any change."

"I told the Doc to make sure they keep him here until we say otherwise."

The Beast nodded his concurrence. "Have we been able to identify any of them yet?" The question was as somber as Zack's tone of voice.

"Not to my knowledge, no. But you should talk to Tyler Lake. He'll know more about that than I would. I know they ran the plates, but beyond that, I couldn't tell you. The bodies were all naked, including the male. There was no immediate identification anywhere."

In the four years Tyler Lake had been an Assistant District Attorney he came to be known for two things. The first was that he was an impeccable dresser. Tailored suits, silk ties, Italian shoes, the works. The second was that he had the highest incarceration rate among the other D.A.'s in his office. However, that was due to his willingness to plea bargain, not because he possessed superior trial skills.

"No we haven't been able to identify the two girls yet." Regardless of how ugly or chaotic a situation ever turned, Tyler had the unique ability to appear unrattled, best exhibited by the effortless grace that remained a constant in his tone of voice. "As for the male suspect, that's a different story. The plates on the car reveal that it's registered to a Louis Hart. A further check revealed that at one time it was registered to a Dottie hart, but she since died . My guess is Louis Hart is her husband, or son, whatever. Either way, according to the Secretary of State, he owns the car."

"Well Tyler, since you've been here awhile, at least longer then me and Zack, let me ask you a stupid question." Max sounded like he was getting ready to make a proposition.

"What's that?" Tyler might have sounded like he was interested in Max's question, but the reticent look in his eyes said otherwise. Maybe it was because the cops had a habit of asking questions, that in the scheme of things, just didn't matter. Oh sure, the questions themselves might have made sense, but what did that have to do with the court system? That was one of the biggest reasons the District Attorney's office had such a high turnover rate. It seemed like the attorneys who did the least amount of hypothesizing, philosophizing and intellectualizing were the ones well grounded in basic common sense. It was already there, it wasn't something they had to search for. They were the attorneys that left every few years or so. Sometimes they went into private practice, sometimes private business, or sometimes they just took a good, long break before starting back up again. The attorneys who didn't leave were the ones who allowed their own sense of fairness to be ground up and reshaped by the often cold finality of the legal system. They were the ones that stuck around ten, even twenty years at a time. They only left because sheer boredom forced them to. Tyler Lake seemed like he was at that crossroad. Do I stay? Do I go? Do I take a break? Does it even matter?

It didn't.

"At this point in time do you think the suspect in the ambulance is the only one responsible for what went on here?" Until Max gathered enough information to form his own opinion he figured it best to get the District Attorney's take on things. That didn't mean Max had to agree with it. Hell, over the years Max was no better then 50-50 when it came to agreeing with the D.A.'s office on anything.

"At this point in time I would consider him the number one suspect." Tyler Lake took a deep breath and exhaled in the form of a long sigh, all in an effort to masquerade his yawn.

Why can't these guy's ever give us a straight answer, the Beast wondered.

By now, EMS attendant Brian Dexter had fallen asleep in the front seat of the ambulance. He was exhausted from a long night of partying and was in no mood, or condition, to monitor someone else's condition. Besides, his partner, Carl Pita, said he'd look after the guy. There was only one catch - Carl had grown weary of babysitting the fat slob and decided he'd rather smoke cigarettes and eavesdrop on police conversations. He went unnoticed as he wandered around the crime scene.

Dave Sanders worked on and off as a freelance cameraman for Channel 12, earning two local Emmy nominations for his "on the scene, up to the minute," camera work. But getting nominated didn't cut it anymore. It was like his dad always told him, some guy's work hard their whole lives to get there, and some guy's just get there. After eight years of working hard, Dave Sanders figured it was time to "just get there."

Earlier in the morning Dave Sanders tried to get the faces of the dead girls on camera but Dr. Murphy and a couple of cops sent him packing. So that it wouldn't be a total loss, Dave Sanders was prepared to settle for a few frames of the body bags being carried away. It wasn't what he wanted, but it would be enough to illicit a measurable response from the viewer, and at the same time, help set the tone of the story. Until then, he would film the killer in his present state, be it passed out, naked, bruised or even bloody. Dave didn't care how the guy looked, just so long as he got him on camera. If the filming went off as planned Dave Sanders would use it in the documentary he was working on, tentatively titled, *Rape, Murder And Videotape - Appendages Of Evolution*.

Louie Hart's ears twitched and his eyelids fluttered when the latch on the ambulance door clicked. He remained perfectly still, not quite sure if he was awake, or merely dreaming. The incessant throbbing in his head was the first clue he was really awake. The ambulance door opening to the daylight outside was the clincher. Louie's eyes burst wide open, his bloodshot, dried out pupils blinded by the sudden exposure to daylight.

Lights, Camera.....and Action! Dave Sanders crouched between the open double doors and started filming.

Louie had no idea what was happening. Where was his ma? Where was his brother Ed? Why did his head hurt? Why did he feel so bad? Who was the guy with the big head? (It was actually a television camera with attached lighting accessories stuck to the eyeball of Dave Sanders). Was he on a space ship? Did this guy take him away from his family? Louie suddenly longed for home. He wanted to see his ma and his brother Ed, his best bud in the whole wide world. The more questions and thoughts that collided in Louie's head, the more his head pounded and the faster the color in his face was washed away by the hysteria filling his big, fat body. Like a wounded dog, Louie wailed uncontrollably. "Maaaaaaaaaa! Maaaa, I'm in here! Maaaaaaaaaa!"

Between Louie's screaming and a few of the cops now heading towards the ambulance (including the one who pointed his finger at him), Dave Sanders realized he'd made a big mistake. He immediately shut off the camera and backed away from the ambulance doors. The open space was all the invitation Louie needed to head for home. No space ships for ol' dumbo.

"I'm comin ma! I'm comin home!"

Louie didn't realize he was naked until he fumbled his way outside and stood on the hard ground. The bottoms of his dirty feet got cold and the brisk morning air caused his peeter to shrink. Nonetheless, as soon as Louie saw people heading his way he forgot about being naked. He turned and ran with the grace of a pregnant cow.

"I can't believe I wore my fucking cowboy boots," Max declared. His words bounced with each stride.

"I can't believe I wore mine either," Zack bounced back.

Seconds later Max reached the ambulance. He darted a couple of steps to his right and tried to plant his shoulder into that stupid son-of-a-bitch cameraman. Luckily for Dave Sanders he was able to veer out of Max's way. Unfortunately it landed him in the direct path of the Beast. (Luck doesn't always run in pairs). The Beast couldn't stop. Not that he planned to, but this way, he figured, at least he'd have an excuse if the question ever came up. Zack lowered his shoulder and bowled Dave Sanders over, camera and all. The Beast never broke stride.

Dave Sanders hit the ground hard. He grunted and his camera rattled. "Fucking asshole," he mumbled.

"Gee, I hope I didn't break anything," Zack called back to him.

Max was bearing down fast. He was now close enough to hear Louie whimpering and carrying on about his mother. The Doc was right, this guy's big, Max thought. Damn it, he might be too big to take up high...I don't want to dive at his legs...I hate diving on the ground...Fuck it...I'm takin' him upstairs. With that, Max leaped forward. He slammed his right forearm into the back of Louie's neck and wrapped his left arm around the front of Louie's chest to hold on. Between the sudden blow from the forearm and the weight of Max's 190 pounds, the impact was enough to drive Louie to the ground, but that was about it.

Max wasn't able to hold on and flew off to the side. Louie rolled forward like a boulder moving in slow motion. When he finally stopped, Louie frantically pulled himself to all fours and scurried around in a circle. Drool hung from both sides of his mouth.

There were just a couple of minor problems. By the time Louie decided which direction he wanted to go in, Max was standing in front of him and the Beast was standing behind him. A third cop was fast approaching.

"Don't you fucking move - Don't you fucking move!" Max commanded. Louie stopped. He didn't know what that guy hit him with, but whatever it was, it made his head feel like it was gonna fall off his shoulders.

"Don't you run! You stand up, but don't you fucking run!" Max commanded again. His words came out quick, his tone came out hard.

In a typical foot chase Max would have already had the barrel of his gun buried inside the guy's nostril. But this wasn't typical. This guy was naked and seemed defenseless. At this point it just didn't make much sense.

Louie pulled himself to his feet. He cocked his head to one side and gazed at Max like he was trying to figure out just what and the hell he was. Drool hung from one side of his mouth. His naked fatness bounced everywhere. Louie still had no idea what was going on. Where was his ma? Where was his brother, Ed? Why weren't they with him? They had to be at home waiting. Louie had to get home. He forgot about what the guy in front of him said and turned to run in the opposite direction. Within two steps, however, Zack introduced him to a solid right to the face.

Louie dropped to the ground. When he woke up he found himself in a holding cell, (with clothes on, compliments of the Chicago taxpayers).

CHAPTER 27

It was almost 10:30 in the morning when Captain Whitaker discovered that Horace Duke, one of the cops working the desk during the graveyard shift, wrote up a missing person's report in the hours leading up to the Louie Hart arrest. It only came about because Larry Buchanan, Rebecca Anderson's divorce attorney, contacted the department and talked to Sergeant Olson. Larry Buchanan and the Sergeant played in a couple of police sponsored golf tournaments together and the attorney decided he knew the sergeant well enough to call him personally.

Larry Buchanan explained to Sergeant Olson that his client had every reason to believe her husband was somehow involved in the disappearance of her two daughters. When Sergeant Olson suggested the attorney bring his client in to fill out a missing person's report, Larry Buchanan told the sergeant that Mrs. Anderson already filed a report earlier that morning. Sergeant Olson walked into Captain Whitaker's office to explain the situation.

The missing person's report was filed shortly after 2:00 a.m.. In essence the report stated the two girls did not return home from school and have not been heard from since. The girls' mother, Mrs. Rebecca Anderson, waited until roughly two o'clock in the morning to file the report because she wasn't able to get in touch with her husband much before then. Up to that point Mrs. Anderson apparently believed Mr. Barry Anderson had the girls with him. Evidently Mr. Anderson told his wife he'd been out drinking and had not seen or talked to the girls all day. Mrs. Anderson insists her husband had something to do with the disappearance, but felt it necessary to come in and file a report just the same.

Horace Duke's response was by the book. Twenty-four hours would have to pass before the girls could be considered missing and the police could begin searching for them.

It may have been a "by the book" response as far as Officer Duke was concerned, but it did little to settle the nerves of Rebecca Anderson. Two more phone calls to her husband produced a busy signal, so by 3:30 in the morning, and with nowhere else to turn, Rebecca Anderson was back in front of the officer to file a second missing person's report. This time she was accompanied by her divorce attorney, Larry Buchanan, who tried to explain why there was not a twenty-four hour waiting period for missing person's, and, why filing a second missing person's report might help to facilitate matters. The more the lawyer carried on, the more Officer Duke realized the attorney shouldn't give up his day job practicing divorce law. A second missing person's report was never filed.

At precisely 5:15 a.m. Officer Winnie Tobinka was ready to go. She used to have the graveyard shift but after Captain Whitaker got word she'd fallen asleep on no less then three occasions he made Horace Duke switch with her. The Captain would have preferred firing her but the department didn't need another discrimination lawsuit filed against it. Instead, she got the early morning shift, often referred to by the cops as the rooster special.

As usual, before Horace Duke left for home he made sure Officer Tobinka was brought up to speed on the activities that occurred throughout the night. Since the night had been extraordinarily slow, there wasn't much for Horace Duke to explain, or for Winnie Tobinka to remember. "Tobinka, if anything comes in about kids, girls to be exact, remember I left a copy of the missing person's report on the dispatch desk. Matter-of-fact, if anything comes in at all about bodies bein' found, what have you, act on the report. Let the Sarge know about it right away. If nothing turns up, we'll just wait the twenty-four hours."

"Don't worry 'bout me Duke."

Horace Duke rolled his eyes and headed for home. At 5:30 a.m. an anonymous caller phoned the police department. He told Officer Winnie Tobinka that during an early morning run he noticed three bodies at Mckenzie Elementary. The anonymous jogger didn't know if they were alive or dead. As soon as Officer Tobinka finished taking down the information she put it on Sergeant Olson's desk. From there she had no idea what happened with the information, nor did she care. Winnie Tobinka was more concerned with her donut, coffee, and the Cosmo article she was reading about sex in the fast lane. When she finished the article some twenty minutes later she could recite a couple of interesting sexual positions, but she forgot all about Officer Duke's missing person's report. Sergeant Olson sat in Captain Whitaker's office, and after reiterating his conversation with Larry Buchanan, watched the Captain's brown eyes turn red with anger.

Two girls were reported missing by a mother who thinks her estranged husband is somehow involved in it all. An anonymous caller phoned in about seeing some bodies. A naked man had been arrested. A search was underway for the victim's identities and the Captain's department had been holding the probable identities for several hours now. "Great, that's just fucking great. Have Cougar and Darwin bring Mrs. Anderson to the coroner's. Get in touch with Doc Murphy and let him know they'll be there sometime before noon. If they get a positive I.D. I want a squad picking up this Mr. Anderson, so find out where he lives, works, whatever, just find him so we can bring him in if we have to. And tell Cougar and Darwin after they've finished with Mrs. Anderson I don't want them wanderin' off. I want them back here when this lady's husband, this Mr. Anderson is brought in. They can worry about the guy they arrested later!"

Captain Whitaker didn't wait for the Sergeant to respond. He stormed out of his office and huffed, puffed and snorted his way down the stairs until he reached his most prized cop, Officer Winnie Tobinka.

"Tobinka! Goddamnit Tobinka, what and the hell are you doing?" The Captain barked.

The Captain's harsh tone caught Winnie Tobinka off guard. "Captain, what's the pra..?"

"Shut your mouth Tobinka, just shut your damn mouth. Does a missing person's report filed by Horace Duke ring any bells? We've been pounding our heads for hours trying to find out the identities of two murdered girls, there's a mother bouncing off walls because she hasn't heard from her daughters since yesterday afternoon, and I got a cop who was so busy doin' nothin' she doesn't have time to remember she's been sitting on the information since early this morning. What the hell is a matter with you, you stupid son-of-a-bitch, you!"

Winnie Tobinka was offended the Captain would take that kind of tone with her. After all they were both black, which also meant she'd look foolish screaming racism, as was her normal protocol. Besides, she still had the male - female thing. It's worked well in the past, no reason to doubt it now. Officer Tobinka stuck her narrow chin forward and narrowed her eyes as she spoke. "Captain, I don't appreciate that tone of voice just 'cause I'm a woman. I 'spect to be treated with the same respect everybody else gets." Winnie Tobinka knew the labor board wouldn't allow her to get fired. She shook her head as though she won some big debate and was daring the Captain to challenge her because of it.

Captain Whitaker lowered his voice to a soft monotone. A scowl dug hard at the female officer. "I've got things that need tending to. We'll talk later. Count on it."

Winnie Tobinka waited until the Captain disappeared back up the stairs. "Like hell," she defiantly whispered.

CHAPTER 28

The moment Rebecca Anderson saw the forehead and blond hair exposed underneath the white sheet, she knew it was her oldest daughter Rachel. Her entire body went limp and she would have crumpled to the tile floor had Max not caught hold of her. As he pulled her up, Rebecca Anderson cried out, "Noooooo! Noooooo! Dear God Almighty, Nooooooooooo!" The words came out like a savage scream.

Max didn't know what else to do so he put his arms around her and gently rocked back and forth, while Rebecca sobbed and gasped out her daughter's name. He peered over at Zack, who was biting his bottom lip and shaking his head. The Beast wanted to respond by winking at his partner but a troubled expression had a strangle hold over his eyes and all he could do was look back.

"Mrs. Anderson," Dr. Murphy said in a soft, reassuring monotone, "I'm sorry, very sorry, but we're gonna need you to identify the other body."

Until now Max had been holding Rebecca Anderson steady. But when she heard the doctor's voice she threw her arms around Max's waist and squeezed as tight as she could. Max could feel her nails digging in to his shirt. "Don't let me go..." she pleaded desperately..."don't let me go."

"It's okay..."Max whispered..."I'm here, I'll stay with you." Max looked back over to his partner. The Beast hung his head low and wept quietly. It caused the lump in Max's throat to quiver and his eyes to moisten. The only thing Max hated more than identifying a body was burying one. Today, he felt like he did both.

When Barry Anderson was told the news about his daughters he never cried or displayed any kind of grief. Almost as big a surprise to Detectives Cougar and Darwin was that he turned down the opportunity to call an attorney. Frankly, Barry Anderson didn't give a damn about attorneys, not while he carried a numb heart and had thoughts of his beautiful baby girls drifting aimlessly in his head. Like a wilted flower he just sat on the couch in Interrogation Room #2, answering questions with a sullen voice and a somber, far away look in his eyes. "Like I told you before detectives, I'm not proud of some of the things I did, but I did them so I could get custody of my girls. I didn't do - couldn't do anything if I thought it was gonna harm my girls in any way."

Max was having a hard time. He didn't know what to think of this Anderson character. For god sakes, the guy had his own house broken into and had his wife tied up. And if you listen to Mrs. Anderson tell it, she claims she was even raped one of the times. What kind of guy pulls that kind of shit? Max certainly didn't know. And when he glanced at his partner the Beast shrugged his shoulders, obviously because he didn't know either.

At that moment the Interrogation Room door swung open and Rebecca Anderson stood in the doorway. Officer Tracy was holding on to her. "Murderer!" She shrieked. "You fucking murderer!"

Barry Anderson started to get up from the couch. He held his arms out like he was making an offering of some kind. "Becca, please Becca," he said, hoping his words sounded like something more than just a futile attempt to appease the situation. "I didn't, I couldn't..."

Rebecca Anderson twisted away from Officer Tracy's grip and charged her husband. "Murderer!" she shrieked. "Fucking murderer!" Before Max and the Beast were able to stop her she was swinging and flailing away at her husband.

Barry Anderson shrugged off the attack and wrapped his arms around his wife. "I'm so sorry for everything," he whispered. "I loved you and the kids, you're all I ever had. I didn't..." his voice broke off and he started to cry like a little boy. At first Rebecca Anderson made a couple of halfhearted attempts to wiggle free from her husband. Barry Anderson just clung tighter, and before long she was hugging him back and mixing his tears with her own.

Officer Tracy figured enough was enough. It was time to let Detectives Cougar and Darwin get on with their questioning. He moved into the room to pull the Andersons apart, but the moment his intentions became obvious, the Beast waved him off. The confused look on Officer Tracy's face caused the Beast to wave him off a second time. He finally got the message and headed out of the room.

Max and the Beast followed.

CHAPTER 29

Eddie Hart was living in the lap of luxury. Big, stupid Louie was gone for good, he had more money than ever before, and for the first time in his life every room in the mobile home trailer was his.

Ain't life grand?

It was late in the afternoon when Max and the Beast pulled up alongside Eddie's green and rusted out pickup truck. The partly sunny sky looked partly not, and a light mist filled the cool air.

Max and the Beast had already spent a hefty chunk of time visiting with Louie Hart in his new abode, but that only proved to be time ill spent. After all, it wasn't like Louie was able to tell them anything. Not that it really mattered. The case against him was quickly building, what with fingerprints, semen samples, blood samples, plus heavy traces of drugs and liquor found all over the Anderson girls, as well as Louie and his Impala. To make matters worse, Louie's court appointed defense attorney was – like most court appointed defense attorneys – constitutionally correct and idealistic, which really meant he was young and stupid. Louie didn't really have much of a chance. Yet, the one thing that struck Max and the Beast as being odd was that Louie kept asking to see his ma and his brother Ed. Asking for his brother was one thing, but in as much as his mother was dead, asking to see her was altogether different. It was as if Louie didn't know she was dead, which the Beast cured by breaking the news to him, (ever so gently, mind you).

"Louie boy, your ma's dead."

That was all it took. Louie heard those words and it was like he got run over by a steamroller. He went to a corner in his cell, sat his big ass on the cold floor and cried like a two year old.

Something just didn't click. "Maybe his brother can clue us in," Max said to the Beast as they left the jail cell.

"Worth a try anyway," the Beast added.

Max was about to knock on the screen door to Eddie's trailer when he got the sudden notion to walk around to the front and peek through the window.

Eddie Hart was laying in the middle of the floor, surrounded by empty beer cans, an assortment of empty soup and chili cans, pizza boxes, newspapers, TV Guides, and a small variety of other unidentifiable garbage. Max figured he was either resting, sleeping or passed out because Eddie's eyes were closed and his body was motionless. "Well, he's a clean motherfucker at any rate," Max said sarcastically.

"Whataya mean?" The Beast walked over and looked through the window. "Yeah, you're right. But I hear it's like that with all great chefs."

"Come on, let's wake the great chef up. Maybe we can get him to cook us something. Maybe we can get the soup du jour."
"That would be a treat."
"Yeah," Max agreed. "It would probably make my day."
"Or end it," the Beast suggested.
Max smiled out of the corner of his mouth and walked back to the screen door. "Ya know my good man, I do believe I feel the need to be gentle," Max said in his best aristocratic imitation.
"Do you now," Zack countered. "By all means then, show me the way, show me the way."
Max hammered the side of his fist against the door with such force the trailer rattled. "Eddie Hart. Mr. Eddie Hart. This is Detective Cougar...open the door please." Max stopped pounding so he could listen. Several seconds later there was still no response.
Eddie was just coming out of one of his headaches and wasn't sure if the pounding he heard was the door, or the inside of his head.
"Indeed you have a gentle touch sir. Some might say it is rather mild. Might I give it a whack?" The Beast asked.
"Do sir, by all means, do sir."
The Beast was just about to tag the door when the detectives heard the hollow sound of empty cans hit the floor. It was followed by what sounded like Eddie Hart stumbling over something, (garbage most likely). "Son-of-a-bitch. Goddamn son-of-a-bitch," shot out an angry voice.
Max glanced at the Beast. "Sounds like he's up."
"Unless it's a big fucking rat, which in this place wouldn't surprise me."
"You think rats can swear like that?"
"Hey Max, with today's technology, who knows." Zack shrugged his shoulders and grinned.
Max rolled his eyes before turning his attention to the front door. Once again he hammered away until the mobile home trailer started to rattle. "Mild my ass." He flashed a quick smile at his partner. "Mr. Hart...Mr. Eddie Hart...This is Detective Cougar...Would you open the door please."
Eddie twirled his head around to face the door. He knew the police were gonna show up sooner or later, but quite frankly was hoping it would be later. At the moment Eddie was somewhere between losing his headache and gettin' another dose of the wild look, so it wasn't the preferred time. Besides, he might've wanted to straighten the place up. (On second thought...Nah!)
"Mr. Hart...it's Detectives Cougar and Darwin. Open the door sir, we know you're inside. You can save us all a lot of trouble if you just open up voluntarily."
"Well whataya know about that. The police have x-ray vision. I'll be a rope

tied, hog eatin' son-of-a-bitch," Eddie shot back. Eddie was much closer to getting that wild look than he figured. It was a situation that was becoming quite the norm. He'd lose the headache and drift right into the wild look. It was almost to the point where he either had one or the other. The in between days were disappearing. "I'm coming officer, sir. Heavens to Bessie, I'm coming, just give me a second."

Max and the Beast looked at each other simultaneously. It was obvious by the looks on their faces that neither one of them liked the tone of voice being thrown at them.

The front door finally opened. "Officers - oops, I'm sorry, you said detectives didn't you. What do you need?" Eddie did a poor job of hiding his contempt.

"We don't need anything, but we would like to ask you a couple of questions about your brother." Max didn't sound like he was asking permission.

Eddie looked at the detective cockeyed and backed away from the door. He motioned for Max to come inside. The Beast followed.

"Jesus, he's filthy," the Beast whispered to his partner.

Max was already standing in the doorway when he quickly turned his head. "Buddy, you ain't seen nothin' yet."

The inside of the trailer was nothing more than a closer view to what Max and the Beast saw from the outside, except much of the garbage came with old, rotted food. It gave the place the feel, and smell, of a little garbage dump, (complete with flies). Eddie grabbed a bottle of Canadian Club from the kitchen counter. The detectives glanced at one another as Eddie took a serious drink from the bottle. As usual, entertainment followed. "Eeeeee - Heeeee! Damn that stuff is me, me, me." Eddie wiped his mouth by dragging his forearm across it. He gave each one of the detectives the once over before settling on Max. "Here boy, try some. Yer gonna like it, I'm sure."

Max shifted his weight forward and pointed his finger at Eddie. "Listen, I ain't your boy and we didn't come here to drink. You get my meaning or would you prefer I spell it out for you on your forehead." A look fell over Max's face just like a dark cloud casting its shadow over the ground when a storm is brewing.

Eddie understood the look. Better ease up, he told himself. Everything's been workin' out up till now. No sense blowin' it, he concluded. Still, when Eddie had the wild look, politeness wasn't part of his repertoire. "I can spell, detective. I don't need you to teach me." He smirked.

Max took a long hard look at Eddie Hart. He was wearing grease or dirt stained jeans, Max wasn't sure which, and a white tee shirt with blotches of pale yellow caused by old, dried out sweat. The shirt was accented by a breast pocket ripped and hanging. Strapped to his feet were a pair of old weather worn work boots tied just above the ankles. His hair, both black and dirty, stood up like it was pointing to the sky. His arms looked working man strong, much like his lean frame, and while one of his dark, piercing eyes twitched east, the other one twitched west.

Bet he gets the babes, Zack thought to himself. He couldn't help but smile at the notion.

"Have a seat," Eddie said to break the silence.

"That's okay, we'll stand," Max countered.

"Suit yerselves, but I'm sittin'," Eddie announced abruptly. He pushed some newspapers aside and hopped up on the kitchen counter. "Shit, I had an open can of beer...it's gotta be here somewhere," he muttered to no one in particular. Eddie turned his head to search behind him. "Yep, there she is, just where I left 'er." He latched on to the can, turned back around and focused his twitching eyes on Max, except Max couldn't tell if Eddie Hart was looking at him or the Beast. "You said you were wantin' to know somethin' about my brother. Well then, what about him?"

Guess he was looking at me, Max thought. "He's being held in jail on a variety of charges pending the outcome of some test results. I would say there's a real good likelihood he's gonna be charged for the rape and murder of two girls sometime in the next 24 to 48 hours."

Eddie was drinking the beer but stopped in mid-swallow the moment he heard Max's words. His hand slowly brought the can away from his mouth and for an instant he looked stunned, almost troubled by what the detective said.

Of course his eyes were driving Max nuts because he couldn't be certain if the look on Eddie's face was for real. Max decided to play it out. What choice did he have anyway? "You didn't know your brother was arrested?"

Eddie was slow to respond. He looked at the linoleum floor, the wall, the couch, almost anything besides Max. "No," he finally began, "I didn't know. 'Course I can't say I'm all that surprised. Louie always used to show a particular interest in young girls, a particular interest indeed."

"I didn't say anything about the girls being young. Why did you, Mr. Hart?" Max unfolded his arms and let them dangle at his sides.

The Beast moved closer to the middle of the room.

Eddie never hesitated. "Because he's always liked young girls. I figured if they was anything, they was young. I was right too, wasn't I?"

Something just doesn't click, Max thought. Don't know what exactly, but it's out there, somewhere.

"How come your brother keeps asking to see his mother?"

Eddie looked at the detective with the deep, raspy voice. "Can't say. Hell, she up and died, ol' Lou, he knows that for sure."

The smelly room fell silent long enough for the three men to trade glances, although with Eddie's twitching eyeballs it looked like he could focus on both detectives simultaneously.

"Maybe that's why he did it. Maybe that's why Lou went crazy like he did," Eddie finally suggested. He wanted to take another swig from the bottle, but decided it best to wait until the detectives left.

"You here all day yesterday?" The Beast asked innocently enough.

"Sure was," floated back a carefree answer.

"Night too?" Max interjected sharply.

Eddie didn't like the question. As a matter-of-fact, he didn't like the cop who asked it. Okay, so the guy's got them Hollywood good looks, but that's it. He ain't got nothin' over on me, Eddie decided.

"I said, night too?"

Eddie hopped off the countertop. "I heard ya the first time," he said, inching closer to Max.

"You may have heard me the first time and even the second time but you still didn't give me an answer. Whataya say we try for a triple play. Night too?" Max asked again. There was a definite edge to his voice.

Eddie Hart stuck his narrow head forward. "Yeah, night too. Ya satisfied now?"

The stench inside the trailer was getting to the Beast. He had to get outside. He looked at Max and motioned towards the door with a nod of his head.

Something didn't click for Max but he couldn't put his finger on it. Maybe he was getting carried away by it all. I mean, what the hell, they had Louie dead to rights, didn't they? What more could there be to it. "Yeah - let's go," Max said.

The second the detectives were outside Eddie Hart took a long pull from the whiskey bottle. It turned out to be one of many.

Ain't life grand!

CHAPTER 30

Boom Boom Larue was a retired stripper turned restaurateur. She had platinum colored hair, dark eyelashes, wore earrings the size of traffic lights, and for a woman in her mid-forties, was still able to give any thirty year old a run for her money. Her real name was Loretta Beasley, but as long as her breasts continued to stick out like two air filled footballs, she'd continue to use her old stage name. Besides, they were good for business.

Boom Boom's Bones was supposed to serve the best ribs in the city, but Max and the Beast only stopped there because it was the first place they came upon after leaving Eddie Hart's trailer home. They were hungry and figured to grab some dinner and kick around a couple of ideas regarding the Anderson murders. It turned out to be somewhere between eating the soggy rainbow trout and watching Boom Boom Larue bring them another round of beers when the two detectives decided to revisit Eddie Hart later that night.

It was a little after 9:00 p.m. when Max turned his Bronco into Lake Cass Mobile Home Park. Lake Cass was a man-made ten acre lake that carried all the trappings of a shallow swamp. It was surrounded by sparsely scattered trailers, owned by people who were willing to put up with dragon flies, frogs, and a summer long stench just to be able to say they lived on the water. The rest of the park was spotted with trailers big and small. For the most part they stood propane to propane, some had wood sheds, some had multi-colored awnings, few had both, a couple had neither. Eddie was one of the couple, although he seemed to make more use of the lake than any of the other residents, fishing whenever the weather permitted, and often catching and eating some strange looking fish.

To Eddie the lake was also a good place to take his wild look, get drunk and watch the moon rest its dreary light on the waveless water, which is exactly what he was doing when Max parked at the boarded up Lake Cass Clubhouse, a brisk fifty yard walk to "Hart Manner."

After peering through the window for a minute or so the two detectives determined Eddie Hart wasn't home. Not to be concerned, Max would just go through the place without him.

"You wait here and I'll check it out, okay?" Max offered.

"Have at it, but watch your ass," the Beast cautioned.

"I will if you watch my back," Max said.

"Always man, always."

The aluminum door was unlocked so Max helped himself to the inside. Not much had changed since the late afternoon. Maybe the cooler night air helped temper the garbage dump odor, but that was about it. Max couldn't say what he was looking for, or why he was even inside, but the feeling he had from the beginning, that something just didn't click, forced him to look anyway. Would a quick search through Eddie Hart's litter infested living quarters change his gut feeling? Max didn't really know, but if at the very least it kept him from losing a night's sleep, and in the process, he was able to extinguish an avenue of possible criminal wrongdoing, then it was worth it. Simply put, the front door was open so why the fuck not?

Zack waited outside and took in the clear night air with some deep breathing and solemn thoughts. He flashed back to Rebecca Anderson. Again he heard the gut wrenching scream and saw the look of death wrestle the life out of her eyes. He felt sad for Rebecca Anderson and started to wonder how she and her husband were going to resolve their differences. Just then he heard a voice singing off in the distance.

"*Jimmy Crack Corn and I don't care, Jimmy Crack Corn and I don't care, Jimmy Crack Corn and I don't care... poor ol' Jimmy Crack Corn.*"

By the second *Jimmy Crack Corn*, the Beast realized it was Eddie Hart's scratchy voice doing the singing. He hustled his way inside to get his partner. "Max, let's shake it, he's on the way." The Beast didn't wait for his partner to respond. He wanted to be outside just in case ol' Jimmy Crack Corn himself showed up before Max made it out. God knows it wouldn't be first time his partner took his sweet ass time after being given proper warning.

It wasn't intentional, it was just Max's way. If he was searching someone's premises without the legal right to do so he didn't leave until the very last second. Max's reasoning was that something could turn up at any second so he had to use up as many of them as he could. Max also had extreme confidence the Beast would do whatever was necessary to protect the situation. This time it didn't make any difference. Max was back outside before Eddie Hart showed up. "Nothin'," he quietly said.

The Beast nodded.

"But as long as we're here we may as well say hello," Max added insincerely.

The Beast snickered.

Eddie Hart sang the same "Jimmy Crack Corn" verse three more times before his face and body became visible in the darkness. At the same time the dull light being thrown off from the trailer's single exterior lightbulb made it easy for Eddie to spot the two detectives. Dim witted motherfuckers, he determined. "What the fuck do you two want?" Eddie Hart snapped from twenty yards away. "I figured when you left here today I wouldn't have to be seein' yer faces anymore."

Max and the Beast watched Eddie but said nothing in return. Instead they listened to him drag his feet over the dirt and gravel path until the distance between them was significantly gobbled up.

Finally Max responded. "We brought you some news." His tone was friendly, like he brought Eddie a present and couldn't wait to give it to him. The Beast was caught off guard. He had no idea what news Max was talking about. Worse than that, he knew Max had no idea either. The Beast didn't know it, but when he glanced over to his partner a look of surprise and confusion caused his eyebrows to come together and his eyes to squint sharply.

"Say what?" Eddie asked curtly.

By now Eddie Hart was close enough for Max to focus in on. His eyes were still twitching, but since Max and the Beast were standing side by side they didn't seem to twitch near as bad as earlier in the day. What Max didn't realize, however, was the deeper Eddie's wild look took hold, the less his eye's twitched and the more beady they turned.

"I said we brought you some news. When we were here this afternoon I didn't see a telephone in your trailer. I figured you'd want to hear the news so me and my partner drove back out to give it to you."

Eddie turned his head on an angle and sneered at Max.

Max ignored the look and continued to speak. "We think someone else may have been involved with your brother. Maybe even put him up to it." Max paused to study Eddie's face. Nothing. "Anyway, like I said, thought you might like to know."

"That it?" Eddie asked impatiently, like he knew the present Max brought him was nothing more than an empty box with wrapping paper.

Max cocked his head and shook it once, "Yep, that's it," he said with a half smile on his face and a full twinkle in his eyes.

"I don't know what yer thinkin' and frankly I don't give an owl's hoot. Now get the fuck oughta here."

Max and the Beast didn't move.

"Go on, I said get the fuck oughta here." Eddie made a backhanded slap like he was swatting the two detectives away. As usual, the wild look made Eddie bold.

The detectives still didn't move so Eddie sauntered up to Max and got in his face. Since they were about the same height it looked like their noses were just inches from touching. "Ya know, I don't like you very much. I think you better get the hell off my property."

Eddie's strong whiskey breath was almost enough to cause Max to take a full step backwards. Whiskey! Fucking Whiskey! Max suddenly realized. Why didn't I think of it when I saw him drinking this afternoon? Son-of-a-bitch, I wonder if it's the same kind of whiskey the Anderson girl's were forced to drink. Not that that would mean anything, but then again, you never know, you just never know. Max's gaze turned cold and the tone in his voice turned hard. "You like whiskey, don't you Eddie? I bet you like it a lot. Probably like valium too. I bet you even like to eat valium and drink whiskey together. You're just like your brother, aren't you? Or is it the other way around? Come on Eddie, which is it?"

Eddie said nothing.

Max didn't let up. "Which is it Eddie, you like him, or is he like you? Were ya with him that night Eddie?"

Because of the twitching eyes, even when they were twitching slow, the Beast didn't figure Eddie Hart had much of a blind spot. Still, he took a couple of steps and squared off on Eddie's right side.

This cop don't know shit, Eddie decided. He's playin' me. The goddamn motherfucker's playin' me. I don't like bein' played. They got Lou but they got nothin' else. It don't matter what this cop says. Everything's turnin' out just like I figgered it would. These ain't problems, these is bumps. This is gonna work out perfect. "No, I ain't like him. And no, I wasn't with him on whatever night it is yer talkin' about." The fuckin' cop was hopin' I'd fuck up and tell him the night, but I'm too fuckin' smart for this guy, Eddie determined. "Now like I said, get the fuck off my property."

"Ya know something Eddie, I don't think I like you either. I also don't think you oughta go running off anywhere 'cause I might be coming back to ask you some more questions. If I do, ya better be here. Ya know what I'm sayin'?" Max's voice was just above a whisper but he was glaring at Eddie with his own kind of wild look.

Eddie didn't recall ever seeing one on someone else before, but one thing was certain, he didn't like it. Not even a little. He returned the glare for a full minute before deciding to back up a couple of feet. When he did, Max turned to his partner. "Come on Beast, let's let this piece of shit alone. The smell is starting to get to me."

Refer to me as a piece of shit? Not in this lifetime, you fucking cop asshole. Not in any lifetime, Eddie told himself. Eddie Hart waited for the detectives to turn and walk away. As soon as they did, he swung wildly at the side of Max's face. At the last second Max saw the fist coming out of the corner of his eye and tried to duck out of the way. It helped some, but Eddie still managed to land a solid blow to the back of Max's head, causing him to stumble forward.

The Beast would have taken Eddie Hart down right then and there, except if he did Max was not likely to speak to him for two or three weeks, something the Beast couldn't bear. It happened once before. Some drunk on the street sucker punched Max, Max went down, and even though he wasn't hurt, he never got a chance to get the drunk back. By the time he jumped to his feet, the Beast was tattooing the drunk's face from chin to forehead, or as the Beast liked to say, "from stern to bow." Over time Max forgot about it, but the Beast knew Max never forgave him. Max needed to get his own piece. That was the way

Max came up and that was the way he'd go down. He didn't need the Beast for protection. He appreciated what the Beast was willing to do for him, but when it came to fighting his battles, Max didn't need it. Not with the drunk, and certainly not now.

Max quickly caught his balance, turned and fired a right hand that landed smack dab in the middle of Eddie's face. It was clean, it was hard, and it set Eddie on his back. "Get up you fuckin' woman," Max bristled.

Eddie's eyes stopped twitching and a snarl came over his face like a five o'clock shadow. He climbed back to his feet and charged forward. Max caught Eddie's head in his gut, twisted his neck and threw him to the ground. Eddie rolled hard and slammed into the side of his trailer. He wasn't on the ground for two seconds before he was up and charging again. This time Max backpedaled on the balls of his feet. As Eddie closed in, Max's fists moved like a jackhammer and he landed a series of vicious uppercuts. Eddie's nose gave out and he yelped. He would have dropped to the ground right then but Max grabbed hold of his hair with both hands and slammed his knee square into Eddie's chin. The blast sent Eddie reeling.

The two detectives stood over Eddie and studied his face, but he was motionless. Not even a whimper.

"Man he looks out," the Beast commented.

"Nah. I hardly got to tag him," Max responded.

"Wanna take him in?" The Beast asked.

"Fuck him. Let's leave him in the dirt where he belongs. Can't charge him with anything worthwhile anyway. He'd be out in a day."

The Beast shrugged his shoulders. "Suits me."

Max and the Beast turned and started to walk back to the blazer.

"Cocksuckers! Eddie bellowed out of nowhere. "Motherfucking cocksuckers!"

Max and the Beast spun around, only to find Eddie coming hard and fast with a switchblade in tow. Max reached for his gun but before he could empty his shoulder holster the Beast let his cowboy boot explode into Eddie's groin. Eddie's knees buckled forward and he grunted, but he didn't drop. The Beast kicked the knife out of his hand and followed it up with a ferocious overhand right to Eddie's head. Eddie dropped and went to sleep, wild look and all.

The following morning Detective Zack Darwin heard the news first. Assistant District Attorney Tyler Lake and Louie Hart's court appointed defense attorney, Simon Ashley, agreed to a plea bargain agreement. In return for a guilty plea to second degree murder, Tyler Lake would drop all rape and other incidental charges. Louie Hart was to receive a total of thirty years in jail. That meant he'd be up for parole in twenty years.

Zack's initial reaction was to find out from Tyler Lake why and the hell he would agree to such an arrangement so quickly, but since he never cared much for Tyler Lake's company, he didn't feel like listening to any of his bullshit. He decided to question Captain Whitaker instead. The Beast tapped lightly on the Captain's door frame. Captain Rudy Whitaker looked up. For the first time in a long time he appeared well rested. "Hey Beast, what can I do for you?"

"Captain, this Louie Hart deal...I understand they're gonna plea him out on second degree murder."

The Captain leaned back in his chair and let his forearms rest on the desk. "That's right Zack, that's right."

The Beast leaned his shoulder against the door frame. "Captain, maybe I'm stupid but could you explain to me why?"

Captain Whitaker sighed. He wanted Louie Hart to die in jail just like everyone else, but his hands were tied when it came to the court thing. Cops arrested bad guys, that's what they did. They didn't do court work. Yet, everytime the cops or detectives in his department arrested some nut case they suddenly couldn't understand how the piece of shit got anything less than life. "What do you want me to tell you Beast?"

"Just tell me why Captain, that's all."

"It's easy Beast. Obviously we've got the guy pegged at the crime scene, as well as with the Anderson girls. At the same time the D.A.'s office was able to get a confession out of him."

"I understand all that Captain. What I don't understand is why they have to plea it out."

Captain Whitaker raised his eyebrows. "Same old reason. The D.A.'s office didn't want to risk losing the case."

"Losing the case, how?" Zack asked. The Beast had been through the same thing a hundred times before, but since he never understood it, he was never able to agree with it.

"Well if you'd quit interrupting me I'd tell you."

"Sorry Captain."

"Sure you are Beast. Anyway, as soon as the lab results showed the levels of valium and alcohol in this Louie Hart character his attorney started barking about how his client couldn't be held responsible, or found guilty, as the case may be. You know, he was lost in space when the crimes were committed. Diminished capacity, temporary insanity, you name it."

Zack took a couple of seconds to digest the Captain's words. "That it Beast?"

"Yeah Cap, that's it." Zack rolled his shoulder away from the door frame and walked down the hall with his head down. Yet, when he explained the situation to Max later that afternoon, Max didn't even hesitate.

"I still wanna go back and see this guy. I mean we both saw what we saw, and I say the guy's a serious head case. Maybe we can get something on him that ties him to the Anderson girls. For god sakes we owe them that much, don't we?"

The Beast folded his big hands together. "Fuck, I'm not arguing that Max. I'm just not sure where it's gonna get us."

"I don't know either Beast," Max said shaking his head. "I just know I wanna go back and see him. I didn't have enough time to look through his trailer, right?"

"Right," Zack agreed.

"Well then maybe I can get another crack at it. I mean it ain't like we'll get the Captain to agree to a search warrant. Not after what he said about Louie Hart."

The Beast nodded and smiled. "Well you know what I always say...in for a donut, in for a donut hole."

Max pushed the hair away from his eyes and laughed. "When and the fuck did you ever say that?"

The Beast didn't answer. He just threw his head back and cracked up.

Between the funeral for Rachel and Jody Anderson, plus all the standard bullshit going on at work it was another three days before Detectives Cougar and Darwin were able to make their way back to the Lake Cass Mobile Home Park. Eddie Hart was standing outside his trailer staring at the full moon and holding a quart of beer when he saw the detectives pull up. Ever since Max and the Beast left Eddie Hart to rot in the dirt he'd been through two headaches, one of his usual ones and one courtesy of the detectives. He was also in the midst of getting another attack of the wild look.

The Beast opened the passenger window. "Hi Eddie, how you doin' this fine evening? You're certainly looking well," he mocked. Zack was referring to the homemade bandage Eddie had plastered across his nose. "Come on over here where I can get a good look at ya. Need to ask you a couple of questions. Won't take but a minute or two."

Eddie tilted his head sideways and glared at the two cops. "Get the fuck oughta here! Get the fuck oughta here now!"

Max put his Bronco in park and turned off the lights. He left the engine running as his response to Eddie's demand.

Eddie pitched his quart of beer off to the side and promptly marched over to the passenger side of the Bronco. The Beast figured Eddie was coming over because he asked him to. The Beast figured wrong. Without hesitation or warning he stuck his hands through the open window and latched on to Zack's thick neck, squeezing as hard as he could. "I'm gonna get you." I'm gonna get you, you motherfucking cocksucker!" There was a frantic edge to Eddie's voice.

The Beast tried to pry Eddie's hands away. He gasped, coughed, and gasped again. Max started to reach for his gun but the sight of his best friend in a choke hold made him nervous. Max was afraid he might fuck up, and with Zack's life hanging in the balance, he wouldn't risk something going wrong.

"I'm gonna get you. I'm gonna get both you motherfucking cocksuckers!"

Max pressed the button to put up the passenger window. "Grab hold of his arms." There was a frantic edge to Max's voice as well. Zack realized what his partner was doing. He held tight to Eddie's hands and pulled him towards the inside of the Bronco until the window went up all the way and Eddie's arms were locked inside.

Eddie shrieked. "Ahhhh...! Goddamn you cocksuckers! Ahhhh!....fucking...Ahhhh!...goddamn.....Ahhhh!"

Max hopped out and ran around to the other side. He grabbed Eddie by the hair and started smashing his forehead against the Bronco. As soon as Eddie's body went limp and the only thing holding him up was the fact that his arms were still locked in the window, Max stopped, (although, he did give him a couple of stiff kidney shots before getting back in the Bronco to release the window).

Eddie fell backwards and was out cold for about fifteen minutes. When he came to his arms felt like they'd been severed with a dull saw, and his head felt like it had been split down the middle with a baseball bat. Blood was all over his scalp and down his face. Other than that, Eddie Hart was okay.

Max and the Beast had been driving home in silence when the Beast suddenly turned to his partner. "That was fun, don't you think?"

Max was still pretty spooked over the thought of Eddie Hart coming out of nowhere and choking the Beast. He ignored Zack's effort at making light of the situation and said, "I'm sorry man. You were right, we should have never gone back. I don't know what I was thinkin', but I'm sorry."

"Shut up," the Beast snapped. "Just shut the fuck up. You didn't do nothing wrong. All you did was try to find out if wacko Eddie Hart was involved with his brother. That's what you're supposed to do. Now I don't want to hear nothin' else like that come out of your mouth."

Max sighed and glanced over at his partner. "Okay...but let me ask you this, did we fuck up by not bringing him in just now?"

The Beast looked out the window at the evening traffic and pondered Max's question. Another quarter mile of road got chewed up before he answered. "No. We would have ended up doing too much explaining. Nobody else saw this guy but us, only they'd take one look at his face and we'd end up being the defendants and he'd end up walkin' clean as a whistle. It just wouldn't have been worth it."

The detectives drove the rest of the way home in silence.

At least they still had their suspicions.

CHAPTER 31

PRESENT DAY:

Susan watched Zack from across the room. He was sitting on the sofa holding a glass of red wine and staring down at the floor as though he was examining the newly installed light gray carpeting. But Susan knew better. From the day they moved into the townhouse Zack never noticed the layout, color scheme, or even a single piece of furniture, unless of course, the big screen was considered furniture. And even then, he only noticed it on "game day."

When Susan first walked in the house she planned on telling Zack she thought someone was watching her as she was walking home. But after observing the lost, almost hopeless expression on Zack's face, she decided against it. Besides, Susan figured, it was probably one of those one time things. Certainly nothing to get worked up about.

Susan and Zack had been living together for a little more than four years. They planned to marry in the near future, although for no particular reason they still hadn't picked a date. Come to think of it they probably never would. Knowing Zack the way she did, he was gonna come home one day, wrap his muscular arms around her, and announce that it was a good day to get married.

To some, it might not have been the most romantic way, but to Susan it was the only way. In the years they'd been together Zack gave her so much love that Susan once confessed to him that he doubled the size of her heart. When Zack heard those words, and when he saw her soft green eyes tear up as she said them, he put his hands on her cheeks and told her she would be the best thing to come along even if he lived a thousand lifetimes. They were words Susan never forgot.

"Zack," Susan called out softly. "Are you okay?"

Zack lifted his head and looked at Susan. He made a weak effort to smile, which only seemed to magnify his pained expression.

"You and Max went to see that guy today, didn't you?"

Zack nodded his head slightly. "Harry Weeble, yeah."

"Didn't turn out so good, huh?"

"No," Zack uttered quietly. "He had nothing to do with killing Max's sister and brother-in-law." Zack fixed his brown, sullen eyes on Susan and sighed. "I feel real bad for Max. I wish I could help him but I don't know how. I don't know what to do."

Susan walked over to the couch, and after kissing Zack hello, sat down beside him. She cupped her hands together, leaned forward and rested her elbows on her thighs. Her dark hair hung aimlessly. "I thought you and Max had more than one guy to go see. I thought there were three of them you wanted to look up."

Zack set the wine glass down on the coffee table and let himself fall backwards. His wide back sunk into the soft cushion. "We do, but I was really hoping it would have been the first guy, Harry Weeble." Zack ran his fingers through his long, sandy colored hair. It was too thick to be so easily rearranged. "Problem is, the longer it takes, the harder it's gonna be on Max."

Susan uncupped her hands and for a moment it looked like a butterfly opening its wings for the first time. "Well...who's the next one on your list? I mean, why can't he be the one?" The simplicity in Susan's question was the result of her candor, not because it was offered as consolation. Her eyes opened wide in anticipation of Zack's response.

"Eddie Hart, his name is Eddie Hart. His brother was arrested for killing two little girls. I might have told you about it. It happened a couple of years ago."

Susan reached for the glass of wine and took a long sip. She didn't remember the name Eddie Hart, but Zack did tell her about the Anderson murders. It was one of those gruesome stories she would just as soon forget.

Zack let his eyes wander around on the ceiling. When he spoke his voice came out in an effortless monotone, as though he was daydreaming and talking at the same time. "The last time I saw Eddie Hart he tried to choke me. He caught me completely off guard and might have killed me if it weren't for Max."

"You never told me that part before." Susan may have sounded surprised, but the combination of concern for Zack and contempt for his job was growing inside her. Had she waited another minute she would have sounded angry, something she didn't want to do.

"I was able to hold on to his hands while Max put up the car window and locked his arms inside."

It used to be that Susan got mad whenever Zack didn't tell her some of the things she thought she was entitled to know. She blamed it on his lack of trust and faith in her. Yet, the real reason was because Zack figured if he mixed Susan in with some of the darker moments in his job, all it would do is take away from the purity she brought to his life. Zack kept things from Susan, not because of her, but because of himself. Time, and a dozen explanations later, Susan understood. (Besides, with each passing day Zack opened up more and more, even if he didn't think so).

"Then once Eddie boy was nice and secure, Max ran out and introduced him to some little stars." Zack grinned, but the grin quickly faded. "Two years ago I thought Eddie Hart was a very dangerous man."

"What about now?" Susan asked.

"I don't know, but I don't think people that dangerous ever change. I guess I'm gonna find out tomorrow."

Susan took another sip of wine and offered the glass to Zack. "Nah. I think I'd rather have a drink."

"What do you want and I'll get it for you."

"That's okay babe, I'll get up and make one in a few minutes. Thanks though."

"Zack...," Susan began, as though analyzing the answer before she even finished the question, "what happens if this Eddie Hart guy didn't kill Kathy and Jack Reed?"

Zack sighed. "I dunno, I really don't." He let his gaze slowly drift down from the ceiling across the barren wall. "At this point I hope he did, because if he didn't, our weak theory gets that much weaker."

"Whataya mean?"

Zack reached over with his hand and cradled Susan's cheek. "Because since day one we've never had anything to go on. Max and I came up with a short list of people, but the list was really based on our hopes and prayers, not because we got any solid leads from the crime scene. It started out weak, which is why if Eddie Hart didn't have anything to do with murdering Max's sister, it gets that much weaker. Then all we'll have left is Billy Turner. After that we're back to square one - literally."

Susan took Zack's hand away from her face. After she kissed it twice she held it in her lap. "I remember him." How could she forget? Billy Turner was one of those stories Zack had to tell her. He was the reason Max and Zack were forced to split up as partners. It made Zack miserable for an entire year, which in turn made her miserable.

Zack gazed over at the wall and shook his head. "Yep, good ol' Billy Turner and his pet monkey, Dino. Quite the pair. Well they used to be until I shot the monkey."

That was another part to another story Susan never heard before. "Why on earth did you shoot his monkey?" She sounded as surprised as she looked bewildered.

"You won't believe me if I tell you...which is why I never told you in the first place."

"Ohhhhh, is THAT why?" Susan said with emphasis. She smirked, thinking she knew the real reason.

Zack answered like he was a little kid caught in a white lie. "That's absolutely why." He snickered.

"Well I promise to believe you, so tell me now." Susan was trying hard not to smile.

"Okay...here goes nothin'. He was standing on a shelf holding a knife and looked like he was about to jump on Max from behind."

"A monkey looked like he was going to attack Max with a knife so you shot him?" Susan repeated in disbelief.

"I thought you said you'd believe me if I told you." Zack pretended to be upset, but it was no use. He was such a shitty actor when it came to play acting with Susan that as soon as he finished talking a mischievous grin sprawled out across his face.

"A monkey looked like he was going to attack Max with a knife so you shot him?" Susan repeated again, only this time she sounded like she believed it even less than the last time she asked.

Zack leaned forward. He wasn't sure if Susan would find the story disgusting because of some silly notion about animal cruelty, but Zack couldn't help it, he was clearly amused. "Yeah, but he was a bad monkey...a real bad monkey. Maybe the worst monkey of all time."

Susan wasn't sure what to think. The thought of killing a monkey somehow seemed strange, but at the same time she too found herself entertained by it all, which is why she decided not to question Zack about it anymore. Instead, she gazed at him with a mischievous grin all her own. "I suppose it wore a black hat too?"

Zack boasted a big smile. "Well...actually, it wore one of those caps ya always see the French guys wearing, you know...like the skunk in that Pepi Lapue cartoon."

Susan abruptly stood up, swung her hair back across her shoulders and headed for the kitchen. "Zack Darwin, you're too much."

"Aw, don't tell me you never saw that cartoon before."

Susan giggled loud enough for Zack to hear.

"You do know the one, don't you?" He called out.

"I do not. You're crazy," she called back to him. Susan giggled again, but this time Zack didn't hear her.

"What'd I do?" He asked in mocked disbelief.

"I'm pouring myself a glass of wine," she announced from the kitchen. "Would you like that drink you never got up to make?"

"Stoli would be terrific." Zack settled back in the couch. He took a deep breath and suddenly realized he was hungry. Maybe he and Susan would eat something after they finished their drinks. Then again, maybe not.

"Where's Max tonight?"

"Taking Clare to dinner."

Susan suddenly appeared in the doorway holding her glass of wine. "What's going on with them. I mean with Max, do you think he's..."

Ever since Max and Clare went on their third date, almost nine months ago, Susan had been asking that same question with increasing regularity. It got to the point where, even though Zack's words were different each time, his answer was always the same. The only thing that changed was that Susan no longer got the full question out without Zack interrupting her with another version of the same automatic response. "I think Max is head over heels in love."

"Good," Susan said, "because Clare would be heartbroken if that weren't the case. She told me she'd wait a hundred years for Max, just as long as there was a chance he loved her."

"Well at the moment I wouldn't worry about it too much. Right now I think Max wants to put all his energy into his sister's murder investigation."

"As well he should, I realize that...but if Clare mentions it again I'll know what to say."

Zack shook his head and rolled his eyes. "Can I have my drink please?"

In the two years since Max and the Beast saw him, Eddie Hart went from 170 pounds of lean toughness, probably able to fight his way down a chimney, to weighing some 235 pounds, with the same likelihood of getting stuck in a chimney as a cork has of getting stuck in a wine bottle.

As it turned out, Eddie Hart wasn't the guy.

But then again, John Henry Stevens knew that all along.

CHAPTER 32

Wanda Seven was 20 years old when she ventured her way out of the dull college life at the University Of Michigan and headed for California. She got as far as Chicago. No matter, Chicago was still better than Ann Arbor, a little city, she concluded, so consumed with its own intellectuality it lost its pulse on the realities of daily life. Besides, Wanda knew if she ever needed anything, or just wanted to visit her folks back in Michigan, it would be much easier from Chicago than it would be from Los Angeles.

Unfortunately, Wanda never figured another Rose Bowl loss by the maize and blue of Michigan would spur some micro biology student into getting so drunk he'd run a red light and slam head on into her parent's car, killing them both instantly.

There was a time, not all that long ago, when Wanda Seven was beautiful. She had light brown eyes as big and round as shiny new copper pennies, jet black hair that hung down to the middle of her back like a gown of silk, and fair colored skin so soft and smooth, it was as if she was cut from velvet. Wanda also possessed the kind of smile that evolved from a look of friendly innocence when she first entered college to a look unequalled in its raw sensuality by the time she found herself living in Chicago.

But that was life before her parent's sudden and tragic death, before the severe drug and alcohol abuse suffocated her mind and feasted on her beauty.

It was life before Billy Turner.

CHAPTER 33

Billy Turner sat behind the wheel of his leased caddie like he was a king and the car was his throne. It was spit shine clean and pearl white, (with red leather interior to match the exterior detail work), had just the right size vanity mirror to allow for the primping of his blow dried, blond streaked hair, and was parked just down the street from the apartment building he last lived in with Wanda Seven. Was she still living there, Billy wondered. And if not, then where? Billy asked himself that same question everyday he was in prison. He even asked his attorney to check on her whereabouts, although Bernard Forest, the self-proclaimed attorney extraordinaire, had no intention of baby-sitting Billy's love life. As Bernard Forest saw it, the only thing that mattered was winning, which meant doing whatever was necessary, legal or otherwise, to get Billy's conviction reversed on appeal.

"Besides..." Billy recalled the fat attorney telling him one day with his usual sly, sarcastic wit..."last I heard one of the detectives that arrested you, Cougar I believe it was, may have moved her somewhere else. I don't really know if it's true or not. Guess you'll just have to find out for yourself."

Billy planned to. He took one last look in the mirror, the fourth time to be exact, fussed with his hair, although not a single one was out of place, then climbed out of the car and headed for the apartment building across the street.

Everything was just the way he remembered it. The lobby had a chair for the doorman, but since a doorman hadn't worked the building since the late 1960's, the chair was growing as old as it was dusty. The chandelier, once a grandiose display that hung from the ceiling like an upside down Christmas tree made of crystal, was really made of plastic and yellowed quite a bit over the years. Now it looked about as grandiose as a flashlight, although it still managed to light up the lobby and throw weak shadows against the tarnished, bronze colored elevator door.

The elevator wasn't much different either. Like a frail old man walking up a long set of steep stairs, it wheezed and whined its way to the 5th floor, where Billy stepped out into the hallway and took a deep breath. Somehow the stale odor creeping up from the decade old carpet started Billy thinking that everything was just the way he left it when he was carted off to prison a year ago, which meant Wanda was still living in the apartment. Billy made his way down the hall, although every couple of steps he grabbed a quick look to make sure no one was behind him. It was a habit he picked up in prison.

The closer Billy got to his old apartment the louder the television blared through the walls and filled the end of the hallway. The familiar sounds tweaked the pit in his stomach. Wanda was still living there. She had to be, Billy reasoned, because there wasn't another soul on the entire fucking planet who could stand to listen to a television as loud as Wanda could, at least without being deaf. Not a soul.

It was true. Whenever Wanda was home alone she cranked up the television so she could hear it from any room in the apartment, even when she was taking a shower. But it wasn't because Wanda liked to watch TV. As a matter-of-fact, she actually despised it for the entertainment value. Wanda only kept it on to hear the voices. Cartoons, sports, (except golf because the announcer's didn't talk enough, and when they did they were always whispering like they were bedroom lovers), MTV, sit-coms, the news, it didn't matter, just so long as she heard the voices. The voices kept her company. The voices were her friends.

By the time Billy was standing in front of the apartment he had himself convinced Wanda was inside. "It's her," he said out loud, almost like it was now time to convince the invisible guy standing next to him. Billy nodded his head. "I know it's her. I know her fucking routine." He half smiled and half snickered at the thought of seeing his girlfriend. Hell, it had been a year and Billy could hardly wait. As a matter-of-fact, just as soon as he finished beating the shit out of her, he planned to fuck her good.

It'd be just like old times.

Instead of knocking, which he knew wouldn't be heard above the stupid television anyway, Billy launched into his trademark front door drumroll. He was certain the moment Wanda heard it she'd know it was him and come running, maybe faster than she ever did before. The only problem was Billy had to repeat his little Buddy Rich repertoire eight times before the television was finally turned down. But when it was, Billy fashioned himself a smile and took a full step back from the door. Like a boxer anticipating the opening bell of a fight he started bouncing up and down on the balls of his feet. The moment she opens it I'm gonna plant my fist in her face. She's got it coming. She didn't visit, she didn't write, she never gave any messages for fat Bernie to give to me. Nothing. Not one damn thing. Billy was so excited about the surprise introduction, by the time the door finally opened, he didn't take the time to focus in on the person standing in the doorway. Instead he leveled a shot square on the chin of Mrs. Tedesco, the 83 year old lady who moved into the apartment about a month after Wanda moved out. She was unconscious before she hit the floor.

Billy's mouth dropped open in disbelief. Not because he knocked out some old bag. For that, he could have cared less. Rather, he was staggered by the sudden realization that it wasn't Wanda Seven lying on the floor, which to Billy meant she no longer lived in the apartment. It also meant Bernard Forest was probably right, Detective Cougar moved her to parts unknown. Billy's eyes quickly filled with the kind of tears that stem from the pain of hopeless frustration. As he stood in the doorway a burning emptiness gnawed away at his belly.

But it was really Billy's own fault. Had he given the situation any thought he might have realized that just because the hallway carpet had a familiar odor and the sounds of a loud television were crashing through the apartment walls, it didn't automatically mean Wanda was inside. But nobody ever accused Billy of being a deep thinker. He was the type who reacted first and put his brain to work second; and so long as he was dealing with the likes of Wanda and the other druggies he hung out with before his short prison visit, it never mattered. They were so out of touch Billy was a genius by comparison.

"Gramma, gramma?" called out a little boy from the other room. The young voice snapped Billy back to attention. He closed his mouth and slanted his eyes in an effort to focus in on 6 year old Markie Tedesco Sanders, who was running over to the unconscious old lady. "Gramma....gramma?"

When his grandmother didn't move little Markie Tedesco Sanders peered up at Billy Turner apprehensively. "Misser, do you know what happened to my gramma?" His chin quivered as he stood there waiting for an answer.

Billy couldn't believe what he was seeing and his mouth dropped open again. He wiped his eyes and focused in on the little boy one more time. Shit, he thought to himself, this kid's face looks just like Joey Dupree, that little nigger I got convicted of kidnapping a year ago. Billy knew it wasn't the same kid but the unexpected, striking resemblance startled him just the same. It took him a couple of seconds before the goose bumps settled back into his arms and neck. "Go back and watch TV you little monkey," he growled.

Billy's abrupt tone of voice sent a tremor through Markie Tedesco Sanders, frightening him to the point where he was shaking like a little kid who had just hopped out of a warm swimming pool into the cold air without a towel. Tears streamed down from his eyes and rolled over his chubby little cheeks.

Billy was in no mood for this crap. Wanda was gone from the apartment, and for the time being, gone from his life. Yet, standing exactly where Billy expected to be looking at her, *in his apartment*, was a little nigger kid crying man-size tears. Billy pointed his finger at the young boy. The rage filling up his body made the skin around his arms so taut it felt like his bones were going to pop through. "If you don't go back and watch TV I'm gonna hurt you just like I hurt your grandma," he growled again.

Markie Tedesco Sanders couldn't hear Billy over his own crying, but when Billy took two short steps forward Markie Tedesco Sanders got so scared he stop crying, scurried around the corner and peed in his pants.

Billy abruptly slammed the apartment door shut and stormed back to the elevator.

"Son-of-a-bitch," he snarled. "Goddamn son-of-a-bitch."

CHAPTER 34

For Joey Dupree, seeing his older brother Elijah stumble through the front door with a face battered and bloodied almost beyond recognition, was something he wouldn't soon forget. Oh sure, Joey knew his brother fought a lot. He even witnessed a couple of the fights himself. But Elijah moved out of the house when he was 18 year's old, and even though he came by regularly in the seven years that followed, it was usually for a home cooked meal, to give his mother some money, or simply visit with his little brother. Never did Joey think he would witness the day when Elijah came back to his mother's house because he'd been beaten so badly his own fear brought him there. And for Joey to see it now, well frankly, that was more than he ever had to deal with before.

"Ya okay E?" Joey asked, as he watched his older brother drop down on the old red couch that rested somewhere between the television and kitchen table. The anxiety in his high pitched voice and the disquieted look in his pale brown eyes was due, in part, because he was concerned for his brother's safety, but mostly because he was scared for himself. Joey was only 10 years old, and while he may not have been able to put his feelings into words just so, the truth was, he was scared because he knew if someone could do this to his older brother they could do it to him and Elijah wouldn't be able to protect him. Joey's stature in the neighborhood had always been one of hands off, but that was only because of Elijah's reputation. How long was that going to last once word of Elijah's ass kicking made its way around the streets?

Not very, Joey feared.

Elijah Dupree first carved out a name for himself walking the halls of South Central High. He didn't get it because he was the biggest or strongest, although his size and strength were never questioned and rarely challenged. Elijah got it because all the students and most of the faculty thought he was crazy. Not because he spent a couple of horizontal hours on a leather couch with a shrink, mind you. They thought Elijah was crazy because he never displayed any respect for human life, be it his own, or anyone else who gave him any kind of shit. It was a reputation that hovered over Elijah like a dark shadow, but it was also one that saved his ass a time or two. Let's face it, who'd want to fuck around with a guy who acts like he doesn't care whether he lives, or you die?

Elijah never set out to be thought of as the toughest or craziest kid in the neighborhood. He grew up wanting what any other little kid wants: a mother, a father and a happy home life. That was until his father went AWOL. From that day on Elijah took it upon himself to look out for his mother's well-being. Maybe not a huge chore for an adult, but at the time Elijah was just a kid. As a result he was carrying around a switchblade by the age of 13 and a Saturday Night Special by the age of 14. And once Joey was born, thanks to dear ol' dad making a surprise Christmas visit for the first time in years, it only added to Elijah's self-imposed burden.

Although with Joey it was different, in many ways even easier because it was so automatic. Elijah loved his mother and wanted to protect her, but that was mostly because he figured he was supposed to. With Joey the relationship was closer to that of a father and son than that of a big brother and little brother. While Elijah may have wanted to see Joey study hard, stay clear of drugs and make something of himself...the thing was, his love for Joey was unconditional, which meant even if Joey strayed off course and chose a path like Elijah's, where drugs, violence and rip-offs were all part of a day's work, it wouldn't have mattered. The bottom line was Elijah would welcome Joey with open arms no matter what he did, simply because he was Joey. Elijah never wondered why he felt that way, nor could he have explained it even if he had the answer. But that's what made the love so pure.

"Ya okay E?" Joey repeated.

Elijah ignored Joey's question and concentrated on asking one of his own. He had to fight to get the words out just so it didn't sound like he was whispering. "Anybody been round lookin' for ya Joe...talkin' to ya, or anything?" A couple of the cuts around Elijah's swollen lips split open again and small amounts of blood and puss trickled out.

Normally the blood on Elijah's face wouldn't have been enough to scare Joey, not after living in a neighborhood where blood was as much a rule as it was an exception. But with Elijah asking if anyone's been by the house, well, suddenly the blood made Joey nervously wonder what kind of trouble his older brother might be in, although he was too afraid to ask. As a matter-of-fact, if Joey was a turtle he might have even considered pulling his head inside the shell and hiding from everything and everybody. But Joey wasn't a turtle. Unfortunately he was just a little boy who was growing increasingly more afraid of the idea that someone might come by the house looking for him. Joey responded to his big brother's question with silence.

Elijah's eye's were glassy and his vision was slightly hazy. He struggled to bring his little brother into focus. "Come on Joe, tell me," he pleaded. Elijah didn't try to mask the urgency in his voice, and he certainly couldn't mask the fear.

An aimless expression danced all over Joey's face, almost like his brain had given birth to a daydream. Finally, he shook his head. It was slow. Had he been an adult it would've looked deliberate.

"You sure Joe...you sure?" Elijah coughed just as he finished asking the question. When his throat jumped forward to let the air out of his mouth a sharp twinge stabbed at his lower back. Elijah's immediate reaction was to reach around, but when he did, the sharp twinge ignited into a series of rapid, piercing-like jolts. Elijah wished Joey didn't have to see the agonizing expression on his face but there was just no way to hide it. After several seconds the excruciating pain settled into a dull vibration, which made it possible for Elijah to go on talking. "Where's Gladys?" He was referring to the mother he often called by first name.

Joey looked like he was still in a daydream, although he managed to respond by shrugging his shoulders.

"When's she 'sposed to be back?"

Joey pulled out one of the yellow vinyl kitchen chairs, the one with the stuffing coming out, and sat down without answering his brother's question.

Elijah tried to meet the silence with an intimidating glare but his swollen face kept the intimidation to a minimum. Still, Elijah sensed, it would be enough to get an answer.

He was wrong. Joey preferred to pick at the chair stuffing and let his silence do the talking.

"Come on Joe think!" Elijah forced out the words as harshly as his sore mouth would allow. "When's she gettin' back boy?!" The blood and puss that trickled from the cuts on his swollen lips grew into a noticeable stream and was now crawling over his chin and down his neck.

It was rare anytime Elijah raised his voice with Joey, which explained why Joey looked so startled. After he settled back down he responded to his big brother's big voice in a quiet cadence. "Dunno...just said she had a few errands to run. Left me here till she got back."

Elijah closed his eyes and shook his head in disgust. At that moment he was thankful his broken right hand was throbbing as bad as it was. Otherwise, the fierce spasms running rampant from his lower back all the way up to his neck and head would have seemed much worse. "Whatya mean she left ya here alone?"

"She just left me here is all," he said innocently.

"Goddamn..." Elijah began. He wanted to say, "Goddamnit, I told her never to leave you home alone," except more blood than words came out of his mouth so he had to stop. Joey jumped up from his chair, grabbed the rag sitting by the kitchen sink and handed it to his brother. He watched pensively while Elijah used his left hand and the next five minutes to dab at the area around his mouth. Until then Elijah didn't realize just how loose his front teeth really were, uppers and lowers. Once again he was thankful for the steady throbbing in his broken right hand.

"Ya okay E?" It was the third time Joey asked the question. This time he thought he might get an answer.

He was wrong.

Either Elijah didn't hear the question, or he decided to ignore it altogether.

Either way Joey's words were left to dangle in the room with the stale air.

Elijah dropped back into a reclining position, although lying on the couch did little to ease his pain. Up to this point he fought desperately to stay conscious, but with his body now trembling and his bone's feeling like they were rattling inside him, Elijah didn't think he had much fight left. His original plan was to explain the Billy Turner situation to his mother then find a doctor for himself. But with his mind and body losing the race against consciousness faster than he'd anticipated, Elijah knew he had no choice but to explain the situation to Joey. This way Joey would be able to hide, or at the very least, look out for himself until Gladys got home. Elijah turned his head to face his little brother. "Joey man."

Joey leaned forward in the kitchen chair and rested his forearms on his thighs. "Ya okay E?"

Elijah was able to force a little smile to turn up at the corners of his bruised and swollen mouth. "I'll be okay Joe, don't you worry none."

Joey smiled back. "Ya gonna get this guy as soon as you're better, ain't ya, E?" He would too. Joey was certain of it.

"Joe, ya gotta listen to me now, ya gotta listen. No more talkin'. I'm gonna be goin' ta sleep in a few minutes and I need ta tell ya something for I do. Gotta promise to do what I tell ya...gotta promise."

Wide-eyed and bewildered Joey nodded his head just like the scared little boy he was.

"There's a white boy named Billy Turner. Says I owe him some money."

"I got some money you can give him," Joey broke in anxiously.

Elijah winced. Where the fuck is Gladys when ya need her, he wondered. "Says I owe him $5,000.00 dollars Joe. Says I owe him 'cause some drug deal went bad. I ain't involved in no drugs Joe, remember that." Elijah wasn't sure what kinds of things Joey might have heard around the neighborhood over the years, but he didn't figure to admit nothin' about no drugs, at least not before he had to. "I ain't got no $5,000.00 for the man Joe. I don't owe him nothin'...told him so myself. He didn't like my answer. Said if I didn't pay him he'd take you in trade. Somethin' 'bout turnin' ya into a junkie, then havin' ya sell drugs for him ta kids your own age. That's when we started fightin'. He's fucked up Joe, fucked up real bad. He might come lookin' for ya. Might make good on his threat. Don't know." Elijah did his best to read the signs on his little brother's face, but thanks to a sudden numbness that crashed over him like a wave, his eye's were fluttering and he found it increasingly more difficult to see.

Joey let his own gaze fall to the floor. "What am I supposed to do if he comes here?" He asked, his high pitched voice cracking with fear.

"If someone comes...I want ya...I want ya ta hide." The numbness also caused Elijah's thoughts to move much slower now and he struggled hard just to gather up enough words to make sentences. "Maybe...Gladys'...room ...her...trunk...you can squeeze...maybe squeeze...her trunk...into her trunk." Elijah stopped talking so he could catch his breath and swallow. The blood all around the area of his throat was dried out and his tongue felt like it was stuck to the roof of his mouth. Joey got up from the chair and kneeled over his brother. As he listened to the words stagger out of Elijah's mouth his eye's went from a look of panic, to one of sad desperation.

"Whatever...whatever ya do...don't let them...find you...little brother... don't let them." Elijah paused to catch his breath and swallow again. A glass of water is just what the doctor would have ordered only Elijah didn't want to waste whatever energy he had left by asking for one, and unfortunately Joey wasn't a doctor so Elijah was left to go without it. "Side's if...if he sees me...here...he might...might figure I got ya...ya out of here...and maybe... he'll...leave...maybe." Elijah closed his mouth and let his eyes drift around the room. The pictures on the walls, the television in the corner, the front door, the window, the table where Joey was sitting, all of them were blurred to the point where Elijah wasn't sure he could distinguish one item from the next. His time was up and he knew it. "Joey..." he said, his voice barely breaking the silence, "Joey."

The last thing Elijah would remember before falling unconscious was the warmth of Joey's tears as they landed about his beaten face and body.

CHAPTER 35

Billy Turner was so furious his face was red and the hair on the back of his neck was standing up. "Listen you stupid fucking bitch," he hurled mercilessly, "five grand may not sound like much to you, but that's only 'cause you're so fucked up ya don't know the difference anyway!" Billy wiped the beads of sweat forming on his temples and across his forehead, then pivoted around to face the open doorway leading out of the bedroom. "Ya know what your fucking problem is - huh, do ya know?" Billy had no intentions of waiting for an answer. Instead he continued on with his verbal assault. "Your problem is you're so busy putting your fucking nose into the piles of coke I bring home, you don't give a shit about nothin' else!"

Wanda hated it when Billy yelled at her like he did. She knew five thousand dollars was a lot of money. She just didn't think it was necessary to kidnap some little kid over it, that's all. Not that what she thought mattered anyway. Billy never listened to Wanda before and he certainly wasn't going to start now, especially when he was in the middle of one of his famous tirades, (they were even more famous than his front door drumrolls). Until Billy was done taking everything Wanda said, plus everything she didn't say, and twisting it all together so it came out just the way he wanted, the tirade would continue. Wanda Seven had been through enough of them to know she was better off simply keeping her mouth shut. But even at that, there were no guaranties.

Billy stormed out of the bedroom to find Wanda. "You don't give a fuck 'bout me," he blasted away. "You don't give a fuck about my money. All you care about is how often you're gonna get high and I'm gettin' sick of it, plenty fuckin' sick of it!"

Wanda was leaning against the refrigerator in the kitchen, wishing she was deaf so she wouldn't have to listen to Billy.

"Ya know what else, I'm gettin' sick of you too," Billy continued, the words flying out of his mouth like bullets. "Ya ain't nothin' but a piece a shit whore. I found you on the street, and if ya don't watch your ass, I'm gonna drop ya back off there. You can go fuck all the rats, you worthless piece of shit fucking whore!"

By now Wanda was sobbing, although she was making every effort to conceal it because the only thing Billy detested more than listening to her opinion, at least when it conflicted with his, was listening to her cry. Not because it made him feel bad. On the contrary, it made Billy want to beat the hell out of her. That's why Wanda would swallow as fast and as many times in a row as she could whenever she felt the tears coming on. The idea was to squelch the gasping sounds she often made whenever she tried to catch her breath between sobs. A couple of years ago she was able to pull it off every so often and forego a beating. But now that the ass kickings were such a brutal and customary event, Wanda's swallowing routine was as much from habit as anything else. She hardly expected it to get her anywhere, (which was a realistic view).

"Where the fuck you hiding, you fucking cunt?!" Billy's tone was vicious. He walked into the kitchen and found Wanda with her back against the refrigerator in the corner. "Didn't you know I was looking for you? Didn't you hear me calling you, you fucking whore cunt! Why didn't you answer, huh, why?"

As Wanda stood witness to Billy's black pupils disappearing behind his rapidly blinking eyelids, her body cowered and trembled simultaneously, for she knew a severe beating was just a matter of...

Whack!

Wanda's head crashed against the refrigerator door as Billy connected with a savage right hand to the side of her face. "You fucking whore bitch," he managed to spit out between clenched teeth. He held her body up against the refrigerator and swung again, only this time Wanda's head snapped backwards from the jolt of a solid uppercut. Her legs buckled and she dropped to the kitchen floor like a sack full of rocks. Billy pretended like he was kicking a football. He backed up and lunged forward with his leg no less than a half a dozen times, connecting on a string of hearty boot shots to Wanda's face and head. Of course this was followed up with two strong minutes of heal plants to the body.

When Billy finished he was sweating profusely. He was also quite horny from all the hard work so he dragged Wanda into the other room and fucked her while she was drifting in and out of consciousness.

But it wasn't rape, mind you. In all the years Billy had been fucking Wanda immediately after beating the shit out of her, it was never rape.

To Billy it was love, and where there was love, there was never rape.

CHAPTER 36

Wanda Seven woke up to discover two things, the fresh cuts and welts on her face, and the fact that Billy made good on his threat, because bound, gagged and slouched over in the opposite corner of the room was the little black kid named Joey Dupree.

Wanda's first reaction was to help Joey but when she thrust her body forward in an effort to stand up a gripping pain burst through her insides; and like an old lady with weary old bones she crumpled back into a fetal position. With her head resting against the floor, the saliva measuring the space between her cut lips and the carpet, Wanda's gaze settled on Joey while her beaten and bewildered mind wandered back to the night she first met Billy.

It was at Boston's house. His real name was Leonard Eastwick but he only answered to the name of Boston. He claimed it to be his nickname from as far back as his junior high school days in Massachusetts. Truth was, Leonard never spent a day of his life in Massachusetts. He was born in Pittsburgh and lived there with his parents until they decided to throw him out of the house. Two days and a bus trip later he found himself in downtown Chicago. Been there ever since.

At any rate, Boston was having a birthday party, one of the two he threw for himself every year. Billy was invited because he told Boston he'd sell him some cocaine at a special birthday discount, (fat chance). Wanda was invited because she needed a place to stay and Boston was hoping to get laid after his pregnant wife went to bed. After all, Wanda couldn't be plannin' to sleep on the couch for free - could she? Naw! No fuckin way, Boston concluded. There ain't no free lunches, and if she don't know it by now, she ought to.

Wanda knew it. She'd been on her own in Chicago long enough to get fired from four pitiful jobs, get evicted from an equal number of seedy apartments, and make the kind of friends that don't do you any favors because they don't expect any in return. Yeah, Wanda knew it all right. She just didn't plan on dealing with it until later.

Turns out, the situation never came up.

Billy saw Wanda's great looking face and tight little ass walk into the room and that was enough for him. Wanda got to pack all the nose candy she could possibly handle and that was enough for her. It may not sound like Romeo and Juliet type magic, but then again, Romeo and Juliet lived in castles so what the hell did they know anyway?

Somewhere in the eight years that followed Wanda's drug and alcohol abuse took on its own parasitic life form, munching away at the clarity in her brain, sucking the oxygen out of her body, drawing her skin tightly to her bones and aging her by one month for each passing day. Billy, on the other hand, went from a pathetic little drug dealer with no place to go but up, to a pathetic little drug dealer with no place to go but up. His biggest problem was that he stopped at nothing to get there, never realizing he was already there.

Together Billy and Wanda's life could be summed up as one that resembled a pretzel. Hard, rigid, tightly, yet delicately twisted together, and capable of breaking into a hundred pieces at any given...

Whack!

The sound of Billy's hand came crashing into Wanda's trip down memory lane like a thunderous hail storm. Her body trembled.

"Well if it ain't my take a lickin', keep on tickin' bitch..." she heard Billy say...

Whack!

"Miss Seven, please meet Mr. Fist..."

Whack!

"Roses are red, violet's are black and..."

Whack!

"Aw, you still love me, don't you baby..."

Whack!

"Tell me you still love me...I said tell me you still..."

Whack!

"Here, do another line of..."

Whack!

"I said do another line of..."

Whack!

Wanda shut her eyes as tight as she could, yanked her long black hair like there was no tomorrow and rolled her head from side to side. Still, she couldn't shake the sound of Billy's voice. She even tried slapping and pinching at the cuts and bruises on her own body, but it was no use.

"Feed 'em drugs and they'll follow ya anywhere..."

Whack!

"Feed 'em drugs and they'll always love ya..."

Whack!

"You fucking cunt..."

Whack!

"You piece of shit whore..."

Whack! Whack!

"Keep feeding 'em drugs you piece of shit whore piece of shit whore piece of shit whore..."

Whack! Whack! Whack!

Wanda's head bolted up from the floor as though she'd been shaken out of a bad dream. She glanced around the apartment, concluded she was still in a bad dream and let her head fall back to the carpet. As she lay there, her hands exploring and taking stock of the cuts and bruises on her body, she no longer saw Joey Dupree as the one bound, gagged and slouched over in the corner. For the first time since she'd been living with Billy Turner, Wanda saw herself. Maybe it was because she was conscious and not high for the first time in eight years, maybe not. Wanda wasn't sure either way. One thing was certain, however, seeing herself as the victim had more to do with the pain in her mind than it did with the pain in her body. The pain in her body would die off as soon as it ran its aimless course. But the pain in her mind, that was something suddenly taking on a life of its own. It now had a voice Wanda could hear. It had muscle she could feel. It had the flutter of a beating heart and dark eyes that bore holes through the middle of her soul. It was a pain that was very much alive and getting stronger with every breath of air. It was also a pain that caused Wanda to spend the next hour letting her tears pour out like blood from an open wound. She would have even cried longer except she heard Billy walk into the apartment.

"Hey Wanda, you sleepin'?" He called out just before slamming the front door. Billy figured she must have been since he didn't hear the television screaming at the top of its lungs from halfway down the hall. "Christ, I've been gone most of the fucking day and you're still sleepin'. Must be nice livin' the life of Riley." Billy's voice was all nice and cheery. Hell, why wouldn't it be? In the last 24 hours he got to do his three favorite activities, beat the shit out of Wanda, fuck the shit out of Wanda, and pick up a quarter pound of his favorite cocaine, (white). "I got ya a present here. Why don't ya get off your lazy ass and come see what it is?"

Wanda wasn't sure if the beatings had grown worse over the years, or whether the last beating just hurt more than the others simply because it was new pain being added to old, unhealed pain. Either way she figured to let the pain soak in while she lay on the floor because she had no intentions of getting up. Besides, Wanda already knew what the little present was. It was her addiction and prison term, gift wrapped, hand delivered, money back guaranteed, and sure..."feed 'em drugs, feed 'em drugs, feed 'em drugs..." to hold her hostage one more time. She kept her eyes closed and prayed Billy wouldn't hit her anymore. In the past she always prayed to god, but since she invariably got her ass kicked again anyway, it obviously didn't do her any good. This time Wanda decided to skip the god part and pray to herself. What did she have to lose anyway? Wanda knew she couldn't end up going to hell just for leaving god out of a prayer, she was already there.

"How the fuck's my little nigger boy doin'?" Billy asked as he strolled into the room like he was walking down a fashion show runway, modeling his new cheap leather outfit. His face was fresh, his steel gray eyes were clear, and the look on his face suggested a cross between plain arrogance and glowing satisfaction with a job well done because he snatched up little Joey Dupree a few hours ago without incident.

Wanda thought Billy's question sounded as much like a general greeting as anything else so she offered no response. Still, the uncertainty as to how he might read the silence caused Wanda enough concern that she nibbled on her bottom lip.

What the fuck is going down, Billy wondered. I come in the apartment, I ask a simple fucking question and I expect a simple fucking answer. It ain't like I'm askin' for the moon, he declared to himself. "Answer the damn question woman." By now Billy's nice and cheery voice had leap frogged to the opposite direction. "How the fuck's my little nigger boy doin'?" Billy kicked at the bottoms of Wanda's feet and the sting from his boot sent a not so subtle reminder that it would be in her best interest to speak up.

"I don't know," she mumbled without looking up from the floor. "I was sleeping until you walked in."

"Uh-huh," Billy said, unsure whether he should lend any credence to the reply. He stepped over her body like it was a fallen tree twig and went to check on Joey Dupree himself.

Anyone who fed Joey the amount of bootleg quaaludes Billy did would have expected the kid to be out of it until sometime the following morning. But Billy Turner wasn't just anyone. If other people had three quarters of their body made up of water, Billy had his made up of ego. He believed people should either eat, sleep and shit when he did, or not at all. Billy squatted down and studied Joey's face. "Fuckin' nig look's just like Dino," he muttered sarcastically. Billy was referring to the pet monkey he was given, courtesy of Janey from Crazy Janey's Wet and Wild Pet Store, where the motto is, "Where crazy people sell pets for crazy prices."

Janey gave up Dino and five blowjobs in lieu of paying off her cocaine debt. Seems Billy was so fascinated by the idea the monkey liked to do cocaine, he agreed to take him instead of the cash. The blowjobs were thrown in as a bonus, interest on Billy's money you might say. It was a deal that worked out well for everyone involved, except Wanda. Wanda hated the monkey with such a passion she asked Billy to keep it locked away in the spare bedroom. The strange thing was, Billy actually agreed to her request, even though it had more to do with the monkey's wildness, than it did with trying to be nice to Wanda.

Billy slapped at Joey's face a couple of times. "Hey nig, you up?"

Wanda couldn't bear to watch, but at the same time she was determined not to bury her chin into her chest and look away. "Why don't you leave him alone," she suggested innocently enough.

Billy abruptly turned around. His menacing glare was almost enough to make her wish the words never left her mouth.

"What? Why don't I what?" he demanded.

Wanda took a slow, deep breath and grimaced as she exhaled. For a brief moment of insanity she actually contemplated telling Billy to go fuck himself. Luckily the thought faded away as quickly as it first entered her mind, otherwise it would have only inflamed...

Whack!

Billy kicked her head with the side of his boot like it was a soccer ball. "Leave him alone eh? You piece of shit whore, I oughta..."

Whack!

This time Billy's boot landed right down the middle, signaling the official start of what promised to be another solid ass kicking performance. Of course, Billy would make love to Wanda right after the game, (just like always).

Maybe he'd even let Dino out to play afterwards.

CHAPTER 37

Not that any time of day was good, but mornings were by far the worst.
By then the cuts, bruises, welts, and any other souvenirs Wanda accumulated from the night before, had been given a nice opportunity to swell up, stretch out and make themselves feel right at home. But that was before today, before Wanda heard the penetrating voice and felt the strength of muscle, before the beating heart pumped life into her mind and the dark eyes burned away the image of Joey Dupree, leaving only the image of herself to dangle like the shadow of a dead body hanging from a rope.
Wanda's gaze danced back and forth across the pale white ceiling as she prepared herself to stand up. She knew her early morning actions would have to be slow and deliberate if she hoped to manage the pain with any degree of success. Any sudden movement or slight gesture the wrong way and the pain could explode into something so intolerable, she might find herself confined to the apartment the rest of the day, something Billy took for granted, something Wanda did not want to happen. Not today...
Whack!
Not tomorrow...
Whack!
Not ever again.
As for little Joey Dupree, Wanda thought about taking him along but he was in no condition to walk and she was in no condition to carry him. For now Joey would have to stay put. It wasn't Wanda's first choice, but since Billy "The Big Time" drug dealer never allowed a phone in the apartment, (something about somebody wanting to tap the phone line), it was her only choice. Besides, even if she had a phone she wasn't gonna call someone and then wait around to get picked up. No way, no how. With Billy gone from the apartment Wanda was gettin' out while the gettin' was good. End of conversation.

It was roughly 10:30 in the morning when Max put down his coffee cup and got up from behind the desk. The Beast was wandering around the precinct looking for someone to bet the Packers - Bear's game with, the bad guy business was unusually slow, even for the morning, the Captain was out of the office, and Max didn't feel like using anymore dead time to catch up on paperwork. Instead, he decided to take a walk and see what was happening on the streets. Max liked to walk outside, especially on days when the sun was having a hard time breaking through the clouds, the temperature was adequate, and there was a mist, so slight, it was hard to feel, even when it took a swipe at your face full blast.
Crazy as it may sound, just about any Chicago cop you ask will tell you

they have gut instinct. The problem is, most of them confuse gut instinct with experience and it's not the same thing. Experience is something of a tool. It enables cops to plod along until enough facts have been defined to allow a puzzle to be pieced together. Gut instinct, on the other hand, has no definable shape or direction. It's something that causes select cops to react to observations other cops don't see, or pick up on. Max was one of the few in his jurisdiction to actually possess gut instinct. The Beast was another one, which explains why they worked so well together.

It also explains why Max stopped, buried his hands in his jean pockets, and leaned against a streetlight in front of the Old Chicago Tobacco Company. He'd been walking for about fifteen minutes when he noticed the figure of a woman heading towards him from about twenty yards away. She was dressed in a full length overcoat and wore a baseball hat and big, bulky sunglasses to shield her eyes. But that's not what tweaked Max's curiosity. The thing that got him was the way she kept looking around, as if afraid someone might sneak up on her. The fact that she was walking as fast as her bad limp would allow didn't go unnoticed either.

When Wanda Seven first left the apartment she planned to head straight for the police station. It'd be easy, she figured, just like washing her hands. She'd walk in, tell them what was happening, then leave. Adios, so long, see ya round sucker, don't call me I'll call you, hasta la vista, baby. There was only one problem: the longer Wanda walked, the more time she had to think, and the more time she had to think, the more confused she became. Maybe it wouldn't be so easy after all, she told herself. Maybe she should go back...she could get high and forget about the whole damn thing...she could do a couple of those bootleg ludes Billy was braggin' about, toot a bunch of coke, she'd be numb in no time...how bad could it be...maybe she should go back. Billy won't bother her...Whack! There was all that coke...Whack! Maybe she'd freebase, she hadn't done that in a while and that was always fun...Whack! What about the kid, what about Joey? Would she be able to ignore the fact he was in the apartment...could she ignore his little body slouched over in the corner? Would she hear the voice again...Whack! Would she look at him and see herself...Whack! Whack! And what if Billy is home when she gets back and he starts asking where she was? What if he doesn't like the answer he hears, then what? Whack! Whack! Whack! No, can't go back. No way...can't go back...no more drugs...no more...never again...gotta keep movin'...gotta keep runnin'...gotta get oughta here...where...dunno...just gotta keep goin'...leave town...dunno...What if Billy gets arrested? What if he finds out she turned him in? Should she turn him in...dunno...if he finds out...Whack! Whack! Whack!

Wanda did her best to go from a limp to a slow jog. Her form wasn't very convincing but the fear and desperation racing through her body still made jogging possible. She no longer looked around for Billy. All she could focus in on was getting away...gotta keep goin'...where...dunno...just gotta get oughta here...gotta keep movin'...

At this point Max wanted to hear her life story, at least the part that gave her the bad limp. He sidestepped a couple of people waiting to cross the street and took a dozen short strides until he came up behind her. "Please stop ma'am, I'm a police officer and I'd like to talk to you."

Wanda was so startled by the sound of Max's voice, friendly as it may have been, that her body jumped forward. As she fought to maintain her balance she bumped into a young, well dressed couple engrossed in a conversation about the unfortunate perils of the homeless. The man and woman quickly locked arms to keep from falling, although from the looks on their faces it appeared as if each one expected to be protected by the other because they had just been brutally attacked by a wretched old bag lady looking for a handout. The couple quickly moved off to the side and let Wanda tumble to the pavement. "Watch where the fuck you're going," the young woman snapped indignantly.

Max rushed to Wanda's aide. As he kneeled down it was obvious by the troubled expression on his face that he was more distressed by the couple's reaction than he was pissed off at himself for needlessly scaring her the way he did. "Get out of here," he said to the couple.

When they didn't move Max looked up at them. "Now," he said earnestly. Max waited until he was satisfied the couple knew how to follow his directions, then refocused his attention on the fallen woman. "Please let me try to help you. You look hurt and I'm a police officer. I can help."

Wanda didn't respond, but she didn't offer any resistance either when Max helped her back to her feet.

"Come on, let's get you inside." Max wrapped his arm around Wanda's waist to keep as much of the pressure off her legs as he possibly could. A couple of steps later and Wanda was resting her head on his shoulder. Somewhere along the way she even started babbling out loud. Max paid close attention, but until he was able to fit the few words he understood into meaningful sentences, most of it would continue to sound like a whole lot of nonsense. Max never thought fifteen minutes constituted much of a walk, that is until Wanda's body all but shut down and collapsed in his arms. At that point, Max couldn't get back to the precinct fast enough. When they finally arrived, he was relieved to discover he still had enough energy to open the door, and at the same time help Wanda inside.

"Jerry," he shot out to the morning Desk Sergeant.

Desk Sergeant Jerry Tatters was talking on the phone to his wife when he looked up and saw Max. "I'll call you back," he declared. He hung up the phone without waiting for his wife to say anything. After eleven years as a cop's wife she was used to it and didn't plan to respond anyway. Jerry Tatters was a big man, stomach included, but when he sprang up from his chair and moved to the other side of the check-in counter he displayed the agility of a shortstop in the middle of a double play. "Jesus Max, what the hell happened?"

Max moved to one side and let Jerry Tatters grab Wanda on the other side. "Thanks man, appreciate it," Max said.

"Hard to believe a skinny little thing could weigh so much."

"Shit, you got no idea Jerry. Let's get her into the conference room. There's a couch in there she can lay down on." It was more a matter of movement than it was a struggle once Jerry Tatters got involved. In no time at all the two men were inside the first floor conference room. Max removed Wanda's baseball hat and sunglasses, revealing the full scope of the cuts and bruises on her face. Someone tattooed her pretty good, Max thought. He glanced at Jerry Tatters and was greeted by a look of disgust. Jerry was obviously thinking the same thing.

"Here now...yeah, that's it," Max said as he eased Wanda onto the couch. It was an ugly, green corduroy couch, but it was also soft and comfortable, something Wanda was no longer used to. Aside from the cuts and bruises her face looked tired and drained. An argument could even be made that her skin was on the outer edges of looking a bit ragged. Still, Max found himself taken by her light brown eyes. To him they sparkled the purity and freshness of a beautiful young woman.

Wanda stared back but said nothing. Yet, for some reason Max was feeling awkward. He wasn't sure if it was because her eyes held him in some kind of trance, or because the silence in the room made him feel like he should say something special in order to comfort her. Either way Max was relieved when Jerry asked a question because his interruption dampened the feeling.

"Whataya think happened?"

Max straightened up so he could face the Desk Sergeant. He sighed before answering. "No idea, Jerry. I'm hoping to find out real soon."

"Well...if ya need anything let me know so I can help."

A concerned, almost apprehensive look settled on Max's face, like he was measuring the sincerity in the Desk Sergeant's words. But just as quickly as the look appeared, it vanished, replaced by a spirited plan to make Wanda smile, giggle, laugh, something - anything to break the hold of her present state of mind. Max waived his thumb in the direction of Jerry Tatters. "Did you hear that. I mean can you believe it," he quipped, "this guy actually thinks he's gonna help us. Hell, we already did all the hard work. This guy just wants to stay in the room cause he sees a pretty lady. He's always like that. Whataya think, should we let him stay?" Max studied Wanda's face. Nothin'. Not even a hint of a smile.

Jerry figured he'd take a crack at it. "Oh hell, you caught me. But think about it, why would I want to do the hard part when you guy's can do it." He turned sideways and patted himself on his ass. "I didn't get this ol' rump of mine 'cause I like hard work ya know." Jerry flashed his big, inviting smile. Still, Wanda offered no reaction.

Time to switch gears, Max decided. He kneeled back down next to the couch and let his eyes settle on the troubled woman beside him. "Jerry, go find the Beast. After that see if you can get in touch with Ricki Jackson in Social Services. If yes, ask her to get down here as quick as she can. Tell her it's for me. If no, then leave a message for her to contact me first chance she gets."

"You want me to get an ambulance lined up?"

Max pulled at the bridge of his nose and Wanda could see that he was thinking about it. She didn't want to go. It might not have looked like it, but she was just starting to feel safe and warm right where she was. Sure, she was banged up, banged up pretty good in fact. But she had been through it so many times before she knew a doctor wasn't necessary. "No, no ambulance." Wanda's pleading voice was faint, but her words were clear.

Max winked at her. "No ambulance," he repeated. "Let's just deal with gettin' the Beast and Ricki Jackson down here."

Jerry Tatters didn't say anything. He figured he'd find the Beast upstairs and hurried out of the room to do just that. Several seconds later, just as he polished off the first three steps with one oversized stride, he heard Max yell, "Hey Jerry, is the Captain back yet?"

Jerry stopped and turned his head. "No..." he shouted back..."as far as I know he's not expected back the rest of the day." He waited a couple of seconds just in case Max said anything else. When all he got was an earful of the usual crap going on inside the building, Jerry took his big smile and promptly finished off the stairs, two at a time.

CHAPTER 38

Social Services didn't have the most sterling reputation, what with the soft stance they were accused of taking whenever it came to issues of domestic violence or child abuse. Still, its reputation was much better than the police department's, even if it was more by default than by design.

Be that as it may, Ricki Jackson was a counselor for Social Services and she was one of the good ones. At least that's how Max described her whenever a description seemed necessary, as was the case when he first told Wanda Seven about her.

Max and the Beast first met Ricki about four years ago. The two detectives were investigating the death of a woman, allegedly bludgeoned to death by her estranged husband. Ricki was brought in to help with the custody issues regarding the six year old daughter who was suddenly and sadly motherless. Seems a battle was brewing between the child's grandparents and the state. The grandparent's wanted the child because they loved her like their own daughter, who was now lying in the morgue pending dental identification. The state, meanwhile, wanted the child put into a foster home pending further investigation because the child's grandfather had charges of aggravated assault and assault and battery staring him in the face. Apparently when Mr. Cunningham got wind of his daughter's murder he went son-in-law hunting, instead of to the morgue with his wife. He found him an hour later sitting on a stool at Rocky's Bar and proceeded to take great delight in beating holy hell out of him with a pool cue. When he was finished Mr. Cunningham called the police to pick the son-of-a-bitch up for the murder of his daughter. Turns out an ambulance picked up the son-in-law and the police picked up Mr. Cunningham.

In any event, after spending an entire afternoon at the crime scene one day, Ricki Jackson asked Max and the Beast out for a couple of beers. Something about wanting to pick their brains. All she really wanted was some company while she let out some of the disgust and aggravation she inhaled from the investigation. It didn't take long before Max and the Beast realized they had a good friend in the works. Ricki took to them much the same way.

Ricki Jackson was an attractive 41 year old woman. Twenty-five pounds lighter and she might have considered trying her hand at modeling again. But that would have required exercise and sweat. It would have also required getting rid of the chocolate bars that grew inside her desk at work, something she wasn't prepared to do. The way Ricki saw it, she had a beautiful teenage daughter named Jamie, two labrador retrievers named Heckyl and Jeckyl, and a husband who routinely told her she was the best lookin' black meat on the planet; point being, why change what don't need changing?

As far as Max was concerned, Ricki Jackson had one other thing going for her. She was as sensitive and compassionate as anyone he'd ever met, something Wanda Seven needed by the truckload, and something she would get just as soon as Ricki showed up. Until then, Max was content to see if he could get Wanda to open up about what happened to her.

The Beast had already been warned about Wanda's fragile state, so when he got to the conference room he made sure to tap lightly on the door with the heel of his palm. Nevertheless, when Wanda heard the muffled sound her head shot up from the couch's armrest.

"It's okay," Max said without taking his eyes away from hers. "It's just my friend. I want you to meet him. There's no need to worry 'cause nothing's gonna happen. I won't let it. I promise you."

Wanda thought about it for a moment then slowly eased her head back on the armrest and watched Max's friend enter the room.

Max didn't even turn around. He knew it was the Beast the second he heard a pair of worn out boot heels smack against the linoleum floor. "Hey Zack."

"How ya doin," Zack responded. One thing about the Beast. The softer he tried to make his raspy voice come out, the more threatening it sounded.

"Zack, I'd like you to meet Wanda Seven. I thought she might need some help so I brought her here. We've been sitting around and getting acquainted a little bit."

The Beast walked over and tipped his head like he was bowing to a queen. It caused his ponytail to fall over the front of his shoulder. "If there's anything you need, anything at all, you just tell us. Don't be afraid either. We'll do whatever we can for you."

For some unknown reason Zack's smile and warm green eyes made Wanda suddenly wonder just how long he could last with Billy Turner. Was he too nice for Billy? Would that give Billy the edge in a fight? Wanda cocked her head and thought about it for a couple of seconds. Naw, on second thought, Max's friend might look nice, he might even use nice words when he talks, but there's something scary about his voice. Besides that, he look's too big and strong for Billy.

Wanda then peered at Max and wondered the same thing. Max had a pretty face and everything, but there was something about him that gave off an intense anger. It's kind of like he was made-up of one part calm, one part rage, and one part something else. Wanda guessed it to be the thing that balanced out the other two parts. Naw, Billy wouldn't stand a chance.

Max took hold of Wanda's hand and held it between the two of his. She trembled slightly and Max was hoping it was because she was afraid of someone on the outside, not because she was afraid of him or the Beast. "Are you sure you're okay?"

"Am I gonna have to leave?" Wanda's eyes were screaming but her voice was barely a whisper.

The question caught Max off guard. Still, it was an indication Wanda wasn't afraid of him or the Beast. "No, you don't have to leave. You can stay here as long as you want to. And don't worry, no one's gonna hurt you. I won't let them." Max winked at her. "And either will that big ugly guy standing behind me."

Wanda smiled...finally! Swollen lips and everything, but she smiled. I'm breaking through, Max thought.

"Are you tired? Do you wanna go to sleep?" The Beast broke in. "If you do, just say so and we can go stand outside the door."

Wanda was tired, even exhausted. But at the moment she wanted Max's company more than she wanted the sleep so she shook her head no.

"Do you want a glass of water. Hell I shoulda asked you that before, I'm sorry. Say Beast..."

"On my way buddy."

Wanda stared at Max while the Beast went to find a glass of water. She liked his face. She liked its hard look, but what she liked even more was that she could still see the softness of his features underneath. She also liked the way his voice sounded. It was quiet and easy, but at the same time carried the strength of unwavering confidence. It moved through her like warm water. It had been a long time since Wanda experienced the security and gentleness she was feeling at that moment, and an even longer time since she smiled because of it.

Max was getting that awkward feeling again and wasn't sure what to do or say as a result. Thank god the Beast came back with the water when he did.

Wanda took hold of the glass with both hands and lifted her head just enough so she could take a couple of small swallows without letting any of it to trickle out the sides of her mouth. "Thank you," she said, offering the glass back to the Beast.

Max liked the idea of Wanda not whispering. It meant she was feeling stronger, more comfortable, or maybe both. Whatever it was, it was bringing her much closer to telling them what happened. "Are you sure you don't want some more water, maybe something to eat?" he asked.

Wanda shook her head. "No thank you."

Max thought about it for a minute, then figured what the hell. If she's not ready she'll say no, that's all. "Talk, do you want to talk, maybe tell us what happened?"

The Beast had a different opinion. He figured Wanda was just about ready to go nonstop, so he pulled up a chair and sat down like some big overgrown kid gettin' ready to hear a bedtime story.

Wanda didn't respond immediately. Her eye's kept moving over Max's face like she was searching for something, thinking if she just kept looking, she'd find it.

Max took hold of Wanda's hand again and squeezed it gently between his. "Please tell us what happened." Max looked deep into Wanda's eyes like he too was searching for something. The difference was, he was searching for information. And by the time Ricki Jackson arrived at the precinct, some ninety minutes later, he got it. But it was almost more than he could stomach.

The two detectives excused themselves from the conference room so Ricki and Wanda could get a little time alone and talk. Some of the conversation touched on Wanda, some on Billy, some on Max, and some of it was just about stuff. Clothes, hairstyles, different uses of makeup, how it can even be used to cover some bad memories of an old boyfriend. It didn't take long before Wanda felt completely at ease with Ricki. Then again, anyone who can't get comfortable with Ricki is probably straitjacket crazy, something Max didn't figure was the case with Wanda. Scared...yeah probably, stressed out and disillusioned...most certainly, but straitjacket crazy? Not a chance. Wanda just needed to get away from a bad life, take some time and rediscover herself.

For the most part Ricki Jackson agreed with Max's take on things. But she also thought Wanda needed to spend some time around a loving and caring family. Only then would she be able to see that good feelings can, and do exist between people. That's why Ricki decided to take Wanda home with her.

"You sure you want to do this?" Max and Ricki had been sitting on the stairs by themselves for all of thirty minutes and Max had already repeated the question three times.

Ricki nodded her head without hesitation. "I've got the right kind of family. I've got the right kind of home life. I want her to see it - to feel it. It's the best way, maybe the only way." Ricki sighed. "Christ Max, look what the fuck she's been through."

Up to that point all Max really knew was that Billy liked to sell drugs and beat and rape his girlfriend whenever he got the urge. It was certainly enough to turn Max's anger loose, but it wasn't enough to make him rush out and arrest the pathetic little bastard. Losers like Billy never go anywhere and Max figured he and the Beast had the rest of the day to bring him in. "I agree," he finally said. "She's been through quite an ordeal. How long ya plannin' on havin' her stay with you?"

Ricki shrugged her shoulders. "I dunno. A few weeks, maybe a month. As long as it takes, I guess."

Max leaned over and kissed Ricki on the side of her head. "You're alright," he declared.

Ricki Jackson appreciated the kiss as well as the compliment, but when she looked at Max she had quite the serious look on her face. "Listen beautiful," she cautioned, "this woman is quite taken with you. I know all you did was talk to her, but in her mind you came riding in on a white horse and saved her. It might not be right, but it's only natural she's gonna feel that way...at least for now."

"You sure about this?" Max sounded troubled by the sudden twist in conversation.

"I'm sure darlin'. I've been doing this a long time. For her sake, even for you're own sake, make sure you watch what you do and say around her. You might not think much of it, but that doesn't mean she won't. Tread softly."

Softly? Max? Wanda, okay. Billy Turner? Whataya kiddin'?

CHAPTER 39

"You wanna announce?" The Beast was referring to that constitutional thing. You know...knock-knock-knock, this is the police. The knock-knock-knock part wasn't bad, but the Beast hated the idea of announcing. To him it was like giving somebody a head start in a race.

Max never liked it either and looked a little annoyed when he was reminded of, what he considered to be, a senseless obligation. "Fuck him, he beats up woman. Besides, why tell him the truth when we can lie and get in the door that much easier?"

The Beast grunted.

The hallway leading to Billy's apartment wasn't as narrow or as dark as the brown wallpaper and various burned out lightbulbs made it appear. Nevertheless, anytime the Beast was in a place darker than he preferred, which didn't take much since he was a big fan of the color white, he found himself a little more wary than usual. Max wasn't any different, except he wasn't as big a fan of the color white. As a result, he didn't think the hallway was particularly dark, all of which explained why the Beast shot one last look behind him while Max gave the door a decent rap. If Billy was home Max wanted to make sure he heard it. At the same time, he didn't want to knock so loud it would cause the little prick to get overly paranoid. After all, he was a drug dealer, and drug dealers have been known to get paranoid. Not that Max and the Beast dealt with them all that much. For the most part it was outside their department. What made this case different was Wanda Seven and the fist and boot marks all over her face.

"Billy," Max called out in a semi-high-pitched voice.

The Beast hung his head and snickered. He knew Max was going to launch into his queen impersonation, and still he couldn't hide his amusement.

Billy Turner happened to be coming out of the spare bedroom when he heard both the knock and the voice behind it. He wasn't sure what to think, so he scanned his memory banks for the names and faces of anyone he knew who might be a faggot. The problem Billy encountered was not being able to come up with a name or face fast enough. It made him all the more frantic about who was at the door. Could it be Wanda fuckin' around? Where the fuck is she anyway? If it ain't her, I bet she put someone up to it. I'm gonna kick her little ass when I see her. The fucking bitch knows I hate surprise visitors.

Max held his ear close to the door but didn't hear a thing. He glanced at his partner and the Beast nodded his head. Max took the suggestion and knocked again. "Billy? Billy?" he repeated in the disguised voice, "My name's Rex, Rex Long. I met Wanda Seven just a little while ago. She told me you're holding. I've got fifteen hundred bucks on me. Cash."

"Shut the fuck up and hold on," Billy snarled from inside.

Max winked at his partner and took a step back.

The Beast fixed his eyes on the door and took a step forward.

Billy slowly turned the knob and pulled the door open just enough to steal a quick peek at Rex Long. If the little fuckhead looks like a fag, I'll let him in and take his money, Billy decided.

Unfortunately for Billy there was no Rex Long. But there was an open door and Max and the Beast charged it like a couple of pissed off rhinos.

Billy was knocked backwards, crashing against the wall before he even knew what happened. One thing about it though, and it surprised Max and the Beast, he came up swinging at a hundred miles an hour. He also went down after the Beast smashed him with three straight thundering overhand rights.

But Billy could take a helluva punch and was far from finished. He scurried to all fours, wrapped his arms around the first pair of legs he could grab hold of and burst forward, growling and panting like a ravenous dog.

Max quickly backpedaled to keep from getting tackled. When he reached the open space of the living room and was able to maneuver he planted his weight firm, grabbed a handful of Billy's perfectly placed, blow dried hair, pulled his head back until his face was all nice and exposed, and proceeded to bang away, like Billy's face was a nail and his right hand was a hammer. By the time Billy's arms fell away from Max's legs, his nose was broken, his eyes were blackening, one of his front teeth was sitting in the back of his throat, and his face was covered as much by blood as it was by skin. Just before stepping away to catch his breath and rest his hand, Max drilled his boot into the side of Billy's rib cage.

Billy coughed and grunted at the same time and the tooth sitting in the back of his throat flew out of his mouth.

"Guess he'll be needin' a cap for that one. Say Bill, how's your dental plan?"

Billy wanted to respond to the big guy with the raspy voice by telling him to go fuck himself, but the sharp pains exploding from his waist to the top of his head put a damper on the thought.

The Beast moved in and proceeded to wedge the toe of his boot under Billy's cheek. He tried to make Billy look straight up, but the more he tried lifting his foot, the harder Billy pressed against it with the side of his bloody face. After a couple of see-saw battles, the Beast retreated and folded his arms. He eyeballed Billy in mock disgust. "Say Bill, it's gonna go somethin' like this. You're gonna turn you're head and face the ceiling, which means of course you'll be looking at my pretty face when I talk to you, or I'm gonna be serving boot for dinner." Zack leaned back for a side view. "So what's it gonna be there Bill?"

Billy figured if he was going to have any chance at all of getting away it was going to take a whole lot of his energy, which meant he was better off lying still for a few minutes and trying to regain some of it. Besides, the thought of eating boot for dinner, especially when it's force fed, wasn't very appealing. Billy faced the ceiling.

"Well now Bill, I guess you're not as dumb as I thought, and to be perfectly honest, I thought you were pretty dumb. Max, whata you think?"

Max walked over and peered down at the bruised, bloodied, and for the moment, tamed Billy Turner. "We haven't been formally introduced, have we?"

Billy looked at the guy with the black leather bomber jacket and long dark hair. His face looked cold, his voice sounded colder. These guy's are friends of Elijah Dupree, they came to get his little nigger brother, Billy concluded. But then, if that's the case, how and the fuck did they know Wanda's name? Did she tell them? Was she helping Elijah? Why would she do that? he wondered. Hell, I never did nothin' to her, the fuckin' bitch. The more Billy thought about it, the more confused it made him. If he could have, he would have shrugged his shoulders in response to his own questions. Instead, he tried blinking away the blood running across his eyelids.

"Say there Bill." Billy's dazed look followed the guy with the thick neck and raspy voice. "Ya know what I think the problem is...I think a guy with a low level of intelligence, a guy like me for instance, figures if another guy can hear and see you, then by all accounts he can talk to you. Which leads us to a little problem with my man Max - Oh!" The Beast declared, as if a new thought just popped into his head and he wanted to put it into words before he forgot the thought. "Just so ya know, my man Max is not to be confused with that character named Mad Max. That guy doesn't have a clue what mad really is." The Beast squinted his eyes as he reconsidered his own words, decided he agreed with them and proceeded talking. "Anyway, my man Max asked you a question and you didn't answer him. I'm sure you have better manners than that." The Beast waited a couple of seconds. "You do, don't you?" The question hung in the room like it was an invitation to a bad party and Billy was expected to R.S.V.P..

Billy opened his mouth to speak but winced from sharp pain as the exposed nerves from his missing front tooth smacked head-on with the air he inhaled.

The Beast rubbed his chin, looking as though he was very much concerned about Billy's condition. A few seconds later he stopped rubbing his chin and the concerned look gave way to a wry grin. "Gee, it's nothin' I did. Come to think of it, it's probably my partner's fault. He's always doin' shit like that. Max, I think you hurt this poor little fella." Zack playfully tapped the toe of his boot against Billy's shoulder. "Hell, he probably didn't mean nothin' by it."

Zack glanced at his partner and nodded his head in the direction of Billy. "Max, tell this nice little fella you didn't mean nothin' by it. Tell him you were just havin' a little fun."

"I'm sorry. I didn't mean nothin' by it," Max deadpanned. "I was just havin' a little fun. And I'm sorry if I knocked your tooth out, but I'll be more than happy to glue it back in for ya. Beast, we have some super-glue don't we?"

Billy sealed his eyes and let his head fall back to one side. Fuck this guy! Fuck both these guys! Rested up or not I've had all the shit I'm takin'! With that, Billy unexpectedly rolled over, placed his palm on top of Zack's boot to keep it on the floor, instead of in his face, and sprang up from the carpet. As he wheeled around he noticed the Beast out of the corner of his eye moving to his left. Billy guessed Max was directly behind him so he abruptly spun around the other way and swung wildly. Max didn't react fast enough and Billy was able to sting him with a pretty solid shot to the side of his face.

The Beast lunged forward, grabbed Billy by the back of his arms and hurled him against the wall. Billy's shoulders hit first, but it was his head that gave way to the loudest thud. It was just about all Billy could do to turn around, keep his back pinned against the wall and slide himself down. But rest was not in the cards. As soon as Billy's knees touched the carpet Max pulled him back up by his red stained hair and introduced his face to the wall again. At that point, whatever part of his face that wasn't bleeding, now was. Billy looked like a staggering drunk trying to decide which spot he wanted to rest in before turning in for the night. Max helped with the decision by throwing him down face first.

The Beast kneeled down and rolled Billy over on his back. He slapped at his face a couple of times, and when Billy protested by sticking his hands in the way, the Beast decided he still had too much spunk for comfort. "Say there Bill, is that how ya used to beat up Wanda? Or, do ya think me and my partner ought to approach it from a different angle?"

The fucking bitch! Billy thought. The motherfucking bitch! Who are these guys? That motherfucking bitch!

"Say Max, did we leave anything out?"

Max cocked his head and thought about an answer. Finally he said, "Ya know, come to think of it, I think we did. Word on the street is Billy here likes cowboy boots. I think we would be remiss not to show him ours."

Zack poked Billy in the chest repeatedly. "Remiss, I like that word. You like that word Bill, remiss?"

Billy tried to grab his finger but the Beast simply pulled it away, smiled and stood up. "Remiss huh? Well goddamnit Max, that means the entire day would be a complete fucking waste of..."

Whack!

Billy grunted loud as hot stabbing pains shot through his groin and stomach.

"You like that you little..."
Whack!
Billy gasped and writhed around on the floor from the crippling pain.
"You're a real tough guy. But somethin' tells me you won't be beatin' anybody up...
Whack!
By now Billy couldn't gather up enough strength to grunt. One more time and he was sure to pass out.
...anytime real soon..."
Whack! Whack! Whack!

CHAPTER 40

It wasn't the pile of drugs or the assortment of drug paraphernalia that rendered Max and the Beast speechless. It wasn't even because the Beast shot and killed Billy Turner's pet monkey, Dino. To tell you the truth, the two detectives shared a good laugh about that one.

What Max and Zack found so disturbing, what overwhelmed them to the point of flushing the color from each of their faces, was opening the bedroom door to find Joey Dupree slumped over in the corner, fresh and dried up vomit plastered to his shirt, human waste saturating just about everything below his belt buckle.

"You remember that day Beast?"

Zack was seated in the booth with his back hunched over, rolling his half filled glass of stoli around in a semi-circle, watching it as if he was studying the movement of the ice cubes. Remembering Joey Dupree, that was easy. Remembering the last time he heard traces of panic in Max's voice, that was hard.

There were two things the Beast figured he could always count on. One was that Max would carry life on his shoulders at a deliberate, unwavering pace. The other was that he'd never apologize for it. The Beast never knew his best friend to be the type who soared with the highs or crashed with the lows. Simply put, it wasn't Max's style. By the same token, it may have been his most potent tool, because for some reason, probably his impassive, cool blue eyes, it gave Max the unique ability to look fearless. Until now, that is, when the Beast glanced up from his drink and noticed a hint of panic also scratching at the surface of Max's face. It was the kind of thing that dug a pit in Zack's gut, partly because he understood the realities of the situation, mostly because there wasn't a damn thing he could do about it.

Hell, think about it:

Max's sister and brother-in-law were savagely murdered. Max and the Beast picked out three people to go after. The first, Harry Weeble, turned out to be the same worthless fruitcake he was on the day they arrested him. The second, Eddie Hart, proved to be nothing more than a big, fat, greasy zero. All of which left Billy Turner as the only person separating the entire investigation from hitting a real shitty bump in the road.

And hell...Zack wondered, as he fidgeted in the booth...what are the chances Billy had anything to do with the murders. Sure, he's a crazed animal. And yeah, maybe he's got a motive. But Billy's no more crazed and has no more a motive than those other two sick losers, and checking them out was a stretch from the word go. Max is thinkin' the same thing. He knows we got nothin'. He knows if Billy goes nowhere, we got nowhere to go. Christ, if that was me sittin' there steada Max, I'd be talkin' to myself by now. The more Zack thought about it, the worse his stomach felt. The answer, he decided, was to fill it up with vodka. So, without further ado, the Beast picked up his glass, tipped it in the direction of his friend, barely uttered, "Here's to ya," and finished off his drink with one large adult size swallow.

Max reached for his own drink. "So, do ya remember the Dupree kid, or not?" he repeated.

The Beast set his glass down on the table, hard. "Yeah, I remember. Who the fuck could forget," he asked rhetorically.

Max answered anyway. "I dunno, probably everyone but us." Max was referring to all the other badges and suits that showed up at Billy Turner's apartment that day to be part of the circus.

And what a circus it was...

Over the years Wanda guessed that Billy raped her dozens of times. She may well have been right, but after the drug and alcohol abuse chewed a nice size hole through the part of her brain that remembers things, Wanda could only recall the last three episodes with enough detail to satisfy the Assistant District Attorney he had a shot at a conviction. Of course, when she failed to show up for court it didn't matter anyway because the judge had no choice but to throw the rape charges out. It's just like basic math, the judge reasoned. One accused minus one accuser equals zero.

The rest of Billy Turner's trial took about four hours. An hour by the State to prove the drug related offenses Billy was charged with, two hours by the Feds to prove Joey Dupree was kidnapped, and one hour of objections by Billy's attorney, Bernard Forest, regarding the admissibility of all the evidence found in Billy's apartment, including Joey Dupree.

Judge Emerson High had served on the bench for over thirty years and was well versed in all areas of constitutional law. Not only did he agree with Bernard Forest on each and every objection the attorney made, he was also convinced any conviction of Billy Turner would get reversed on appeal. But, Judge Emerson High didn't have the nickname, Judge Hang Em High, for nothing. Black, white, red, yellow, the Judge couldn't care less about color. To him it was all good guy - bad guy, and if he thought someone was a bad guy, then it was goodbye. On top of that, Judge High didn't give a shit what the Court Of Appeals or the State Supreme Court did anyway, especially since he planned to retire at the end of his current term. His attitude was simple and to the point. "They wanna reverse me, great, but I'm not setting this stinkin' little wretch free." As a result, Billy Turner was sentenced to thirty years in prison, five for all the drug related bullshit and twenty-five for kidnapping Joey Dupree.

And what a circus it became...

The State Supreme Court agreed with Bernard Forest. In short, the panel of judges concluded that Wanda Sevens' lengthy history of severe drug and alcohol dependency, skillfully documented and introduced to the court by Bernard Forest, affected her credibility to the point that Detectives Cougar and Darwin could not have reasonably relied upon her statements in order to investigate whether a crime was in fact taking place in Billy Turner's apartment. (No one would say it, but Wanda's failure to appear in court in order to pursue the rape charges against Billy didn't help her credibility either).

The court also found, as inconclusive, any evidence suggesting Wanda Seven had the legal right to be in Billy's apartment. Notwithstanding the possibility that Wanda may have lived in the apartment, the court pointed to the fact that Billy Turner was the only tenant on the lease agreement itself. As such, he was the only individual entitled to the rights provided for under the lease. Therefore, Wanda could not give the detectives permission to enter premises she herself had no legal right to enter.

Lastly, the court dismissed the argument that Billy opened his door and voluntarily invited the police detectives inside. The court ignored the affidavits of Detectives Cougar and Darwin, suggesting instead the affidavits were self-serving. In essence it was the court's opinion that nobody in their right mind would have opened the door to expose criminal activity on the inside if they knew it was the police on the outside. Suffice it to say, the court determined that access to the apartment was gained under false pretenses.

Therefore, the court concluded Detectives Max Cougar and Zack Darwin violated Billy Turner's Fourth Amendment rights by conducting an illegal search of the defendant's premises. As a result, nothing found on the premises should have been allowed to be used as evidence in court, Billy's conviction was reversed, and he was set free.

And what a circus it would become...

Billy was gunning for Max, Max and the Beast were gunning for the killer of Kathy and Jack Reed, and John Henry Stevens was gunning for just about anybody.

CHAPTER 41

THE ADVENTURES OF JOHN HENRY STEVENS
(get ready, 'cause he ain't no Huck Finn)

Even as a kid, John Henry Stevens was a nasty motherfucker. Maybe it was because his old man walked out when he was three years old; maybe it was because his mother blamed him for it every chance she got; maybe it was because his mother kept him locked up in the crawl-space basement so she could go to the bar and pick up strange meat, (which was at least twice a week); maybe it was because his mother kept him locked up in the crawl-space basement when she was home because she didn't feel like dealing with him, (which was at least three times a week); maybe it was because John Henry got so used to the crawl-space basement he ate most of his meals down there, at times even choosing to sleep there instead of in his bedroom; maybe it was because John Henry's mother wouldn't let him out of the house to play with the other neighborhood kids; maybe it was because none of the neighborhood kids were allowed to come over to his house; maybe it was because John Henry's mother used to let some of her midnight boyfriends hold him down and fondle his privates; maybe it was because John Henry's mother died when he was ten years old and his aunt and uncle begrudgingly took him in; maybe it was because his aunt and uncle hated everything about him and treated him like the family dog, feeding him table scraps after the rest of the family had finished eating, sometimes even forcing him to go to the bathroom outdoors; maybe it was because none of John Henry's four cousins would talk to him for weeks at a time; maybe it was because his aunt and uncle blamed him for everything, whether it be the missing dog (although that one was true 'cause John Henry buried it alive), or the funny tasting lemonade, (okay, so he did, but only because the colors were so close together he didn't think anybody would know); maybe it was because his aunt and uncle used to blindfold and lock him in the closet for hours on end; maybe it was because John Henry never had more than two shirts and two pair of pants to wear during any given school year; maybe it was because he had an IQ of 172; maybe it was because he had unusually violent mood swings, one minute smiling at some evilness only he could appreciate, the next minute scowling and banging his head with his fists; maybe it was because John Henry delighted in sticking pins under his fingernails and in the tip of his tongue just to see if he could stand the pain; maybe it was because after awhile he could; maybe it was because he was thirteen when he got his first piece of ass, but in order to get it, used a knife to slice a little part of it off; maybe it was because nobody wanted to report him to the police for fear he might retaliate; maybe it was because John Henry didn't care about being reported one way or the other because the retaliation would have made it all worthwhile; maybe it was because the only thing he ever got for Christmas was a kick in the ass and a crack across the face; maybe it was because the word deplorable wouldn't begin to describe his family life; maybe it was because John Henry never felt loved as a child; maybe it was because after awhile he was so drunk with hatred he didn't care about being loved anyway; or maybe, just maybe it was because John Henry Stevens was one insane son-of-a-bitch.

Whatever the reason(s), it was in the middle of a hot and sticky July 4th afternoon when John Henry hit the road. He was eighteen years old at the time.

Of course, he didn't leave without first taking the time to give his heartfelt goodbyes to each of his cousins, as well as to his aunt and uncle.

The twins, Lyle and Eric, were cordially introduced to each other's dicks, ("loads too fellas"). At first they balked. Then John Henry brandished the little revolver he borrowed from his uncle and all but buried it in one of Lyle's nostrils. At that point, cousin Lyle was able to convince cousin Eric that a little beef was better than a little dying. Before he left, John Henry bid the twins adieu by giving each of them a kiss on the forehead with a two-by-four. It wasn't bad, just enough to dull the senses and slow them up for a few hours.

Cousin Maggie, she got her goodbye in the form of a longneck, beer bottle butt-fuck, although truth be told, John Henry was a little taken aback because she seemed to enjoy it so much. I mean what the hell, she kept grunting out the name Joe Faster, or maybe it was Faster Joe, John Henry couldn't remember. Nevertheless, after a while it kinda pissed him off so he yanked the bottle out of her ass and smashed it over her head. Again, it wasn't very serious - just a take six aspirins and call me in the morning type of thing.

Cousin Buck Teeth was John Henry's favorite. Consequently, she got to eat an itty-bitty gardener snake, six inches, tops. Actually, it wouldn't have been all that bad except it was alive when he fed it to her. As soon as she swallowed the last chewy morsel John Henry intended to give her the same two-by-four kiss goodbye he gave to the twins. But as luck would have it, it wasn't necessary. Cousin Buck Teeth passed out on her own. (It must've been something she ate).

As for Aunt Rose, after being stripped of every stitch of clothing, she was left in the bed, bound, gagged and covered with honey from toe to chin. John Henry figured the bed full of cockroaches would enjoy it. Oh yeah, so would the two or three honey bees floating around the room.

Last, but certainly not least, was Uncle Ray. He was bound, gagged and left on the kitchen floor with a handful of worms and at least a half dozen good sized leeches to explore the variety of razor blade cuts decorating his naked body. It was fitting, in light of the fact John Henry always thought of his uncle as a bloodsucker.

CHAPTER 42

Abilene, Kansas resembled the other "nothing special cities" John Henry traveled through in the four months since he left his aunt and uncle's house. Except for one thing, the waitress at Chuck & Buck's Diner. At first John Henry hardly noticed her. Oh sure, he saw that she was pretty alright, maybe even sexy. It's just that John Henry hadn't had a decent meal in two days, so when the old man offered to buy, he couldn't think of anything else but eating. Not only that, but the way he was shoveling the food in his mouth, it was a small wonder he even had time to look up from his plate.

Yet, at some point John Henry must have found the time, because as soon as they were back on the road he envisioned himself in the company of the waitress' young, healthy chest. First he pictured them from a side angle. There they were in full blossom, standing straight out, pushing her waitress uniform to its maximum stretch. Then he pictured them from the front. Still in full blossom and still standing straight out, only now they were just a button away from falling out altogether. John Henry started by unbuttoning her uniform from the bottom up (save the best button for last). In no time at all he was unbuttoning the top button first (why wait?). Before long John Henry saw himself pawing, clawing and ripping the uniform completely off (fuck the buttons!). It got to the point where the hardness in John Henry's pants made him forget he was even in the truck.

Leave it to the old fart to bring him back to earth. "Did I tell ya I'm headin' ta Lincoln ta see my sister. She's purdy bad off. Got the cancer and all. Husband died a year ago for the same thing. Damn shame. Gotta couple kids but they ain't nowhere ta be found. Damn shame alright, damn shame." The old man paused long enough to clear his throat and swallow whatever it was he had in it. "Say, ya got any family?"

Yes, John Henry knew the old man was going to Lincoln. He was also heading in that direction, which is why he asked the old fart if he could hitch a ride in the first place. No, John Henry didn't know about the sister with the cancer, nor did he care for that matter. And as for his own family, not that it was any of the old fart's business, as far as John Henry was concerned, they all died the moment he was born. For a couple of seconds John Henry thought about verbalizing his answer. Then he figured, why bother, it's like talking to an idiot.

The old man glanced at his hitchhiking passenger half expecting to hear a little conversation. When all he got in return was the silence of somebody staring off into space, he shrugged his shoulders and wrote it off as rude behavior.

Twenty miles later, just as the old Ford pickup exited off Interstate 70, the

Shell gas station sign jumped into view like a big fluorescent yellow balloon and broke John Henry's tranquil gaze and relaxed, but thirsty, always thirsty state of mind. At that moment he realized how much he preferred total darkness over everything else. Maybe it had something to do with all the time spent locked away in the crawl-space basement and closet. The thought had merit, John Henry would concede to that, but not as much as he would to the belief there was more to it than that. What, he didn't know exactly. But, there was definitely something. It was as if the answer was wandering around in the darkness, waiting to be found.

"I'm gonna see 'bout takin' me a shit. That blueberry pie I had when we was back in Abilene is wantinna poke its head out," the old man announced with a slight case of urgency.

John Henry would have liked to ignore the old fart, but after being with him for the last five hours the sound of his hillbilly twang had become, pathetically, all too familiar. It clung to his every word just like the foul stench of stale tobacco clung to his three day old cigar stub, which, by the way, looked like a chewed up tootsie roll hanging from his lips.

"Long as we're here we oughta filler up. 'Course she only needs 'bout a quarter tank." The old man pulled into the gas station like he was heading for the finish line. It was a whiplash waiting to happen and John Henry braced his hand against the dash to keep his upper body from jumping forward. It turned out to be a good move because the old man stopped so suddenly, his own fat ass almost lifted off the seat, and he was at least a hundred pounds heavier than John Henry.

John Henry covered his eyes and shook his head.

"Wallet's inside the glove box," the old man said nonchalantly.

John Henry uncovered his eyes.

The old man was far too busy huffing and puffing his way out of the truck to give his words, or the hitchhiking traveler he said them to, a second thought. It wasn't as if the truck was high off the ground or anything. It was a normal size pickup. It's just that it was driven by a real short guy with a real hefty appetite. It made getting in and getting out look more like climbing up and climbing down.

John Henry watched the old man waddle his shit filled ass towards the gas station. When he disappeared inside the debate started.

Abilene, huh? Hell, Abilene's got a rich cowpoke history. And it can't be, what, twenty, maybe twenty-five miles back the other way. Fuck, by the time the old fart gets done telling the cops I'm heading east, I'll already be back there lookin' at those beautiful tits. Wonder what they look like bouncing up and down anyway?

Lincoln...I don't even know why I was going there, come to think of it. It's not like there's anything to do...and as far as I know there ain't dick to see but a bunch of stinkin' cows. Sure, I gotta head in that direction eventually. But so what, it's still just a direction, it's not a destination. And what the hell, eventually means eventually, it doesn't mean today. Still, I am halfway there and it'd probably be a helluva lot easier if I just keep going that way.

By now the old man had to either be pulling down his drawers or filling up the porcelain so John Henry grabbed the wallet out of the glove compartment. After counting out four hundred big ones he snickered quietly and slid over to the driver's side.

End of debate. Abilene it was.

CHAPTER 43

Cindy Joe Lyons moved with her family from Oklahoma City to Abilene when she was 16 years old, although she didn't go quietly. After all, in the course of a single family barbecue, complete with hotdogs, baked beans, potato chips, Budweiser for her mama and daddy, flies the size of helicopters, and humidity thick enough to choke a desert lizard, Cindy Joe went from being an incoming senior in high school, complete with friends, the prom, homecoming (she was even thinking about running for Homecoming Queen), graduation and all the other bells and whistles that went with being a senior, to a new city, with new faces, no friends, no prom, no homecoming (certainly no shot at becoming Homecoming Queen), and no bells to chime or whistles to blow.

Yet, all her mama could say after watching Cindy break down, in what seemed like an endless parade of tears, was, "don't worry sugar, you'll meet lot's of friends. You're such a pretty girl. You'll be popular in no time at all. Girls'll be callin' to go shoppin'. Boys'll be callin' for dates. Just you wait-n-see."

Boys? Cindy Joe didn't wanna hear nothin' about no boys! She already had Bobby Galloway. Had him ever since the tenth grade. Now her mama and daddy expected her to leave him. Leave Bobby? How could they do that to her? How could they be so damn cruel. It wasn't fair! She and Bobby were in love. It wasn't fair! And what happens when all the other girls start chasin' after him? Oh, they'll chase him alright, never you mind about that. Hell, it happened to Donna Lynn last year, didn't it? Donna said it even happened to Mary Jean the year before, and she was the prettiest girl in school. Worse yet, Mary Jean didn't even move away when it happened to her. She only went on a summer vacation to Yellow Stone Park in Colorado, or maybe it was Idaho. Oh what difference does it make where the stupid park was anyway. Cindy Joe wasn't goin' to no damn park. She was movin' away and Bobby was gonna be up for grabs. And why on earth not? He's real cute. He even has his own pickup. And when he ain't at football practice he's got a real good job workin' at his daddy's hardware store.

Since most of Cindy Joe's crying time had already been spent with her head buried, in what had become a tear soggy pillow, she used the last of the Kleenex to blow her nose. No matter, as soon as Cindy Joe started thinking about her and Bobby doing the wild thing she started blubbering all over again and no amount of Kleenex in the house would've made a dent.

"Come on over here," Bobby used to say. "Come on and sit on my lap. Come on here and let me lick your ears. Oooh baby, you're so yummy, you're my little sweet like cider Cindy girl, that's what ya are, my sweet like cider Cindy girl." Cindy Joe loved the ear licking routine because it invariably lead to the wild thing, something Cindy Joe really liked doing. Even more than Bobby. Come to think of it, a helluva lot more than Bobby, and he was a healthy teenage boy.

But that was four years behind her, and until John Henry Stevens walked back into Chuck & Buck's Diner to hunt out the waitress with the beautiful tits, all but forgotten about.

Cindy Joe had just slipped through the two-way aluminum doors separating the kitchen from the rest of the diner when she caught sight of John Henry planting his ass in one side of the booth and his backpack in the other. "My god," she uttered, loud enough for the counter waitress to hear, but quiet enough to hide the words from anyone else in the restaurant, "for a second that guy over there reminded me of my old boyfriend Bobby."

The other waitress, the one with the beautiful tits, her real name was Sherry Sharp. She glanced at John Henry, then looked over her shoulder to her best friend. "Well I'd say if he looks anything like your old boyfriend then your old boyfriend was pretty cute."

"He was," Cindy Joe assured her, "but now that I've had a couple of seconds ta look, this guy don't look nothin' like Bobby. For one thing, this guy's cuter."

"Well he must think your kinda cute too 'cause he ain't stopped starin' at ya since he sat down."

It was true. John Henry might have come all the way back to Chuck & Buck's Diner because of the waitress with the beautiful tits, but as soon as he sat down he saw a pair he liked better. What John Henry liked even more was watching them bounce as Cindy Joe latched on to a pot of coffee and made her way over to the booth.

One thing about it, as soon as she got within close-up viewing distance she forgot all about the coffee, focusing her attention on John Henry's features instead. She was quick to notice the smooth skin and straight, baby fine blond hair, but the two things Cindy Joe found most intriguing were John Henry's chin and green eyes. There was something about the way his chin narrowed, which forced his cheekbones to angle upwards, creating a tapered, but resolute appearance on his face. Cindy Joe wasn't sure if she saw that kind of look on a guy before. Then there were his green eyes. On the one hand they were clear and bright, warm and inviting. On the other hand, the overly large black pupils made them look icy and dark, isolated and inaccessible. They were eyes that looked at you on their way to looking through you. Cindy Joe was certain she never saw that kind of look before on anyone. Yet, she liked it because the eyes intimidated and desired her simultaneously.

John Henry cracked a crooked little smile and it broke Cindy Joe's concentration. "Oh, I'm sorry," she said, suddenly embarrassed by the fact she was standing there like an idiot holding a pot of coffee and doing nothing with it. "You look...I mean, for a second there you reminded me of someone." Cindy Joe was hoping her bullshit response wasn't as noticeable to John Henry as it was to her.

"Who?" John Henry may have asked a one word question but it was more than enough to make the edge in his voice obvious.

Cindy Joe moved out of her parents' house on her eighteenth birthday. In the two years that followed her biggest concern was picking between all the guys that wanted to get in her shorts, not how to go about making them interested. She may've been a babe in the woods when her family first moved to Abilene, but it wasn't long before she discovered how to shake it for the guys she wanted. And right then she wanted John Henry Stevens. "You look like you could use a cup of coffee," Cindy Joe said, fully aware that she didn't answer his question.

John Henry was aware of it also, but frankly didn't give a fuck.

Cindy Joe could have easily grabbed the coffee cup on John Henry's place setting but purposely reached for the cup on the place setting beside him. It allowed for maximum stretch appeal.

Figuring it would be impossible to see much before morning, John Henry had dumped the old fart's pickup truck behind one of those big advertising signs along the highway. From there he lugged his backpack three miles to the diner, working up quite a thirst in the process, all of which made coffee the last thing he wanted. Still he waited until she finished pouring the coffee, (let's face it, who wouldn't), before he said, "I'd rather have a glass of water."

Cindy Joe gave John Henry her best sexy smile and said, "sure."

John Henry took great delight in watching the tight little ass inside the tight little uniform sway from side to side as she went to find a pitcher of water. In the process Cindy Joe decided to bring John Henry a piece of blueberry pie.

For his part John Henry would've welcomed just about any kind of pie, except a piece of the same shit initiating blueberry pie the old man ate not all that long ago. Hells bells, he got it anyway. Of course his tune quickly changed once Cindy Joe set the plate down, tossed her tinted blond curls over her shoulders and launched into her best silky voice routine. "My name's Cindy Joe, if ya need help eatin' that, let me know. I'll be glad to show you how." She paused long enough to let the ends of her mouth curl up. "On me," she added, with a wink.

John Henry may have had an IQ of 172 in his brain and dry ice in his bones, but in his eighteen years of living nothing he'd ever read or felt made him feel like a happy little puppy dog, until that very moment. Was it the sultry voice? Could be. The suggestive look in her dark brown eyes? Perhaps. The way she swung her ass when she walked? Possibly. Or maybe it was a combination of all three...then again, maybe it was something altogether different. Let's face it, one never knows, does one?

Whatever the case, John Henry was certain of one thing. Cindy Joe could make his tail wag.

CHAPTER 44

Chuck & Buck's Diner had all the trappings of a typical serve it up, slop it down, truck stop. Bright, yet nondescript to the eye, accommodating to the nose, hot and greasy to the stomach.

One other thing about Chuck & Buck's Diner, due to its centralized location and the kind of people that wandered in during the wee hours of the night, it slowly gained a reputation as being a good place to find drugs. We're not just talkin' marijuana and hashish here, we're talkin' drugs such as LSD, peyote and psilocybin. We're talkin' the space-age stuff, drugs with an oomph, drugs with a personality, drugs tailor-made to be swallowed, snorted and smoked by anyone looking to go from warp drive to hyperspace, which at times included none other than the owner and operator of Chuck & Buck's Diner himself, the irrepressible Chuck Buckley.

Chuck Buckley stood five feet, ten inches, had a long ponytail wrapped up in a tight braid, a full set of tattoos on each arm, wide shoulders, and a belly that looked like it was carrying around a keg of beer. His jeans, hanging halfway down his little ass, always looked two sizes too big, while his tee shirts, all with the same yellow stains under the armpits, even though they were difficult to see because all of his tee shirts were black, always looked two sizes too small. He had a nasty scar running the length of his forehead, the result of introducing his motorcycle to a car windshield, a mustache and beard that hid some of the rough skin on his face, brown eyes that often squinted, seldom blinked, but forever exaggerated his slightly twisted nose, and a loud, rugged voice to top it off. Chuck also had the heart of three people, especially when it came to doing favors for Cindy Joe and Sherry Sharp.

He did them for Sherry because she was roommates and best gal pals with Cindy Joe. He did them for Cindy Joe because he was in love with her. Had been from the moment she walked into the diner looking for a job. Unfortunately for Chuck, Cindy Joe didn't love him back. Sad? Yeah, it was actually. Sad enough for Chuck to anguish over it every now and again. Surprised? Nah, not even a little. Hell, Chuck looked in the mirror. He knew that guys like him didn't get girls like Cindy Joe, especially when the guys like him were almost twice as old. It just wasn't in the cards. Suffice it to say, Chuck played the hand he was dealt. He fed her all the drugs she wanted, (free of course), ran whatever personal errands Cindy Joe might bat her eyes and request, gave her cash, above and beyond the money she earned waiting tables at the diner, and did it all knowing full well the only thing he was gonna get in return was the chance to play big brother whenever he found it necessary, which is exactly how he found it after meeting John Henry Stevens.

It started with the limp handshake. Chuck figured any normal eighteen year old kid just starting to grow workman size calluses like John Henry would have way too much ego not to squeeze as hard as he could, especially with a girl like Cindy Joe standing there watching. Two weeks later it moved to the lack of sparkle in his eyes. Forget the color green. Everytime Chuck Buckley locked eyeballs with John Henry all he could see was his big pupils and their likeness to dull black glass. They made John Henry look preoccupied in thought, most times even distant, as if he embodied the spirit of a stranger rather than an acquaintance, of a foe rather than a friend. Not only that, but when blended with the self-restraint he carried around so effortlessly, his glass-like pupils made him look older than he really was. It ended ten days after that. One minute John Henry was sitting on the floor in Cindy Joe's apartment taking a regular turn on one of the many hash oil soaked joints making the rounds, the next minute he was up and out the door. No goodbye, no see ya in a while, no wave of the hand, no tip of the hat, no nothin'. Just up and gone. Poof!

But that's not what convinced Chuck Buckley he had cause for concern. Let's face it, if John Henry was just stepping outside to get some air, no big deal, right? Right. Chuck Buckley's concern didn't settle in for another four hours, when his own marijuana induced sleep was awakened to the sight of John Henry hovering over him like the room darkness itself. His immediate reaction was to spring up from Cindy Joe's couch, but sensing that very response, as well as wanting to play the game by his rules, John Henry moved quickly. He steadied his right knee on the side of the couch, firmly planted his right glove covered hand on top of Chuck Buckley's chest and brought his left index finger to Chuck's lips to signal for quiet. John Henry closed in to search for a reaction, but half-groggy with sleep and half-foggy from all the reefer he smoked earlier that night, Chuck exhibited no signs of intelligent life.

John Henry returned from the cool black night a tad chilled and a little bit weathered, but his body had so much adrenaline racing through it, it was impossible to determine if his body's faint trembling had to do with the elements on the outside, or the elements on the inside. Yet, when he whispered to Chuck his voice sounded as poised and confident as ever. "You know, I've discovered something. You wanna know what it is?"

By now Chuck had grown accustomed to the room darkness and he could see that John Henry's eyes were wide open, or as Chuck liked to say, "open for life." That meant John Henry was tripping, probably from the LSD Chuck gave Cindy Joe earlier that day. Now every sight and sound, thought and feeling, be it real or imagined, loud or delicate, trite or unusual, plain or colorful, had the potential to alter John Henry's mind. It also meant the fastest way for Chuck to get back to sleep was by humoring John Henry. Don't do nothin' to agitate him. Don't do nothin' to make him laugh. Don't do nothin' to make him cry. Just let 'em talk until he's all talked out. Otherwise, we could be up all fucking night.

"Sure John Henry, what is it?"

John Henry pointed his index finger to the ceiling and wagged it back and forth. "Did ya ever stop to think about the darkness, 'cause I think about it a lot. It's really an amazing thing. People are born in darkness, people die in darkness, but the whole time they're alive they walk around like they're afraid of it. Like something's hiding inside it waiting to eat 'em up or something." John Henry jut his neck out like it was a periscope, glanced from side to side - stopped - snuck a quick peek over his shoulder - stopped again - then suddenly, and without provocation, rotated his head one time in a rapid, circular motion.

Chuck's mouth dropped open, and a bewildered look settled in.

John Henry continued talking, unaware that Chuck found his bizarre head movements so captivating. "I think the strangest thing of all might even be that people don't realize that the darkness is inside them, whether they like it or not. It's inside everyone. You know what I mean?"

There was a momentary pause but Chuck had no intentions of using the time to answer John Henry's question. What would be the point? John Henry was just like anybody else whoever got high on acid. He wasn't waitin' on no answer. On the contrary, he probably wants to ramble on about how the effects of the LSD lead him to some great mystic discovery about the truth of man, heaven and earth.

Chuck was right, John Henry wasn't waiting for an answer. But it had nothing to do with any newly discovered drug prophecy. It couldn't. John Henry wasn't high. He cocked his head to the left and lowered his voice until it was a shade above a whisper. "People sleep when it's dark, that's it. They don't live where it's dark, they don't live when it's dark. But I have, and I know there's nothing to be afraid of. No matter what people think, there's nothing to be afraid of."

Chuck decided as long as he was gonna have to listen to this line of crap his bad back would be much better off if he was sitting up. He initiated movement but John Henry would have none of it.

John Henry stopped wagging his finger and pointed it half an inch away from the bridge of Chuck's nose. "Uh-uh," he cautioned, "or the sky's gonna fall in all around you." John Henry cocked his head to the right and peered down at Chuck like he was an alien from another planet. "I don't think you want that. I don't think it'd be healthy." John Henry narrowed his eyelids until his eyeballs almost disappeared. He curled his upper lip just enough to expose an eyetooth.

Chuck found the threat to be a little chilling. Nevertheless, he did his best to hide any expression of fear or self-doubt, all the while making certain his body stayed relaxed and still.

John Henry pulled his finger away from Chuck's nose and tapped himself on the side of his head. "The darkness lives in here." He paused briefly, then brought his hand down and tapped at the spot where his heart was supposed to be. "Here too."

In another couple of seconds the silence grew to a nice uncomfortable level. John Henry pointed his V shaped fingers towards his eyes. "And here," he whispered with a sneer.

That's it. I've had it, my backs had it, I'm getting up, Chuck declared to himself. Once again he initiated movement, and once again John Henry put a little muscle behind his glove covered hand to suggest to Chuck he remain in place.

Chuck's instincts told him otherwise. He ignored John Henry's subtle suggestion and continued to lift himself up, resting on his elbows only when John Henry started talking again. "You know the wind at night is nothing more than the darkness breathing... the rain at night is only its tears. Did you know when it snows at night it's really an angel giving its blessing to earth."

Chuck sighed and rolled his eyes. Why me lord? What the fuck did I ever do to you? he silently asked.

John Henry didn't pay Chuck's exasperated look any mind. He just added a little more muscle behind his glove covered hand and kept talking. "Did you know the darkness has eyes. It can see through me as well as I can see through you - you think I'm crazy don't you?" John Henry leaned towards Chuck until their noses were almost touching. "The whole time you've been watching me, I've been watching you. You think you know me...eh partner? Well guess what, I know you a helluva lot better." John Henry straightened back up, although his hand remained firm on Chuck's upper torso.

There hadn't been a day in the last three plus weeks when Chuck Buckley didn't walk away from John Henry, mumbling, "this fucker's weird, this fucker's weird, this fucker's weird," as if the more he repeated it to himself, the sooner he'd be convinced of it. This time Chuck mumbled to himself, "this fucker's eerie." He didn't need to repeat the words in order to convince himself either. Chuck also didn't need anymore convincing that he'd had enough of John Henry. "I tried to do it the nice way John Henry. I tried listenin' to ya, but now your talk is turnin' ta bullshit and I ain't gonna stay here and listen ta anymore of it neither. Now either get up so I can get up, or I'm gonna move ya."

John Henry snickered at the thought. "Really, how ya gonna do that?"

John Henry's sarcasm rang in Chuck's ears like an obnoxious bell.

"Move John Henry."

John Henry didn't bat an eye.

"Now, move now." Chuck's menacing glare and warning were met by a smirk and a shake of the head.

"John Henry, I ain't gonna say it again."

"Fuck you Chuckie."

Suddenly the strength and anger of Chuck Buckley's 38 years came roaring into his arms like an avalanche. His chest swelled and his heart beat strong and fast. Without warning, Chuck latched on to the lapels of John Henry's jacket, launched himself up, and at the same time drove John Henry backwards. John Henry was caught by surprise and his arms flailed in the air as he tried to catch his balance. It didn't help. Chuck Buckley's weight and muscle mass were too much and John Henry dropped to the floor. Chuck scrambled to his feet, but since he was a pretty hefty guy, quick for him was slow for John Henry, who, by now, had rolled over, popped back up and moved in to take first crack. He lunged forward and grabbed hold of Chuck's neck. The momentum forced Chuck back a couple of feet but he quickly regained his footing and held firm. He slammed his forearm into the underside of John Henry's arms, causing them to buckle. He followed it up with another forearm and this time John Henry's arms collapsed altogether.

John Henry retreated a full two steps so he could study Chuck's eyes and plan his next move.

Chuck hunched over into his version of a boxing stance, and now flat-footed with knees slightly bent, he rocked back and forth. With his left fist standing guard a good three inches below his chin, Chuck held his right fist down at his side and twirled it around in tight, little circles...waiting for his opponent to climb into the ring...waiting to strike...waiting...waiting...

John Henry stretched his arms out halfway, got up on the balls of his feet...waiting...waiting...

Chuck brought his right fist up to waist level. The twirling got faster, the circles bigger...waiting...waiting...

John Henry swayed back and forth, inching forward on the balls of his feet...waiting to leap forward...waiting...waiting...

Chuck moved to his left. He brought his right hand up a little higher and dropped his left hand a little lower...waiting...waiting...

John Henry brought his arms closer to his body, still inching forward on the balls of his feet...waiting...waiting...waiting...

Bam!

John Henry lunged forward and slammed his hands around Chuck's throat like he was trying to smash a fly between his palms.

The move was so sudden Chuck couldn't react fast enough. But just like before Chuck rammed his forearm into the underside of John Henry's arms, only this time John Henry had a grip worth talking about and his arms, lean and strong, didn't budge. Chuck coughed and gasped but he was a long way from the panic button. He figured if he couldn't break the hold from underneath, he'd go over the top. He reached up and grabbed John Henry by the wrists, squeezing them with such fury it was only a matter of seconds before John Henry's fingers started to loosen, all the invitation Chuck needed to push down on his wrists, utilizing every one of his two hundred and twenty pounds for leverage. Slowly, but ever so surely, John Henry's hands, shaking with their own fervor and rage, came loose. Once free, Chuck charged forward until he slammed John Henry against the makeshift cinder block-plywood wall unit, causing the stereo, record albums, books never read, and a host of other garbage to come crashing to the floor.

By the time Cindy Joe came running out of her room to see what all the noise and commotion was about, John Henry was doing a lousy job fending off the rest of Chuck's blistering attack.

Sherry, on the other hand, never woke up, which was just as well since it was her stereo anyway.

CHAPTER 45

"Ya prouda yourself, ya big, fat ape?" Cindy Joe might have been a helluva lot younger, but when she barked at him like that - whoa Nellie - Chuck would've preferred dealing with Lizzie Borden herself. At least Lizzie used an ax for cutting people in two, not her tongue.

"Naw hell...I'm not proud. You know me better than that. But hell, the son-of-a-bitch is nuts. He tried to choke me to death. What the hell ya expect me ta do?"

John Henry lay stretched out on the floor trying to listen to the conversation between Chuck Buckley and Cindy Joe. But John Henry was never one to forget the past, and with a head throbbing like it was about to explode, he started to reflect back to the time his mother beat him senseless with a frying pan. He was four years old at the time. It certainly wasn't the first beating, it just happened to be the one John Henry remembered as being the first. Maybe it had something to do with his mother tossing him in the crawl-space basement to recuperate. No food, no bandages, no blanket to keep warm. Just him in a cold dark place with a low ceiling. (But hey, who's afraid of the big bad dark anyway?).

John Henry kept his eyes closed until the image of his mother finally disappeared into the image of Cindy Joe, until the musty odor in his mother's house was overtaken by the smell of the marijuana parked in the walls and furniture in Cindy Joe's apartment, until the sound of his mother's bitter, often vociferous tone of voice was lost to the sounds of Chuck Buckley and Cindy Joe Lyons' conversation.

"I didn't expect ya ta do that, that's for sure." Cindy Joe was clearly alarmed. Having never witnessed the results of a real ass kicking before, and with a propensity to talk herself into just about anything, it was easy for her to turn the smallest cuts into the deadliest wounds.

Chuck already defended himself once. He'd be goddamned if he was gonna do it again! "Well it's like I said, the son-of-a-bitch is nuts. He had it coming," he replied indignantly.

"Look at him...my god. Charles Buckley you should be ashamed of yourself!"

Chuck Buckley didn't know what it was about Cindy Joe, but in the twitch of a nose, she could build him up, or crush him like a pretzel. He buried his hands in his pockets, kicked at the carpet and offered nothing in response.

Sounds like she's taking my side, John Henry thought. If she is, at least I'll get a day inside to heal up, which is all John Henry wanted because after that he was planning to leave.

And why not?

John Henry had already been there a month. Stayed for free, ate for free, fucked Cindy Joe, what could be so bad? Although truth be told, John Henry discovered that he didn't give a rat's ass about fucking Cindy Joe anymore. It started out okay, although after the first couple of times it got to be the same old thing. She was always willing to spread 'em, but it was her willingness that dampened John Henry's passion. Plus, with his first college term set to begin in the middle of January, John Henry figured he would arrive six weeks early and use the time to familiarize himself with the new surroundings.

Then, of course, there was the money. John Henry still had the $1,500.00 he ripped off from his aunt, uncle and four cousins after bidding them bon voyage. On top of that he had the $400.00 he lifted from the old fart's wallet inside the old fart's pickup truck. And thanks to Cindy Joe's stupid hiding places in the apartment, John Henry was able to help himself to another $300.00. It was a tidy little circle. John Henry would rip off Cindy Joe, Cindy Joe would think she spent the money, only 'cause she was always too high to think otherwise, Chuck would end up giving her more, and John Henry would take that too.

Yeah, it was definitely a good time to part company.

Besides, it wasn't like John Henry couldn't come back for a little visit.

CHAPTER 46

Who would've thunk it. An insane eighteen year old with a terrific grasp of the Three R's, and the unique ability to place out on every test he ever took, gets a full academic scholarship to Iowa State, and almost immediately, things start to happen. A couple of them strange, a couple of them perverse, all of them outrageous, all of them pathetic.

Lilly Otis had been a Professor at the University for over 27 years. At one time she was even offered the deanship of the English Department. Unfortunately it was just after her fiancee left her standing at the altar. Hurt and troubled, she declined the added pressures of the new position, instead seeking refuge in her house, where she found solace in her cats and peace of mind in the placid setting of her garden.

Professor Otis lived a mile from campus in a subdivision largely populated with other faculty members, professional types and old Victorian style houses with large wrap around porches. It was one of the few subdivisions John Henry Stevens found suitable for his customary midnight strolls. The streetlights were too few and far between to screw up the darkness, the trees were tall, round and numerous, lending a variety of interesting shadows and shapes to the concrete terrain, and the only noise heard was from the prowling wind...except when John Henry passed by Professor Otis' house and her cats were outside screeching, meowing, and carrying on.

But John Henry wasn't giving up on the area just because a few disgusting little furry creatures were ruining it for him. Nosireee Bob, he knew how to take care of them.

It was roughly 12:30 a.m. and due to a charitable function at the University, one of the few times during the year when Professor Otis was out so late. Since the professor never went to bed until sometime after one o'clock in the morning anyway, it was not unusual for her cats to be wandering around in the front or back of the house. It simply depended on the weather. If it was warm enough she let them outside to play. If it was too cold they stayed inside and the whole lot of them curled up on the couch together.

It was late February, and until earlier tonight, extremely cold. Something about a southerly wind kicking up, carrying itself across the country's midsection and dumping unseasonably warm temperatures in the process. It wasn't suntan weather, mind you, but it was 45 degrees, which was certainly warm enough for the cats to play outside until Lilly Otis returned from the school.

Dressed in all black, John Henry's streamlined body was almost impossible to see as he cut through the heavy, mist-like fog lingering close to the ground. When he reached Lilly Otis' porch, all it took was a small plastic container of tuna fish and within seconds all four of the professor's cats appeared.

John Henry waited patiently. Okay, here they come, get ready, he said to himself. Just another second or two. Okay..here they come..."Come on kitty," he mumbled as if he was talking to a baby, "Come on. That's it...there ya go...that's it." John Henry started to pet two of the cats with his glove covered hands. "That's it...that's a nice kitty...you like that...then die ya little fuck!" John Henry snarled. He snatched them up, snapped their necks and dropped their limp bodies back to the porch quicker than a butterfly changes direction. The other two cats got away but John Henry only figured on getting two of the little furry fucks anyway so he really didn't care.

Before he left John Henry tied guitar string slipknots around their necks and hung each cat from the doorknob, where they remained to greet Professor Lilly Otis upon her return.

By the following evening the story was all over the local news. *Professor Lilly Otis Lies Critical From Stroke. Paralysis Feared.* The story went on to say something about how the police think the gruesome murder of two of her cats might have played a role.

John Henry Stevens finished the article and shrugged his shoulders. "Gee I wonder who's gonna feed her other cats while she's laid up?"

CHAPTER 47

Dougie Royal.

As far as John Henry was concerned he was a royal pain in the ass. A real schmuck indeed, straight from his mommy's tit. Never mind if it was cold outside. Dougie always showed up to sociology class looking like he just stepped out of a prep school catalogue, complete with golf shirt, turned up collar, hair ruffled up just so, and a nice, even tan to compliment the tortoise-shell horn rims sitting on his nose.

One look and John Henry hated him.

As if that wasn't bad enough, once in a while Dougie Royal found a seat in the back of the room...next to where John Henry usually had his own ass parked. It was one thing for John Henry to have to look at a squirrely little fuck trying to look smart by pretending to look bored, it was quite another having to endure the squirrely little fuck's nose piercing cologne. As a result, as soon as Dougie would sit down, John Henry would snarl at him and get up to find another seat.

Being the deep thinker he was, it didn't take long for Dougie to figure out why John Henry always scowled at him and moved to another seat. Being the idiot he was, Dougie thought he'd amuse himself, and at the same time, get the best of John Henry by sitting next to him every chance he could, even if it meant following him around the room.

Then one day, about six weeks into the semester, it went from bad to worse. Dougie Royal offered his opinion about the sociological and economic impact of using tax dollars to provide shelters for the homeless. Country club bred looks were one thing. But the smirk on his face, coupled with the condescending attitude in an opinion, long winded, poorly conceived, and crammed with big words that made little sense, was all it took to spring John Henry's madness loose.

It was just after 2:00 a.m. and the last thing John Henry wanted to do was bring life to the apartment building so he made sure to tap lightly on Dougie's first floor apartment door. It might've taken a little longer this way but John Henry wasn't going anywhere. Sooner or later the door was going to open. When it did Dougie Royal would have no more than a second to see a masked figure dressed in black.

John Henry was right. For a split second that's exactly what Dougie saw. What he didn't see was John Henry's glove covered fist come crashing forward, sending his ass to the apartment floor. John Henry stepped inside, pushed the door shut with the back of his heel and introduced Dougie's stunned head to a big, juicy two-by-four. One pop and it was lights out, (which was a good thing).

Actually, it was a very good thing. That way Dougie couldn't feel the two inch Frankenstein-like zipper scar being inscribed into the middle of his forehead with the tip of John Henry's knife. Although, he would get to look at it for the rest of his life.

For that matter, so would everybody else.

CHAPTER 48

Like any other petty thief John Henry always appreciated easy access. That's the one thing he liked about dorm life. On any given day he could explore the hallways and find a handful of unlocked doors. Some of the students might have been forgetful, while others might have been brought up a little too trusting. Either way John Henry had no intentions of analyzing the minds of the ignorant. He was just glad they were, especially when know-it-all Gary Maddin's little brothers came for a weekend visit.

Gary Maddin lived in the dorm room that adjoined John Henry's. Maddin wasn't such a bad guy, he just liked to hear himself talk. His little brothers, on the other hand, were a much different story. Scotty was eight and Trevor was six. Once a month they came to spend the weekend, bringing with them all the noise and spoiled manners they could pack their sloppy little bodies with.

For the most part John Henry stayed clear of the dorm, mainly showing up to change clothes, shower and sleep. Nevertheless, whenever the Maddin brothers were visiting, even the limited time John Henry spent in his room seemed like an eternity. If John Henry was in the shower, they were pounding on the walls. If John Henry was changing clothes, they were outside in the hallway, waiting to attack him with dirty, sticky fingers. Worse yet, if John Henry was out on one of his patented midnight ventures he usually wouldn't get back to his room until three-thirty or four in the morning. By four-thirty he'd be asleep, and two to three hours later the wild little Maddin brothers would be screaming him awake.

But being a man of obscene imagination and wit, John Henry wasted little time in formulating a suitable plan to combat the situation. "If those fucking little Maddin rats wanna make noise, I'll give 'em something to make noise about. When I'm done, they'll never wanna visit big brother again."

Larry Leinenjack lived on the second floor of the eight story dorm, known around campus as The Suites. Larry was considered a little weird, although he was one of the few guys John Henry seemed to have something in common with. Not that John Henry liked him. On the contrary, John Henry thought Larry was an idiot, just like he did everyone else. The thing about Larry was that he had some exotic pets that John Henry liked to visit with every now and then. He had a Piranha named Elvis, a nice furry Tarantula named Spider Man, a small, but rapidly growing Python named Huey, and his most recent purchase, two bite-size baby alligators named Duey and Louie. John Henry got such a kick out of watching the two little gators rip their goldfish dinners to shreds, Larry kept his door open just so John Henry could come in and feed them whenever he felt like it. Even when Larry wasn't home. And with a Python to stand guard who was going to come in Larry's room and rip him off anyway? The answer, of course, was John Henry Stevens. Only John Henry didn't take the stereo, the albums, or any of the standard bullshit that usually gets ripped off. John Henry nabbed Huey, Duey and Louie.

Just because Gary Maddin's little brat brothers came for a weekend visit didn't mean Gary wasn't going out to play. Hell, it was Saturday night! It was drunk night! It was Ladies night! And with his brothers finally sound asleep, it was time! He tried to talk John Henry into going with him, but John Henry had other plans.

It was shortly after midnight when John Henry slipped inside Gary Maddin's room. As usual he was dressed in head to toe black to resemble the other lifeless shadows growing out of the dark. John Henry was somewhat relieved knowing Maddin was one of the ignorant ones and he wouldn't have to break into his room. Having to carry the Huey, Duey and Louie filled pillow case was pain in the ass enough. Of course, it mattered not to Huey, Duey and Louie. That's because it only took a couple of minutes before they grew accustomed to the two little bodies sleeping in the makeshift bed on the floor. Fat, slimy Huey curled up next to the boys' feet, Duey snuggled up under the blanket between Scotty's legs, and Louie found himself a nice warm spot next to Trevor's ear.

Huey's long tongue was flirting with the air, but when it slapped against Scotty's toes his body had a reactionary twitch. So did Duey's. He latched on to Scotty Maddin's underwear covered testicles and the next sound heard was a piercing scream shooting down the hall.

In most cases if Trevor heard his older brother scream he would've started crying instantly. But with Louie hanging from his ear, Trevor had his own screaming to do.

Meanwhile, John Henry sat in the middle of his floor, surrounded by the darkness in his room and the darkness in his mind, laughing quietly.

As it turned out, the entire little episode was good for John Henry because the little Maddin kids never wanted to visit their brother again, bad for Larry Leinenjack because he had to get rid of all his pets, and even worse for the rest of the campus because there was still an animal on the loose.

Gee, who could that be?

CHAPTER 49

Bonnie Bartush and Philly Giles loved to fuck in the backseat of Philly's old Buick. It never mattered where, just so long as the stars in the sky were their only company. It would have been a helluva lot more comfortable if they went at it inside Philly's rented house, but Philly's roommate was Bonnie's boyfriend. The same could also be said about fucking in Bonnie's apartment, but she lived with her boyfriend's sister. Besides, Bonnie and Philly liked the intrigue of sneaking around. It was sleazy. So were they.

Ergo, the Buick.

For the most part John Henry Stevens never had a destination in mind when he set out on one of his midnight adventures. Tonight was no different so it was purely coincidental when his legs carried him to the same lonely street where Philly and Bonnie were parked for some backseat magic. From twenty-five yards out John Henry's crisp night vision honed in on the car's fog covered rear window. He stood motionless, his eyes squinting as though the car itself was made out of sunlight.

Then out of nowhere the voice returned. Again.

Some of the words may have been different from years past...

"Kill the spider. What? No. Kill the spider, kill it! What? Kill it...bury the dog, kill it, bury it alive! What? No. Kill it. Bury it alive, bury it, bury it, bury it...Cut it hard. What? Cut it deep. What? Do it! Cut it hard, cut it deep. Do it. Do it now! Make her bleed. What? Make her bleed. Feel it. What? Wash in it. Wash it away. Do it now!"

But the voice was the same...

John Henry couldn't recall the last time he heard it, but tonight, tonight it kept coming back, greeting him with all the sincerity and comfort of the long lost friend it was. Once an hour, twice an hour, a word here and a word there. John Henry's body went rigid and hard, soft and limp. Three times an hour, four times an hour, bits and pieces of sentences. John Henry's body turned hot and cold, warm and cool. Over and over the same voice, over and over the same words, the same bits and pieces, until finally, the words swelled up and burst in his head. *"To be whole. Inside no shadow lives. No father to be, no mother. No baby to be, no mother. No soul, no mother. Wash in it, wash it away."*

John Henry gazed up at the moon, its glow muted by overcast skies, and rolled his head around until the voice died off like a distant echo in a barren canyon. The nonexistent wind suddenly came alive, swirled through his body, then vanished just as suddenly, leaving its damp residue to rot in his spine. "No shadow," John Henry whispered, "No soul." The words fresh off his tongue, John Henry proceeded towards the car, his long, fluid strides swallowing up the street effortlessly. He stopped when he heard grunting and squealing coming from the inside.

Hopping in the front seat, now that would be a novel approach. So would jumping on the hood and doing a little lovebird tap dance. A cockeyed grin formed at the ends of John Henry's mouth as he dispatched the two choices, and for a second, thought about pressing his face against one of the fog covered windows and giving a Minnie Pearl rendition of the word "howdy."

Maybe next time.

Instead, John Henry put on his trusty ski mask, crouched a few feet behind the car and pointed his thin lips towards the black sky. What began as a soft, melodic whistle, quickly faded to the emptiness of a dull monotone.

The grunting and squealing stopped immediately.

John Henry waited for the silence to settle in before whistling again. He wanted to make sure whoever was inside the car heard exactly what they were afraid they heard.

They did.

"What was that? Someone's out there," Bonnie whispered frantically. She was clutching Philly around his back, the fear in her eyes as revealing as her naked body.

Philly didn't say a word. He was so rattled someone might actually be outside, his hardness melted away without him even realizing it.

"Get off me and go see who's out there," Bonnie pleaded.

"No...no way." For a moment Philly thought his hard charging heart was going to pop out of his chest. He slammed his eyes shut and buried his head in Bonnie's shoulder.

"C'mon, get off me. You're hurting me."

"No. Now just shut up and maybe they'll go away," Philly hushed.

John Henry whistled again.

"Who's there? Whataya want?" Bonnie blurted out.

The stench from the anxiety in her voice was a sweet smelling invitation to John Henry. He sprang to his feet and dashed over to the passenger side of the car to introduce himself. "Howwwwwww-Deeeeeee!" He shrieked. (Minnie Pearl wasn't out of the running after all)

Phillip Giles was a junior at Iowa State. He was majoring in Communications. Known to his friends as Philly, he was found dead early Tuesday morning. An autopsy has been scheduled, although according to police officials, speaking on the condition of anonymity, his death had to do with severe head injuries, caused, in all likelihood, by repeated blows with a blunt object.

The naked body of a young woman was also found. Her identity is being withheld pending further investigation and notification to her family. However, police officials do believe she is a student and was with Phillip Giles at the time of the assault. The extent of her injuries has not been determined and she remains in the hospital in intensive care.

Reading the newspaper article and seeing the images of Philly Giles and Bonnie Bartush come back to life, he with his flattened skull, she in all her bloody nakedness, praying to John Henry, as if he was Jesus Christ himself, inflated John Henry with all the fervor and excitement he felt while standing over them the night before. His body trembled slightly and for an instant the paper rattled in his hand. After all, this wasn't like burying the dog alive or hanging a couple of cats with guitar string. It wasn't even like slapping his cousins around with a two-by-four, or covering his aunt and uncle with bugs and worms. That kind of behavior might have squeezed out a little adrenaline, but when it was over with it was time to go to bed, period. This feeling was different. This was like a frenzied orgasm racing through his bloodstream as fast as it could, settling down only because it grew weary from bouncing off the walls of his veins.

John Henry steadied the paper and continued reading.

Although no motive has been given for the attack the police have thus far ruled out robbery. At this point it is unclear if the female was sexually assaulted. A search is underway for possible witnesses and an earlier report about a pair of bloody gloves found near the scene of the crime has not been confirmed. Beyond that the police appear to have very little to go...

It sure didn't take long. Without reading another word John Henry fired the paper against the wall in disgust, sending with it all the exhilaration, that up to that point, he'd been digesting like oxygen. Suddenly it was clear. A little voice went off in his head - and boom! - he found himself hopelessly dangling in front of the world, about as conspicuous as a fireworks display on the Fourth of July. And it didn't have to be this way. All John Henry had to do was read the signs. If he had, there wouldn't be anything to investigate but the invisibility of the darkness itself. Yet, it wasn't the Bonnie Bartush, Philly Giles episode that triggered the anger and frustration. Oh sure, it complicated matters, but what really upset him was that it started with Lilly Otis and he was too blind to see it, until now. Fucking pitiful, John Henry thought. A couple of cats hang dead, the old lady strokes out and the next thing you know it gets so much local TV play, one would've thought Martian's landed. With Dougie Royal it was the same goddamn thing. One night a little cosmetic surgery on his forehead, and the next day all hell breaks loose in the paper about some midnight assailant with a black face and a sharp knife. It was all there to see and I missed the fucking boat.

What John Henry failed to understand, however, was that he didn't miss the boat because he was too blind to see what was happening, (like he wanted to believe). He missed the boat because of the arrogance mounting inside him.

John Henry's hardened glare burrowed into the floor carpeting as he continued to linger in thought. Too close to home, that's the problem. He shrugged his shoulders without realizing his body moved an inch. Gotta learn to control it, gotta learn to work the darkness better than that. Especially now, 'cause now I heard the voice and felt the words. And it's got nothing to do with hanging cats or drawing scars. It's about life. It's about death. It's about how each becomes the other. It's about washing away impurities. It's about rinsing my body and cleansing my soul. It's all about becoming pure...only no one's gonna understand. They'll try to suffocate me like they suffocate themselves. Sooner or later they'll come for me. But when they do they'll be coming for the darkness. And there won't be anymore closet or crawl-space to hide in. And there won't be anymore darkness to protect me. And there won't be anymore purity out there for me to breath. John Henry dropped his head back until it touched the top of his spine. His bloodshot green eyes scurried back and forth across the ceiling and his breathing picked up to keep pace. It can't happen, I can't let it. I can't die. Gotta live in one place and play in another. Live in one place, play in another. Live in one place, play in another.

With mass transit and plenty of unlocked cars to borrow, he would too, just as soon as he exchanged greetings and salutations with Ginger Brown.

After all, John Henry had arrogance to pacify.

CHAPTER 50

After watching Ginger Brown serve beer for an entire semester, John Henry knew she wouldn't be home before 2:30 in the morning. That's why, despite being thirsty with anticipation, having hand picked her weeks ago, John Henry's uncharacteristically nonchalant attitude was still bright and shiny when it came to hopping her backyard fence and slipping through an unlatched window at 2:00 a.m.

"There's gonna be trouble brewin' in the henhouse tonight," he said, the words playfully skipping off his tongue.

On nights when Ginger was working at the bar, her ex-mother-in-law, Fritzy Cooper, babysat eight month old Chelsea. Ever since Fritzy's son got himself thrown in jail for the third time on drug related charges, Fritzy figured it was the least she could do. It would have been easier for Ginger if her ex-mother-in-law did the babysitting at Ginger's house, but hey, babysitting was babysitting, and if Fritzy didn't mind waking up at 2:30 in the morning when Ginger came to pick up Chelsea, so be it. Besides, it wasn't like Ginger was blessed with a bunch of ready-made alternatives.

Unless she was suffering through a restless night, little Chelsea was usually sound asleep by the time her mother arrived. Tonight was no exception. Chelsea didn't even wake up when Ginger carried her from the warm crib into the night air, wrestled to get the car door open and strapped her into the car seat. As a matter-of-fact, the only time Chelsea woke up the entire night was when she heard her mother scream. It was a short scream, but Ginger's lungs were healthy so it was still a pretty good effort. It happened just as she opened up her bedroom closet and saw the figure of a man standing inside, dressed in black from head to toe.

Ginger darted for the door but John Henry was quicker. He seized her arm and hurled her against the wall, so hard in fact, she almost lost consciousness. Normally John Henry would have pounced on Ginger right then and there, only this time he hesitated long enough to soak up her helpless condition. It served as another endorsement of his new found strength, which in the last few months alone, seemed to have almost doubled. What used to take effort now took sweatless energy, and John Henry was both delighted and dazzled by it.

Ginger tried desperately to catch her breath so she could at least give screaming another shot, but John Henry had other plans. He three stepped his way over to her quivering body and proceeded to bang her head against the wall with relentless fury. "No mother, no soul, no mother, no soul, no mother, no soul." What started out as a whisper, ended deep and raspy.

Before long, Ginger was rendered unconscious. Before long, Ginger was just this side of death. Before long, Ginger was perfect rape material. That was another thing John Henry discovered about himself. A good, hearty rape was the only kind of sex that got his rocks off.

And let there be no mistake. John Henry was so proud of his strength he decided to let it rip one more time. As soon as he finished with sweet Ginger Brown, he sauntered into Chelsea's room, picked up the antique rocking crib, baby and all, and launched it against the wall.

Not to worry. Baby Chelsea only suffered a broken arm and a broken leg. It could've been worse. She could've ended up a rape victim with a concussion, as well as a lifelong member of the trauma club like her mother. Actually it could've been much worse. She could've ended up like Bonnie Bartush.

Oh yeah, Bonnie never made it out of intensive care.

CHAPTER 51

By the time John Henry Stevens was in the middle of his senior year at Iowa State, having completed his undergraduate work in just three years, he murdered six more people, five of whom lived anywhere from 250 to 300 miles away from the university. And the voice that first whispered to John Henry as a child, soothing him like the warm blanket he never had, the same voice that disappeared for months and months at a time as he got older, returning just when he figured it deserted him for good, the same voice that invited him to the surprise party for Philly Giles and Bonnie Bartush, was with John Henry every step of the way...

There was Dianne Wheaton. She was a pretty little thing, with two young kids, a healthy marriage, a strangled neck and a skull smashed to pieces by a sledge hammer.

"No soul, no mother. Wash in it. Wash it away."

There was Joy Gooden. Another pretty little thing, especially since her pregnant condition brought, what looked like a warm glow to an already warm smile. Nonetheless, she wasn't glowing the morning she was discovered face up in a parking lot with a broken neck and a body split open from eyeball to gizzard.

"No baby to be, no mother. No baby to be, no father."

There was Elaine Keebler, owner of Elaine's Tanning Salon and wife of Dr. William Keebler. He was a prominent psychiatrist, highly sought after speaker, and moderately successful author, having penned two books about the social interaction of straight and gay couples over fifty. Unfortunately his credentials were useless when it came to helping the police figure out why someone would want to strangle his wife, then char-grill the rest of her body by sealing it inside a tanning bed.

"No shadow. No soul."

There was Lucinda Reynolds. John Henry decided to kill her only because he never killed a nigger before. Much to his dismay, John Henry discovered her body bled, her bones bruised, and her neck snapped just like everyone else's.

"No..."

And of course, there was the irrepressible Chuck Buckley.

You didn't really think John Henry was going to forget about him now, did you? Well parish the thought. Not a day went by since John Henry left Abilene when the Chuckster didn't cross his mind. And for good reason. Chuck Buckley not only beat the living shit out of him, he humiliated him something fierce in the process. It was bad enough John Henry had to endure being humiliated everyday of his life while growing up, first by his loving mother, then by his loving aunt, uncle and cousins. But Chuck Buckley? Nah! It wasn't in the cards.

It was spring break and two weeks before classes were scheduled to start up again. John Henry didn't get the entire time off because he had a job as an administrative assistant in the university library. But that was okay. He got a few days, more than enough time to slip into Abilene, pay his respects to Chuck, and slip back out without anyone ever knowing he was there. Except, of course, for Chuck. He'd know. By all means, he'd know.

Not much had changed about Chuck and Buck's Diner on the outside. The sign still flickered on and off as though the skinny fluorescent tube lettering was running out of gas. The parking lot still had more deteriorating asphalt than not. The dirty windows were still dirty, even filthy, depending on who you ask, and a greasy odor continued to emanate from the vents, welcoming anyone with an appetite for bad food.

From what John Henry could tell, not much had changed on the inside either. Sherry Sharp still had a nice set of tits. Cindy Joe still shook her ass from New York to Los Angeles when she walked, and Chuck Buckley was still a fat tub of shit who preferred closing up the diner all by his lonesome.

John Henry waited outside the back door, dug in like a batter at homeplate with a three-two count and the bases loaded.

The seconds evaporated into the late night air as Chuck fumbled with the doorknob from the inside. Finally the exit light clicked off, the door swung open, and Chuck Buckley lumbered outside.

"Hi Chuckie."

"Huh?"

"Eeeeeeoughhhhh!" John Henry wailed, making solid contact between the steal pipe in his hands and the teeth in Chuck's mouth. Chuck's head slammed against the door frame, but before it could follow the rest of his crumpled body to the ground, John Henry clamped down around his rubbery neck and squeezed every ounce of life from his lungs. After which, John Henry hammered a rough carpentry nail into each one of Chuck's temples and dragged him over to a tree. As strong as he was, in addition to how strong he thought he was, John Henry found hoisting Chuck's dead fat ass off the ground to be quite a chore. He settled on standing Chuckie on his head, where he secured him by tying his ankles to the tree. Still, it did the job. Yesireeee Bob, it did the job all right.

By morning the pressure in Chuck's head was so intense one of his eyes popped out while the other one waited its turn in the on-deck circle. It made for a helluva sight. Yet, rather than stick around until morning so he could gawk at it like Cindy Joe and the rest of them were bound to do, John Henry preferred, instead, to quietly slip away into the night. Although when he did, the voice no longer followed him like a shadow.

It didn't have to anymore. Its soul was waltzing in his mind, and its spirit was mingling with his blood. It was with John Henry to stay...for good.

Of course, it always had been. It was him.

CHAPTER 52

What if Cain was Able and Moses was the Pharaoh? What if Robin Hood was the Sheriff Of Nottingham? What if Jack The Ripper was the King Of England? What if Napoleon was the Pope? What if Jeckyl and Hyde were Hyde and Jeckyl? What if there was no Jeckyl? What if the Lone Ranger was Wild Bill and Tonto was Crazy Horse? What if Hamilton was Burr and Arnold was Washington? What if Lincoln was Davis? What if Grant was Lee? What if Zorro had no sword and Bowie no knife? What if Lucas McCane had no rifle? What if Custer had nuclear power? What if Leopold was Lobe and Lobe was Lindbergh? What if Lindbergh was Luciano? What if Oppenheimer was Einstein and Einstein was Hitler? What if Harpo was Bozo and Groucho was Carl? What if Larry was Moe, Moe was Curly and Curly was Shemp? What if Pan was Hook? What if Elvis was the Walrus? What if Spock was Vader? What if Darwin was Adams and Spokes was Cheetah? What if Bryan was Darrow? What if the Holy Grail was the Anti-Christ? What if Merlin was Oz and Oz was Houdini? What if day was night? What if Houdini was me? What if I was a lizard and could shed my skin?

Would I be Houdini or would I be a lizard? Would I be night or would I be day? Or would I still be me???

As John Henry sat naked in the middle of his tiny closet, arms draped across his shoulders, knees digging into his chest, and darkness raging from every corner, it was as if a lightbulb went on in his head...

And a Dissertation was born.

CHAPTER 53

In summation, poly-mesh, as I have termed it, can be defined simply as a nylon based material made to resemble skin. Name notwithstanding, the concept remains rather basic, albeit the existence of certain technical complexities.

As I have previously suggested in the facts and data, this process can best be accomplished by embedding skin cells in a nylon-mesh culture. These cells will send off proteins and growth hormones to help generate new tissue. The molecular weight can thereafter be reduced by oxidizing the mixture until such time as it can absorb, contain and allow moisture to permeate its synthetic structure. This synthetic structure, while it embodies strong adhesive-like qualities, similar to the way skin tissue binds itself to other skin tissue, would seemingly encompass a more natural feel of skin if real tissue samples had been introduced into the chemical balance, although that was not done here. As a result, it remains speculative at this juncture.

Nevertheless, the synthetic structure is economical in that, like a polymer (poly), it has the ability to be re-used simply by thawing it out and reheating it. Therefore, its functions and purposes could be endless, bound only, perhaps, by the limitations of man's own imagination.

After finishing the brief conclusion to John Henry's dissertation, Physics Professor Randall P. Rooney stroked his baggy chin, swayed his head back and forth to the tick-tock sounds coming from the wall clock, and pondered the subject matter. Of course, since the professor only read the conclusion there wasn't much to ponder. As if that wasn't bad enough, had the school not required all grades to be turned into the administration office by 10:00 a.m. the following morning for processing, Professor Rooney wouldn't have even read that much. For the past several months he'd been far too busy to read much of anything, what with his own experiments involving under the tongue injections of speedballs, a potentially deadly combination of heroin and speed. And with only three more conclusions to get through and three more dissertations to grade, it would only be another thirty minutes, (start counting), before the bald headed, short legged, overstuffed, bespectacled, one time bible fearing mama's boy and ex-hippie, conducted another such experiment.

Of course, it was just as well the professor didn't read John Henry's dissertation anyway. The data wasn't all inclusive.

For example, there wasn't any data included about the two people John Henry sliced, diced, and turned into his own little experiments.

CHAPTER 54

Maybe it was because of his deep sense of commitment to society; maybe it was because of his strong belief in right versus wrong; maybe it was because he felt a kinship with the moral fiber of a cohesive system, rather than one of utter chaos; maybe it was because no one ever figured he'd amount to much; maybe it was because he felt comfortable knowing his level of intelligence would allow him to pull it off without much trouble; maybe it was because it would give him a chance to play on both sides of the fence; maybe it was because it would give him an opportunity to study the criminal mind; maybe it was because it would provide him with the ability to make a good living and buy the kinds of things he never had before, clothes for instance; maybe it was because he'd be entering a field of work that would spare him from the kind of humiliation he received as a kid; maybe it was because it was another step in some self-serving grandiose scheme; maybe it was a combination of all these things, some of these things, none of these things, or maybe, just maybe, it was because he wanted to.

Whatever the reason(s), John Henry decided to go to law school at Iowa State.

He quit two years later...

Maybe it was because he got bored with life in Iowa and wanted to move; maybe it was because he hated the smell of cowshit; maybe it was because after two years he figured he knew enough law to get by; maybe it was because when John Henry threw a dart at a map it landed on Madison, Wisconsin, which was good since he'd always been a Green Bay Packers fan and carried around the silly notion of donning a cheese hat on his head; maybe it was because he had a dream one night of Big Ten dancing girls singing the University Of Wisconsin fight song while doing the shimmy-shimmy-shake-shake; maybe it was because he wanted to be a stranger in a strange land; maybe it was because he wanted to use fake names and phony I.D.s; maybe it was because John Henry wanted to be Houdini, maybe it was because he wanted to be two people at once; maybe it was because he wanted to be a lizard and shed his skin; maybe it was because he wanted to be both day and night; maybe it was because he wanted to be both night and day; maybe it was because John Henry decided the time was right to make good on the subject matter of his dissertation; maybe it was because he still wanted to be a lawyer; maybe it was because John Henry believed in order to do both, all he had to do was introduce skin tissue from the fingers of a law school student to a batch of his homemade, chemically enriched, poly-mesh material and he would be; maybe it was a combination of all these things, some of these things, none of these things, or maybe, just maybe, it was because he wanted to.

Whatever the reason(s), John Henry Stevens moved to Wisconsin, where under the name and guise of Hank Connors, he rented a cheap, slab house on a secluded street from some old lady, took a job in the library at the University of Wisconsin Law School, and searched out an unsuspecting law school student to befriend.

In no time at all Hank Connors...er, excuse me, John Henry Stevens, found him too. He was 26 years old with a little less than a year to graduation. He was also pigeon-toed, short limbed, carried twenty pounds more than he should have, didn't have enough hair to make it to his 40th birthday, but had firmly entrenched crows-feet, which made him look as if turning forty was already a thing of the past. Other than that he was a soft spoken, well mannered, "I'll do anything you wanna do," type of guy. Best of all he had no family, and except for Hank Connors, no friends to attend his graduation, or to come looking for him when he disappeared, which of course, allowed Hank Connors...oops, I mean John Henry, to strangle him, cut off his fingers for skin tissue use, bury him in the homemade grave he dug underneath the old lady's house, and slip into the person of his victim without incident.

Abracadabra!

The night becomes the day.

CHAPTER 55

PRESENT DAY

The thing Keona Raven remembered most about the Arizona desert was the way the sun changed from blazing yellow to deep orange as it gradually slipped below the horizon, a horizon where endless mountains of sand stood like broad shoulders neath the spirits of twilight's desolate shadows.

But that was another time, a time when Keona's formative years were filled with stories about the lives and cultures of his Apache ancestors, even though Keona himself would've been treated like an outcast half-breed had he been born a hundred years earlier.

As it was Keona was still considered somewhat of an outcast, at least by those who couldn't understand why he would give up making good money playing pro football for the Chicago Bears to making no money running a nonprofit drug rehabilitation center in Wisconsin. Then again, those same people probably couldn't understand how, for the last five or so years, Keona was still able to see his vision of the desert sun while watching the early morning summer fog stretch its body across the tranquil waters of Lake Kegonsa, a short distance from Madison.

But Zack Darwin was never one to question Keona Raven about the things he did or the things he saw, which, in a sentence, best explains why the two remained friends long after their college football days at Illinois were over.

It also helps explain why Keona never questioned Zack about who Billy Turner was and why it was so important he juggle a couple of people around just to make room in the rehab center for Wanda Seven.

Of course, the answer was simple.

Billy Turner's appeal was granted, his conviction overturned, and after spending the first two months of freedom re-establishing his seedy drug presence on the streets, he was back on the prowl looking for the one great love of his life. The one he turned into a junkie, beat the shit out of more often than he raped, and whose disappearance he blamed on Max Cougar simply because his fat attorney, Bernard Forest, suggested as much.

Now all he had to do was find her. Okay, so he struck out when he went looking for her in the apartment they once shared, so what? How hard could finding Wanda really be, Billy wondered. Hell, to find her all he really had to do was find Max Cougar, a nothing cop with an everyday office.

Besides, Max never hid from anybody so that made it even easier.

The collision on the other hand, now that was hard.

CHAPTER 56

Billy Turner parked his bright and shiny, three year new caddy down the street from the police station, took a quick peak at himself in the visor mirror, then settled back in his seat as if he was at a drive-in and the movie wasn't gonna start for another hour or so. Five minutes later his hands tightened around the steering wheel, his back turned rigid and the hair on the back of his neck stood at attention. It was 8:30 in the morning and Max Cougar just swallowed the steps leading into the police precinct.

At noon Billy was still sitting there, tinted hair, electric tan, numb ass, simmering anger and all, when finally, Max came back out of the building. He was with the Beast and the two of them hurried across the street and headed to the Curbside Tavern for a quick lunch. Billy slowly climbed out of the caddy, dusted off the stiffness in his back, and followed.

Now that Eddie Hart turned out to be nothing more than a pathetic dead-end lead and their attention was focused on finding Billy Turner, the last of the three suspects in the murder investigation of Kathy and Jack Reed, Max and the Beast sat at a corner table trying to decide where to look for him first.

One thing was for sure. They certainly didn't figure on finding him in the restaurant. As a result, when Max looked up from his menu and saw Billy Turner standing spitting distance behind the waitress he was getting ready to give his order to, a stunned look filled his face about as quick as the water from a fire hydrant would fill a hose.

The Beast saw his partner's expression and knew it was more than just a Kodak moment. It was an invitation to turn around. When he did, his head and entire upper body moved as one large unit. "Son-of-a-bitch," he mumbled in his deep, raspy voice to no one in particular, "son-of-a-bitch."

The waitress backed up a couple of steps, peered over the glasses sitting halfway down her pug nose and said, "excuse me." She wasn't exactly certain what it was she heard, but it was obvious by the tone in her voice she was preparing to get mad just in case it was something she didn't like.

Max peeled his eyes away from Billy and let them crash head-on with the waitress. He realized the waitress didn't have any idea about Billy Turner, or his murdered sister and brother-in-law. Just the same, the insignificance of her concern over what the Beast might have said was enough to trigger a stern response. "My friend wasn't talking to you. He was talking to that low life standing behind you. I suggest you not waste too much time gettin' all fired up over nothing. You might even think about steppin' aside."

The waitress peered over her shoulder, saw Billy and his contempt filled eyes stuck on Max, turned back around, watched as Max stood up and pushed his chair away as though he was preparing for a gunfight, took notice of the

Beast, who appeared ready, willing and able to spring to his feet at the drop of anything, added it all up in her head, and promptly backed away.

Now the only thing separating Billy Turner from Max Cougar, the prick cop Billy guessed to be fucking Wanda before, during and after moving her to parts unknown, was ten feet of worn-out floor space.

"Well, well. If it isn't my dear, old friend Billy Turner. It's really a displeasure to see you again. Maybe ya wanna sit down for a minute or two and have a cup of coffee while me and the Beast here ask ya a couple of questions."

Billy ignored Max's caustic wit and shot a quick one at the Beast (as if looking at him was really gonna make a difference). The Beast winked. "Hi there honey, how ya been? Gosh, I've missed ya."

Billy scoffed.

"I betcha he's fine Beast. Maybe a few pounds light, but other than that I betcha he's fine. Hell, get a look at him partner. He's got the blond streaks happenin'. He's got the Malibu Coast tan happenin'. He's got some fine lookin' leather threads on. Billy's so fine I betcha he thinks he's doing us a favor by coming here and breakin' bread with us." Max cocked his head, then added, "on second thought who gives a fuck. I'm not breakin' bread with him. About all I intend to do with this piece of shit is find out if he had anything to do with my sister's murder."

Billy Turner didn't know a goddamn thing about any goddamn murder. Hell, he didn't even know Cougar had a sister, much less a dead one. All he really wanted was to find Wanda, and come hell or high water, that's what he was gonna do. Billy squared up his shoulders and dropped his hands to his sides. "Where'd she go? Where'd ya move her to?" He demanded.

"Fuck you!" Max growled loudly. "I said I've got some questions about my sister's murder."

The entire year Billy Turner was in jail all he could think about was Wanda Seven, and kicking the shit out of the two cops who busted him. Yet, now that the two cops were in front of him memories of their last encounter began stirring in his head. It was an episode he didn't wish to see repeated. If he could get either one of them alone, that'd be one thing. But that two against one crap? Nothin' doing. Billy decided he'd already had all of that shit he wanted. Of course, he couldn't let the cops know that, otherwise he'd never get anywhere with 'em. "Shove your questions up your ass Cougar. I got question's of my own. Questions about Wanda. I figure you got the answers." There was no fear in Billy's voice, but what he failed to realize was that his eyes kept darting back and forth between Max and the Beast, making his concern over confronting both cops at once somewhat obvious.

"Say what?"

Billy ignored the question but not the fact that Max took a step closer when he asked it. As far as he was concerned Max Cougar was marking off territory like he was preparing to challenge for dominance, a sure sign of the inevitable. He gave Zack Darwin the once over. "You plannin' on jumpin' in, or do I get a shot with Cougar alone?"

Zack shrugged his shoulders. "You'd probably be better off taken a shot with me...but hey," he said, directing his open palm towards Max..."be my guest."

"Don't bullshit me Darwin. If I gotta take both of you cowards on at once then tell me now."

Coward, huh? Had it been up to the Beast he would have gotten up right then and there and beat the living shit out of Billy. But he couldn't. It was Max's sister, and so long as Max wanted it, his fight. "No. No bullshit," Zack said in earnest, his open palm still directed towards his partner. "Have a ball."

Before responding Billy held his breath for a second or two in an effort to temper the look of relief that broke across his face. "You gonna cry out for help Cougar, or you gonna take it like the big man you think you are?"

"Wrong question. The question's whether you're gonna go crying off to that fat piece-a-shit attorney of yours once they scrape you off the floor?"

"Don't worry 'bout me Cougar."

Max held his hands out to his sides like he was offering himself up. "You want me Billy, you got me."

Billy took a step closer to Max. "You gonna tell me where you moved Wanda to?" The thought of going one on one with Cougar had Billy pumped so full of adrenaline he couldn't help but twitch when he finished asking the question.

Max shook his head. "Ya know somethin' Billy, one of the differences between you and me is that after I finish with you, I'm still gonna get my answers. But you? Not a chance."

Max's response was like a pistol going off to signal the start of a race.

Billy charged forward. "A fucking year!" he bellowed. "I waited a fucking year!"

Max sidestepped Billy's rush, but when he backed into a table it stunned his movement and Billy caught him with a solid blow to the side of his face. Max stumbled over a chair but quickly regained his balance. His lip opened up and his jaw started screaming, but they could wait until later.

Again Billy charged, this time swinging with reckless abandon. Max eluded a left jab, spun away from an overhand right, ducked underneath a wild left cross, then lunged forward, driving his shoulder into the exposed area between Billy's armpit and ribcage. The impact catapulted Billy over a table for two and he crashed to the floor. Yet, no sooner did he fall when he sprang up with chair in hand, poking and prodding at the stale bar air between him and

Max. "Come on motherfucker, let's go," he snarled.

By now the Beast was on his feet. He had no intentions of joining in the dance, but what the hell you gonna do, reflexes are reflexes. Nevertheless, now that he was standing Zack figured he might as well stay that way. If nothing else it could give Billy something to think about.

Max grabbed his own chair and hurled it forward. Billy crouched down and let it sail by. It crashed against a waitress station and the pitchers of water and coffee split apart like bowling pins. By now all patron's sitting in the area had taken refuge on the sidelines.

Head down, ass up and chair legs pointed at Max, Billy made like a bull. Waiting...waiting..waiting. Now! Max stepped to his right, grabbed the chair by one of its legs and swung it around, sending Billy crashing into a wood column. By the sound of his agonizing groan, the column didn't give much either.

Max turned three steps into one, dug his knee in Billy's chest, but Billy up and stung him with a left hook. It surprised Max almost as much as it hurt him. It also gave Billy the opportunity to push Max off to the side and climb back to his feet. When he did, however, Max was waiting for him. So was his cowboy boot, and the next thing Billy knew, he was doubled over, pain shooting in and out of his testicles, lower back and abdomen.

But Max was just getting warmed up. He stood Billy against the wood column and proceeded to let his fists dance over Billy's face and midsection. By the time the Beast intervened the only thing keeping Billy upright was Max's ability to hold him by the hair with one hand and punch him with the other.

It was a nasty sight. Worse yet, it was only the beginning.

CHAPTER 57

Captain Rudy Whitaker lifted his head up from the soft, leathery palms of his hands and let the disappointed look in his eyes fall on Max. He was running thin on patience but yelling at his detective wasn't gonna do any good. Threatening him would do even less. More than anything else Captain Whitaker simply wanted to understand why Max allowed himself to be baited by a cheap punk like Billy Turner. Sure, Max was hurting over his sister, and yeah he was playing with a whole lot of anger and frustration. But as far as Captain Whitaker was concerned none of that mattered. Not when everything Max had been working for was hanging by a thread.

Captain Whitaker shook his head. When he spoke it sounded as if the words rode out of his mouth on the tail of a long, steady sigh. "What you did just doesn't make any sense Max. What were you thinkin'?"

As far back as Max could remember he always appreciated Captain Whitaker's input and concern, regardless of the investigation he was involved with. And why not? The captain was a smart man, gruff maybe, at times even curt, but always insightful, always clever, and always true to his word. Yet, since the murder of his sister Max no longer felt the need to oblige Captain Whitaker's concerns simply because he appreciated him. Part of it was because the evidence in his sister's case was essentially worthless. As a result, the longer the investigation dragged on the quicker Max's short fuse burned and the less time he had to deal with, what he considered to be, extracurricular bullshit. It was at a point where, for the first time in his life, Max found himself standing toe to toe with odds so overwhelming, he felt as if he was traveling full speed into a brick wall and couldn't do a goddamn thing about it.

The other part, the part Max couldn't shake and chose not to explain, simply because he didn't think anyone else would understand it, was the image of his sister. When Max saw Harry Weeble, he saw Kathy. When he saw Eddie Hart, he saw Kathy. It wasn't as if they were one person. It was more like they were attached and Max couldn't set the image of his sister free, (or, for that matter, free himself from his own pain), until he killed the image of her murderer. With Billy Turner it was more of the same thing. You see him, you get her. That's why Max decided it was pointless to do anymore than shrug his shoulders in response to the Captain's question.

Captain Whitaker leaned his well padded cheekbone against his fist and waited for Max to toss out a better answer. Unfortunately the only thing he got was an empty stare, causing what little patience the Captain had left, to all but disappear. "Damnit Max, that isn't an answer...and I need answers." Captain Whitaker's voice was caught somewhere between a plea and a demand.

Max momentarily closed his eyes and tried to roll the tension out of his neck. He had about as much luck doing that as he did trying to roll the tension out of his voice. "What the hell you want me to tell you Captain? My sister was 35 years old. My brother-in-law was my age. They're both dead. Now all that's left of my family is a little boy. What am I supposed to tell him when he wants to know what happened to his parents? That his uncle the cop couldn't stop his mommy and daddy from getting killed in the first place, or, that his uncle the cop was sitting in a restaurant staring at the guy who might've killed them, but couldn't do anything about it 'cause he might get in trouble for it?"

Captain Whitaker was determined not to be swayed by the somewhat staggering impact of Max's answer. "Look Max, you've put yourself under a lot of unnecessary pressure. I know you wanna find the crazy bastard who killed your sister, but ya can't go about it like you have been."

Max wanted to ask the Captain just how and the fuck he was supposed to go about it, but the puzzled expression on his face beat his mouth to the punch.

Captain Whitaker let his hefty forearms and open palms crash to the table. "For Chirst's sake Max, think about it. You put that son-of-a-bitch Billy Turner in the hospital, and your partner there, he stood by and watched the whole damn thing. Made no effort to stop it. I'm not sure which one is dumber. A cop who beats the hell out of some guy he knows he shouldn't touch, and does it in the middle of a crowded restaurant, or his partner, who stands in the middle of the same goddamn restaurant and watches the thing like he's at a boxing match."

"It wasn't like that," Zack offered. He gave the Captain one of those subtle, reassuring nods for good measure.

With anger in tow Captain Whitaker ignored the Beast and kept on talking. "As for me, in case either one of you forgot, I was the one who fought against the Commissioner splitting you up after you arrested Turner a year ago...AND," he added with emphasis, "I was also the one who convinced the Commissioner that putting you back together on this case would be okay. Only guess what? According to the Commissioner I was wrong."

The Beast all but jumped out of his seat. "Whoa, whoa, whoa. Hold on a second. Are you saying me and Max are gettin' split up again?" It might not have sounded like it but Zack was actually afraid to hear the answer.

Captain Whitaker responded with one of those subtle, reassuring nods, only his was meant to be sarcastic.

"Give me a break Captain, what'd the Commissioner tell you. Are we getting split up again, or what?"

Zack's voice reeked of petulance, something Captain Whitaker didn't expect to hear, or intend to tolerate.

"Well Cap?" The Beast asked impatiently, "Are we, or aren't we?"

"Damnit Darwin, enough!" Captain Whitaker snapped. "Number one, I don't have to give you a break, and number two, what the Commissioner and

I talk about becomes your concern when I tell you it's your concern. Understood?"

Zack frowned.

"And ya know what else Darwin, it's a little goddamn late for you to start worrying about it now."

"I'll quit," Max interjected, the bullheaded nature of his response matched only by the uncompromising look in his eyes.

Captain Whitaker leaned as far back as the vinyl covered chair would allow him to, and let Max's anticipated threat hang out there for a couple of seconds. By the time he replied a thick, uneasy silence was settling over the conference room. "If a couple of things don't go our way Max, you may not have to quit. You'll probably get suspended."

"Oh, now that makes a helluva lot of sense," Zack quipped.

"You too Darwin."

Max shook his head in disgust. "Ya know what Captain, if that's the case, fine. I'll survive. Hell, me-n-Zack'll both survive. But if it's gonna happen then tell me why. Explain to me how physically defending myself against the only suspect I got left in a murder investigation gets my ass tossed?"

"Tell me why you quitting is any different?" Captain Whitaker countered.

"Principle," Max retaliated. "The same goddamn principle that gets me up every morning and drags my ass in here. The same goddamn principle that makes me hate all the crap on the streets. You know exactly what it is Captain. It's the same goddamn principle that makes me glad when worthless pricks like Billy Turner wind up dead."

Captain Whitaker sensed the conversation was headed for orbit so he softened his approach. "Look, Max, I don't want to sit here and argue, okay?"

"Yeah, fine. I don't want to either."

"But I think it's important that you understand what your principle's doing for you now."

"I thought you didn't want to argue?"

"I don't. I want you to sit there and listen," Captain Whitaker rebuked.

Max said nothing, although frankly he was quite annoyed. If they agreed not to argue with each other then why and the fuck was Captain Whitaker hellbent intent on backing him into a corner?

"For starters, your old pal Bernard Forest has been making noise about suing the department. Seems while Billy Turner's been healing up in the hospital the last couple of days, Forest has been working overtime, trying to get the D.A.'s office to bring you before a grand jury. He figures if he can get you in front of a grand jury and get an indictment for something involving excessive or unwarranted force, be it brutality or any kind of assault or battery, he might be able to parlay it into a civil action. You guy's know how it works. You get indicted and found guilty on one level and all Forest has to do is convince a civil jury to pay off on another level." Captain Whitaker's chest heaved as he blew all the air out of his nose. "Principle you say? Well Max, lemme be the first to tell ya, your principle probably gave him the case on a silver platter."

Argument or not Max wasn't about to let himself get steamrolled by the Captain's inaccurate assumption of the facts. "Fuck that, Captain! He came at me first!"

The Beast was about to pipe in his concurrence but a solid knock at the door stopped him.

"Yeah, what. Who is it?" Captain Whitaker called out. He hated intrusions. This one was no exception.

Assistant District Attorney Tyler Lake ignored the less than cordial greeting and breezed inside the room with all the cockiness one would expect from a good looking, well dressed, well educated attorney. Fellow Assistant D. A. John Perry followed close behind, although his appearance wasn't near as polished as Tyler Lake's. He had the expensive clothes and all, it's just that he looked uncomfortable wearing them. Who knows, maybe it was because his tie was too tight, or his underwear was pulled up too high. On top of that it didn't look like John Perry got much sun, resulting in a clash between his blond hair and pale complexion.

"Captain, how are you?"

"Fine Tyler." Captain Whitaker didn't expect to see anyone from the D.A.'s office and immediately wondered if he had a scheduled appointment. "Did we..."

Tyler cut the Captain off like he wasn't even there. "Cougar... Darwin, nice to see you."

The Beast eyeballed the two attorneys and nodded.

"Always a pleasure Lake." Of course, Max was lying through his teeth. Nothing against Tyler Lake, mind you. It's just that he represented a system, that as far as Max was concerned, played fast and loose with itself.

"You gentlemen remember John Perry, don't you?"

"Yeah, sure. But hell, I haven't seen you in about two years. Don't they ever let you out of the office?" Zack queried.

"Normally we keep him chained up inside a small, dark office, but today I needed his brain power so I dragged him with me," Tyler explained.

John Perry smiled at the comment, while Captain Whitaker slid his question in before there was room for anymore idle chit-chat. "We didn't have an appointment, did we Tyler?"

"No Captain and I apologize for the interruption. However, John and I had to be upstairs on another matter, and as long as we did, I figured I'd stop by and tell you firsthand what I've already recommended the D.A.'s office do regarding the Billy Turner situation. The actual report is still in type, but I thought you might like to know now." Tyler Lake paused and looked around the conference room. He wanted to be certain that once he continued on with his story the level of anxiety had climaxed to the point where each person in the room was ready to cling to his every word. "As you fellas may or may not know, I was the one assigned to look into Billy Turner's allegations. To make a long story short I conducted eighteen interviews. From those eighteen interviews I took a dozen statements from people who are prepared to testify that they were in the restaurant and witnessed the confrontation from the beginning. The other six people claim that they only witnessed the fight after it was in progress. Be that as it may, not only did each of the dozen statements unconditionally affirm for us that Billy Turner initiated the fight, but they made it quite clear that Detective Cougar was only defending himself as a result."

"Meaning what?"

"Meaning Captain that Max Cougar is not going to brought before a grand jury. There's just no basis for it."

Captain Whitaker digested the words for a moment, then exclaimed, "Well goddamnit, alright! It's about time somethin' went our way for a change."

Max showed little emotion but immediately felt some tension drain from his neck and shoulders.

"I bet that'll make Forest's day." Unlike his partner, Zack let his relief pour out in the form of a big, juicy smile.

Tyler Lake attacked Zack's meaningless declaration with a stimulating dose of reality, somehow believing if he didn't, the significance of what he'd already told them would be lost. "Whether it does, or doesn't, is immaterial. What's most important is that Bernard Forest doesn't have enough evidence to pursue anything, including a civil action for money damages. Believe me, as far as Billy Turner goes, and as far as the D.A.'s office is concerned, the entire matter is closed."

Somewhere between his third and fourth beer Max drifted back to the words Tyler spoke earlier that afternoon. "Ya know what I don't understand Beast?"

Zack cut off his intake valve and set down his bottle of Molson. "What?"

"I don't understand why the D.A.'s office seemed so...what's the word...hell, I dunno...inclined to wanna help me out."

Zack gazed up at the ceiling, thought about it, then abruptly shook his head. "I disagree. I think it's more like they were disinclined to help out Billy boy and that pig attorney of his."

"I dunno," Max said, reluctant to think otherwise. "Usually the D.A.'s office gives as much a fuck about us as they do the man on the moon. But suddenly it's different. Suddenly out of the clear blue Tyler Lake shows up and tells me I'm off the hook. And when he say's it, he say's it in such a way that I couldn't help but get the feeling the D.A.'s office was on my side from the beginning, rather than investigating the other side like you'd expect them to. I mean, hell, they never even questioned either of us." Max took a quick swallow of beer. "Ya know what I mean?"

"Hard to say. Maybe you're just thinkin' too much...makin' too much of it. Don't forget Max, the D.A.'s office hates guys like Billy Turner. They know he's scum as much as we do. And how much can they like the attorneys who represent guys like that. Yeah, maybe on the outside they get along with those kind of lawyers. But on the inside, after awhile it's got to eat away at them. I mean yeah, maybe Lake acted like he was in your corner, but he's a lawyer, he's used to acting." Before Zack downed the rest of his beer he held the bottle off to the side of his mouth and added, "Personally, I don't think it's anything more than giving you the benefit of the doubt where they found a way to give it. Maybe it's just their way of helping you out because of Kathy's murder. I mean it's not like there's a conspiracy against Billy Turner or anything."

Or was there?

CHAPTER 58

As John Henry watched him walk out of the hospital he couldn't help but notice the similarities between Billy Turner's swagger and that of his old pal, Whipley Horatio Sneed.

Whipley Horatio Sneed, the self-proclaimed King of Kill, although affectionately referred to by the news media as "The Whip" and "The Whipper Snatcher," was the last piece of business John Henry took care of before moving to the vast city streets of Chicago a few years back.

Whipley was one of those people who loved to see his name in the paper. Front page too. Matter-of-fact, front page, or else. Or else what? Yeah, one of the local newspaper's asked the same thing. Shortly after they got their answer. Assistant Editor Cynthia Hornsby was found blindfolded, gagged and tied to a tree. Bruises and welts covered much of her face and a note was left pinned to her chest. It read,

I perfer page 1
have yorselfs a nice day
xoxo,
guess who?

Much to his delight "The Whip" made the front page eight more times in the next two years, although unbeknownst to Whipley, he had John Henry Stevens to thank for at least three of them. Hey, but who cares? The important thing was making the headlines. If that meant getting blamed for every gruesome murder in Wisconsin, so be it. The funny thing was, Whipley Horatio Sneed never killed anyone. He simply waited for a dead body to be discovered, decided if it was something suitably horrifying for the King of Kill, then sent one of the local newspapers a typewritten note accepting responsibility, for what Whipley always described as, *"a joyful act, one born from the glories of Jesus hisself."* A note here, a letter there, and before long "The Whip," "The Whipper Snatcher," and the self-proclaimed King of Kill, reached household name status.

Of course being popular isn't always a good thing. The heat gets turned up, the dog's get turned loose, and before another sentence can conclude with the words, *"a joyful act, one born from the glories of Jesus hisself,"* the police have had an opportunity to match the fingerprints found on one of the typewritten notes with a set of prints already on file from a three year old assault charge. Suddenly, Mr. Popularity is brought in for questioning.

The problem was, since Whipley Horatio Sneed never actually killed anyone the police never uncovered any credible evidence to prove otherwise.

All they had were the fingerprints on the typewritten note. It might have been enough to hold and question "The Whipper Snatcher", but that was about it. After two days and no other charges forthcoming, the police had to let him go. That was the good news for Whipley. Of course, since John Henry Stevens was in the interrogation room from the moment the King of Kill offered up his real name and home address until his release from custody, the bad news was just a dark night away.

Whipley Horatio Sneed's naked body was discovered by a couple of teenagers two weeks after it was left sitting upright against a tree. His neck had been snapped in two, his eyeball's scooped clean out of their sockets, and a note had been nailed into his chest. It read,

Here lies Whipley Horatio Sneed.
He claims he saw the Darkness,
poor Whipper Snatcher Sneed.
Say's he gave himself to the Darkness,
he pretended to live my deed.
The king of kill was nothing,
born from a hollow seed...
Darkness he wanted to live
but Darkness made Mr. Whip bleed.

Still, that was yesterday's news...old, stale, and until John Henry was reminded of it because of Billy Turner's pathetic swagger, almost forgotten about altogether. Not to worry. With Billy heading straight for Wisconsin, (courtesy of an anonymous tip regarding Wanda Seven's whereabouts), and with John Henry following close behind, he couldn't help but be excited about what news might be shed tomorrow.

CHAPTER 59

The first five rings...nothin'. Not even a twitch from the eyelids. On the sixth ring you would have thought the telephone was an air raid siren. Zack sprang up, but in his frantic rush to shake off the effects of his afternoon nap, and at the same time grab the phone before it stopped ringing, lost his balance and rolled off the couch. The telephone didn't fare much better. It landed next to him, unit on one side, receiver on the other.

"Hello...hello." The caller sounded like he was in a wind tunnel. Zack picked up the receiver as fast as he could. "What-yeah-hello."

"Gee, you sound out of breath. Anything wrong my brother?"

Zack grinned at the friendly locker room sarcasm, then responded in much the same way. "Why no Kee. What on earth would give you that idea?"

By his own admission Keona Raven didn't talk much. Taught by his grandfather and father alike that fulfillment in conversation came from digesting the words of another, not by shoving your own words at somebody else, Keona spent much of his adult life maligned as being standoffish. Yet, all he really was, was quiet. Nevertheless the label followed him, courtesy of those who practiced the fine art of assumptive understanding. But Keona didn't mind, not so long as he could open up around the few good friends he had, Zack Darwin among them. "I woke you, didn't I? I can hear it in your voice. You were in the middle of a fuckin' nap, weren't you? Matter-a-fact, I bet your ass is lyin' on the couch right now."

The Beast snickered. "Actually it was but I fell off trying to grab the damn phone. Believe me, if I knew I was gonna have to listen to your bullshit it'd still be ringing. What the hell do you want from me anyway?" he quipped.

"Oh yeah, here ya go..." Keona bounced back..."I call up and all of a sudden you act like you're doing me a favor just by talking to me. I don't know what they're feeding you down there but you're gettin' awful cocky for a little fella."

The Beast promptly stood up. "Yeah...well this little fella's a helluva lot bigger than you. Just to prove it I think I'm gonna drive up there and whip your ass."

Keona tossed his head back and cackled. "Hell brother, you're bigger than everybody, but whippin' my ass...nah! You know you can't whip my ass."

Zack shook his finger at the ceiling as if getting ready to deliver a great proposition of truth. "Ya know you little guy's are all the same," he chaffed. "You, Max, it doesn't matter. Y'alway's think you can stand toe to toe with real men, tough men like me. But deep down you guy's know you can't. The Keona's and Max's of the world are really nothing but a bunch of women."

The moment Keona heard Max's name mentioned his smile faded, the potential for any smart-ass response disappeared, and his thought's returned to the reason he phoned Zack in the first place. He fixed his dark, naturally brooding eyes on the crisp autumn colors outside his office window. "Speaking of Max, I got a message he called."

After a couple of seconds the Beast finally said, "And?"

"The message said something about me staying alert because Billy Turner was on his way up here to get Wanda."

Zack was pacing back and forth, unaware that he was stretching the phone cord and pulling the phone box across the floor at the same time. "Gimme that one again Kee."

Keona calmly repeated himself, then added, "I thought this Turner character..."

"Is a sick motherfucker, yes he is," Zack hastily concluded.

"How'd he find out where she...?"

"I don't know Kee, but it bothers me."

"Yeah, you sound a little troubled," Keona responded.

"Frankly I just don't understand why Max would leave that kind of message for you."

Keona shrugged his shoulders but said nothing.

"You two haven't talked at all?"

Keona moved closer to the window to get a better look outside. "Naw, I wasn't here when he called, and unfortunately my receptionist didn't get his number so I could call him back." Keona steadied the phone receiver between his jaw and shoulder blade and slid the window open to get a dose of fresh autumn air. "Where's this all heading my brother?" If Keona was concerned about Billy Turner showing up at the rehab center the unwavering firmness in his voice certainly did a good job of hiding it.

The Beast rubbed his forehead. "Jesus, I wish I knew the answer. The first thing I'm gonna have to do is call Max and see what the deal is. I'll call you back as soon as I find out."

"I'll be here."

An hour later the Beast called, but only to tell Keona he hadn't been able to get in touch with Max.

And he wouldn't get in touch with him either. Max went to Wisconsin for the weekend.

CHAPTER 60

It was late evening, almost a week after Wanda arrived, when she and Keona first spent time alone. The sky was clear, the stars scattered, a light breeze rode in and out, and in her soft brown eyes Keona saw the kind of staggering beauty he'd only experienced when gazing at the desert mountains. Then he kissed her, and it was as if the warmth from one of his beloved Arizona sunsets came down to greet him in person.

With the memory of that night as fresh in his mind as the moment he drifted back to it, with his love for Wanda stronger than anything that's ever filled his heart, with the understanding that Wanda's only desire was to remain by his side and love him back, there wasn't much for Keona to think about. The fact that the Beast never got in touch with Max to find out anymore details about the phone message didn't matter either. Plain and simple, if Billy Turner thought he was gonna come to Wisconsin and take Wanda away, then as far as Keona was concerned, Billy's best bet was to start praying to his maker. End of story.

Actually, it was just the beginning.

CHAPTER 61

Billy figured he'd waltz up to the front door, announce himself, (as if the very sound of his name was enough to part the Red Sea), walk inside, grab Wanda and leave. No muss, no fuss, and in no time at all, it'd be just like old times.

Whack!

There were only two problems with that scenario, although the first one wasn't a big problem. Actually it was a rather small problem, and only a problem because, like so many other things, it was something that never dawned on Billy. The rehabilitation center was a private facility and the doors closed at 6:00 p.m.. Billy showed up at 7:00.

Ah, but what the hell. With his left eye still tender, (thanks to Max Cougar mistaking it for a pin cushion), the thought of picking up Wanda and driving several more hours against the glare of headlights wasn't very appealing. As such, Billy decided it'd be better not to huff, puff and blow the house down just yet. Instead he'd wait for morning. Besides, this way he could find a motel room, do a couple of fat lines, then head to one of the titty bars he passed on his way into the city. Maybe even latch on to a couple of dancers for a little late night entertainment.

And find a motel room he did; a nice secluded dump. Although, with a pile of coke by his side and two cellulite thighed, saggy titted carpet-munchers rolling around on the floor at 2:30 in the morning, the room pretty much had all the decor Billy could possibly want.

The second problem...now that was a problem. That's because Max Cougar, John Henry Stevens and Keona Raven were all in Wisconsin and one of them had been following Billy ever since he left the rehab center. He was peeking through the window watching Billy pack his nose while the two fat, ugly broads took turns humping each other. He tapped at the window. "Well hi there kids. Can I come in?"

Billy's head movement was so abrupt a sharp pain poked him in the neck. He grimaced, grabbed the back of his neck, and at the same time, tried to focus his bloodshot, paranoid stricken eyes on the window where he thought he heard the muffled voice coming from. No luck.

The two dancers had worked each other into such a frenzy they didn't hear a thing. They just kept humping, moaning and murmuring like a couple of giant sea groupers in heat.

"Shut the fuck up," Billy hissed.

"Ohhh...ohhh. God...honey...touch...yeah, right, yeah...oooh that fee—eel's so-oh..."

Billy took his boot off and fired it at the two girls. As a pair they were too big to miss. "Shut up," he hissed again. "I think someone's here." Billy sat perfectly still, listening...waiting, his eyes sailing around the room as he tried to anticipate where the next sound might come from.

Nothing. Not even a goddamn peep out of a fuckin' cricket.

Billy still wasn't convinced, however, and hurried to turn off the room light so he could look outside. He stuck his head between the plaid drapes, but the moment his forehead touched the seldom cleaned windowpane he heard a loud thud behind him and his head snapped back as if the window itself was made out of fire. It was Dominique, the girl with the tattoos plastered on her tits. She tried scrambling to her feet faster than her body was willing to move and ended up falling on her ass. "What the fuck's a matter with you. I said shut the fuck up! Now shut the fuck up 'cause you're ruinin' my concentration." Billy turned to look back out the window. "Goddamn fuckin' whores are all the same," he muttered.

Dominique stood up and struck an indignant pose. As long as Billy had drugs she could tolerate his strange behavior. But drugs or no drugs she wouldn't tolerate his lack of respect. "Hey you," she bristled. "Just who and the fuck ya think yer talkin' to, huh?" She shook her head like a ten year old know-it-all.

Billy kept looking out the window, infuriating Dominique even further. "I said who and the fuck ya think yer talkin' to, huh buster... huh?"

Without warning Billy took a step back, whirled around and blasted Dominique with a backhand to her double chin. She stumbled backwards and fell across the bed. "Don't fuck with me," he warned. He held his hand like it was a gun, pointed it at Dominique and pretended to pull the trigger. "Don't ever fuck with me."

Satisfied he made his point, and ever mindful of the voice he thought he heard outside, Billy was quick to move back to the window and scan the night. That's when China decided to stick up for her friend. She rushed Billy from behind, hitting and scratching him several times before he was able to duck to the side, grab her by the back of her gnarly hair and smash her head against the wall. China landed on the carpet just this side of consciousness, although one good shot took care of that shit.

Next up, the whore with the painted tits. Yet, just as Billy moved in her direction the faceless voice returned, this time as clear as the moon itself. "Hey Billy boy, why don't ya come outside to play?"

With his cocaine induced adrenaline now feeding off the rage of his mindless anger, Billy spun around and bolted for the door. "You motherfucker," he erupted, "I don't know who the fuck you are but if you wanna piece of me you got it!"

Famous last words.

At least for Billy they were...well maybe not famous, but they were his last words. No sooner did he charge out into the darkness when a hand came out of nowhere and planted a kiss on the back of his head with a brick. When Billy awoke, he was bound, gagged and riding back to Chicago in the trunk of a car. He was found early the next morning, dead from a single gunshot wound from a Gluck 9mm revolver. His mouth was swollen and a couple of teeth were missing but the coroner chalked that up to little more than the calm before the storm. Hey, easy for the coroner to say. It wasn't his mouth, and they weren't his teeth.

CHAPTER 62

As a man Rudy Whitaker lived it. As the Captain it was something he saw virtually everyday. The thing that separated cop's like Max Cougar from criminal's like Billy Turner was the instinctive desire to form judgments and draw logical conclusions when faced with moral dilemmas on the job. That's why Captain Whitaker laughed when District Attorney Julian Sweet told the Captain he wanted Max brought in for questioning in the Turner murder investigation. Sure Max had a temper, so what? In a situation involving murder he also knew when to draw the line.

District Attorney Sweet ignored the Captain's nervous laughter, pulled the phone away from his ear and grabbed himself a quick peek in the mirror. He brushed at the freshly painted gray highlights decorating his short dark hair and toasted himself with a proud smile. Yep, he liked the new look. It landed him somewhere between distinguished and youthful. Better yet, he thought to himself, while tipping his head to catch a side angle, he looked dashing. Good for the upcoming campaign. With that settled the District Attorney put his game face back on and his serious voice back in. "Look Captain, you may or may not want to admit certain things about your detective, that's your headache. But the uncontested facts, thus far, are these: Cougar's sister and brother-in-law were murdered. Billy Turner was a suspect. Cougar wanted to question Turner about it and in the process put him in the hospital. A day after Turner was released from the hospital his body was found in the trunk of an unmarked police car, something Cougar could easily have gained access to. A single bullet from a Gluck 9mm was found in Turner's head. Stop me if I'm wrong Captain but a standard police revolver is a Gluck 9mm, is it not? Something Cougar carries, yes?"

District Attorney Sweet waited for an answer until it became obvious Captain Whitaker's silence was meant to be just that. "Look Captain, let's be realistic. Cougar's temper does not come with a sterling reputation. Plus, Cougar and Turner had a history of bad blood. Now, when you add that up, then throw in the fact that Cougar thinks Turner might've had something to do with his sister's murder, motive isn't a problem."

As soon as Captain Whitaker pushed his chair away from the desk and stood up, his breathing, heightened because he was getting increasingly more pissed off at the D.A., revealed that either his oversized belly was being stretched to the hilt with each breath, or his shirt was two sizes too small. "Realistic?" He countered in disbelief. "You think if Cougar killed Turner he would've used his own gun and then stuck the body in the trunk of a police car? You don't find that the least bit convenient?" The Captain didn't pause long enough for the D.A. to respond. "And motive, that ain't no motive. For Christ's sake, there's bad blood between every cop whose ever busted a Billy Turner type," he said emphatically. "Besides, Cougar only wanted to question Turner. If you recall it was your office that chose not to press charges against Cougar for the fight they got in. According to you guys Turner was the one who started it."

Julian Sweet did not appreciate the Captain's sudden and ill-advised attempt to challenge him intellectually. But what was the use in getting mad? After all, he was holding the trump card. As such, he calmly dispatched Captain Whitaker's argument as insignificant, and smiled, exposing two perfect rows of white. "Captain, I can place Cougar and Turner in Wisconsin at the same time."

"What the hell does..."

"Don't interrupt me Captain, I'm not finished. There's a couple of other things you may want to be advised of before responding. The first is that according to the coroner's report the victim suffered a blow to the head, sufficient enough to render him unconscious. The second is that the report also indicates the victim's ankles and wrists carried markings characteristic of one being bound for several hours. By all means ample time to drive from Wisconsin to Chicago."

"So what's the point?" Captain Whitaker broke in. He did his best to sound unimpressed by the circumstantial evidence.

Julian Sweet knew enough to know better. "I'll paint it for you this way. Turner was knocked out, tied up and transported in the trunk of a car from Wisconsin to Chicago."

Rudy Whitaker took a long, deep breath, hoping it would help quash the anger that had been mounting inside him from the moment he heard the D.A.'s arrogant stuffed voice on the other end of the telephone. It only worked half-assed. "Ya know what...you guys have a habit of taking a pretzel, untying it, then putting it back together to make it look like something else. Yet, all it ever is, is a pretzel, not what you've made it."

As far as Julian Sweet was concerned playtime was over. "It would seem as though your detective has some explaining to do. Either you bring him in or I will."

"Fuck you, you back stabbing son-of-a-bitch," the Captain bellowed, (although it was probably just as well he waited until the D.A. hung up the phone before saying it).

CHAPTER 63

District Attorney Julian Sweet carefully studied each of the four faces sitting in the interrogation room.

First there was Assistant D.A. Tyler Lake. He was brought on board so District Attorney Sweet could offer him up to the public because of his previous screw-up, i.e., the recommendation that charges not be filed against Max Cougar as a result of his fight with Billy Turner. The D.A. figured it was either this or having to answer for it himself.

Julian Sweet could hear the reporters now:

"Mr. District Attorney, isn't it true if Detective Cougar was arrested for his altercation with Billy Turner in the first place, that he might not have been in a position to get to him the second time around? And if Detective Cougar wasn't in a position to get the victim the second time around then Billy Turner would, in all likelihood, be alive today. Will there be an investigation into your department sir?" There was no way on god's green earth District Attorney Julian Sweet planned to put himself in that position, not with the election looming just around the corner. And, by appointing Tyler Lake to assist him, he wouldn't have to. It had already been arranged. Tyler would stand at the podium with his hands in his pockets, a sullen look on his face, and say, in a somber tone, "I didn't divulge all the facts to District Attorney Sweet, not because I tried to hide them, because I didn't feel they were necessary in order for the District Attorney to make an informed decision as to what charges to consider filing against the police department, and in particular, Detective Cougar. Although I didn't think so at the time, I now feel this was a mistake on my part."

It wasn't perfect by any means, but goddamn if it wasn't a plan with a purpose. Tyler Lake takes the heat, Julian Sweet gets re-elected, and some time after all the shit dies down, Tyler Lake gets a hefty raise. It's a quid pro quo kind of thing.

Then there was Captain Rudy Whitaker. He kept his eyes pretty much in front of him, listening to the questions and answers without expression. It was as if he was bored with the story because he already knew the ending.

Next came the Beast, Zack Darwin. The D.A. figured it was a good idea to let Zack in the room, maybe take some of the legal stiffness out of the air. The more comfortable Max felt, the easier it might be to get him to tell the truth. Yet, as Zack sat at the table it was clear by the redness in his face and the swelling veins in his neck that he was helping to provide the District Attorney with anything but a comfortable setting.

Last, but not least, there was Max. A portrait of calm and storm, intelligence and intolerance. Just the slightest insinuation was enough to unchain Max's hostilities. "Go fuck yourself! If you think you've got something on me then have at it. I've been at this job long enough to know you've got shit. As a matter-of-fact, unless you're planning on chargin' me with that little prick's murder, I'm outta here."

The District Attorney was put off by Max's contemptuous outburst almost as much as he was enthused by it. On the one hand he didn't approve of a detective, any detective, treating him with such disrespect. (After all, he was the District Attorney). On the other hand, it appeared to be a defensive response, an indication to Julian Sweet that he was on the right track. "All I asked you is where you were over the weekend. I didn't accuse you of anything," he said with a smirk.

"Spare me the bullshit, okay?"

"What bullshit? I just want you to answer the questions, that's all."

In Julian Sweet's four years as District Attorney Max never had any dealings with him. As a matter-of-fact, if it wasn't for television or newspapers, Max wasn't certain he'd even know what the D.A. looked like. That's because the Assistant D.A.'s, people like Tyler Lake, Samantha Edwards and John Perry, handled the brunt of the cases. The District Attorney usually didn't get directly involved unless it was something high-profiled, or it happened to be an election year, distinctions prevalent in the Billy Turner case.

Max folded his hands across his lap and gave Julian Sweet the once over. He was taller than Max figured he'd be. No giant, but his square shoulders and lanky frame had Max convinced he was pushing six-one. Well dressed too. Come to think of it, his electric tan, carefully sculpted hair and well manicured fingernails made him look downright expensive. Still, Max realized it took a helluva lot more than that to ascend to the position of District Attorney. It took steel balls, razor sharp teeth and a cunning, calculating mind, characteristics well hidden behind the District Attorney's magazine-like facade.

"I gave you an answer. I said I went away for the weekend with my girlfriend and my nephew."

"Yes, but your answer wasn't very conclusive. For instance, I understand your nephew is two years old. If that's the case and you took him with you...as you say you did, then it wouldn't be too far fetched to think you might have taken some pictures of him, you know, being that he's growing up and all. If so, I want to see them, maybe the dates are stamped on the pictures or the negatives themselves. I also want to know where you went, where you stayed, what you did, and where you ate. I want receipts for all of it. Of course you'd only have those things if you really were up there with your girlfriend and nephew." Julian Sweet folded his arms like a proud warrior, leaned against the wall and waited for a reaction. It didn't have to be much, maybe a twitch of the eyes, staggered breathing, anything, just so long as it was a further indication he was on the right track.

Max didn't even blink.

Okay, so now Julian Sweet would have to play one of his trump cards. He didn't mind. He loved playing his trump cards. Their slam-dunk impact gave him a rush and put a shit eating grin on his face at the same time. "Listen Detective, if you don't know the answers, don't have the answers, can't find the answers, don't want to look for the answers, or don't want to give me the answers, I can ask your girlfriend the same questions. I'm sure after questioning her for several hours she'll somehow help me retrace your entire weekend. And lord knows, if she really was with you I'll be able to retrace her steps as well." Once again the D.A. paused to get a reaction out of Max and once again he came away empty handed.

Suddenly the D.A. wagged his finger in the air, as if struck with a brilliant notion. "Ya know...now that I think of it, maybe I can get your nephew to tell me what you did all weekend. Whata you think detective, think your nephew can tell me anything? Is he intelligent enough to talk yet?"

That was the clincher.

Max got up from the chair and moved away from the table until he was standing in full view of the D.A. He squared up his shoulders and let oxygen fill his lungs to exaggerate the width of what was already a sturdy chest. Maybe he wasn't there to protect his sister Kathy when she needed it, but he'd be damned if he wasn't going to do everything in his power to protect Clare and Matthew. He gave Tyler Lake a long look before letting the chill in his eyes lock onto District Attorney Sweet. "I don't know what you have stirring upstairs in that head of yours, but it's like I said before, unless you're planning on chargin' me with that little prick's murder, I'm outta here."

The District Attorney loved it. Here he was hoping to get a little reaction out of Max, when instead, Max was posturing himself like a cave man protecting his territory. How entertaining it was going to be for a jury too. Mention the girlfriend a couple of times, throw in the nephew's name here and there, and before long he'd be taking Max apart on the stand, one bloody piece at a time. Of course, he'd have to take it slow...very slow. After all, accurate reporting means giving the media ample time to keep pace with the morsels of his genius.

Man, oh man. Talk about what a long day that would be.

CHAPTER 64

On a Saturday morning, almost three weeks after Max's little encounter with the District Attorney, Captain Whitaker summoned Zack Darwin to his office. In the preceding 24 hours rumors began circulating around the precinct that the grand jury concluded hearing the evidence adduced on behalf of the State against Max Cougar in the murder investigation of Billy Turner. Zack knew the D.A.'s office had nothing but circumstantial evidence. Yet, since he also knew that nothing of any substance was introduced to the grand jury to deflect the appearance of guilt away from Max, coupled with the fact the D.A. had the media in a feeding frenzy, he feared the worst when he took a seat opposite the Captain.

At first the Captain didn't look directly at Zack, although he didn't look away from him either. His eyes kind of strayed back and forth until the words he'd been searching for stopped tumbling around in his head and spilled out of his mouth. "Beast, thing's aren't lookin' very good. I'm afraid an indictment's been issued. In all likelihood Max will be arrested sometime today. When he is, he'll be suspended with pay pending the outcome of his trial."

Zack immediately closed his eyes and hung his head in prayer.

Captain Whitaker let him have a couple of moments before continuing. "I know that what I'm about to say isn't good, but I think it's the best alternative we have."

"What?" the Beast asked without looking up.

"Beast..." Captain Whitaker stopped to clear his throat because there wasn't enough kick in his voice to get it much above a whisper. "Beast...Zack, it might be best if you brought him in. Otherwise I'm afraid that..."

"You want me to what?" Zack interrupted. He wasn't sure if he felt more betrayed, or more surprised by the statement.

The Captain shrugged his round, meaty shoulders. "I know it's bad, but I don't know what else to do. I don't want a uniform to cuff him and bring him in. He doesn't deserve that."

The Beast let it fly. "He doesn't deserve any of this Captain and you know it. It's nothing but a bunch of crap. All of it, nothing but crap! Goddamnit, how could you ask me to do that?" Zack dabbed at the water forming in his eyes. "Jesus, whose side are you on anyway?"

In all his years as Captain, Rudy Whitaker only saw two other cops brought up on charges. One for selling heroin and another for taking part in a robbery. But those cases were different. They involved a couple of uniforms, policemen the Captain didn't see much of, and talked to even less. With Max, the Captain felt like he'd been kicked in the gut. Max was one of his boys. He watched him grow into a good cop, one of the best he'd ever seen. Sure, the Captain argued with him. He argued with him a lot. Everything from criminal procedure to whether Gale Sayers was a better running back than Walter Payton. But the Captain also broke bread with him, joked with him, laughed with him, and, as much as his position would permit, befriended him. The Beast was absolutely right, it wasn't fair. But like it or not, the problem also wasn't going away. As a result, Captain Whitaker realized no matter what he tried to do to make it easy on Max, he'd still end up somewhere between the devil and the bottom of the deep blue sea. "I'm on Max's side," he replied, somewhat irritated at Zack's implication to the contrary. "That's why I made the suggestion in the first place. That's why I want your help on this."

There were a lot of things Zack could endure. The sight of his best friend and partner being led to jail because some slick and slimy, power hungry lawyer was willing to rush to judgment and sacrifice Max, all for the sake of his pathetic re-election, was not one of them. The Beast calmed himself, although the clarity of his thoughts was lost amidst his anger and confusion. "Forget it Captain. It ain't ever gonna happen. I'll be with Max when they come for him, but they may as well bring a set of cuffs for me too. As far as I'm concerned, Max goes on his own terms."

Captain Whitaker could've tried convincing Zack until cows started barking and Zack's reaction wouldn't have changed. And it wasn't like the Captain didn't know it. He just figured with so few options he had no other choice but to offer the suggestion up anyway. "Look, Beast, I don't like this anymore than you do. But frankly, what else can I do with this thing? I can tell you this much, by not doing it you're sure as hell not making it any easier."

"Thing Captain? This isn't a thing. This is Max. And to be honest with you I have no intentions of making it easy. But guess what? You're not making it easy either." Thinking he should be on his way to Max's apartment instead of sitting in a stupid chair inside the Captain's office escalated Zack's restlessness. He untied his ponytail, let his thick hair fall about his shoulders, then promptly gathered it back up and re-tied it.

Captain Whitaker ignored, what he assumed was nothing more than Zack's mindless attempt to appease some nervous energy, and tried appealing to him again. "Beast, I'm asking you for your partner. More importantly I'm asking you for your friend. He's in trouble and he needs your help. Now. He needs it now." The Captain hesitated for a few seconds then threw up his arms in the hopes of initiating a response.

At some point in time Zack Darwin might have agreed with the proposition that Max's sister, Kathy, was the only person in the world who knew and understood Max better than he did. Maybe. But even at that, it would've been when the two detectives first partnered up several years ago. Since that time Zack didn't think there was a soul on earth closer to Max than he. And even if there was, it certainly wasn't the Captain. As far as Zack was concerned, the moment Captain Whitaker asked him to bring in Max, was the moment he heard the Captain say, job first - friend second. "Captain, I have no intentions of sitting here discussing what you think Max needs. But I will say one thing." Zack held up his forefinger for emphasis. "Right now Max has enough of the world against him. What he needs from me is to help get him out of this little jam. And that's exactly what I aim to do. Matter-a-fact, no matter what it takes, that's all I aim to do."

Between the stoic look on Zack's face, the icy firmness in his voice, and the fact he knew Zack as well as he did, Captain Whitaker was quick to appreciate the magnitude of the detective's unflinching resolve. Nevertheless, the Captain decided to throw out one last plea. "Beast, please...for Max, for you, for his nephew...for everyone concerned, don't do anything stupid."

The Beast calmly shook his head. "Look Captain, maybe you're doin' what you think is right, what ya think ya have to do. But, I'm sorry. I can't do what you want. Orders or not, I don't agree with it and I ain't doin' it. It's nothing personal with you. It's something personal between me and Max."

Captain Whitaker grudgingly nodded, not because he agreed, because as much as he may not have wanted to, he understood.

"Besides, I don't intend to do anything stupid. About the only thing I can think of now is helping Max find himself a lawyer. After that, who knows? I guess I'll have to find out who really killed that son-of-a-bitch Turner."

Once Zack left the office Rudy Whitaker leaned back in his chair, gazed up at the paint chipped ceiling, and said, impassively, "God help them."

A little luck wouldn't hurt either.

CHAPTER 65

Clare Adams clicked off the television and lifted her head up from Max's shoulder. Shortly after the murder of Kathy and Jack Reed, Clare came to understand how important it was to Max that their life together remain separate from his life as a detective on the streets. Often times his job was dirty, ruthless, and obviously with the murder of his sister and brother-in-law, quite ugly. Yet, Clare was the one person in the world who continued to represent something beautiful and pure to him. Unfortunately, ever since the grand jury narrowed in on her testimony in its investigation of Max, she felt as if that same beauty and innocence was lost forever. And as she gazed at him, in her violet colored eyes, once glistening with the eagerness and anticipation of a young girl hopelessly in love, was a look of profound sadness.

Clare started to say something but her voice caved in under the weight of her despair. Instead of words, Max heard gentle sobbing. He brushed his thumb against the warm tears on her cheek. He knew Clare felt bad, although frankly he couldn't understand why. After all, the only thing they were guilty of was taking Matthew to her parents' summer house on the lake.

"So what if the house happened to be in Wisconsin? So what if we happened to go on the same weekend as Billy Turner? So what if we used a summer house and it wasn't summer? So what if I went to bed earlier than Max? So what if I woke up at six o'clock one morning and Max wasn't there? So what if the car was missing? So what if he left Matthew with me? Why wouldn't he? Besides, I love taking care of him. So what if Max didn't return until after ten in the morning? So what if he had his revolver with him. He's a detective, he's supposed to. He also had pancake mix so he could make pancakes for his nephew. So what if I can't account for his whereabouts every minute of the time we were there, so what?" Looking back, it seemed as if Clare grilled District Attorney Sweet and Assistant D. A. Tyler Lake almost as bad as they grilled her. The difference was, she was the one on the witness stand and the direction of Max's immediate future swung from her words.

Max tried to convince Clare one last time. "It'll be okay...okay? There was nothing else you could've done. Believe me, you said nothing wrong, okay? As a matter-of-fact I'm proud of the way you didn't let those bastards push you around. I'm proud of the way you stuck up for me. Now...don't worry," he said, although the pretense of his smile and the sleepless red in his otherwise blue eyes said differently.

Clare rested her head back down on Max's shoulder and took a deep breath to try and settle her nerves. "What's gonna happen now?" She asked, the strain in her voice obvious.

Max kissed the top of her head and tightened his hold around her waist. "I don't know," he answered with a sigh, "but it won't be long before they figure out I'm at your place. Not that it really matters...I've gotta go in either way. I don't want to, but at the same time I can't see becoming a fugitive over the likes of Billy Turner. I asked Zack to pick me up. He said he didn't think he'd be able to handle it, but you know Zack, he'll handle it okay. Says he's already gotta line on an attorney for me...a bulldog type. Hopefully we won't kill each other."

Clare grabbed hold of Max's hand and squeezed like she had no intentions of ever letting go.

Max squeezed back the same way.

CHAPTER 66

Anthony David Stokes, (A.D., for short) came up the hard way. His father died of a heart attack when he was ten and his mother was left to raise him and his two sisters alone. Obviously it was tough on the old lady as well, what with working two jobs, one as a secretary and the other as a cook/maid combo for private parties. Nevertheless, she managed to spend quality time with her kids, making sure they grew up reading books instead of flirting with drugs and gangs. And it worked. By all accounts A.D. and his sisters stayed clean, worked hard and turned out to be good students, although A.D. was in a class by himself. By the time he graduated high school he'd been offered partial academic scholarships to a handful of small colleges, and been accepted by each of the three major universities he applied to.

Mrs. Stokes pleaded with A.D. to accept one of the partial scholarships because it meant her son wouldn't have to work full-time while going to school. More importantly, it meant he wouldn't have to borrow as much money as would otherwise be necessary. "Don't ya understand son, iffin you don't borrow so much, ya don't have to pay so much back? Be less of a headache for you after ya graduate."

A.D. didn't care. If he had to work full-time, so be it. He'd been working everyday since he was thirteen years old, so what was the big deal? And if he had to take out school loans to cover his tuition and the like, that was okay too. "It's Northwestern ma. It's the only school I've ever wanted to go to. And they accepted me, so I'm goin'."

Mrs. Stokes didn't come to grips with her son's choice of colleges until he graduated from Northwestern's law school some years later. At that point she figured A.D. would end up with a good job and be able to pay off his debts. And as far as Mrs. Stokes was concerned, nothing was more important than her son paying off his debts.

Of course, when A.D. told his mother his plans were to borrow more money so he could open up his own law office, rather than accept one of the many job offers he received, she was beside herself all over again. "Are you nuts, you crazy boy. Are you nuts?"

"Look ma, I'm independent. That's the way you raised me."

"Yeah I guess I did, didn't I? But I didn't raise you to be no fool idiot either. And what the hell does your independence have to do with it?"

"I just think I'd be stifled working in some high-rise office building doing research on hand-me-down cases, that's all. It's not like I want to borrow more money. But short of finding buried treasure somewhere, I just don't see as I have much choice."

Same old thing - Mrs. Stokes didn't come to grips with her son's business decision until it was obvious A.D. was well on his way to carving out a solid career as a criminal defense attorney.

A career furthered along by Keona Raven.

Keona's grandfather died, in what turned out to be Keona's final year of playing professional football. Initially he accepted his grandfather's death as life taking on another form. As a result, Keona was prepared to find his grandfather's spirit in visions, just the way he was taught. However, when the visions didn't materialize as soon as Keona would've liked, he sought the aid of hallucinogenics. Unfortunately, they offered little more than wild colors and dancing flowers, and it was then, for the first time in his life, that Keona felt a deep and staggering sense of loss. Like a wildfire it raged out of control, and the next thing Keona knew, he was getting fried on cocaine and martinis just so he could deal with it. Keona figured it like this: If he could keep to himself and numb his mind, at least until he was over the hump, then with any luck no one would find out and ultimately the pain would pass.

That theory lasted until Keona was pulled over by a police officer after running into a mailbox with his corvette. Of course, the situation escalated when the cop explained to Keona that he didn't care who he was, pointing out that anyone who played professional football wasn't worth knowing anyway because they probably had rocks in their head.

Just as Keona attempted to convince the police officer that his fists were every bit as hard as the rocks in his head, he stumbled and the officer nailed him over the head with his flashlight.

That's where A.D. came in. He happened to be posting bail for one of his clients when he saw a handcuffed and bloody Keona Raven being jabbed in the small of the back because Officer Joe Boyd didn't think he was walking through the precinct with the greatest of ease. A.D. might not have had a father growing up, but that didn't mean he wasn't a football fan. Besides, from the looks of things Keona Raven needed a lawyer, and needed him right then.

"Say Boyd," A.D. called out, "did Mr. Raven tell you how he got that cut on his head, or shall I assume he fell down due to a lack of coordination on his part, something I've always associated with professional athletes, especially cornerbacks that play for the Chicago Bears." A.D. loved his own sarcasm and snickered.

Keona must've loved it also because he cracked up.

About the only one who didn't appreciate it was, you guessed it, Officer Joe Boyd. He ignored A.D., shoved Keona in the back and said, "Keep movin' and shut your mouth till I tell you otherwise."

"Whoa, whoa, whoa. Hold on there big fella," A.D. cautioned. "That's my client. Now either keep your hand off his person or I'll see to it a judge keeps that badge off your lapel."

Like so many other police officers, Joe Boyd disliked criminal defense attorneys because they represented the same people the cops put their lives on the line to arrest. Yet, there were few he disliked as much as A.D. Stokes. For one, A.D. Stokes was one of those lawyers who took it upon himself to learn the names of every cop in the joint, which, as far as Joe Boyd was concerned, made him look like a phony son-of-a-bitch, rather than a friendly son-of-a-bitch. For another, when it came to representing his clients, A.D. Stokes was known to be absolutely fearless, never afraid to make a witness look like an out and out fool in open court, especially when it came to cops. And last, but most important of all, A.D. Stokes was a very smart, very good looking, well dressed nigger who forgot where he came from.

Officer Boyd kept his eyes fixed on the back of Keona's head until he finished with what he had to say. "Why I'm sorry counselor, I didn't know this drunk, er, I mean Mr. Raven, was your client. If I did, then I probably wouldn't have protected myself like I was forced to."

In typical fashion A.D. strolled towards Officer Boyd and his "new" client with the kind of casual grace reserved for one who is confident with, but does not flaunt, his own success. "Yes indeed, I can see by your perfectly clean uniform and my client's bloody scalp that you were forced to protect yourself. After I get a couple of pictures I'll take it up with the D.A. Hopefully I can get with him before Mr. Raven is arraigned. Now, what was it you were planning to charge him with anyway?" A.D. cupped his hands and waited for an answer, the cherubic look on his face purposely designed to piss off the officer.

It did too, because Officer Boyd took one look at the uppity nigger and wanted to spit in his face. "He'll be charged with drunk driving, disorderly conduct and resisting arrest."

Joe Boyd's attitude did not go unnoticed. "Wanna bet?" A.D. asked, although his austere delivery made the question sound more like a statement.

It was a good thing Joe Boyd didn't bet because he would've lost.

Not only was Keona released with little more than a token slap on the wrist, but Officer Boyd was taken off the streets and given a desk job. It had something to do with his flashlight and the pictures of Keona's head. Although, more than anything else, it had to do with the fact A.D. Stokes was a bulldog.

The same bulldog, that thanks to Keona's assistance, Zack was able to line up for Max at a minimal rate.

CHAPTER 67

In the hours leading up to Max Cougar's arraignment:
The Beast was looking out the living room window, his eyes pacing the darkness, his mind racing through facts and situations, faces and personalities, conversations and first impressions, anything that might lead to answers and help Max, answers the Beast knew he wasn't going to find overnight.

Captain Whitaker was lying in his bed doing much the same thing. Except, the longer he thought about Max's plight, the more nervous he became and the hungrier he got. It wasn't long before the Captain was heading to the kitchen for something to eat.

Keona was sitting in his hotel room thinking about Wanda Seven. Before Zack mentioned something about lending moral support, Keona hadn't planned on driving down from Wisconsin until Max's trial. Of course, after giving it some thought, he realized he should. After all, had it not been for Max finding Wanda roaming the streets in the first place, Keona seriously doubted he would have ever met her. And even though he'd only been with Wanda for a relatively short period of time, Keona couldn't imagine the rest of his life without her. So yes, if his presence could help in some way, even if just to let Max know he was pulling for him, then Keona was glad to do it. Absolutely.

A.D. Stokes was in his office drinking coffee and pouring over the motions he planned to file immediately following the arraignment. For the most part they were your typical motions in that they challenged the validity of the grand jury proceedings and the weight and sufficiency of the case evidence. A.D. was also planning to file a motion to have all charges dropped and the case thrown out. However, before he could do that he needed copies of the prosecution's evidence, a request the judge was going to hear just as soon as Max's plea of not guilty was entered into the court record.

Meanwhile, Clare was leaning against the wall opposite her bed, the bedroom light casting a dim shadow across the pages of the book sitting open in her lap. As she read out loud, the melancholy in her voice made the words sound as if they were floating across the room, only to disappear into the night's dark loneliness.

> *When that day comes and I find you,*
> *birds will sail, they will not fly*
> *the sun will forever glow, it will not rise*
> *and the moon will dip,*
> *but only my heart will set,*
> *for it will take its place inside of yours.*

When that day comes, I will feel you
inside me stay, you will,
from the freshness of morning
to the endless light of a burning sun,
eternally blessed,
my life with you will be.

When Clare could recite the poem no longer, when all she could conjure up was an image of Max wasting away in a jail cell, his love for her eroding under the strains of bitterness, her love for him confined to the anguish of a life apart, she cried hard.

Then there was Max, whose night was pathetic altogether. Whereas Zack had a window to look out of, Captain Whitaker a bed to lie in, and Clare the opportunity to read at her leisure, Max had concrete floors to walk on, steel bars to look through, and a urine stained toilet to smell. And, when a damp chill wasn't creeping up his spine, or a wretched fear of the unknown wasn't gnawing away on his insides, a mixed dose of good old fashioned despondency and confusion was there to greet him every step of the way.

As if that wasn't enough, Max had to listen to some crazy bastard five empty jail cells down talk to a fly. To make matters worse, when Max told him to shut up, he got louder.

"Now Wilbur, why don't ya fly over here and keep me company. Now Wilbur, ya know I hate it when ya fly around. Now Wilbur, I'm over here Wilbur. Where are you? I know you can see me cause flies got eyes everywhere. They can see everything. Can't sneak up on ol' Wilbur, can they big fella? Can't sneak up on no fly. They can see everything cause they got eyes everywhere. They do, they do, they really, really do."

When the following morning rolled around and Officer Sweeney came to escort Max into court, the crazy bastard was still at it. Sweeney got a laugh out of it, but that's only because he didn't have to listen to it...all fucking night.

"Listen Larry, before we go into court, how 'bout walking me down to that guy's cell."

Officer Sweeney didn't mind. Max was a cop and it was an innocent request. Besides, yesterday the crazy bastard pled guilty to rape charges - triplets, boys eight years old. If Max wanted to harass him a little bit before the crazy s.o.b. was sentenced and moved from the courthouse jail, what did he care. "Sure, what the hell," Sweeney responded.

The crazy bastard was on all fours searching for Wilbur in the far corner of the cell and didn't notice Max and Officer Sweeney as they approached. "Hey you, jackass," Max called out. His voice was scratchy from a night of no sleep.

The crazy bastard spun his head around and the drool hanging from his mouth flew up and landed across the side of his face.

"Check it out." With that said, Max smacked his palm against the wall, and with a look of utter disgust, added "Sorry, but I just snuck up on ol' Wilbur. I guess flies don't see everything after all."

Little did Max know the crazy bastard was so distraught over Wilbur's death he hanged himself the first chance he got.

Little did the crazy bastard know, Max hit nothing but wall.

CHAPTER 68

Prudence Deere learned three basic rules since becoming an associate clerk for Judge Elias Riley. The first, always get to work before the Judge. The second, make sure the Judge receives all his messages promptly, even if it means interrupting him while he's on the bench. The third, and most important, if you screw up either of the first two rules, show him a little leg or cleavage. Better yet, show him a little anyway.

Truth be told, Pru didn't mind the third rule. As a law school student she figured it was incumbent upon her to witness the wheels of justice spin firsthand. If that meant being a party to an innocent trade-off, that was fine by her.

Be that as it may, on the day of Max Cougar's ten o'clock arraignment Prudence Deere didn't break any of the three rules. Oh, don't get me wrong, she didn't get to work on time. It's just that Judge Riley was unusually late so she got away with it.

Of course, by the time the Judge walked into the receptionist area and saw his sexy young law clerk leaning over a desk to sign for a package, he immediately forgot about his car trouble, ("goddamn German piece of shit!"), thinking instead that his timing was perfect. "Whataya have there Prudence?" What the Judge really wanted to ask her is if he could rub up against her while she stayed in that position.

Pru worked for the Judge long enough to know that at that precise moment he was gazing at her ass, inquiring about the package only as a matter of course, not because he was interested in its contents. She smiled to herself before turning around with the signed receipt in her outstretched hand. "Thank you," she said, looking past the postal deliveryman and flashing her pearly whites at the Judge. "Good morning Judge Riley. How are ya?" Prudence let her voice bask in the flirtatious glow she generally reserved for the Judge and other stepping stones like him.

The Judge waited for the postman to leave the room before responding. "I'm fine Prudence and how are you? You're certainly looking well this morning. Healthy, very healthy." Judge Riley wanted to look as dignified as he sounded when he was on the bench, but with his eyeballs running up and down her curvy frame he had a hard time pulling it off.

"I'm fine, and thank you," Pru said. She let the Judge have one last look-see before adding, "pretty busy day today, your Honor. It starts with that detective's arraignment."

Yep! Nothing like a good old fashioned murder charge to bring you back to earth. Nothing quite like it anywhere, Judge Riley thought to himself. He shook his head, clearly disappointed that he couldn't stare at Prudence any longer, and headed for his office, his tongue flapping every step of the way. "Yes, the case with the police officer, it's drawn quite a bit of media attention, wouldn't you say? Of course, it's nothing I haven't seen before, but at this point, it's only the beginning, so who knows how out of hand it might get? Bring me some coffee, and grab yourself a pad and pen. There's a few things we need to discuss before I take the bench and we only have a few minutes...oh, and don't forget to bring in that package. My birthday's coming up. Maybe somebody sent me a gift."

The package wasn't much bigger than a shoebox, but goddamnit if it wasn't a heavy little bugger. And after peeling away the four layers of wrapping paper and opening it up, Judge Elias Riley discovered why.

CHAPTER 69

Circuit Court Judge Elias Riley was famous for bellowing out the same phrase at the start of each proceeding. "Let's get to the facts and dispose of her, shall we?"

At first none of the lawyers or other judges thought much of it, although it wasn't long before they realized just how quickly the judge's court docket moved, saving the taxpayers a bundle of money in the process and earning Judge Riley the decade old campaign slogan, *Swift And Conclusive. A Judge For Taxpayers' Justice.*

But today was different. Today the Judge didn't start off Max Cougar's arraignment by bellowing out a thing. Instead he summoned District Attorney Julian Sweet and Defense Attorney A.D. Stokes to his chambers. "Mr. Sweet, Mr. Stokes, sit...please." After the two attorneys found chairs for their asses, Judge Riley wondered if he looked as bewildered pouring the dirt out of the box as they did surveying it piled up on the newspaper beside his desk. "The dirt was one part of a four part package I received. The second and third parts are here." Judge Riley set two plastic bags on his desk so the attorneys could examine their contents.

In all the years A.D. Stokes had been going to court not once could he remember being witness to such an unusual demonstration. And sensing that it might prove beneficial to Max, he eagerly inquired, "What's the fourth part?"

The Judge grabbed the letter he'd already read several times, situated himself until he was sitting in his big leather highback posture perfect, cleared his throat, and proceeded to deliver each word with the austerity one would expect from a judge imposing a life sentence on a serial rapist.

"*Dear Judge:*

Besides the dirt, enclosed in this box you will find the actual gun used to kill Billy Turner. It's a Gluck 9mm. I wrapped it in aluminum foil, sealed it in a plastic baggy and stuck the plastic baggy inside a brown paper bag. Pretty neat wrapping job if I do say so myself. Almost as neat, but not nearly as fun, as the single bullet I put behind his right ear.

Wait...that ain't all. Besides the gun you will find two of Billy Turner's teeth. I pulled them out myself. I used a small pocket knife and a needle nose pliers to do it. The coroner claims the missing teeth didn't have much to do with the murder, kind of like it was part and parcel to the whole thing. Since I killed him before I pulled out his teeth, I guess that would make for a true statement. However, that doesn't mean the dental work didn't have something to do with Billy Turner's murderer......me! And I'll be honest, part and parcel doesn't make it sound like it was fun. But I assure you, yanking them out of his mouth most certainly was.

As you can see I didn't wrap the knife, the pliers, or the teeth in aluminum foil. The teeth looked kind of rotten so I decided another plastic baggy was good enough for the three items combined. I just hope the "tooth blood" didn't get all over everything.

Mr. Judge, sir, do you realize I'm on the outside looking in, while the detective you arrested is on the inside wondering, justifiably so I might add, why he's there?

I guess since it was I who killed Billy Turner, I'm wondering the same thing.

Yours forever...(and then some), MR. OUTSIDE LOOKING IN.

P.S. (that's postscript for all you idiots); Just to make sure you and I are clear on this, here's a few more facts no one besides me knows, unless of course you consider the schmuck who found the body, assuming he's alive, well and somewhere to be found, the coroner, and if the District Attorney was smart enough to ask, (which from what I hear is debatable), the District Attorney. I highly doubt the lawyer representing Detective Cougar has any knowledge of the information I'm about to divulge simply because the District Attorney probably wouldn't have turned it over to him even if he had it.

Anyway, contrary to rumors, reports and innuendoes:

Billy Turner was found face down, his hands were cuffed behind his back, not tied. His feet were bound at the ankles with nylon rope and duct tape, not just rope. His crotch zipper was cut out of his leather pants, not unzipped. Oh, and for the record, it wasn't because of any sexual perversion on my part. It was because I thought about cutting his dick off. Obviously I decided against it. Though I probably should have followed through with it...eh? Besides all that, the lump Billy was sporting on the back of his head came from a brick. Although I read somewhere that a blunt object was used, I have to be honest with you, I don't consider a brick a blunt object.

Oh yeah, one other thing. I peed on him when he was in the trunk. I'm quite certain his dead-ass body would've accounted for most of the stench, but rest assure, when I left him I left piss stains all over his clothes, dead hair and the trunk carpet lining.

Bye. So long. Arrivederci.

HASTA LA VISTA!"

Judge Riley set the letter down, pulled off his bifocals, and after rubbing his eyes, said, clearly exasperated, "Well...it would appear we have an interesting situation on our hands."

District Attorney Sweet motioned for the letter with a dip of his head. "May I see that your honor?"

The Judge ignored the D.A.'s question and asked a couple of his own. "Tell me something Mr. Sweet. Is there truth to this letter. Do you possess knowledge of certain facts, and have you failed to turn over that knowledge to Mr. Stokes so that he might use it for the benefit of his client?" Judge Riley firmly believed in the concept that a person is innocent until proven guilty. Yet, when he frowned at the District Attorney he seemed to be suggesting just the opposite.

For his part Julian Sweet believed silence was tantamount to a tacit admission when used as a response to an accusation. As such, he answered immediately. "No sir, your honor. I don't and I didn't. Though, I will admit, I don't appreciate the meaning of your question." Julian Sweet glanced at A.D. Stokes just to make sure A.D. understood the comment was also meant for him in the event he was thinking about making the same accusation.

Not the least bit concerned with the message Julian Sweet was trying to send, A.D. turned to face his counterpart. "You're not trying to tell the Judge and me that you're stupid?" Amused his question caught the District Attorney off guard, he winked at him for good measure.

Julian Sweet turned a sharp glare on A.D. Stokes. "Ya know what? Enough already. I'm the District Attorney, and I'll be damned if I'm going to sit here and put up with your sarcasm."

A.D. touched his chest and shrugged. "Me?" He asked the question with all the innocence of a child trying to convince his mother it wasn't really his hand she saw inside the cookie jar. "I'm not talking about anything. Whoever wrote the letter said you either had the information and wouldn't turn it over, or you were too stupid to find the information. Since you already told the Judge you didn't have the information, I just assumed you were telling us you were stupid. I certainly didn't mean to offend you. After all," A.D. said with a sardonic grin, "It's like you said, you're the District Attorney."

"And as such, you may have a problem that could well prove embarrassing for you and your office if not handled correctly," Judge Riley added.

With a comment like that District Attorney Sweet had no problem shrugging off A.D.'s caustic wit and turning his attention to the Judge. "I'm not sure what you mean your Honor. How so?"

"How so?" Judge Riley repeated. "That's easy. You played your cards in the media, but I'm not sure you were playing with the right cards. I suppose it's possible, although right now it appears we have a lot more questions than answers. And until..."

"Wait, wait, wait. Hold on a second." The D.A. boldly interrupted. "Just because you received an anonymous letter from an obvious quack is no reason..."

Judge Riley slammed his palm down on the desk like it was a gavel. "I wasn't finished!" he roared. He allowed the sudden room silence to simmer for a couple of moments before continuing. "As I was saying, until these answers are provided I don't know what authority I have, legal or moral, to keep Mr. Stokes' client in jail. Now, Mr. Sweet, I will say this: If I decide to believe that you haven't withheld any evidence, it's because I choose to believe you overlooked some things and a more thorough investigation is now needed. On the other hand, if it turns out you were withholding evidence, evidence to suggest somebody else may be responsible for the victim's murder, then the only reason I won't order an investigation into you and your department is because I do not want shenanigans out of your office to have the detrimental impact on the state of the judiciary it would most certainly have. The court system has enough problems without you adding to it. But know and understand this, either way Detective Cougar is going to walk."

"Fuck you, you condescending son-of-a-bitch!" That's what District Attorney Sweet wanted to say. Yet, the bite in his words and the self-assurance in his thoughts headed due south the moment he opened up his mouth. "May I ask a question, your Honor?"

"Ask away Mr. Sweet."

"What if I want to proceed to the arraignment and make my case on the record?"

"Mr. Sweet, the anonymous letter poses enough questions and creates enough doubt to make me personally want to know if what the writer claims is true. If it is, who then is the writer? And until I get some satisfactory answers, it's like I previously indicated, I find no legal or moral authority that allows me to hold Detective Cougar." Judge Riley leaned back in his chair and contemplated what had been rolling around in the back of his head one last time. Satisfied it was the quick and proper resolution, one in keeping with his all too important campaign slogan, *Swift And Conclusive. A Judge For Taxpayers' Justice*, he threw it out on the table. "Might I recommend that instead of trying to save face by making a hopeless argument, you explain to the media that newly discovered evidence suggests the impropriety of continued custody for Detective Cougar. That way..."

The District Attorney looked like he was about to interrupt again so Judge Riley cut him off with a wave of his hand. "That way when we go into court Mr. Stokes can bring an uncontested motion to have all charges against his client dropped. At the same time I won't have to waste the court's time and the taxpayers' money by conducting an investigation into you and your office."

Julian Sweet scowled.

A.D. Stokes smiled.

Max waited until Judge Riley's gavel pounded his freedom into the court record and immediately pumped his fist in the air. Zack closed his eyes and breathed a heartfelt sigh of relief, Keona slapped him on the back while nodding his head in concurrence, Captain Whitaker pulled out a pack of Tums, Susan and Clare hugged each other...

And after thinking about it later that night, John Henry Stevens laughed like hell.

CHAPTER 70

Sure, John Henry Stevens liked summers. With hot, sticky days winding into long, sweaty nights, nights filled with the sounds of crickets and the company of mosquitoes, what more could someone like John Henry want? What? The company of Kathy and Jack Reed? Shit they were nothin' but a little family tune-up to get him ready for the holiday season.

Ah yes, the good old holiday season. For John Henry Stevens there was nothing quite like it. Beginning shortly after Halloween and ending the first day of January, in between lived a world where winter darkness devoured the light of day like it was a late afternoon snack, where snow, ice and bone chilling winds turned neighborhood streets into desolate alleys, where the twinkling of starlight was muted by thick, billowy clouds, and, most importantly, where John Henry's mind numbing abyss of horror filled with an unquenchable desire to bury the annual celebration of family.

And for the most part it didn't matter what kind of family. Wrinkled old folks, pimple covered, tattoo stamped young folks, wining, crying, tantrum throwing baby folks, martini mingling, cigar chomping, fruitcake eating parental folks, rich folks, poor folks, middle class folks, even welfare folks. To John Henry they were all the same - "one for none and none for all."

Yep, the good old holiday season. A time for pickin' and choosin', searchin' and destroyin'. A time to pay homage to the Lord Almighty. "Yeah, right!" John Henry cracked to the full-length mirror.

Now who, pray tell, was it gonna be?

There were the Langstons. They lived three doors down from where the Reeds used to live. Mommy Langston was about the same age as Kathy Reed, Daddy Langston looked a couple of years older than Jack Reed, even though John Henry would be the first to admit, looks can be deceiving, and the two kids, little boy Langston and little girl Langston looked to be about six and three years old respectively. One thing was certain, if John Henry paid the Langstons a midnight visit, by the following morning the entire subdivision would be one big ball of hysteria, a scene John Henry would surely find amusing.

Yeah, the Langstons could be just the right ticket.

Then again there was the Wally clan across town. Mom and dad Wally in their late forties, two daughters in high school, one snotty looking boy in elementary, and Granny Wally who stayed inside most of the time. How bad could they be? Especially since John Henry figured after taking out Daddy Wally it would make ripping into a couple of young, tight asses, interruption free. It might be so easy, in fact, he probably wouldn't even work up a sweat.

Come to think of it, the Wally girls were too ugly to work up much of a sweat over. Nice tits and all, but ugly. Definitely ugly.

Maybe the Berman family. They lived in a nice secluded sub. Well spaced houses, hundred year old trees to decorate big rolling lots, minimal traffic. Actually it might be as good a setting as the Langstons' house. Plus, with three girls, ranging in ages from thirteen to seventeen, John Henry had entertainment for the taking. That's if his appetite wasn't completely satiated after taking down Mommy Berman, something he'd been thinking about on and off since he started watching and studying the Berman family five weeks ago. She certainly wasn't as pretty, but there was something about her face that reminded John Henry of Susan Jacobs, and Susan...well, Susan was another story altogether.

Susan Jacobs did for John Henry what Cindy Joe Lyons did for him the first time they met several years back, only tenfold. To put it bluntly, John Henry took one look at Susan and realized the term "rockets red glare" had to do with the firepower in his dick. Of course, Susan had one minor problem. It was holiday season, a time when John Henry had an undeniable hankering for wanting to embrace a family, and from all appearances, Susan didn't have any. She only had that cop, Zack Darwin, to call family. Maybe down the road - and soon, very soon - but right now John Henry needed kids, he needed mommies, and he needed daddies.

So who the hell's it gonna be? The Langstons or The Bermans?

Eenie, meanie, miney...

CHAPTER 71

Mo!

Alan Berman sold medical supplies, lots of them, as a matter-of-fact. He also spent four months a year on the road doing it. At first he didn't mind, but that was fifteen years ago when he was younger and a helluva lot more energetic. Then one day he was on an airplane bound for Cleveland when he was struck with the guilt infested realization that his kids were growing up and he was too busy working to share in their childhood experiences.

On the one hand, Alan thought about cutting back on the travel so he could spend a little more time at home. Yet, doing that would mean the family would have to cut back on expenses and give up some things. On the other hand, he could keep to his present work pace and continue to miss out on the kids. Although, they, in turn, wouldn't miss out on anything.

When all was said and done, Alan Berman didn't change a thing, preferring instead to blame his wife's spending habits for his work schedule. True or not, the fact remains he was out of town on business the one night in early November when John Henry Stevens decided to pay a little visit.

Front doors and first floor windows provided such easy access John Henry didn't think they were fun anymore. No pizzazz and only a minimal element of surprise. Breaking in through the basement or an upstairs window, coming down a chimney or lying in wait in a bedroom closet, at least that wasn't mundane. Mundane was for common thieves, not for those whose blood pumped to the heartbeat of darkness. Although, at two o'clock in the morning when everyone was tucked neatly away for the night, the real surprise was waking up to find out someone was in the house, not how they got in.

Unless, of course, someone had insomnia, in which case waking up wouldn't enter into the equation. Just ask seventeen year old Stacy Berman. She was downstairs in the family room reading a collection of short stories by Edgar Allen Poe, (high school assignment, don't you know), when out of nowhere she heard a noise. Startled, she lowered the book and examined everywhere her eyes could reach, thinking what she didn't hear, she'd at least be able to see.

The longer Stacy listened, the deeper, it seemed, the silence dug in. After several moments of hearing nothing but the heavy sounds of her own staggered breathing, Stacy decided the present state of her nerves probably had more to do with *The Tell-Tale Heart* than it did anything else. Cautiously relieved, she went back to her book.

"-but the noise steadily increased. Oh God! What could I do? I foamed - I raved - I swore."

Again! There it was again! Were the stairs creaking? The house settling? Was it coming from upstairs? Downstairs? Did somebody get up to go to the bathroom? Maybe get a drink of water? What? Was her imagination running wild? What? Stacy propped herself up, but like a doe smelling the intruding aroma of a hunter's stench, she otherwise remained paralyzed from the uncertainty of her own fear.

Again she waited...

Again nothing.

Again the heavy sounds of her own staggered breathing permeated the room. But this time Stacy continued to wait...

And wait...

And wait...

And wait...

Finally she heard water running and immediately found herself exhaling from the deep breath she didn't even realize she took. Now thoroughly satisfied the noise of one of her sisters using the upstairs bathroom frightened her only because she didn't expect to hear anyone else up that time of night, Stacy settled back in, determined to finish the Poe story once and for all.

"*It grew louder - louder - louder! And still the men chatted pleasantly and smiled. Was it possible they heard not? Almighty God! - No, no! They heard! - They suspected! - They knew! - They were making a mockery of my horror! - This I thought, and...*"

In a single, unsuspecting moment of terror, Stacy's eyes bugged out, her mouth popped open, and her young body twitched from top to bottom.

John Henry snuck up behind her so quick and effortlessly, it was as if he was a shadow leaping out of the floor. He hadn't planned on breaking her neck until he took care of the daddy - the daddy first - always, the daddy first - but when he saw Stacy sitting with her back to him, her short hair exposing a neck deliciously ripe and tender, he strapped his powerful hands around it, yanked her up from the couch - and whamo! - snapped it in two.

Death certain, John Henry contemplated slicing her open from Adam's apple to vagina. Yet, as Stacy lay there, her limp neck dangling over the couch armrest, her lifeless blue eyes staring up at the ceiling, she reminded John Henry of a dream he had long ago about an angel with no wings. The angel couldn't fly, but everytime he tried to touch her, the angel vanished right before his eyes. On and off the dream played until the sun broke through John Henry's window the following morning. Yet, when he awoke John Henry was more concerned with his sweat soaked bed than he was the angel with no wings. And it wasn't as if he was all that concerned about it now. It's just that he found it somewhat impressive to be peering down at the face of a young girl lying peacefully dead, and realizing for the first time, his memory of the angel with no wings wasn't as distant as it was intact.

    Somewhat impressive, I said. Christ, it ain't like the angel with no wings was the light in darkness and could welcome John Henry with the same warm embrace as the darkness awaiting him upstairs. Matter-of-fact, it wasn't even close!

    Don't think John Henry didn't know it either.

CHAPTER 72

Arms folded, shoulder against the wall, and perfectly content to let Zack do the talking, Max watched the precinct activity from Captain Whitaker's office window and let his mind wander through the recent string of events in his life. Could he have done something different? Maybe. But then again a person can always do something different. The real question is whether doing something different would have changed anything? Would his sister and brother-in-law still be alive? Would the insane motherfucker who killed them still be on the loose? Then of course, there's Billy Turner. What would've happened to him? Would he have been killed regardless of the situation he was in? And who would've landed in jail because of it? Who knows. Hell, at this point, did it really matter?

"How'd the guy enter their house? It wasn't the chimney, was it Captain? Or didn't anybody bother to check?" The Beast queried.

Yeah - and then there's the Berman family. What about them? Max wondered. Where would they be?

Captain Rudy Whitaker moved around to the front of his desk and rested his full size ass on the corner of it. He couldn't remember the last time he'd seen Max so quiet, but with everything Max had been through the last couple of months, he wasn't entirely surprised either. By the same token Captain Whitaker thought it important to get his input. Granted, discussing the similarities between the Berman family murders with that of Max's sister and brother-in-law was going to turn over a couple of the emotional rocks. Unfortunate indeed, but something that couldn't be helped. Not when the Reed investigation was in dire need of catching a few breaks.

"Did your sister know this Berman woman, Max?"

Since Max and the Beast played social geography earlier that morning, Zack didn't feel like having his question ignored just so the Captain could explore dead-end territory. Nevertheless, he was the Captain so there wasn't a whole lot Zack could do about it except roll his eyes and keep quiet.

"Were they friends Max? Acquaintances maybe? Could there have been a common thread between them that we don't know about?"

From the moment Max was able to digest the particulars of his sisters' murder he realized the deranged bastard who killed Kathy would likely kill again. And again - and again - and again. Yet, that didn't make talking about her any easier. Nor did the image of Alan Berman coming home to find one child with a broken neck, two others gutted, and his wife, savagely beaten, raped and strangled. Max hesitated and swallowed hard. Satisfied the pain and bitterness rolling around inside him wasn't going to reach up and tug on his voice, he responded, "No captain. Beast and I talked about this shit already. I don't think so."

Captain Whitaker folded his arms across his droopy belly and pressed on anyway. "What about your brother-in-law. Any connection to this Berman guy? Maybe common business interests or business associates? Could that be possible?"

Why the fuck he's gotta ask me what I already told him I discussed with Beast is beyond me, Max thought to himself. Be that as it may, Max peered over his shoulder and said, "I suppose anything's possible Captain, but no, I don't think so." Then, wanting to be certain the subject of who knew who was put to rest for good, added cogently, "and before you ask captain - no - my sister didn't know Alan Berman anymore than my brother-in-law knew his wife."

Had it been any other situation Captain Whitaker would've gladly told Max to chill his detective ass out. But it wasn't, so he didn't. Instead, he promptly directed his attention to Zack and answered his long lost question. "Yeah Beast, according to the information given me, there's evidence to suggest somebody was on the roof. Maybe somebody tried, but couldn't get down it. Then again I'm told there's a few shingles that don't exactly match, so for all we know someone could've been up there doing roof work."

"Do we know if anyone measured the chimney opening? If not, someone ought to. That way we can at least compare..."

"Don't know that," Captain Whitaker interjected. "What I do know, at least what they told me, is that entry was made through the doorwall in the lower level walkout - although I'm not sure how significant that is. Now there may be a few things..."

Max dipped his head and gazed down at the floor. If only for a moment, the scene still packed enough punch to make it clear to Captain Whitaker that turning over a couple of emotional rocks might be tougher on Max than he originally thought. He pursed his lips and debated over how best to proceed.

By the time Zack thought enough to twist his head around and find out what his partner did to make the Captain stop talking, Max was locked onto the precinct activity, never having noticed the little battles being waged between the words that wanted to be spoken, and the pensive looks second guessing their probable impact. He did, however, pick up on the room silence, and without looking away from the window, calmly addressed it. "Listen, I know it's tough on everybody, but say what needs to be said and let's not worry about it - Okay? Otherwise, I'm afraid we'll never get anywhere."

What else was the Captain going to do? Keep force-feeding the evidence to Max? Pull him off the investigation because some of the conversation might make him testy? Or better yet, maybe he should stick a couple more detectives on the case and take some of the pressure of him. Yeah, right. Like he'd actually stand for that kind of shit.

Realistically speaking, short of having a crystal ball to lead the way, the Captain figured his best bet was to proceed with business as usual, just the way Max suggested. And with that, he cupped his hands down by the crotch of his pants and said, "Okay, then here's what we have. The Berman house was left in a bloody mess much like the Reed house. And, though I'm sorry I have to say it Max, the Berman woman was found in a condition very similar to your sister. I'm told that blood and semen samples were taken but results haven't come back. Prints were also pulled up, but again, results haven't come back. Now remember," the Captain cautioned, "even if all the samples come back positive, it only indicates the same guy is likely responsible for the Berman and Reed homicides. It still isn't gonna bring us any closer to finding him, because so far, we haven't been able to match the prints and samples taken from the Reed house to anything else we have on record."

"The bodies been removed yet?"

"Yeah, but you and Max can still go and check out the rest of the house. Captain Dooley said jurisdiction won't be a problem. You may want to see it too. I'm told the furniture was knocked over in each of the kid's rooms and a couple of stuffed animals were ripped apart. Fairly similar to the way the Reed house was left. Photographs were taken and I've requested copies. I've been assured they'll be dropped off sometime this afternoon."

"Speaking of Captain Dooley, is his precinct giving us all the information they have? Or they doing their usual song and dance routine?"

Captain Tom Dooley did a lot of charitable things throughout his redheaded Irish life. Giving evidence to another police precinct wasn't one of them, however. Yet, there wasn't much anyone could do about it, (except maybe bitch for the sake of bitching), because four of the last five years his precinct had the highest arrest to conviction ratio, a record he intended to keep. And the worse off the competition, the better his precinct's chances.

Nevertheless, Rudy Whitaker wanted to think in a situation such as this one, a situation involving a fellow cop, Tom Dooley would forego his personal agenda and share the evidence.

He did too - but it wasn't because of any cop. Hell, there's nothing Tom Dooley would've liked more than to be credited with arresting a sick ticket like the one who killed the Bermans. Problem was, between city wide cutbacks and one too many criminal investigations firmly in progress, his precinct was strapped for competent manpower. It certainly wasn't what he wanted, but why take on an investigation when there's a chance his own guys, (already stretched to the hilt with overtime) could screw it up. Nope! No point in that. Not when there's somebody else willing to take it on. But not to worry. Tom Dooley planned to keep his hand deep enough in the shit-pile to be able to angle for some of the credit if Rudy Whitaker's investigation went well, but not so deep he couldn't pull his hand out and point to Whitaker if things went awry.

"Yeah Beast, I think Dooley's being straight," the Captain responded, a hint of trepidation still lurking in the shadows of his robust voice.

"Well then, unless I'm missing something Captain it doesn't sound like Dooley's got a whole lot to give."

"I dunno, there may be something else. Something we didn't get from Dooley."

"Like what?"

Captain Whitaker didn't think he ever heard two words jump out of someone's mouth so quickly, and yet, the Beast looked even more impatient than he sounded. "It may be nothing, it may be something." The Captain held up his big empty palm as if it was a stop sign. "But, whatever it is, hear me out before you start firing questions, okay? 'Cause I'm still working through it myself."

The Beast nodded.

Max turned away from the office window, but otherwise appeared indifferent to the request.

"Between this case and the Reed case we have a few similarities, right? Both houses trashed, trails of blood, fingerprints all over the place, women assaulted in the same manner, and stuffed animals torn apart. Does it mean anything? I dunno. What I do know is that both these cases involve families. Sure, Max's nephew got lucky because he wasn't home when the attack on his parents occurred. Either was Alan Berman when his wife and kids were killed. But so far no one's convinced me they weren't supposed to be victims along with everyone else." Captain Whitaker let Max and the Beast chew on his words for a couple of seconds before continuing. "Do either of you ever remember me talking about my first cousin Manny?"

"Yeah, isn't he the chef over at Trudy & Al's Nuberry Steak House?"

Sincere question notwithstanding, Captain Whitaker rolled his eyes at the ceiling, sighed, then looked at his detective and shook his head. "No Beast. Manny works homicide in Milwaukee."

Zack glanced at his partner and shrugged.

The answer sounded good to Max so he shrugged back.

"Anyway, Manny happened to call me last night. Wants us, you know, me, Norma and the kids to come up there for Thanksgiving in a couple of weeks. Thing is, hearing Manny's voice made me think about a case he worked on six years ago. It involved a family named the Littlefields. It got some local news coverage but nothing we would've heard about down here. At any rate, The Littlefields were a young couple. Nice little house, couple of kids, a dog...the whole nine yards. Turns out, two days after that particular Christmas one of the neighbors got curious enough about their whereabouts to call the police. To make a long story short, Manny shows up as one of the investigators, walks in the house and finds the entire family murdered."

Max took a couple of steps towards the middle of the room and waited on the Captain's next words like a beggar waiting for a food handout.

"Anyway, shortly after Manny and I got off the phone yesterday I called him back. Six years is a long time and I wanted to make sure I remembered the relevant particulars just the way he explained them to me back then. I was pretty close."

Zack arched his eyebrows and held out his hands, as if to say, "okay great, so lets have it."

"Turns out the house was ransacked. Blood everywhere. Stuffed animals torn apart. And the Littlefield woman beaten to a pulp and raped. Those are the common denominators with what we have here. What isn't common is that they found no evidence of semen. Didn't get any clean prints either."

"How were they killed Captain?"

"The Littlefield woman was strangled and the rest of them were hacked up with an ax. On top of that, all of them had their mouths stuffed with crushed up Christmas ornaments, you know, those bulbs, that kind of shit."

Zack laced his fingers together behind his head and stared at the ceiling.

"The point I'm making is after I came in this morning I had Lemke do a little computer search. I asked her to see if she could find all the unsolved murders of families in a two hundred and fifty mile radius in the past two and a half years. Now bear in mind, there was nothing magical about picking out the distance or the time frame. I don't know if one was too long and the other too short. What I do know is that one case turned up."

That was all it took for Max to feel the hair on the back of his neck come to life.

Captain Whitaker continued. "It was in Springfield, two years back. Lemke had a copy of the investigation report faxed here a couple hours ago."

The Beast lowered his head. "What's it say Cap?"

"You guys ever hear of Donald Blair?"

"No."

"Me neither Cap."

"Well, Donald Blair owns radio stations. He also owns television stations and newspapers. As you might guess, he's extremely wealthy and powerful. In any event, it turns out his daughter, son-in-law and grandchild were murdered on New Years Eve. The daughter wasn't raped but she was stabbed repeatedly and strangled, as were her husband and little boy. After I read the information I contacted a Sergeant Baker. According to the report he was one of the original officers assigned to the case. He didn't really tell me anything different from what I read, although he did confirm that they found a stuffed animal with the stuffing pulled out."

"Say anything about prints?"

"Yeah, said there was a lot of blood and that they didn't pick up any clean ones. He, in turn, wanted to know why I was asking, so I told him what we were looking at up here. He asked if we'd keep him apprised of the situation if it appears we're dealing with the same guy. I assured him just as soon as he sent me a copy of the entire case file for our review, I'd let him know where we stood at all times...if anywhere. I also told Manny to send me a copy of his records. I woulda picked it up when I was up there for Thanksgiving, but didn't want to wait any longer than necessary."

"I'm kinda surprised we didn't hear about this case before."

"Don't be. From what this Sergeant Baker told me it was all pretty hush hush because Donald Blair wanted it that way. Something about not giving the killer the benefit of the doubt by glorifying what he did in the media. Let the victims rest in peace while the cops did their work behind closed doors kind of thing. Besides," Captain Whitaker added, "even if you heard about it, ya probably wouldn't have remembered a thing. I mean, why would you? Until now it had no meaning for you."

The Beast looked at his partner. "Whataya think?" He had to wait until the faraway look disappeared from Max's eyes before he got an answer.

"I think there may be something to the trail of blood this guy seems to be leaving everywhere he goes."

"Such as?" Captain Whitaker asked.

"Such as, there's so much of it, it's probably responsible for washing away more fingerprints than anyone's been able to find. At the same time this prick keeps leaving these trails of blood like he don't give a fuck if we're pullin' up clean prints or not. And that's the part that bothers me. His nonchalance is beyond fucking reason."

So far Captain Whitaker didn't agree with what he was hearing. Yet, never one to summarily dismiss what one of his detectives obviously thought necessary to explore, he proceeded with caution. "Meaning what Max, he's daring somebody to catch him? Beast and I discussed that very thing when we were walking through your sister's house. Frankly, I don't see where it makes any sense. If he's daring us, why leave such a big mess behind? Why don't he just leave us some kinda note? He keeps leaving a mess of blood, sooner or later we gotta find something in the mess that takes us to him. Yes?" Captain Whitaker knew better, but took a shot anyway. "Don't you think so Beast?"

"On the contrary Cap. It's probably something we need to re-think." The Beast spoke softly, yet the firmness in his raspy voice revealed an unwavering conviction to follow his partner's lead - no matter where it took him.

"Maybe we're lookin at this the wrong way. Maybe we gotta look at it like this guy's not daring anyone," Max said, both his voice and his blue eyes jumping with signs of life.

"Meaning what?"

"Meaning he doesn't think he can get caught...period."

Captain Whitaker frowned. Max thought it was because the Captain still disagreed with what he said, when in reality it was because the Captain's big ass was getting numb from sitting in the same position for too long. Yet, rather than stand up, Captain Whitaker pushed himself further back on the desk, figuring a broader seat was all it really needed. Once situated the frown disappeared. "Well if he doesn't think he can get caught then he must think he's invisible."

"Precisely Captain."

Captain Whitaker scoffed. "C'mon Max, crazy's one thing, but invisible? I don't know about that."

Max shook his head and quickly waived off the Captain's remark. "No, no, I don't mean literally. What I'm saying is that this guy doesn't think of himself as part of the trail, which is why he doesn't care about leaving one wherever he goes. He thinks of the trail as having one identity, and himself as having another. He's there, but at the same time he's not there kinda thing. So yeah, in a sense Cap, he thinks he's invisible, not because he can't be seen, because he can't be found. Now we may think otherwise, but what we think isn't an issue. The issue is what he thinks. And maybe that's the part we've been overlookin' all along."

The Beast stroked his chin and kicked it around. Okay, so maybe it didn't provide him and Max with any kind of physical evidence to go on - but maybe, just maybe, it gave them a peek inside the killer's mind, which is a helluva lot more than they had the day before.

Truth be told, getting a little peek at something is a lot like getting a tiny scrap of food when you're starving. Neither one does a goddamn thing...except make you crave more. And we all know how unhealthy craving can be.

CHAPTER 73

After their meeting with Captain Whitaker, Max and the Beast went to work.

They visited the Berman crime scene, poured over the Littlefield and Blair case files, talked at length with the officers, crime lab technicians and surviving family members involved in each case, including media mogul Donald Blair, (who flew in from New York just to make himself available), revisited the Berman crime scene, inspected, dissected and compared every piece of evidence imaginable, theorized, rationalized, hypothesized, dramatized, and then, when none of that worked, extended the boundaries of Captain Whitaker's self-imposed two hundred-fifty mile, two and a half year search of unsolved murders of families, to five hundred miles and five years.

But, it was all for naught because nothing turned up.

Worse than that, their optimism, resurrected from the presumption that somewhere in all the bullshit they were sifting through something was bound to turn up, once again waned.

Then one night a couple of weeks later, Zack was at home trying to steal a couple hours of quiet time for Susan and himself, when the phone rang. It was Keona Raven.

"Hey, Kee, how ya doin'?"

"Beast, you'll never guess who they found dead up here?"

"Who?"

Yep, wouldn't ya know it. Max and Zack did all that work to find one good lead, when all it took was a simple phone call.

CHAPTER 74

From the time she was a little girl the only thing Beatrice Mead ever wanted was a house to call her very own. That's because she grew up poor, so poor in fact, that throughout her childhood, her parents, Ben and Zelda, often had to choose food over rent. Suffice it to say, while Beatrice may not have gone hungry, her family moved from house to house with such regularity, she once described her life in a school paper as resembling that of a revolving door.

Bess Mead was different. To Bess, owning a house wasn't that big a deal. She didn't take it lightly, she simply didn't spend every night dreaming about it. Instead, Bess dreamt of having a husband and kids, particularly a son. If she could just have that, she'd be comfortable no matter where she lived.

Two sisters, two choices, and as it turned out, two dreams fulfilled.

Beatrice Mead not only ended up owning her own house, she òwned and rented out thirteen others.

Bess, on the other hand, only had one house, although she had the good fortune to share it with her husband and son. Of course Franklin Jr. only lived with his parents until he went off to college, and from college to medical school.

Beatrice and Bess remained close throughout their lives, and when Bess died, having survived her husband of fifty-two years, Beatrice changed her will so that her nephew, Franklin Jr., was the sole beneficiary of her estate. And it was none too soon because Beatrice died within months of her sister.

Franklin Jr. kept the house his aunt lived in as a testament to her, and sold twelve. As for the thirteenth house...well, it just so happens it sat on a beautiful lot at the end of a cul-de-sac, in an area where Franklin Jr. and his wife had hoped to move, but until then, couldn't find a lot anywhere in the vicinity for less than a $150,000.00. Eight, ten years ago, no problem. But today, with the way everything was so built up, not a chance.

The one thing nobody counted on, however, not Franklin Jr., not his architect, builder, not even the excavator, was that the skeleton of a young man would be found when the old house was leveled and a new foundation was dug. But that's because nobody knew, including Aunt Beatrice when she was alive, that her tenant, Hank Connors, (oh - excuse me, John Henry Stevens), would bury some poor, unsuspecting son-of-a-bitch underneath the house before he moved out of it years ago.

But he did, and lo and behold, the skeleton showed up as one of the stories on the local evening news.

Nice smile too.

CHAPTER 75

When he was born William Lake insisted that his son be named in honor of his great grandfather, Livingston Tyler Lake, who in turn had been named for both, Livingston Beasley, a would-be explorer and beaver pelt merchant who drank himself to death, and Sebastian Tyler, a self-proclaimed bounty hunter, riverboat gambler, and great lover of women who keeled over dead in a Minnesota bordello, a syphilitic wreck.

Mary Elizabeth, on the other hand, figured since her own father, Clifford Benjamin Wiley, American history buff and high school English teacher, died three months into her pregnancy it would have been nice to name the child after him. William Lake snickered at the thought, spit at her audacity to suggest such a thing, and boldly asserted like the drunken, swashbuckling pirate he always dreamed of being, "By God woman, Tyler it is!"

So, Tyler it was - although naming him was about the extent of Williams' influence on his son because shortly after Tyler's name hit the birth certificate, William disappeared to parts unknown.

At first Mary Elizabeth thought William was on one of his typical three day drinking binges. However, when the fourth day rolled around and William still hadn't showed up for work, (even though William and work had always been an iffy combo), or brought his hung over, dehydrated, disheveled and dead-ass tired self back to their front door, she figured something was wrong.

Yet, in reality, nothing was...at least not from William's point of view. When Tyler was a week old and smack dab in the middle of spitting up on dear ol' dad, dear ol' dad abruptly decided between work and marriage his life had become far too rigid and unfulfilling to be further confined by the pathetic smell of dirty diapers, the off-key melody of stupid bedtime lullabies, and the inhumane schedule of bottled feedings. Not to mention baby puke.

For cryin' out loud man! There were seas to sail and sandy beaches to roam! Native girls to eyeball and afternoons to nap away! Soothing tropical breezes and moonlight serenades! Dreams to live and rainbows to chase! And Goddamnit! William Lake was determined to chase them all!

So, without further adieu William put his son in the bassinet, where his mother would find him upon her return from the store, and made haste for the great outdoors. Of course he stopped off at the bank to withdraw half of the eighteen thousand dollars Mary Elizabeth received from her father's estate. It certainly wasn't a fortune, but it was all the money they had in the bank. More importantly, half of it was more than enough to get William's ass down to the Canary Islands, where, when he wasn't soaking up the sun, he was filling his days working part-time in a bait shop, while filling his nights listening to something resembling calypso music and soaking his head with dark rum.

Despite the stark realization her husband was never going to return, Mary Elizabeth, in turn, followed her best friend's advise regarding life, liberty and the pursuit of deadbeat husbands, and filed a missing person's report, which the police promptly filed away under "husband took the money and ran." Besides that, about all Mary Elizabeth could do was tend to her son, cry whenever she felt the urge, and try as best she could to get on with the rest of her life.

And a sad, empty life it turned out to be. A life burdened with the emotional and economic hardships of being a single parent, a life riddled with guilt (because try as she might, the love for her son was severely tempered simply because of the physical resemblance he bore to his father), a life replete with cynicism for every man whoever approached her, a life where sexual satisfaction came from the fantasy filled pages of romance novels, a life, where everyday, Mary Elizabeth wanted to be someone else.

Given the fact Tyler grew up the unwanted victim of a situation he knew nothing about, much less had any control over, his formative years weren't any better. With no family besides a long gone father and a mother who talked to him only because she had to, it wasn't hard for Tyler's personality, somewhat quiet by nature, to cascade into reticence. He spoke only when someone spoke to him first, (which generally meant he answered a few questions every now and then), laughed only when he told himself jokes, (which meant he only laughed once and a great while because he wasn't all that funny to begin with), and played or hung out with the other neighborhood kids only when he was invited, (which wasn't all that often because the other kids wouldn't invite him anywhere unless somebody's mother forced them into it).

Suffice it to say, Tyler grew up a loner, finding his only real companionship and comfort in books. It started out as a simple curiosity. One day his mother left one of her romance novels, *The Tremor Inside*, on the kitchen table, and after running his bony fingers over the picture of the seductive looking woman with the big time cleavage, Tyler couldn't help but ignore his mothers longstanding insistence...

"Don't you ever touch my things! Not ever! Especially my books!"

From there it wasn't long before Tyler was in the library everyday after school and on weekends, reading as many as three books a week. By the time he graduated high school the number was up to four books a week, although the subject matter was generally the same. He liked American history, science fiction and even the occasional book about animals in the wild. Yet, his absolute favorites were whodunit murder mysteries, where the intrigue and legal eagle drama was so captivating, he often found himself playing both tough guy and sap, villain and hero, prosecutor and criminal, predator and prey.

When Tyler was nineteen years old his mother died of heart failure at the ripe young age of 49, an event which unleashed a myriad of thoughts and feelings he never had to deal with before. Should he be sad? After all, lousy relationship notwithstanding, Mary Elizabeth was still his mother. But then if Tyler was supposed to be sad - how sad? Crying kind of sad? Sullen look and dab at the eyes once in awhile kind of sad? Or, oh woe is me kind of sad?

What about angry? Should he be angry at his mother because she never seemed to want him around? Should he be angry at the father he never saw because that was at the root of his mother's ugly attitude? Or, maybe Tyler should be angry with himself. Maybe he didn't do enough to get along better with his mother.

Then again, what if Tyler felt happy? Should he smile? Giggle, perhaps? Or should he hold back altogether for fear it wouldn't look right? The bigger, more confusing question was why Tyler would be happy in the first place? Because his mother, the woman who seemed to begrudge his very existence, was dead? Because the finality of her death was the first step in prying him loose from his lonely Wisconsin life? Or, because his mother, as it turned out, actually did something parental, like make him the beneficiary of a $50,000.00 life insurance policy, money that would enable him to go to college - and with any luck, from college to law school, where, upon graduation, he could get involved in his own legal eagle whodunits?

Tyler Lake never did come to grips with all the questions rolling around in his head. But he did end up dragging his scrawny little body and pigeon-toed clumsiness to law school. And he did end up in his own whodunit.

Problem was, it wasn't the legal eagle kind.

CHAPTER 76

Tyler Lake pulled out of the drugstore parking lot feeling pretty good about himself. And why not? He was a lifetime removed from his mother's death, and, as of that morning, a proud law school graduate from the University of Wisconsin, (graduating with flying colors to boot). But that's not even the best part. The best part, the reason he walked out of the store carrying a big shit eating grin and whistling like some happy-go-lucky kid with a shiny new quarter was because he and his best bud, Hank Connors, were gonna do a little celebrating.

The celebration was Hank's idea. Had it all planned, he said. "Just stop at the store on your way back over and pick up a couple of cigars. I already got the beer and whiskey. Ordered a pizza too."

That was the thing about Hank. He was always doing stuff for Tyler, stuff no one ever did for him before. And that was one of the things about Tyler. Having been starved of friendship his entire life he never knew how to react when Hank did something nice for him. As a result, even springing for a six pack of beer and a small cheese pizza was enough to push Tyler up and down the emotional ladder. One minute he was smiling and whistling, the next, he was all choked up. Another thing about Tyler was that in all the books he read, or movies he saw growing up, guys weren't supposed to cry. That's why he was scared shitless Hank wouldn't want to be best buds with him anymore if he saw him in that condition. Let's face it, if guys aren't supposed to cry, then being best buds with one who does would make that guy a crybaby too. And since Tyler was so certain Hank was no crybaby - FOR GOSH SAKES, NO WAY! NO HOW! - Tyler figured his best bet, his only bet if he didn't want to get caught, was to pull the car over and dry his eyes. Unfortunately it didn't do a helluva lot of good because one teary eyed thought lead to another, and within seconds, he was thinking about the handful of times Hank stuck himself on the back burner just so the two of them could talk about Tyler's life. You name it, if it had to do with Tyler, Hank was eager to know about it. And it didn't stop with listening to Tyler go on about his past either. Hank also took great interest in Tyler's law school education, even convincing him to follow the curriculum set forth by the State Supreme Court so he wouldn't have to sit for a bar exam after graduation. It was all so thoughtful and genuine of him. But hey, watching out and caring for one another was just the kind of thing best buds did. At least that's what Hank always said.

Be that as it may, Tyler continued to agonize over the prospect of loosing his best bud to a couple of tears, and as a result, didn't move the car another inch until satisfied his eyes were nice and dry.

The one bedroom slab house Hank Connors rented from an old lady sat alone at the end of a dirt cul-de-sac. There were three other houses scattered along the street, but due to the overcast skies and thick, misty-like humidity, the moonlight didn't serve as much of a guide past them. Not only that, Tyler had to slow the car down considerably in an attempt to avoid all the potholes and ruts. Not an easy task considering one or both popped up every couple of feet. Still, it was Hank's car and if going slow meant not screwing it up, slow it was.

Tyler had been to Hank's several times before, though most of his visits came during the afternoon so he never realized just how desolate his house could look, especially since all the lights appeared to be off. Strange too, because his best bud was supposed to be inside waiting for him. Tyler was prepared to shrug it off, except when he got out of the car and found himself no longer sitting within its protective 2-door confines, strange turned to eerie and he couldn't shrug off shit. It was the kind of eerie where you'd expect the hoot of an owl, or the screech of a cat to pierce the stillness of the dark night - the kind of eerie where you'd expect doors to slowly creak open and windows to slam shut - the kind off eerie where you'd expect to be greeted at the bottom of a winding concrete stairway by Vincent Price dressed in a long, flowing black robe and hood.

It was the kind of eerie where, despite the gripping summer humidity, spine tingling chills dug deep, goosebumps ran wild, and Tyler decided to turn around to see if someone was sneaking up behind him.

Unfortunately, Tyler didn't move quick enough, which was too bad, because someone else did. It was his best bud, Hank - "my real name is John Henry Stevens and I'm gonna kill, cut and bury your sorry, worthless ass under the house" - Connors.

But hey! What are best buds for?

CHAPTER 77

If somebody had told Max or Zack they wouldn't have said more than a mouthful of words to each other on their way to Wisconsin, each one acceding to the quiet stranglehold of his own ambivalence, an ambivalence brought about by the unexpected discovery of a skeleton, apparently identified as one, Tyler Lake, neither one would've ever believed it. But that's the way it went. Other than the basic... "I told Susan we'd probably be gone for a couple, three days - what'd you tell Clare?" kind of thing... and..."I spoke to the Captain and he said he'd keep a lid on everything until we had more information," nothing was said. Zack kept his eyes on the road, every now and then dipping his head from side to side for a little stretch and crack of the neck, and Max gazed out the passenger window, the look on his face as barren as the expression on the face of the distant pale moon.

Keona figured to have Zack and Max meet him at his rehab center in Madison. Yet, no sooner did the suggestion leave his mouth when he said, "On second thought, let's meet at my house. That way we won't have to worry about anyone with nose trouble. And by the time you guys get up here, it'll be to late to go lookin' for a bed anyway. You'll crash at my place. It beats the hell out of a hotel, even if my cooking is for shit."

Staying at Keona's house was easy. Finding it was a bitch. It's not that it was out in the boonies, or anything like that. Although with Keona that was somewhat surprising. It's just that there wasn't any sign to identify his street. As a result, unless someone was well acquainted with the area they stood a good chance of passing right by it - at least once. Unfortunately, the Beast passed it three times, which took him ten minutes and three "motherfuckers!" out of the way.

Having been stuck in the car some two hours, Max wasn't any more thrilled about the extra drive time than Zack was. By the same token he couldn't help but laugh each time the Beast spewed forth one of his frustrated induced, temper laden "motherfuckers." The first two times were quick outbursts Zack was able to ignore. But the third time Max's laughter was punctuated by the kind of shoulder shaking cackle that caused him to snort when he tried to catch his breath.

Rather than ask Max what the hell was so funny, the Beast nonchalantly reached for the stereo and cranked up the volume. I'll drown the son-of-a-bitch out. That'll get him, he thought to himself.

Oh yeah? Not so fast. As soon as Max calmed down he nonchalantly reached for the volume control and turned it down, at which point he looked out the window, pretending as if he'd done nothing at all.

Four, five, even six times, the music went up and down, up and down, up and down, each time bringing back a small dose of the kind of lighthearted, little kid spirit the two friends often shared, but hadn't had much of since the murder of Max's sister and brother-in-law.

Finally, just as the Beast realized he was on Keona's street, he plastered his big mitt across, what seemed like half the dashboard, and the stereo was suddenly off limits. End of the road - Victory was his! Zack flashed a big, juicy smile, then winked at his friend and nodded his one-upmanship.

Max acquiesced and settled back in his seat, if only for the time being. When it appeared Zack's concentration was locked somewhere between pulling up the drive and turning off the ignition, he decided to lunge for the volume control one last time.

Nothing doing. Knowing his friend the way he did Zack anticipated the move and beat Max to the punch. "Hah! Gottcha you motherfucker! Didn't think I was payin' attention did ya?"

"What? What the hell are you talkin' about? I was just reaching for my gloves." Max did his best to smother the mirth in his voice and the grin breaking in on the corners of his mouth.

The Beast looked around the front seat. "Gloves? What gloves Max? I don't see any gloves." Then tapping lightly across the top of the dashboard, "Why lord have mercy, I don't feel any gloves either."

Max leaned against the passenger door and looked at his friend in feigned disbelief. "Well they were there a minute ago - whadya do with em?" Not wanting to give the Beast a chance to respond, he quickly added, "Ya stole 'em, didn't ya? Ya always liked 'em and now ya went ahead and stole 'em right off the dash. I'll tell ya, ya can't trust anybody these days."

The Beast laughed and climbed out of his jeep.

Max followed close behind, snickering all the way.

CHAPTER 78

By the time December rolled in just about every place around Madison was usually covered with snow. Yet, this year had been mild in comparison to years past. Oh, don't get me wrong. The air was brisk, the overcast skies looked like they could split open anytime and let it rip, and the grass, frosted over nice and firm from the night before, crunched under the weight of Max, Zack and Keona as they made their way down to a little stream running through Keona's one acre back yard.

"It's like I was tellin' you guys last night after you got in. When I heard them say his name on the news, I had to think about it for a minute. I knew I heard it before, I just couldn't place where. Then it dawned on me. He was the lawyer who assisted the D. A. when Max was arraigned for that Billy Turner crap."

"Only one problem..." the Beast chimed in..."as of yesterday the Tyler Lake we know was still working as an Assistant D.A.. He sure as hell ain't no dug up skeleton."

"I know, that's why I called," Keona responded, his gentle voice a stark contrast to the reflective glare in his brooding, dark eyes. "I mean, once I realized I saw this guy at Max's arraignment - what a month ago? I knew something was off. Let's face it. You don't turn into a skeleton overnight. At least not where I'm from."

When they reached the stream Max kneeled down to get a closer look at the clear, shallow water as it trickled by. A few seconds later he looked up, glanced to his left, glanced to his right, and announced, "You gotta nice place here Kee. Peaceful, ya know?"

Because Keona didn't know Max well enough to know better, he was somewhat surprised to hear him talk scenery when a situation involving the identity of an Assistant D.A. and that of a skeleton long dead was sitting front and center. Nevertheless, Keona responded as if there was nothing unusual about it. "Yeah, I like it Max. Between the stream and the trees I get a little taste of seclusion."

The Beast, on the other hand, didn't find anything unusual about the comment. That's because he knew Max didn't give a shit about the scenery. Something was floating around inside his head and talking small talk was just his way of killing time until he had his thoughts sorted out. Of course, that didn't mean Zack planned to stand around until Max was ready to clue him in on what he was thinking. Hell, if that were the case he'd be standing around all the time. "C'mon Max. What's up?"

Max arched his eyebrows and shook his head slowly. "Frankly Beast, I'm probably wondering the same shit as you. Do we have two guys with the name Tyler Lake? Which, to me, would be about as unusual as the name itself - or do we have one Tyler Lake and two bodies, one dead, god only knows how long, and one alive, well and playin' lawyer in Chicago?" Max stood up and brushed at his jeans as if the December weather made them dusty. "More importantly, if it turns out there's one Tyler Lake and two bodies, can we safely assume the one in Chicago had something to do with the one they dug up here?"

"I don't know Max. But I think we need more information before we get to the point where we're assuming things," the Beast cautioned.

"Listen," Keona broke in, "I don't know what you guys plan to do in terms of checking out police records and that sort of thing. But if you're looking for information I can probably get you whatever's out there."

Max and the Beast were at Keona's house only because Tyler Lake, the Assistant District Attorney in Chicago, Illinois, and Tyler Lake, the skeleton dug up outside Madison, Wisconsin, had the bizarre makings of one helluva case. Compelling to be sure. By the same token, if it was going to take any significant amount of time away from the murder investigation of Kathy and Jack Reed, a priority second to none, then bizarre and compelling would have to wait in line. No ifs, ands, or buts about it. So yes, if Keona had a way of getting the most information in the least amount of time, which would be the likely scenario if it meant Max and the Beast wouldn't have to introduce their curiosities or out of state presence to the "suddenly interested," jurisdictional red tape bullshit of the local police department, then by all means Max was interested. "How so?" he queried.

"Because I know the reporter who covered the story. He's cousins with a guy named Curtis Webber."

Zack burrowed his hands inside the pockets of his leather bomber jacket, hunched up his broad shoulders to keep the cold from slipping through his long hair and reaching down his back, and tried to place a name with a face. When that didn't work he asked the obvious. "Who the fuck is Curtis Webber?"

Keona turned up the collar on his jacket, then followed Zack's lead by hunching up his own broad shoulders. "Curtis Webber was a guy I played ball with. He was drafted out of Wisconsin in my second to last season with the Bears. Played a couple of years on special teams, got hurt, then moved back here to try his hand at sportscasting. Did that for a couple of years before taking a job as sports director for another station. Same one his cousin works for as a reporter. Anyway, Webber and I fish during the summer and every so often he brings his dad or cousin along. And that's how I know him."

Zack smiled. "Shit Kee, that's the most I ever heard you say at one time."

Keona returned the smile. "So whataya think? Want me to get in touch with him and set something up?"

Zack grunted his answer in typical Beast fashion.

Max gathered up a healthy dose of the still, winter air, and said, "I agree, it certainly can't hurt."

Man, talk about speculating.

CHAPTER 79

*S*am Quiz. Helluva name, ain't it?

Anyway, Sam Quiz wasn't just a reporter. He was a reporter's reporter. We're talking about a guy whose favorite slogan is, *"There's More To The Story Than Meets The Eye."* We're talking about a guy who believes that getting to the heart of a matter, (any matter, for that matter), is all that matters. We're talking about a guy who doesn't watch the 10:00 p.m. news unless one of his stories is on it, and even then his story has to be one of the top three. We're talking about a guy who eats breakfast, lunch and dinner wherever his feet are planted, but always in the company of a pen and pad of paper. We're talking about a guy who would have more time to give guest lectures at the University if he wasn't so busy writing the most widely read newspaper column in Wisconsin. We're talking about a guy, who, for each of his twelve nationally published magazine articles, has received a job offer in a different state, yet remains in Madison where much of his family is scattered throughout.

We're talking about a guy whose utter persistence to find the truth once uncovered a conspiracy to frame the police commissioner's brother for insider trading - which, strangely enough, evolved into Sam somehow having a head start on the other reporters in Madison whenever a unique set of facts were unveiled, like that of a skeleton in a homemade grave.

We're talking about a guy who sat across the table from Max and Zack, looked them head-on and said, "Ya know, try as I might, sometimes I just don't understand. Why and the hell would someone chop off the fingers and thumbs of somebody else if all they were planning to do was bury them anyway? Hell, you guys are cops. You should know the answer to that."

Max looked as puzzled as he sounded. "I'm sorry, but I'm not sure what you mean. I mean all we were told was that a skeleton was dug up and identified as someone named Tyler Lake."

Sam scratched at his patchy head of short black hair and smirked. When he did his brown eyes just about disappeared inside their narrow shaped eye sockets. "Yeah, but only because that's what I gave the news department for a story. I had to give 'em something. If I didn't, sooner or later another station woulda got their hands on it and reported it first. So I waited as long as I could, then gave 'em just enough to get a jump on the other stations, which is all they're interested in anyway. The important thing is that I was able to preserve the story for myself. None of the other reporters around town will jump on it now because they know I already did. Now I can take the time to find out what really went down with this thing. Which, I might add, is all just as well since the cops around here will likely conduct an obligatory investigation and nothing more. You know, their desks are full with new unsolved crap, why waste time looking into old unsolved crap? Especially when there doesn't seem to be any family or friends pressing to find out what happened to the dear departed." Sam stuck his chin forward. "What about you big city guys? Do you get a case like this and wait around, hoping some reporter like me takes enough of an interest to do your investigative work for ya?"

While Zack mused over the distinction between what Sam's news department was interested in, and what Sam sought to preserve for himself, Max dismissed the reporter's arrogance and said, "No, I'm afraid not. Now how 'bout we get back to what you said about the fingers, and thumbs?"

"Oh, that's right. You did say you hadn't heard that, didn't you? I'm sorry. I forgot." Sam Quiz flashed a friendly enough smile, then leaned back in the padded leather chair and searched the restaurant until he spotted Millie, at which point he signaled for more coffee.

Underwhelmed by his apology, Max sensed that Sam liked to blow it hot and cold. And until he was comfortable Sam wasn't dealing from the bottom of the deck, Max figured it was one more reason not to tell him anything he didn't have to.

"So, you two been partners long?"

Zack muttered something underneath his breath.

"What...ain't you got better English than that?" Sam joked.

Maybe Zack was being a tad sensitive. Then again, maybe not. Either way, he wasn't the least bit amused by Sam's comment. But then, Sam only need look at the scowl on his face to realize that - that and the fact it might be best if he rekindled his conversation with Max. "Yes, the thing about the missing fingers and thumbs is true. Saw it myself."

Max raised his eyebrows and glanced at his partner, which Sam promptly interpreted to mean one of two things. It was either an indication that something was out there the detectives weren't coming clean with, or, Max was simply appalled by the horror of the act itself. But being that Max was a cop and likely saw horrific shit all the time, Sam took a stab at the former. "What's up? Whata you guys know that you don't want to talk about?" The question was innocent enough, yet, the only response it drew was a blank stare, compelling him to take a stab at something else. "Look, Keona said you guys are good cops and good people. Now I hope you don't take this the wrong way, but the good people part can wait. I'm interested in the part about the good out of state cops. Why are they here? What do they know that I don't? What is it they can tell me?"

Enough of this crap, Max concluded. Either Zack and I get some info or we're going back to Chicago. "Look Quiz, we're here to listen. Not the other way around. Now if you talk to us maybe we'll know if we've got something. And if we do, we'll let you know. But if you're gonna sit there and play hard to get, we're oughta here. Got more important things to do. Know what I'm sayin'?"

Sam Quiz stroked his clean shaven face. Max might've looked and sounded impatient, a character trait Sam generally associated with weakness, but Max wasn't coming across as the weak type. Intense? Likely. Resolute? Possibly. Weak? Naw. And Sam realized it was pointless to try and fool himself into thinking otherwise. So too was making an enemy out of Keona, which is exactly what would happen if he didn't tell the detectives what he knew. It wasn't that Sam was so against it, mind you. He was merely looking to get information in return, that's all. "Listen Max, I gather facts for a living. Sure, I write, but so do a lot of people. Uncovering the substance that becomes a story," he said with his forefinger tick-tocking in the air for emphasis, "that's the hard part. Believe me, I'm not trying to stonewall you guys. I'm just trying to protect my interest. It's my bread and butter. That's why if you know somethin', I'd like to hear about it."

"Believe me, we understand that Quiz. We're not looking for a story to write. Regardless of what my partner and I uncover, you can have it. The story is yours. Do you understand that? More importantly, now that I've said all that, were you able to understand my English?"

Okay, so maybe Zack's question was a little bit of a jab. But it was the gleam in his eyes and the crooked grin on his face that had Sam visualizing how a big ol' alley cat must look when it's getting ready to pounce on a canary with clipped wings.

And guess who was playing the part of the bird?

Yeah, that's what Sam thought too. He also thought it might be a good idea to laugh off Zack's question. Take the starch out of it, if you will - remind Zack his previous sarcasm was all in good fun.

The Beast always enjoyed watching the Sam Quizzes of the world. They come charging from the gate full of piss and vinegar, and yet, when they can't figure out a way to dance around someone who won't back-up, they just sort of fizzle out altogether. What Zack enjoyed even more was that it changed the momentum of their conversation. "So, how bout spittin' out this skeleton shit. Max and I don't have all day ya know."

Sam leaned forward until his flat chest rested against the edge of the table and opened up like he never had any trepidation at all. "It's the strangest fucking thing. The body was actually uncovered three, maybe almost four weeks before I gave the story to the news department. I get a call from a cop I know. He tells me, Sam head on over to so and so street. There's a guy digging a foundation for a new house. You won't believe what they found. So I go over and in between knocking down the old house and digging a foundation for a new house, pop goes the weasel and up comes a skeleton. And the son-of-a-bitch of it all was that the fingers and thumbs were missing."

"How did..."

"Hold on now, hold on. I said I was gonna tell you, and I'm gonna tell you, okay?"

Silence.

Sam's eyes darted back and forth. "Okay, now check it out. According to the medical wizards, bone size and density indicated the skeleton to be male. They also determined this skeleton, this guy, his joints, you know, his fingers and thumbs, they were cut with shears, or bolt cutters, something of that nature. Of course for all I care they could've been cut with a butter knife. The important thing is that the fingers and thumbs were nowhere to be found. Intentionally removed, right? But why? Was it some kind of occult crap? Someone lookin' for a new pair of hands? What?" Sam fell back in his chair and sealed his lips.

Max took the silence and made it his invitation to talk. "What about I.D. How'd they figure out who it was?"

"Shit, that was easy. Dental records. The son-of-a-bitch might not've had any fingers or thumbs, but he had a mouthful of teeth."

"How long ago?"

"They estimate he's been dead about seven years. They figure he was between 26 and 28 years old at the time, which would put him in his mid thirties today. I pretty much confirmed it at 35, but I'll get to that in a minute."

Once again Max raised his eyebrows and glanced at his partner, and once again Sam interpreted it to mean there was something out there the detectives weren't coming clean with. Yet, rather than ask them about it, this time Sam carried on with the facts. "After they aged and identified this guy, I spent the next two weeks or so, round-the-clock I might add, chasing his past. I started with the Secretary of State. Not the office, mind you. I mean, I ended up getting information from the office, but I needed the Secretary himself to make sure his staff cooperated with me." Sam shook his head and sighed. "I'll tell ya, it's a good thing I wrote a couple of favorable articles about him during the last election. Without his help, I doubt I would've gotten the shit I was after. Not as easily, that's for sure."

"And?"

"And using his name and what was determined to be his approximate age, I plugged in a time frame. Went back nine years and ran a computer check to see if he had a driver's license." Sam paused momentarily, then added, "Bingo."

"Interesting," Zack deadpanned.

Interesting? That's all he's got to say is interesting? Sam was truly insulted, but kept his feelings in check. That's because he was willing to bet the Chicago twosome would be singing a much louder tune just as soon as they heard the rest of the story. "Either of you guys ever look at your driver's license?"

"Sure," Zack responded, the question itself striking him as a no-brainer. "I mean we're cops. We've seen tons of licenses."

"So then you know what kind of information is on it?"

Zack scoffed. "What is this, a test? C'mon Quiz, get real."

Sam shook his head no, the placid expression on his face slightly distorted by his earnest reply. "I wouldn't ask if I didn't have good reason."

Zack thought about it for a second, figured, what the hell, and spit out the words in rapid succession. "Address, driver's license number, date of issue, date of expiration, date of birth, height, sex, restrictions, and some half-assed photograph." The Beast grabbed himself a handful of air. "Okay?"

Sam grinned, exposing a full set of white, yet slightly crooked teeth. "Okay, but like I said, I asked because I had reason to ask."

"Which is?" Max interjected.

Sam's teeth disappeared, in turn, narrowing his jaw line and rounding out his small head. "Well remember when I said I spent a couple of weeks chasing this guy's past?"

"Of course."

"I did it by tracing the information on his license as far as I could. You'd be surprised where it took me."

"We're all ears Sam."

Suddenly, telling a story wasn't all that bad. It gave Sam the rare opportunity to witness the arousing effects of his words as they were being said, something he couldn't get, (though often imagined), from his writing. "For starters, the address on his license took me to an apartment complex close to, as a matter-of-fact, within walking distance to the University of Wisconsin. I got in touch with the apartment management and tried to find out if someone named Tyler Lake was ever a tenant. Now as far as I'm concerned there's no doubt he lived there because that was the address listed on his license. Unfortunately their lease records didn't go back far enough, so there was no way of getting a copy of the lease to prove it."

"Did anybody remember him, remember the name?"

"Uh-uh. Not a chance. Nobody working there now was working there back then. The person whose been there the longest is the manager, and she's only been there two years. Pretty steady turnover rate, ya know?"

"So then what?" the Beast questioned.

The heedful look on the face of his two person audience - small yes, but an audience nonetheless - finally made its way to Sam's ego. He responded by crafting an expression of a sympathetic philosopher contemplating Shakespeare's, *"To be, or not to be,"* and remained in silent pose until fairly certain he could amplify the look of his self-proclaimed genius no more. "Then it dawned on me. Most kids, when they graduate college, are 22 years old. And they don't stick around. They're hellbent on getting a job and joining all the happy horseshit of the real world. But this Tyler Lake guy was somewhere between 26 and 28 years old at the time of his death, and was still living in an apartment complex within walking distance to the University. Why would he be there if he wasn't still in school? Maybe the kid was working on his Ph.D. Maybe he was in med school, or law school. Then again, maybe he wasn't in any graduate school and was still living there because he liked it. Whatever the case, I figured it was worth followin' up." Sam paused momentarily, then added, "Bingo."

What's up with this bingo shit? Max wondered. "Bingo what?"

Sam sat in his chair straight and proud. "You want the long story or the short story?"

"Let's start with the short one."

"Bingo, the administration offices had records showing he graduated college and law school. Now here's the thing," Sam said, his forefinger pointing to the ceiling, "the law school tries to keep tabs on its graduates, if for no other reason than to grow the alumni and beg for money, so there's generally a current address on file. Yet, the last thing they had in this kid's file was a list of all the places he requested his transcripts be sent...for job interviews I would guess. Now there's certainly no crime in not providing your school with current info about yourself, but maybe he didn't provide any 'cause he wasn't around to provide it...if ya know what I mean. That assumption is also how I figure he'd be thirty-five if he were alive today. Ya know, if you use the year he graduated and subtract the birthdate shown on his license, you come up with thirty-five." Sam winked. "It's the new math."

Max ignored Sam's attempt at humor, and asked, "You get a look at anything else in this kid's file. His school application for instance."

"Yes, I got a look at his entire file. But don't think it's something anyone could've done," he advised. "The law school administration office isn't in the habit of turning over information to any Tom, Dick or Harry who asks for it. I doubt a family member could even get it. At least, not without getting a court order first." With the backdrop of this difficult task now laid out nice and puffy like, Sam thrust himself back on the familiar settings of his self-ordained pedestal and added, "It's a good thing I'm well known around these parts. People like to do you favors when you're well known. Not only that, but it seems like everyone wants to be friends with you too. They see you as someone who stands out from the crowd - someone who knows, and who's friends with all the right people - the kind of people they themselves want to be friends with. They must think if they're friends with you it makes them stand out in the crowd also. I guess you can't really blame them for that, can you?"

Max shook his head. "I don't know, I've never been around anybody famous."

The Beast decided his partner was being far to kind in his response, and offered up what he saw as the only logical answer. "Hey, that only means stupidity knows no bounds."

"Oh really? Well, I think you're missing the point," Sam countered, clearly pissed off by Zack's remark. "The point is, because I'm well known the Dean of the law school let me have a copy of Tyler Lake's file. Now let's face it, aren't you two here because you want information I've got? Information I've come by only because of who I am and who I know? Isn't that right?"

Zack held up an open palm. "Take it easy Quiz. I was just having a little fun with you, that's all. You're right, Max and I are here because you have information." Zack waited for Sam's expression to soften up, turned his palm into a pointed finger, and in his best gyrating Elvis, half sang, half joked, "You-da-man, Sammy boy. A-just-a hunka, hunka, hunka, you-da-man."

Sam didn't want to give Zack the satisfaction of laughing, but when Max gasped, stifling his own laughter, he couldn't help himself. It started off a slow, deep rumble, like it originated in his toes, caught fire somewhere around his midsection, and skyrocketed out of his mouth in a high-pitched cackle. And an obnoxious motherfucker it was. Within seconds everyone in the restaurant was staring at the table.

As for Max and the Beast? What else could they do but roll their eyes at one another and wait for Sam to settle down.

At least the information they got was worth the wait.

CHAPTER 80

Max would've never guessed that seeing Wanda Seven again could be so rewarding. But there she was beside him - eyes, bright and clear, smile, soft and genuine, overall appearance, that of a young woman bristling with happiness. It was a happiness brought about by the calm and loving hand of Keona Raven, yes. But, if it wasn't for Max, it was a happiness never born. Let's face it, had he not grabbed her from the streets and returned her to life among the living, there she would've most certainly died, courtesy of the drugs and beatings bestowed upon her by the late, great, Billy Turner. And for the few minutes that Max entertained the thought, his face lit up - and when it did, words no longer seemed necessary. Wanda understood.

So did Keona. Which, of course, is why he was able to walk in the room, summarily dismiss the sight of Wanda's hand curled around Max's, and do his best to sound like John Wayne living in the ice age. "Hey pilgrim, you makin' time with my woman?"

"She looks great Kee." Max sounded like a proud papa.

Zack agreed. "Yes she does, doesn't she."

"Hey, what is this? Just because you two animals sprung for chow doesn't mean you can start making moves on this beautiful woman here." Keona gently squeezed Wanda's shoulder as he lead Zack and two overstuffed bags of Chinese carryout to the dining room table.

"Hush. I think I like it," she playfully responded.

"You should," Keona tossed back. "You deserve it. As a matter-of-fact, I'd like to spend the next hour telling you how terrific you are...but we have a problem and I can't. A rather large problem at that," he added sincerely.

"What do you mean large problem? What large problem?" Wanda's soft voice might have made her sound like the girl next store, but since she wasn't altogether convinced Keona wasn't just fucking around, the wary look in her eyes made her look like anything but.

Keona waited until Wanda and Max were standing at the table before wagging his thumb at the Beast. "Well you see this big moose here? He eats fast and he eats a lot. I'm not even sure if he chews. I think he just breaks his food in big pieces and swallows. Hell Max, you probably know, which is it?"

Max gave the question the once over, then replied, "Ya know, I gotta be honest Kee. I think I saw him chew one time. But he was eating scrambled eggs so it was kinda hard to tell."

"See Wan, that's what I mean. When food and Zack are at a table together, you can't spend much time talking."

"Now wait a minute," Zack protested. "You two keep talkin' and it won't be long before Wanda's thinkin' big guys like me actually pay attention to scrawny, little guys like you. And the truth is, we take scrawny, little guys like you with a grain of salt." The Beast winked at a smiling Wanda and proceeded to rip open one of the carryout bags.

Keona threw his leg over the chair and sat down. "Not to change subjects, but speaking of scrawny, little guys, how'd your afternoon with Sam Quiz turn out?"

"I'll say this much Kee, he sure does like to hear himself talk. And when he laughs - man, you'd think..."

"Yeah, like a pack of wild hyenas, I know. But did he give you anything good? Anything to sink your teeth into?"

As Max reached across the table to hand Wanda a bottle of water, he replied, "Well he appears to do his homework, that's for sure."

"Then he must've had something, yeah? I figured he would."

In between swallowing food and beverage Max and Zack took turns repeating what Sam Quiz told them in the restaurant. And when they were finished, Keona tilted his chair back on its hind legs, folded his arms, and asked, "So whata you guys think. Is the guy they dug up in Madison and the lawyer in Chicago one and the same?"

Max arched his eyebrows and shrugged his shoulders simultaneously. "That's the sixty-four thousand dollar question Kee. Hell, right now about all I can tell you with any degree of certainty is that if you go by the picture on his license, plus the one the law school has on file, the Tyler Lake we know is a lot better looking."

"Older, too," Zack added.

"Probably, although I'm not sure that makes anymore of a difference than the idea of him being better looking?"

"How ya figurin' partner?"

"I dunno. I guess I'm saying if nobody sees the ugly guy because he's buried, then he doesn't exist. In which case no one ever knows who the better lookin' one is. And with the age thing, he can be older and younger at the same time. You know, he can be 40, 45 in reality, but if he passes for 35, and there's no reason to say otherwise, hell, he can be that too."

Despite having half an eggroll stuffed in his mouth the Beast managed to grunt his concurrence. But that was it. As far as he was concerned, no more conversation. It was time to finish eating. If Keona wanted to find out anything else he was going to have to get it from Max.

"What about the kid's background. Quiz know anything?"

"Uh-uh, I don't think so."

"Not even family?"

Max hemmed and hawed for a couple of seconds before responding with, "I guess the best way to explain it is like this. A law school application has one spot to list your parents names, and another spot asking for the name of a family member to contact in case of an emergency. For both questions he answered none living. So, no, based on that I don't think there's any family to know about. Quiz said he's gonna keep looking, although I'm not holding my breath."

Keona's eyebrows drew together. "Hmmmm, that's kind of interesting, isn't it? How about the one in Chicago. Anything on him?"

Having just slurped up some of the longest lo-mein noodles he'd ever seen, Max had to wipe off his chin before answering. "Naw. Me-n'-Zack figured we'd find out what the deal was with this guy before we started ruffling feathers with our own guy. Figured tomorrow morning we'd check out a couple of things around here, maybe talk to Quiz again, then head back to Chicago. Once we get there we'll check out our guy. Our biggest problem is not having enough time to spend on this thing because of my sister's investigation. That's why we figured if we can put a couple of solid leads together real quick, then dish it off to someone else, why not?"

Chinese food was the only American food Keona could eat three times a week. He liked eggrolls best, although fried shrimp ran a close second. As a result, as soon as he noticed all the eggrolls had disappeared, (thanks to the Beast) he didn't hesitate in pulling the carton of fried shrimp out of future harm's way. "See what happens Wan. While Max and I are talkin', Moose here's chomping away."

The Beast gently patted his stomach. "Man, they were good too."

CHAPTER 81

One o'clock in the middle of a Wisconsin winter morning is no time to be walking around outside. Who cares if there's a bright moon, a calm wind, or a gurgling stream? Who cares if the sound of a crackling fire and the smell of steaks cooking over burning pine were the last ingredients needed to turn Keona's backyard into the perfect setting for a beer commercial? The point is, cold is cold is cold, so who cares?

Evidently Max, because that's where he was. Had been ever since Keona left the house a half-hour earlier to take Wanda back to the rehab center. He even tried getting the Beast to go outside with him, but with a coffee table for his feet and a little crown for his head, Zack wanted no part of it. As a matter-of-fact, had it been a star filled summer night he still wouldn't have gone. With so few opportunities for any real quiet time, what with the crazy pace of his job and all, Zack had to pick his moments - and right then his moment was on the couch. And a grand moment it was. He closed his eyes, sipped at his drink and thought back to the same time last year when he and Susan were soaking up a little Key West sun.

Of course, that's the unfortunate thing about moments. Just as a trip down memory lane can make one linger, the feeling someone is staring at you can make one vanish. Which is precisely what happened because the Beast opened his eyes and found Max standing in the doorway. And never mind that his face was all red. The single digit winter air took care of that. It was the disconcerting look in his eyes which prompted the Beast to straighten up and take notice. "What's up bud?"

Max didn't answer, and it wasn't until he took a seat on the couch opposite Zack, where, closer to the light, Zack was able to get a better feel for just how deep his partner's troubled expression was. "You alright man?" After a short silence, Zack set his glass on the table and narrowed his focus. "C'mon Max. Something's up. I can see it in your face. Talk to me man. Tell me what you're thinkin'."

Max remained quiet until satisfied the words rolling around in his head would make sense when they fell out of his mouth. At that point he gave his day old beard a quick genie lamp rub, and said, "Beast, you remember that day we were in the Captain's office talking about the Berman and Blair murders? How we were comparing the similarities of those cases with my sister's?"

The Beast nodded.

"You remember what we talked about?"

Knowing how impatient Max could get once he started chomping at the bit, like now, the last thing Zack wanted to do was guess, and guess wrong. "Yeah, sure. Probably. I mean, we talked about a few things so I'm not really sure what you're after."

Max pressed down on his thighs, as if that was supposed to suffocate the bounce in his legs. "The evidence Beast. Remember I said that maybe we're dealing with a guy who isn't all that concerned about leaving evidence behind. If he doesn't leave it, great. But if he does, that's okay too."

The urgency in Max's voice was like an underlying current, one so profound, the more he talked, the more Zack could feel his own anxiety starting to swell up. Nevertheless, he did his best to remain calm. "I remember. You thought maybe the guy didn't give a shit about what he may or may not have left behind, because in his mind, it wouldn't lead to him anyway. He couldn't get caught."

"Right. Exactly. Couldn't get caught because he doesn't think he can be found. The guy thinks he has an identity different from any identity we might uncover in the evidence left at the murder scenes. Don't matter if it's fingerprints, semen. In his mind, it ain't his, 'cause in his mind, it ain't him." Unable to sit still any longer Max popped up from the couch and dug his hands in his pockets. He kept them there for about half a second. "Now, that being the case, think about what Sam Quiz said this afternoon after we told him about the other Tyler Lake in Chicago."

Zack's eyes darted back and forth as he reflected back to the conversation with the Wisconsin reporter. Yet, when he repeated it, he spoke slowly, almost gingerly, as if making every effort to keep his thoughts no more than a step ahead of his words. "Quiz said he's intrigued at the possibility a person could actually murder somebody else, steal his identity, and in his mind..." Suddenly, the significance of what Zack was thinking overwhelmed his ability to finish his sentence.

"And in his mind, be two people at the same time," Max injected.

The Beast bit his lower lip and swallowed hard. As he steadied his gaze on Max, the thoughts in his head now running at what seemed like a hundred miles an hour, the color in his face drained and the words, "the press conference," fell out of his mouth.

"Huh? Whata you talkin' about?"

"The press conference the D.A.'s office had after they dropped those charges against you."

"What about it Beast? I was with Clare and didn't see it."

"I caught it on the news that night. Tyler Lake said something to the effect that you got charged with Billy Turner's murder because things appeared one way, when in reality they turned out to be altogether different. But then he said the D.A.'s office shouldn't be held accountable because, often times, it's difficult to know when things are different than they appear. Then he just sort of smiled. At the time I wrote the whole thing off as just another politician doing his best to look good in a situation gone bad. But now, now with all this other bullshit..." Zack arched his eyebrows and took a quick breath, "I gotta tell ya Max, when it comes to murder, I've never been a big believer in coincidence. I think of Lake's statement now and I think it's real easy for it to take on a whole new meaning. And when I picture him smiling, I'm thinkin' maybe in his own mind it was all he could do to keep from laughing."

"Yeah, well ya know what I think Beast? I think it's time to pay Lake a little visit."

Zack nodded. "We'll call Keona from the car and let him know we're heading back to Chicago."

CHAPTER 82

The Berman clan didn't do a fucking thing for him. I repeat, not one fucking thing. Oh sure, John Henry got the family bug out of his system, but that wasn't because of anything the Bermans did. Hell, any family could've done that. What made the Berman family so appealing in the first place were the three daughters, all tush biting cute and talcum powder fresh, and that heart stopping, good looking bitch who called herself mommy. They were the added attraction. They were the reason John Henry picked them over the other families.

The thing of it was, he got so jacked up thinking about them, by the time that special night actually rolled around, John Henry already had a clear picture of how the evening's activities would turn out. He'd slither inside the house on a cold, dark night, move along the hallways and inside the rooms like a shadow, strap his hands around each of the three girl's young, deliciously ripe necks, watch them succumb before the darkness of his piercing glare, get all nice and goose bumpy in the process, maybe even get a hot flash or two, then turn his cravings on the mommy, who, in turn, would make his dick come alive like a lightning bolt in an electrical storm.

But goddamnit, the fucking whores didn't do their jobs. Not a single one of them. And all the slashing, cutting, chopping and choking by John Henry did little to change it. To a bitch, the Berman broads bowed out quietly. No fighting. No scratching or kicking. No biting or pulling hair. No screaming. Nobody tried to run. Nobody tried to hide. Not even a single dirty look. They just laid perfectly still, as if they were already dead, which is why killing them, although inevitable, turned out to be a fucking bore.

Well it 'tweren't gonna happen that way this time around!

No way!

No how!

With Christmas only spitting distance away, John Henry was going to give himself the kind of present he knew wouldn't disappoint. The kind of present that would chill his spine, warm his blood, and jingle his balls. The kind of present that would satiate his crave, which, after his encounter with the lowly, miserable Bermans, stood on the brink of seething rage. The kind of present he could rip open and suck out the spirit. The kind of present that would allow him to bathe in the darkness, cleanse his soul, and once again, become whole.

And if you think John Henry was concerned about the oversized prick she lived with, to hell with you. Aside from the thumping in his head and the throbbing going on in his pants, only one thing concerned him - how soon he'd be inside her house.

Well don't fret John Henry. You'll be there soon. Long before the sun comes up kind of soon.

CHAPTER 83

When she left the doctor's office that afternoon the first thing Susan wanted to do was call Zack and tell him the unexpected, good news. Yet, by the time she got home she had a change of heart, deciding instead to wait until she could tell him face to face. She knew the instant Zack heard the word pregnant his expression was going to turn into a Kodak moment too precious to miss. So why miss it?

Generally speaking, Susan was a pretty good sleeper. But on a night when Zack was in Wisconsin, a night she wished to share with him more than any other, she slept plain lousy. So lousy, in fact, that by 2:30 in the morning she'd gotten fed up with all her tossing and turning and decided to get up and read. Unfortunately, she just finished a book and didn't have any other new ones in the house. The idea of browsing through old Cosmo magazines didn't exactly excite her. Either did reading any of Zack's Sports Illustrateds, even though the most recent issue had an article about downhill racers she would've found interesting. But that's only because she used to race in college. Other than that the article was only a few pages, which meant, even if she read it, ten minutes later she'd be looking for something else to occupy her time with. And figuring she was going to be up for quite awhile, she wanted something more - like maybe an old movie on TV. Or better still, something she hadn't done, in what seemed like years, making it all the more reason to do it now.

Susan found the photo albums on the top shelf of the walk-in closet. Both were covered with a thin skin of dust so she grabbed one of "those" shirts Zack never wore, yet refused to part with, and wiped them off.

Although much of the day and night had been a trade-off between a nothing breeze and a few scattered flurries, almost from the moment Susan climbed back into bed and started looking at pictures, a robust wind reared up its ugly head and came roaring in from the west. Still, no matter how many times a window rattled, or the wind just flat out whistled, it never really bothered her, not like the sound of...let's say...creaky stairs. But that's because, no matter what sound the wind makes, it's still just a product of the wind. Stairs, on the other hand, only make one sound...they creak. And they only do that when someone is using them. The other thing about stairs is they always seem to creak loudest at night...when you're home alone...like Susan.

Of course, that sounds like quite the paradox, because if Susan was home alone and the stairs suddenly creaked, wouldn't that mean someone else was in the house?

Yeah, that's what Susan figured too. That's why she popped her head up from the photo album and called out, "Zack, honey?"

Two...three...four...

"Zack?"

Again, no answer. Just the squeaky, squawky sound of creaky stairs.

"Zack, honey? That you?"

Still, no answer. Only the stairs, moaning and groaning...a little slower...a little louder.

Close, and closing in, John Henry curled his upper lip.

Waiting...waiting...

Susan scanned the room.

Waiting...waiting...

Her eyes locked onto the doorknob.

Waiting...waiting...

She tugged nervously at the ends of her hair. Something was wrong. Something had to be. Zack would've heard her. By now he would've surely answered.

But there was no answer, only the stairs crying out, as if in agony. Goosebumps. First her arms. Then across her shoulders and down her back. Damp. Chilling. Susan quivered.

Closer, and closing in, John Henry bared his teeth.

Standing perspiration now trickled across Susan's temples. She ignored it, pushed the photo album aside and forced herself from the confines of her warm bed.

And then...

Bang! The upstairs erupted as John Henry smacked his hands against the hallway walls.

Oh God, what now? What do I do? The gun, the gun - Oh God, please god - the drawer - hurry, hurry - the drawer - open the drawer - the gun - Oh God - hurry, hurry.

Closer...

Closer...

Closing in...

Closed!

With shadow looming overhead, and dark, glistening pupils, John Henry stood on one side of the bedroom door, his long, outstretched fingers craving to stretch until they split skin, his breathing hastened - and Susan stood on the other side, her trembling hand squeezing the handle of the gun, at that moment she wished she never convinced Zack to unload, her breathing, all but paralyzed with fear.

And as the door crept open, pushed in from the hand of night itself, all that remained was for darkness to invade darkness, hatred to invade hope, death to invade life.

Yet, and no matter what John Henry might've been thinking, it was a life Susan had no intentions of giving up anytime soon.

CHAPTER 84

Take the burning flame from a gut reaction, stick it in a car for an hour plus, and one of two things will likely happen. Either the flame will intensify with each highway mile, or it'll quietly simmer down. And when Max pulled his eyes from the passenger window, turned to his partner, and declared, "I plan to be sittin' on Tyler Lake's doorstep before the little prick wakes up," there was little doubt which way he was leaning.

Of course, it certainly didn't come as any surprise - at least not as far as Zack was concerned. Hell, from the moment Kathy Reed's body was discovered, Zack knew Max was going to go headhunting. It was his sister for Christ's sake! Who wouldn't want to see the murdering son-of-a-bitch dead?! That's why killing him, whoever "him" turned out to be, had never been an issue Zack felt the need to resolve. Granted, Zack didn't want to see Max lose his job, or worse yet, end up in jail over it. But Max was gonna do what Max was gonna do, and that's all there was to it. Period!

As for the Beast? The most important thing he could do was help his best friend and partner make the entire episode look nice and tidy like - in a justifiable sort of way. That meant coming up with the kind of game plan that would allow Max to blow the motherfucker away and look like a hero in the process. And since they wouldn't be back in Chicago for close to another hour, Zack decided now was as good a time as any to start thinking one up. "Can I ask you a question bro?"

"What's that?" Max replied, his attention once again resting on the passing night.

"If in fact it turns out Tyler Lake is the guy, have you given any thought about how you wanna do this thing?"

It wasn't so much the way Zack asked the question, but the uncertainty in the words he used that proved troubling for Max, prompting him to answer the question with one of his own. "Tell me something Beast, where do you think Tyler Lake really fits in all of this?"

The Beast shrugged his big, square shoulders. "I don't know yet. I think it's still too early to tell. For either of us."

Zack's response was a whole lot easier for him to say than it was for Max to listen to. That's because Max spent the last 75 miles convincing himself Tyler Lake murdered his sister and brother-in-law. Unfortunately, it was a conviction, so perilous in foundation, that in one compromising breath Zack managed to rehang it by the thinnest of rope. And once that happened, the only thing left was for Max to wait until his insides finished crashing to the pit of his stomach, (heart, guts, psyche and all). It wasn't something that was easily lost inside the jeep's hollow darkness either, as Zack jerked his attention from the road long enough to find Max staring at him with the eyes of a bewildered child. "What's eatin' you?"

"What the fuck you talkin' about Beast? What happened to all that happy horseshit you said about not being a big believer in coincidence when it came to murder?"

Zack could hear the tension in Max's voice and went out of his way to sound just the opposite. "Listen Max, all I'm saying is that we have to find out if Tyler Lake did it for sure. And if we find out he did, then we have to have some kind of plan already in place so that killing him looks justified. I mean, obviously, you can't just walk up to him and shoot him."

Everything the Beast said made sense. Thing was, Max only clung to the part that pissed him off the most. "Yeah? Well don't bet on it," he snapped.

Now Zack could either make an assumption and leave it go at that, or ask, and know for sure, but at the same time, risk stoking the fire once again. Needless to say, in a situation like this, what choice did he really have? "You are just fucking around...right?"

His eyebrows drawing closer together, his tired blue eyes now lost somewhere between a look of disbelief and one of righteous indignation, Max grumbled, "You know damn well I wouldn't fuck around about something like that?!"

"C'mon Max, don't be ridiculous. You can't just walk up to the guy and kill him. No matter what you say, you can't! And if you think otherwise, then I'm here to tell ya, ya need some fresh air."

Listening to the Beast suddenly insist on following the law, when, in this particular instance, following the law carried all the insanity and immorality of the killer himself, was more than Max was willing to tolerate. "Fuck you Beast. Don't tell me what I can and can't do. Okay?"

Stung by his response, Zack was ready to hit back with, "Yeah, well fuck you too!" Problem was, if he did that, a thick, uneasy silence was going to crawl between them like a fat, unwanted passenger with a nasty case of body odor. Not exactly the kind of plan Zack had in mind. Nor was it the ideal way to spend the rest of the drive back to Chicago. As a result, he decided to suck it up - treat his partner's belligerence as nothing more than nervous energy gone haywire, if you will.

Of course, it was a helluva lot easier to swallow once Max hung his head and did an unexpected about-face. "Sorry man. I didn't mean that. I got carried away. This whole thing's got me crazy. Believe me, I know what you're sayin'. I know it has to look clean."

Zack waived off the apology as if the outburst never crossed his mind. "Forget about it. Let's just see if we can come up with something just in case it turns out Lake's the one we're after."

Yeah? And what if it turns out he isn't? A possibility, had it not been for Zack's cautious approach, Max would have never entertained. "Christ, Beast. I know this crap ain't the best lead we've ever had to go on, but this whole time I've been teasing myself into thinking it is. What's worse, what if I killed Lake and it turns out he didn't have anything to do with my sister? Where would I be then?"

Zack kicked the question around for a couple of seconds, then replied, "I dunno. I guess they'd throw you in the can. Then again, if it turns out he is the guy and ya kill him on the spot, the D.A.'s office is gonna cry foul and you'll probably end up there anyway. And let's face it, if that happens, Lake may be dead, but if you end up in jail, he takes your life away too. And quite frankly, I don't want to see that happen. You've got a life worth living and I think it's time you got back to it."

Having finally said what had been on the tip of his tongue, for what seemed like close to forever, Zack found himself somewhat apprehensive over the uncertainty of how Max would now react. He could get all pissed off again, simply because he was flirting with that kind of mood anyway. He could crawl into his tough guy shell and swear his life away in return for the life of his sister's murderer. Better yet, he could crawl into that other shell of his, the loner shell, the place he hides whenever it dawns on him he'll never see his sister Kathy again. Or, and as it turned out, he could take the blank look on his face, stick it on his partner, and ask, "Whataya mean?"

Zack rolled his eyeballs and thought, for a guy whose been looking out for other people longer than I've known him, when it comes to looking out for himself, he can be so goddamn dumb it's amazing. "I mean Clare and your nephew, Matthew."

Boy oh boy, mention Clare and the little kid to Max, and Bing! Bing! Bing!, lights go off in his head like a slot machine. Still, you wouldn't know it to look at him, as both the deeply rooted twinkle in his eye for Matthew and the heartfelt longing to be with Clare remained muted under the weight of his anger, although temporarily on hold, still dying to get out. "Fuck, Beast. I'm sorry. I don't know what I was thinkin'. I must be a fucking moron or something."

Now it was Zack who wore the eyes of a bewildered child. "Sorry? Whata you sorry for?"

"I'm sorry because I'm a selfish idiot, and I'm a selfish idiot because I got you doin' something you got no business doin'."

Zack responded with an exaggerated nod of the head and a sarcastic, "Well, that certainly clears it up for me."

Max grinned. "You obviously missed my point."
"To put it mildly."
"Hey, I can't help it if you don't understand English."

"What can I say? I studied the arts in college. English ain't considered an art."

Max's grin spilled into laughter.

The Beast pretended to look serious, and kept his eyes glued to the lines in the highway to help him do just that. Try as he might, however, he still ended up swallowing back his own yucks, culminating in a shake of the shoulders and a squeaky gasp for air, which, when you consider his raspy voice and largeness, sounded as stupid as it looked.

Funny thing, this laughing business. Especially when it emanates from nerves and necessity, not some mindless hilarity. It's not as pure that way, granted, but it's a helluva lot more medicinal. At least it was for Max. That's why after the laughter died down and the Beast asked him to explain again why it was he apologized, Max was able to answer without the least bit of hesitancy in his thinking, or strain in his voice. "The point I was trying to make was this: We can try and make this thing look clean, but you know as well as I do there's always the chance we could fuck up and get caught. Now I don't see where I have a choice in the matter, but that's no reason for you to put your ass on the line. And before you say anything, I understand the part about Clare and Matthew. I really do. But you've got an entire family to think about. Hell, you guys are like The Waltons. Plus there's Susan, and I know you wanna get married and have kids. So maybe you oughta take more of a backseat on this shit and let me see it through alone."

Strange thing, this conversation business. One minute it moves along without a hitch, and the next, the most innocent idea can be conveyed by the simplest of words, and yet, out of the blue it takes off in a whole different direction.

"Max, do you remember that time we were in Harvey's Bar shootin' pool? Actually I was playing some guy and you were waiting on the winner. He and I bet five bucks on the game. He lost, paid up and disappeared. Then about ten minutes later he came back with some big hairy lookin' goofball. Remember? You even asked the guy if his name was Big Foot."

Max smiled. He remembered the story alright. He just didn't know where Zack was going with it.

"Anyway, the guy wanted his five bucks back and when I told him to go fuck himself his goofball friend pulled out a switchblade. Remember what you did? You broke a pool stick over his head and had your boot planted in the other guys nuts before I even got my hands out of my pockets."

"Big deal. I was drunk."

"That's not the point Max. The point is, you stood between me and a knife, and did so because we're friends. Who knows, I could've been killed. So could've you. But that didn't stop you for a second. So please, before you insult me by telling me not to put my ass on the line, remember that. Okay?"

"Yeah, but this is different," Max protested.

"You're right, it is." Zack deadpanned. "This time we're working a murder case that happens to involve your sister and brother-in-law. We were only playing pool then."

Max chewed on his partner's words, before mumbling, "Point taken."

"Good. Now there's one other thing." Zack waited for Max to ask what it was, then replied, "I want you to be my best man."

Wow! Talk about being bowled over. Max went from nondescript to looking about as wide-eyed and open-mouthed as a blow fish.

"Little surprised, eh?"

Hell yeah, he was a little surprised. Sure, he knew the Beast wanted to get married. He even brought it up a minute ago himself. But, so what? That didn't mean he expected to hear something like that now. And just 'cause he did, that certainly didn't mean he was going to be able to respond right away. Hell no. It took Max several seconds to digest the news and break into that big, beautiful shit eating grin of his. "Goddamn, you sneaky son-of-a-bitch. Why didn't you tell me?"

With a big, beautiful shit eating grin of his own, the Beast said, "Whataya mean? I just did."

"Yeah, but how long this thing been coming? I mean, when did you and Susan decide? And why didn't I know that day?"

Zack pulled his hand off the wheel and tapped his fist into the one Max offered for congratulations. "We haven't decided. I haven't asked her yet. I figured since we'll be getting in, in about 45 minutes or so, I'll stop by the house and leave her a note telling her I'm back in town early and I wanna take her out to dinner. I'll ask her then."

"Why risk waking her up? Why don't you just call her later?"

"Cause we may get tied up with this Tyler Lake thing and I may not get the chance. Besides, she'll wanna know what the special occasion is and I'll have to come up with some bullshit reason. And she can always tell when I'm lying. This way, I'll leave her note and be done with it."

"Yeah, but what happens if we're still looking into Tyler Lake when the dinner bell sounds?"

Zack gave the question a casual shrug. "If I can't break away, I'll worry about it then. The worst case scenario is that I'll put it off until tomorrow."

"Sounds like a plan to me."

Zack nodded his concurrence, before adding, "Now all we gotta do is come up with another one for Tyler Lake."

Max didn't respond. Instead he turned his focus back to the darkness racing by his window, hoping somewhere within its endless mysteries, there was indeed, a plan for the making.

CHAPTER 85

Fear: A feeling of anxiety and agitation, dread and despair, timidity and terror, caused, of course, by the presence of danger and evil.

Oh yeah, there's one other thing about fear, to John Henry Stevens, its very essence...

You can smell it!

Although, with Susan hiding behind the bedroom door, her body pressing against the wall with such force it was as if she was trying to become one with the paint, smelling it was almost too easy. Consequently, John Henry thought it might be fun to take a few steps away from the door, and simply stand in place. Let his pretty little bitch soak up his presence without beholding the image of his dark figure. Allow his glorious uncertainty to reek havoc on her imagination. Oblige her with the whispered words of an epitaph to be. Then witness her crumble under the strength of her own weakness.

There was only one problem with that. Susan understood the gravity of the situation all too well. She certainly didn't need her imagination to explain it. What's more, she had no intentions of listening to the maundering incantations of some depraved madman. Okay, so maybe she was trembling like a frightened child, and breathing as if the taste of oxygen was a precious new discovery. But that aside, the continuation of life remained a mere flight of stairs and front door away. And as long as her legs were working, that's exactly where she intended to have them carry her.

Susan rode the back of her shoulders along the wall as she inched herself away from behind the bedroom door. "I have a gun, and I'll use it," she warned, her eyes bug-eye wide, her voice one big quiver.

John Henry snickered.

"I swear, I'll shoot you." This time Susan tried to add a little oomph to her warning, but there's only so much oomph you can add when you're scared shitless, and holding an unloaded gun to boot.

Not only that, but once inside the bosom of his mind's own darkness, John Henry stood, at what he considered to be, the pinnacle of strength and greatness, and frankly, didn't give a shit about any oomph. Just to prove it, he moved into Susan's line of sight, twisted up his face until he became a caricature of himself, and in his best schoolgirl impersonation, mocked, "Ooooh, Auntie Em, Auntie Em. I've got a gun and I'll shoot. Auntie Em, Auntie Em."

Twisted up face, or not, if the light on the nightstand was good enough to look at photo albums, it was certainly good enough to recognize a face from the past. "I know you," Susan said, her terrified expression melting away just enough to make her look as stunned as she sounded. "You're a lawyer for the city. I saw you in court. I was there that day."

"You're a lawyer for the city. I saw you in court. I was there that day," John Henry mimicked, immediately after which, he stomped his foot and bellowed, "You don't know shit!"

So much for the "stunned" look. As a matter-of-fact, it was all Susan could do just to harness her runaway adrenaline long enough to string a couple of sentences together without sounding completely out of breath. But even at that, there was no way she could minimize the desperation in her voice. "I live with Zack Darwin. You know him. I know you know him. He'll kill you if you touch me."

John Henry snickered. First it was the insignificance of the gun, which, as it turned out, was an obvious decoy, otherwise he would've been shot at by now. Now it's the insignificance of Zack Darwin, who was nowhere around anyway. What next? he wondered. Was he going to get struck down by a bolt of lighting? Better yet, was a bolt of lighting gonna fly up his ass and take him to a galaxy far, far away? John Henry found the thought so comical, it took but the blink of an eye for his ominous laughter to fill the room, where it hovered, for what seemed like an eternity, before it came to a crashing halt, and he growled, "Darwin'll do the same thing to me that Cougar did after I killed his sister...Nothing!"

Okay, so up until now, John Henry was obviously doing a helluva number on Susan. But, it wasn't until his chilling revelation that her blood ran cold and body shuddered, first causing her knees to buckle, then washing away her vision, if only for a second, by the tears she could no longer hold back. "It...It... It was... It was... It was you," she stammered.

John Henry took a step forward, and bowed like a regal gent. "At your service, me lady."

Instinctively, Susan stepped backwards. At the same time, she bit her bottom lip so hard, she actually bit a piece off. Yet, it was the severity of the pain itself that continued to feed her consciousness, in turn, keeping John Henry's madness from overpowering her want for survival, a survival, that Susan believed, depended solely on her ability to get out of the house. The stairs! Gotta get to the stairs! Gotta do it while I've got the chance! Gotta do it before he kills you! Gotta do it now! And with that, Susan threw the gun at John Henry and bolted for the door.

The gun was a minor irritation. John Henry wasn't. He half-stepped his way into her path and tagged Susan with a vicious backhand across the face.

Susan stumbled backwards, but thanks to the wall, managed to remain standing.

John Henry sneered. "Now why would you think you could escape me? Did you think I wasn't paying attention just because I was bowing down like a faggoty royal? Is that what you thought?"

Susan said nothing, her watery eyes, nose and bloody lip, doing all the talking for her.

John Henry cocked his head, the faraway look in his glassy eyes the perfect rendering of the madman he was. "I asked you a question, you pathetic little whore. And I want an answer!" He demanded.

Susan shook her head no, but the movement was so subtle, it wasn't until her quivering voice muttered, "go fuck yourself," that John Henry got his answer.

Of course, it wasn't an answer John Henry expected. And it certainly wasn't one he appreciated. But hey! Even John Henry Stevens, in all his darkness and glory, has to take a little shit every now and then. The thing is, in a situation like this, he won't take it for very long - very long being defined as about three, maybe four seconds. Either way, hardly enough time for Susan to do anything, but wait...and react.

Wait... and react.

Wait and...Susan grit her teeth, and with all the fight and fury she could muster up, drove her foot between the only opening she saw. It wasn't the cleanest of shots, but she still managed to catch John Henry's two little boys with a pretty good wallop. Good enough to drop him to one knee.

Nevertheless, John Henry's lunacy prevailed, allowing him to sidestep the intensity of his pain long enough to reach back and trip Susan just as she was about to skirt by. Susan lunged for the bed in the hopes of breaking her fall, but in the process, stumbled awkwardly, butting heads with the cherry wood bedpost instead. It was a bad break too. If she hadn't, she might've been able to recover from the fall fast enough to make another mad dash for the stairs before it was too late.

Unfortunately, Susan did butt heads, it did hurt, and by the time she shook out the cobwebs...it was too late.

CHAPTER 86

Maybe John Henry Stevens pretended to be somebody else because a part of him always wanted to be. Maybe he carved another person's name into his mind because a part of him cringed at the memory of his mother and aunt screaming his own. Maybe he sported fancy duds because a part of him could still feel his skin crawling under the filthy clothes he was forced to wear as a kid. Maybe when he looked in the mirror and saw the reflection of an important attorney it was because a part of him didn't want to endure the otherwise dark eyes and spiritless face staring back at him. And maybe, just maybe, John Henry dressed his fingertips, his sense of touch, his stimuli, in what he believed to be the skin of another, because a part of him believed he might feel things differently.

Yeah? Well guess what? Even if true, none of that shit matters. What matters, what consistency can never be flushed from John Henry's mind, or stripped from his body, is the impurity of his very essence. As a result, when the energy racing through his veins jump with life, or collapse from exhaustion, when his wordless conversations with the night cease, or cease to end, when the light in his maddening gaze brightly burns, or barely flickers, John Henry Stevens, remains. Sometimes a bit weaker, sometimes a bit stronger, but always John Henry Stevens, and always ready, willing and able to take delight from the pain he inflicts on others.

The one thing John Henry has never realized, mind you, what he's never understood his entire life, what he would never admit to himself as being true, even if by some miracle he did understand it, is that the pain he inflicts on others, no matter how deep, or how profound, will never wash away that of his own. And without that happening, he can never escape himself.

Ya know what though? None of that shit matters either. Think about it. Who cares what John Henry Stevens understands, or is willing to admit to himself? Who cares what he might want, think, or feel? For that matter, who gives a rat's ass about John Henry altogether? As far as I'm concerned, the only thing that has any bearing whatsoever, is the motherfucker's self-indulgent abyss of horror.

And ya know why? 'Cause the son-of-a-bitch is still at it. It isn't enough that he spent the last half-hour beating Susan to death, strangling life from her unborn child in the process. It isn't enough that he used Susan's lipstick to scribble on the wall the epitaph he never got to say. It isn't enough that the pain he caused Susan in death, will become pain for others to carry around in life. No, no. For John Henry Stevens, none of that's enough. Now, on top of everything else, he has to throw her on the same bed she once shared with Zack, and violate her once again.

CHAPTER 87

Zack glanced at the familiar houses off the driver's side of the jeep, and said, "Man, the ride back seemed to go pretty quick."

Max grinned. "Yeah, that's because you got love on the brain."

"Whataya mean?" The Beast did a lousy job imitating clueless.

Max threw his hands against his cheeks and exclaimed, "Oh, gee. I dunno! Maybe 'cause it's 3:30 in the morning and we're stopping off at your house just so you can leave a love note for your little love muffin."

Zack wanted to give Max the evil eye, but couldn't wipe the "aw shucks" smile off his face. "Well, yeah...but I'm also gonna drop off my shit while I'm there. So..."

"So your ass together," Max chimed in.

Zack laughed.

"Whata you laughing at?"

"Nothin'."

"You liked that one, didn't you Beast?" Max pursed his lips together and nodded his head as if proud of it himself.

"No. Actually it's the dumbest thing I ever heard."

Max shrugged. "You laughed, didn't you?"

After Zack pulled his jeep along the curb opposite his house, he turned to Max and said. "Yeah, but I was only laughing 'cause it was so stupid."

"Yeah, uh-huh. Meanwhile, take your house keys and leave the jeep runnin' so I don't freeze my balls off waitin for you."

"Awww. You afraid of a little cold little boy?" The Beast snickered at his own sarcasm, before adding, "Cause if you are, you can come in the house with me and I'll make you some hot cocoa."

Max folded his arms like he was taking part in a sit-in. "Fuck that. Ain't no way I'm waking up the future Mrs. Beast."

Zack rolled his eyes. "C'mon man, you ain't gonna wake her up."

"Easy for you to say. Besides, all this shows is that I'm obviously more concerned she gets a good night sleep than you are."

Zack rolled his eyes again. "See you in a minute."

"Adios."

CHAPTER 88

When Zack walked inside the house he did his damndest to be quiet, even tiptoeing across portions of the floor he was certain creaked. But when you stand 6'- 3" and weigh 225 pounds in your birthday suit, quiet doesn't always come easy. And when she was alive, no one understood that better than Susan. Over the years there were times when she'd be upstairs and the dull thud from Zack's heavy footsteps would follow him as he wandered around downstairs. She'd lie in bed, and though she'd call out his name every now and then to let him know she was awake and it was okay to make noise, most of the time she'd say nothing, preferring, instead, to bathe in the warmth of his efforts not to disturb her.

If only Susan could call out to him now.

Unfortunately, she couldn't, so there isn't anything more to talk about. Besides, the longer John Henry stayed upstairs, breathing too hard to notice much of anything except his own sweat, and Zack stayed in the kitchen writing Susan a note, there wasn't a problem.

The problem didn't start until Zack decided to bring Max some hot chocolate as a joke, and accidentally knocked a coffee mug off the counter searching the cupboards for cocoa mix. It didn't explode in a thousand pieces, or anything, but when it crashed to the wood floor, it certainly got John Henry's attention.

"Shit," Zack whispered. "I wonder if I woke Susan up?" It was a question his curiosity would only debate for as long as it took him to clean up the small mess. After that, he headed for the stairs to find out.

Debate - Schmate! With his cold, clammy hand draped firmly around his gun, John Henry moved through the hallway in a matter of a few long, fluid strides, waiting for the stairs to play music, music he so elegantly orchestrated under his own shifting weight not more than an hour ago himself.

It was a three step wait...

And then - in one furious, unforgiving moment - the stairway lit up, Zack's eyes locked onto John Henry, and before he could say the name Tyler Lake...

Bang! Bang!

CHAPTER 89

Max didn't remember cutting his hand diving through the picture window to get in the house. He didn't remember dropping his gun, or getting dry heaves the moment he laid eyes on the fallen figure of his best friend. He didn't remember racing upstairs, only to throw up at the sight of Susan's terribly bruised and bloodstained body. He didn't remember how long it took before realizing whoever was responsible was already gone. He didn't remember how long it took before calling for help, or if one of the horrified neighbors made the call before he did. As a matter-of-fact, Max couldn't even remember if he'd been with Zack for three seconds or three hours before anyone else showed up. All Max could think about was the way Zack - The Beast - "His Beast," looked at him. His eyes flickered. His body quivered, and after struggling just to whisper, "It's...him, Max...Lake," he grasped desperately at one last hint of a smile, then closed his eyes and went to sleep.

And now, as Max cradled Zack's head with his left hand, and with his right, wiped away tears, Captain Whitaker leaned over, and in a voice barely able to choke back the pain his eyes could not, said, "C'mon Max...c'mon son. Let...let these people take him... now. There's nothing you can do for...there's nothing you can do anymore," it was only then, Max realized he had to let Zack go.

Still, it wasn't until Captain Whitaker and one of the ambulance attendants gently tugged on Max's arms that he actually stood up, at which point, he promptly turned to the Captain and collapsed in his embrace.

CHAPTER 90

Captain Whitaker waited for all the ugliness to die down before asking Max to meet him for coffee.

For much of that same week, other than paying his sad, but necessary respects, Max went from painfully drunk, to painfully sober, then started the process all over again. So it was on this early morning, with Christmas just around the corner, that he took a seat in the booth, saw the weariness and hurt in Captain Whitaker's eyes, and figured, even on a good day like today, he probably didn't fare as well.

"How's your girlfriend Max? How's Clare?"

Max knew the Captain didn't ask to meet him because he wanted to talk about his love life. Yet, rather than concern himself with some motive he really didn't care about, on top of waiting for the appropriate time to bring up his own agenda, Max was perfectly content to sit back and absorb the small talk. "She's fine Captain. As a matter-of-fact, she's the only thing keeping me alive. Frankly, I don't know what I'd do without her."

"Loves an important thing, isn't it Max?"

Max nodded. "Yes sir, it is. Very important."

Captain Whitaker set his coffee cup down and gazed out the window. "Sometimes none of us ever know just how important until we lose it. Doesn't matter what the relationship is either. Sad, don't you think?"

The Captain's voice tailed off sharply and Max wasn't quite sure if the Captain was asking him a question, or reaffirming some long lost notion to himself. He answered anyway. "Yes, it is. It's actually quite pathetic when you think about it."

Soothed by the quiet calm of the snow falling outside, it wasn't until Captain Whitaker broke free of his hypnotic stare that he responded. And when he did, the sadness Max first saw in his eyes appeared to have been swallowed up by a look of tempered anger. The slight edge to his voice confirmed it. "Oh, I've thought about it Max. I've thought about it a lot. To be perfectly honest, that's all I've been doing. But, I'm glad I did. It gave me a chance to re-evaluate some things."

"Yeah, thinking has a way of doin' that Captain."

Captain Whitaker did a once around the restaurant to make sure no one was sitting too close to their booth. Nobody was, but he leaned forward and lowered his voice anyway. "I'm only going to say this to you one time Max. I know you haven't been around lately, but as you'd probably guess, we haven't finished the investigation at Zack's house. Now, regardless of what evidence is ultimately found, it doesn't take a genius to see the similarities between the way Susan and your sister were both beaten and violated. More so than the other cases you looked into. Enough that I think it was the same son-of-a-bitch. With that in mind, this is what I wanna tell you. No matter what you have to do to find this guy, you find him. And if you need anything from me, anything at all, you just say the word. And then, when you do find him, I want..."

"I know who it is Captain."

Wow! Talk about the eye-poppin', jaw-droppin' impact of getting smacked upside the head with a two-by-four (without actually getting hit), and you've pretty much described Rudy Whitaker's reaction. "Huh? What'd you say?"

"I said I know who it is Captain. Zack got a look at him. The Beast, he stayed around long enough to tell me." Max quickly looked away, as if that would somehow hide the glistening water resting in his eyes.

Captain Whitaker didn't know which direction to go in first. Part of him was troubled because Max should have conveyed that information to him the moment he got it. Part of him was surprised to learn Max knew the persons identity, yet, hadn't made any effort to go after the son-of-a-bitch. And still, another part, was simply plain ol' curious to find out who it was. After the Captain gathered in a decent chunk of air to help quash his angst, he went for the obvious. "Who is it?"

Ah yes. The opportunity Max had been waiting for. The magic question he wouldn't answer. Not just yet anyway. Sure, Captain Whitaker instructed Max to do whatever he had to, to find the killer. Yet, since Max already knew who it was and where to find him, the Captain's instructions, and more importantly, the assistance he indicated a willingness to lend, were, by and large, useless. But, now there was a new tune to be sung. Now, Max had a chance to find out just how far the Captain would go to legitimately help him, something Max wanted, almost as much as he figured to need. And until Captain Whitaker professed his full and unwavering support to do just that, Max would remain content to wail the name, Tyler Lake, like a wounded dog, do so in the confines of his own mind, and let his dubious response inflame the Captain's curiosity all the more. "I'm not sure I can tell you Captain. Not sure I should."

And inflame it did, because the only thing keeping Captain Whitaker on the "north side" of beside himself was the stark and sad reality of the situation itself. "Excuse me, Max. Whata you mean, not tell me?"

Max didn't budge. Nor, by the steadfast look in his eyes, was he going to.

"For Christ's sake, Max. That doesn't make any sense."

Max shrugged. "Maybe not, but at this point I don't really give a shit."

Captain Whitaker proceeded to count to five, slowly. Although, he could've counted to one hundred and it wouldn't have made any difference. Like it, or not, after twenty-seven years on the force, the Captain couldn't escape the fact that bits and pieces of his patience had either chipped away, or rotted. "Now you listen, goddamnit, you're not the only one affected here. And you sure as hell ain't the only one hurting. Now, I want this guy, want him bad. Not just for me. I want him for every family he's ever torn up. Yours, mine, Zack's, all of 'em. But, if I can't get him 'cause you don't trust me enough to help you, then maybe it's time I take you off this case. You hear what I'm sayin'?"

Being jerked off the case wasn't going to get Max where he wanted to go - not with his badge, that is. Nevertheless, he responded full steam ahead. "Yeah, I hear ya fine Captain. You want this guy bad. And you wanna help me get him. Well, that's not a problem, 'cause I'm probably gonna need it. But if you wanna help me, then what I really need is for you to sit there and tell me something - and you've never fed me a line of shit before, so I'm not expecting one now. I just want the truth...your truth. And I trust you enough to give it. Okay?"

Captain Whitaker took hold of the olive branch. "Like I said Max, I wanna help."

Max nodded. "Okay, then tell me this...and I'm only asking because if I can't hide certain information or evidence, it's bound to come out before I want it to. You know investigations as well as I do Captain. It'll only be a matter of time before someone gets hold of it. And if that happens...right, wrong, or otherwise, I'm gonna be backed into a corner. And, I'd rather not be. I'd rather know where I stand goin' in."

"Well than why don't you ask the damn question already."

"Fine. What if I said I had reason to believe the person we're looking for committed murder in at least one other state. Possibly more. What happens then Captain?"

It was a simple question, one, by virtue of the answer generally attached to it, clarified everything for Captain Whitaker. "You think the Feds are gonna find out, don't ya? You're worried someone in the department, or more likely the D.A.'s office is gonna catch wind of something and bring 'em in? Afraid of losing control of the case, aren't you, Max?"

"How 'bout an answer Captain?"

Captain Whitaker threw up his hands, and said, "Sure, I suppose me or someone else could tell 'em we've got an investigation that just went interstate. So what? Nothing would change. You'd still take the risk and go after the son-of-a-bitch yourself. And don't say you wouldn't, 'cause I know you would. Ya want me ta keep a lid on everything so no one else finds out. Kinda like lettin' me protect you from yourself...wouldn't ya say?"

"Look, Captain..."

"Hang on Max and let me finish. Now I asked you to meet me here because I wanted to say something to you. Something I'll never say again, or admit that I ever said at all. I'm prepared to turn my head. I'm prepared to help you any way I can, including keeping the case away from the Feds. But," the Captain warned, his forefinger tick-tocking back and forth...

"But what, Captain?"

"But, only if you have a plan that'll insulate the department from wrongdoing. Including you Max. I mean that too. You owe that much to me. You owe it to the people you have left. And, more importantly, you owe it to yourself. Now, with that said, do what you have to do, just make sure you look like a white knight doing it. Understood?"

Hey, the Captain's much needed assistance in return for a plan of action Max was already in the process of working on. What more could he ask for?

"Understood Captain."

"Good. We'll discuss the plan once you come up with it. Right now, let's discuss who did it."

CHAPTER 91

The Players:

Media and business mogul, Donald Blair. Here was a guy who'd been haunted by the strangled images of his daughter and grandson ever since they were murdered on New Years Eve some two years back; a guy who suffered from the torturous uncertainty of a murder case that remained unsolved; a guy, so eager and determined to bury that uncertainty, he embraced the Tyler Lake theory with open arms; a guy Max wanted because of his considerable clout and power, a power that would breath its judicious fire on the front page of every newspaper and through the airwaves of every television station he owned across the country in the pathetic event Max was arrested for killing Tyler Lake; a guy willing to endorse his own culpability twofold: One, by agreeing, in writing, to set up a college fund for Max's nephew, in return for Tyler Lake's head. And two, by offering Max the services of his long time friend, confidant and business associate, Miles Simon.

Which, of course, brings us to Miles Simon, a one-time high society jewel thief turned mastermind in the art of business espionage. The work might not have been as glamorous, but with Donald Blair's international holdings, the intrigue and pay were second to none.

Nevertheless, when it came to the dirty work of setting up a crazed killer, Max wasn't thrilled at the prospect of using a spy. The guy might have been a pro among pros - hell, Max could even picture him ordering his martinis shaken, not stirred, but that didn't mean stealing files suddenly qualified him for planting evidence. And yet, after Max expressed his concerns, Miles Simon flashed a discerning smile in the direction of Donald Blair, then with the confidence of a man who thought he'd seen it all a thousand times before, looked at Max and proceeded to undress the situation. "At this juncture, you're concerned that you don't have enough evidence to obtain an arrest warrant. You're of the opinion that because this Tyler Lake animal is an Assistant District Attorney, one with a solid record to boot, he'll receive the benefit of every doubt...meaning, your partner's identification of him, and you'll excuse me for saying this, will be shrugged off as little more than the incoherent mutterings of a guy fading fast. It also means you'd likely have a hard time getting a search warrant. Although, even if you did, without an arrest warrant being issued simultaneously, all it'll do is let this creature know you're on to him. And since you don't want to give him an opportunity for escape, what's the point in tipping your hand. Correct?"

Max may have been impressed with the way Miles Simon pieced everything together so quickly, but given that he was so damn cocky about it, Max wouldn't respond with anymore than a casual, if not altogether unimpressive nod of the head.

"As such, you've come to the conclusion, an appropriate one I might add, that you need to create a situation where, what is supposed to look like an ordinary break-in by a common criminal, is simply a way to plant enough evidence to insure that the District Attorney's office has no choice but to go along with you. And if they do that, a judge will most certainly issue arrest and search warrants simultaneously. Correct?"

Again, Max nodded, (barely).

"The problem is, even if you arrest him, should he somehow die, in a manner, shall we say, deemed questionable, the D.A.'s office can still jump off the bandwagon and come after you. As such, you're banking on the premise that somewhere between the evidence produced, be it real or planted, and Mr. Blair's media machine, you'll elicit so much public sentiment and support, they'd be hard pressed to do much of anything because no jury in the world would convict you. Correct?"

Again Max nodded, but this time Miles Simon was too busy strolling his debonair charm across the marble floor to notice. And Max refused to offer him anything verbal. Not that saying anything would have made a difference. On the contrary. Miles Simon was going to finish what he started come hell or high water. And the very moment his hoity-toity ass sank into the thick, forest green leather chair sitting across the table from Max and Donald Blair, he did just that. "Well then, if you need an unrelated third party to do this, which you do, why pluck one of your pigeons off the street to do it, when you can have me? A man of many faces and talents, no prior record, no traceable past, and, no known ties to the police."

It was a good question, one put to rest three days later, when Miles Simon, with the grace of a skilled surgeon and the appearance of an everyday crook looking to steal whatever might feed a drug habit, neutralized Tyler Lake's alarm and slipped inside his house in the middle of a workday afternoon. And surprisingly enough, that was the hard part. The easy part turned out to be planting the evidence. That's because Miles Simon discovered Tyler Lake's basement, and with it, evidence so compelling, planting it wasn't necessary. Now all he had to do was finish playing the role of Joe Tripp, the penny ante thief, who, after breaking into a house to steal a stereo, happens upon such horrifying looking shit, he forgets all about the stereo and goes running to the cops instead.

And who better a cop to run to than Rudy Whitaker. Better because it was obviously part of the plan. Better still, because as a Police Captain, he was in the best position to deal with District Attorney Julian Sweet. The way Max and the Captain had it figured, with Julian Sweet's personal, albeit unwitting, involvement, the department, and in particular, Max, would likely face far less scrutiny from the D.A.'s office for any actions deemed questionable. Perhaps none at all.

It goes something like this: Ever since the District Attorney was forced to abandon the charges brought against Max for the highly touted murder of Billy Turner, the bottom of his political career dropped out, stranding him with nowhere to go and nothing to cling to. Nothing but the sorry ass belief that every courtroom whisper was a knife twisting in his back, every hallway snicker, a joke at his lame duck expense.

Then, as if by magic, Captain Rudy Whitaker shows up, and suddenly Julian Sweet sees a chance to redeem himself, and at the same time, reclaim a once flourishing career. And considering his greed was both enormous and blind, he'd do anything for another shot at the brass ring. Going along with the Captain's efforts to secure a couple of warrants? Big deal. Tyler Lake? Who fucking cares. As far as Julian Sweet was concerned, Tyler Lake could have been the Pope. It still wouldn't have made a damn bit of difference.

All of which was fine by Captain Whitaker. It spared him from embellishing the District Attorney with details regarding the severed fingers sitting in a basement freezer, or of the thumb floating in a bowl of, what looked like water, smelled like formaldehyde, and sat alongside that which resembled a chemistry set. The Captain didn't even find it necessary to mention the bloodstained knives, gloves, or other assorted goodies laying around. The only thing Julian Sweet seemed interested in was the basement wall decorated with newspaper articles about old, unsolved murders. In particular, the one about Billy Turner. Somehow that article lead to the premise that Tyler Lake set up Billy Turner's murder as a means to create trouble and chaos for the District Attorney. Never mind that Tyler Lake may have simply been trying to entertain his abominable self. As far as District Attorney Sweet was concerned, it was all about him, not Tyler Lake.

Who knows. Maybe it was...maybe it wasn't. Either way, the only thing Captain Whitaker cared about was getting a judge to issue the warrants, which, as it turned out, was fairly easy. Now, all he had to do was send somebody to pick up Tyler Lake.

Gee, you'll never guess who just happened to be on duty.

CHAPTER 92

Tentative? Not on your life.
Nervous? Maybe a touch.
Psychotic? Always a slight possibility.
Intense? Count on it.
Enraged? From the moment he saw the body of his murdered sister.
Ready? Absolutely. And once Detective Todd Dodd signaled the two uniforms out back were also ready, Max calmly stepped forward, tapped on the front door, and called out, "Hey Tyler. It's Max Cougar. How 'bout openin' up. I got somethin' I wanna show you."

John Henry was catching a few hard zzz's in his favorite recliner and reacted with the kind of eye twitching, puppy dog whimpering generally reserved for a nightmare. As if John Henry having a nightmare was even possible. Christ Almighty, when you consider the fact that everything about the son-of-a-bitch was a nightmare, it's hard to imagine he could actually have one himself. But it's true. He did...and often. Unlike most normal people he didn't have to wait for nighttime to roll around either. Of course, since so many of John Henry's nights were spent prowling the darkness, it only stood to reason that most of his nightmares would occur during his twilight nap ritual.

Suffice it to say, it took a solid minute before John Henry's eyes flickered open to the sounds of some asshole banging on his front door. "What the fuck," he growled, his body snapping to attention, his mind racing to catch up.

"Hey Tyler. It's Max Cougar. C'mon man, it's cold outside. Open up. I got a little Christmas present for you that I think you're gonna like."

Max Cougar? Christmas present? Here? Now? What the hell is he talking about?

"C'mon Tyler. I know you're home. It's cold man. Open up," Max pleaded.

What choice did he have? His car was parked in the drive, the house lights were on, and chances are Cougar saw him through the window. The way it stands, things would look awfully strange if he didn't open the door. Worse yet, Cougar (fucking cop that he was), would probably resort to snooping around out back. And, since there was no way of knowing where that could lead, it was a risk John Henry wanted no part of. Besides, it's not like he had anything to worry about. If Cougar was on to him for something he certainly wouldn't be knocking on the door boasting about some stupid Christmas gift. He'd be charging into it like a wounded bull. And speaking of stupid Christmas gifts, what the hell is up with that? Is the motherfucker that desperate for a new friend? After John Henry cackled at his own twisted sarcasm, he bounced up from the chair, and barked, "Quit the goddamn banging already. I hear ya."

Max buried his contemptuous expression under the guise of a friendly smile the moment the doorknob started to turn. Although keeping it buried required great discipline once he was standing eyeball to eyeball with the man he intended to kill. "Hey Tyler, I hope I'm not disturbing you or anything."

John Henry smiled back because it was the friendly thing to do. Though when he did, he noticed something change in Max Cougar's expression that somehow belied just how friendly the situation really was, And as much as he may have wanted to, he couldn't very well stand there and dwell on it. If he did, sooner or later, (likely sooner), a look of concern would show up all over his face. Just the sort of thing he couldn't afford to give away. "No. I mean I was taking a nap, but you're not disturbing me. Although, I must admit, your being here is quite the surprise."

"Yeah, I know you weren't expecting me and I promise I won't stay long. Actually, I just came by to give you these." Max promptly retrieved the two warrants from the inside pocket of his bomber jacket and handed them to John Henry.

Ever the Assistant District Attorney, John Henry didn't have to study them too long to realize what he was looking at. Nevertheless, his immediate desire was to laugh the whole thing off as a practical joke. Yet, the look of concern he was hoping to avoid arrived full throttle, making it impossible. And any thoughts of leap frogging into the innocent victim routine, were just as quickly dispelled when Max winked at him and said, "Don't worry. I'm not here to search your house or arrest you. I'm here to interrupt your breathing. Forever."

It wasn't the threat of words that staggered John Henry, but the sudden explosion they created between flesh and fantasy. He winced, and his cold, penetrating eyes, always a match for the depth of night's seamless darkness, revealed pain. His body, always simmering in the strength of insanity, now lay shelter to floundering rage. And there, in the bleakness of what seemed like one endless moment, he felt the desolation of uncertainty, depriving him of all but a sense of numb.

"Did you hear what I said?" The first time Max asked the question the words carried all the impact of a distant echo. The second time John Henry bugged his eyes out as far as he could and rolled his head around like the delirious madman he was. There was no third time. Instead, Max rushed through the doorway and slammed John Henry to the floor with such driving force, it pushed out all the air inside his lungs. "Hope you like backseats, 'cause we're goin' for a little ride," Max snarled in his ear.

Still struggling to catch his breath all John Henry could do was cough.

"Dodd, get your ass in here!" Max yelled.

By the time Detective Dodd and Officers Conway and Gordon were all inside the house, John Henry was sprawled on the floor face first, his hands tied behind his back with a pair of cuffs. Nice, loose cuffs to keep his wrists free of bruises, cuts and other incidental markings.

"That's the motherfucker who shot Beast, eh?" Randy Conway asked.

"That's him Connie." Max clamped his hands around John Henry's hair and pulled it as hard as he could. "How's that feel pal, you like that?"

"May I?"

It was a deliberate question, one Max responded to by yanking John Henry to his feet and hurling him against the wall.

Randy Conway would never admit it, at least not to another man, but he loved Zack Darwin. Not man - woman kind of love. Admiration - respect kind of love. As a result, he found great satisfaction tagging John Henry in the stomach with, what had to be, the hardest punch he'd ever thrown before.

John Henry didn't care for it either. Although, he didn't have much time to think about it. At Johnny Gordon's beckoned request, Max straightened him back up and Johnny Gordon whacked him in the groin with his police baton. At that point, any effort to keep John Henry on his feet was pretty much useless. So much so, Max tossed him towards Detective Dodd, who, in turn, stepped aside to let him fall to the floor, though, not without first spitting in his face.

"Okay. Anyone want more?" The question was met with the silence of three stoic expressions, so Max continued. "No mistakes guys. And, no tainted evidence. This piece of shit ain't walkin'. Just go slow and make sure you bag everything that even thinks about looking suspicious. Especially when you're in the basement. And don't forget to have his car impounded."

"You stickin' around?"

"Nope. I came here to arrest this motherfucker, and that's exactly what I intend to do!" Max replied emphatically.

"You want me to ride with you? Ya know, case lawyer here has visions of gettin' away."

"No Connie, there's plenty of work for you guys here. Besides, he ain't gonna do nothin'." Max gave John Henry's ribs a nice little toe tap with his boot, and said, "Are ya big fella?"

With the darkness - his darkness - just starting to come back around like the dear old friend it was, John Henry didn't figure that was something Max should count on just yet.

John Henry wasn't...that's for sure.

CHAPTER 93

Although he might have guessed as much, it wasn't until the stranger left the pickup truck on the side of the road and sped away in a waiting limousine that John Henry was convinced. The accident between the truck and Max Cougar's unmarked cop car, the same pickup Cougar followed for countless miles, was no accident at all. It was a staged event. So too was the pickup truck's flat tire. And now, after a long, confining hour in the backseat of that same unmarked cop car, John Henry suddenly found himself under the spotlight of a ghostly white winter moon, smack dab in the middle of nowhere, wondering just where and the hell he was supposed to be heading when the tire blew out and he was left to escape on foot. It was a question his curiosity wouldn't let go of. One, that so long as he and Max Cougar were gonna spend some time circling each other like a couple of cheap club fighters, he felt inclined to ask.

Max didn't mind answering either. As a matter-of-fact, he wanted to explain how charades pulled off by this killer in life, would now be pulled off by Max in his death. "Don't really know. The likely theory'll be the train station, since it's only a few miles up the road. Maybe you figured with security at airports being what it is, you'd have a better chance on a train. Doesn't really matter though, I don't figure I'll have to explain it away."

"That a fact?" John Henry asked, as if he knew better.

"Yeah," Max declared, "that's a fact. Contrary to the little accident we created. That was done so I'd have a way to explain how you got out of the car. And the truck? You rushed the driver and stole it before I could stop you - what else? After that, all I could do was give chase. Fortunately for me, the truck blew out a tire and you had to continue on foot. Gave me a chance to catch your sorry ass."

John Henry sneered. "And now you're gonna shoot me in the back, is that it?"

Max smiled. "You ain't that lucky. First I'm gonna beat you to within an inch of death."

"That a fact?"

"Then you're actually gonna take a couple of shots at me. Theoretically, of course. You'll be holding the gun, but I'll be pointing it, so you'll only hit the car. Me? Naturally, I'll have no choice but to return the fire. At which point, you'll die. Get it?"

"Pretty cocky for a guy whose had just about everything fall by the wayside 'cause of me." Figuring to make the ugly reality of his truth linger all the more, John Henry topped off the reply with a wretched little smile.

"Sticks and stones baby."

John Henry shrugged. "Well, if that's the case, then there's something I've been wondering."

"Ask now while your mouth still works."

John Henry snickered, and said, "Do you think I'd enjoy fucking your girlfriend as much as I enjoyed fucking your sister?"

WHAMO! The wait was over.

Bellowing the primal scream of a man willing to die, in order that he may kill, Max charged forward.

John Henry went low and tried to take Max out at the knees. All he got for his efforts was a thigh in the face that sent him reeling. Problem was, even without snow, the ground was still winter hard and a tad slick, so Max fell on his ass as well.

John Henry was the first to scramble to his feet, but instead of going on the attack, slouched forward and let his arms dangle from side to side, as if a chimpanzee. It mattered not that his choice of action, or lack thereof, gave Max the freedom to get up. Having realized this was the one instance when he wasn't in control of the situation, simply because it was the first time in his life he didn't bear the element of surprise, it only mattered to John Henry that he take a deep breath, and a moment to plan his next move.

Nothing doing!

Back on his feet, Max charged again. John Henry backpedaled but Max caught him flush on the cheek with an overhand right that jumped with the sound of a cracking whip.

John Henry stumbled and staggered, but it was the two point-blank shots Max followed up with, that made him fall down - go boom. It was unfamiliar territory too, this fallin' down shit. Not since the days of the irrepressible Chuck Buckley to be exact. Still, the harmless anxiety he remembered feeling back then, was lost under waves of adrenaline filling him now. And as his dark, penetrating eyes looked up, only to dance with the ever mindful glare of Max Cougar, and the throbbing in his head exploded from the roar..."I didn't take the cuffs off you for nothin' – now get up you piece of shit coward, 'cause you gotta ways to go yet..." John Henry ignored the winter chill and trembled from its warmth.

Now he was ready!

Now he would stand!

Now it was he who would attack, and Cougar who would die!

But Max wasn't going anywhere. Even when John Henry looked up at the moon and wailed like a wild dog. Even when he launched into the nonsensical mutterings of a crazed madman, or laughed the effusive laugh of the insane. Even when he rocked forwards, backwards, and forwards again, only to come to an abrupt halt, look sharply to his left, sharply to his right, then sharply at

Max, and whisper, "My names John Henry Stevens, and now, I'm gonna kill you."

It was a nice introduction to be sure. One followed by a lunging, wild right cross.

Max was far enough away for John Henry to miss, yet close enough to feel his fist swoosh by and set him back on his heels. It also meant John Henry got another crack at it - which he made good on by connecting with a lunging, not so wild, left cross that stunned Max long enough for John Henry to devour the remaining ground between them, and seize him by the throat.

Instantly Max took hold, squeezing John Henry's wrists with such ferocity, it was only a short matter of time before John Henry realized this particular choke hold wasn't going to cut it. But it wasn't until Max wrestled the quivering hands away from his neck that John Henry's expression unveiled the strained blemish of a losing struggle - at which point, Max's sardonic grin suggested he knew it too. But, just in case that wasn't clue enough, Max dropped his grip, stepped back, and promptly fired off a couple of stiff jabs.

Now here's the thing. John Henry wasn't much of a fighter, much less a boxer. Never had much call for it. He mangled and choked, stabbed and used blunt objects on people. He even got a kick out of the occasional shooting. But fighting someone face to face? Man, that just wasn't his forte. Be that as it may, his ego, pathetically distorted as it was, wouldn't accept it. Consequently, John Henry figured he was never more than a proverbial sock in the jaw away from getting another crack at Max Cougar's neck.

And a sock to the jaw he landed. A few of them, as a matter-of-fact. Certainly enough to lend credence to the theory Max was forced to defend himself.

Of course, defend himself, Max did. When John Henry managed to get in a couple of decent pokes, Max responded with three thunderous shots of his own. When John Henry caught him with a lucky left hook, Max answered back with a solid right/left combo. When two of John Henry's jabs were followed by a combination that resulted in nothing but air, Max unleashed a flurry of blows to the head and body that lasted as long as John Henry remained standing. Even when the fog cleared and John Henry wobbled back to his feet in a veiled attempt to lull Max off guard while he lunged for his throat, Max lunged right back.

And so it was, with glazed eyeballs and churning teeth, arms shaking and fingers digging into flesh, that the two grappled with the hellbent mind of one. John Henry driven by the same vicious hatred as always - Max, by the timeless memory of his sister, the vivid pain of his best friend, and the bitterness of loss, his nephew Matthew would be lucky to never know.

And so the struggled continued, with lonely, seamless shadows lurking under frigid December skies - the will for life, the clutches of death, and the tenacious wind howling between.

And in the manner it all began, so the struggle would end - eyes frozen wide with the fear of a newborn child, and body still...

Just like the earth below.

EPILOGUE

In the three months following John Henry Stevens' death, no charges were brought against Max Cougar. Nor, would any be brought in the future. District Attorney Julian Sweet would seek re-election, where, a year into his new term, he would be forced to resign in disgrace, following a Grand Jury's indictment on several counts of embezzlement and money laundering.

Sam Quiz had been successful in tracing John Henry's life as far back as college. He would continue his search until he learned about John Henry's childhood and upbringing. At that time, he would quit the newspaper to begin work on his first novel.

A.D. Stokes was still practicing law, but would ultimately turn to the political scene, where he would gain distinction and prominence as a member of the House Of Representatives.

Captain Rudy Whitaker was still captain. His 30th wedding anniversary happened to coincide with the successful outcome of John Henry's death. And though his wife didn't realize it, he happily celebrated both by taking her on an extended trip to the Bahamas.

Wanda Seven would soon move in with Keona Raven full time, where she would remain his best friend and lover, as well as become an important asset in the running of the rehabilitation center.

Max and Clare married, and after filing the necessary documents to legally adopt his nephew Matthew, the three of them spent a month in Maui, Hawaii, courtesy of Donald Blair.

Upon their return, a message from Keona was waiting for Max on the answering machine. "Glad you're back. Hope you guys had a great time. I'll be in town on Sunday and wanna meet you at the cemetery. I'll be there around noon. Won't be around for you to get back to me, so I'll just plan to see you then. Bye."

In as much as Susan didn't have any family of her own to speak of, and since no one from Zack's family offered, Max saw to it that she, along with the unborn child she shared with Zack, were buried next to his sister and brother-in-law. As far as Max was concerned, it was the very least he could do. The only thing that proved troubling for him was the sight of the unborn child's gravestone. If he went to visit his sister Kathy, he was able to visit with Susan as well. But a gravestone inscribed with the words, *The Darwin Baby. Sweet light for the Angels*, was almost more than he could bear, and invariably, his throat would grow tight, his chin would quiver, and chills would fill his body.

Nevertheless, he and Clare showed up on Sunday just like Keona requested. As usual, after Clare paid her respects she went back to the car. Max needed time alone, just as he'd need her steady hand when he finished with his visit.

She provided both.

And Max? During most visits he never knew what to say. He'd generally just stand with his shoulders hunched over and go from sad to sadder. This time, however, he was telling his sister and brother-in-law about their plans to adopt Matthew. "Your parents gave their blessing Jack, otherwise Clare and I would have never considered it," he whispered. "Now I know we'll never be able to replace you guys, but you gotta know, we'll do our best. Matty's crazy about Clare...almost as much as she is about him." Max suddenly wanted Clare by his side, but when he turned to wave for her, his attention was diverted to the limousine pulling up behind his Bronco.

A few moments later Keona climbed out of the car and stood by the door. He was soon followed by the Beast.

Zack Darwin awakened from his coma with his memory intact and the full use of his faculties a week after Max and Clare headed to Hawaii. He refused to allow Keona, or anyone else for that matter, to disturb their well deserved time alone. Besides, upon hearing the news about his beloved Susan and the baby he'd never know, it was time alone he needed as well. Even if he had to spend it in a godforsaken hospital.

Susan and the unborn baby were buried a relatively short walk up a little hill. Yet, since it was Zack's first visit, the walk seemed like an eternity.

An eternity that came to rest when a tearful Max and Zack embraced.